**W9-CLY-300**

## Angela Thirkell

Angela Thirkell, granddaughter of Edward Burne-Jones, was born in London in 1890. At the age of twenty-eight she moved to Melbourne, Australia where she became involved in broadcasting and was a frequent contributor to the British periodicals. Mrs. Thirkell did not begin writing novels until her return to Britain in 1930; then, for the rest of her life, she produced a new book almost every year. Her stylish prose and deft portrayal of the human comedy in the imaginary county of Barsetshire have amused readers for decades. She died in 1961, just before her seventy-first birthday.

Altogether, Mrs. Thirkell is in form, and equal even to the dire contingencies of Peace.
— *The New York Herald Tribune*

Delightfully gay, charming, humorous — at once troubled and serene.
— *The New York Times*

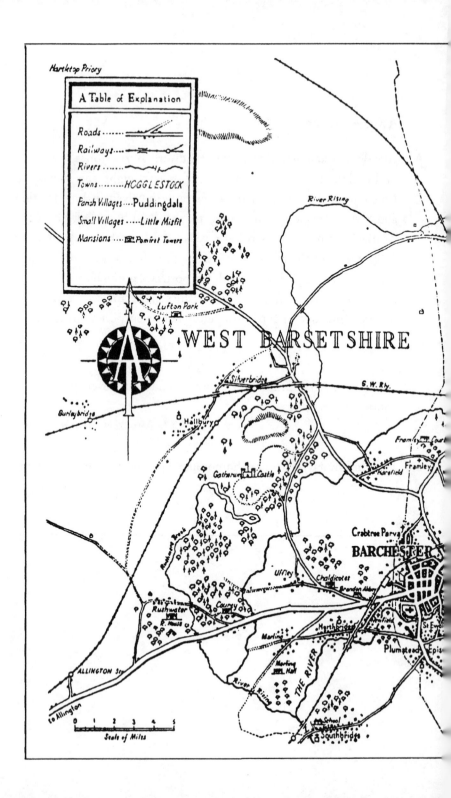

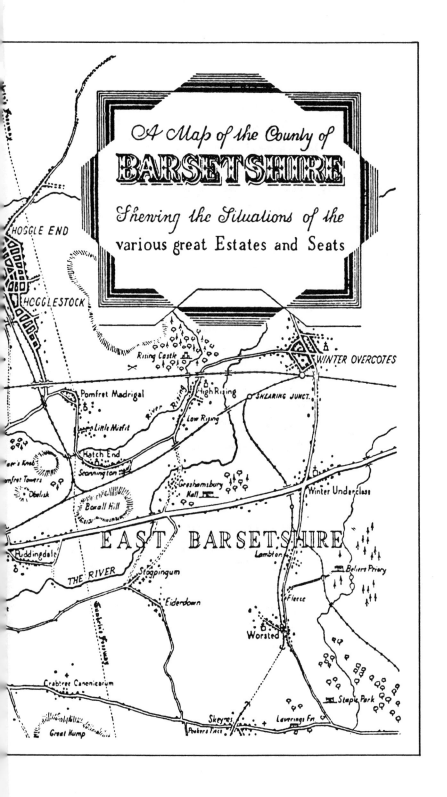

Other books by Angela Thirkell

Three Houses (1931)

Ankle Deep (1933)

High Rising (1933)

Demon in the House, The (1934)

Wild Strawberries (1934)

O, These Men, These Men (1935)

August Folly (1936)

Coronation Summer (1937)

Summer Half (1937)

Pomfret Towers (1938)

Before Lunch (1939)

The Brandons (1939))

Cheerfulness Breaks In (1940)

Northbridge Rectory (1941)

Marling Hall (1942)

Growing Up (1943)

Headmistress, The (1944)

Miss Bunting (1945)

Peace Breaks Out (1946)

Private Enterprise (1947)

Love Among the Ruins (1948)

Old Bank House, The (1949)

County Chronicle (1950)

Duke's Daughter, The (1951)

Happy Returns (1952)

Jutland Cottage (1953)

What Did It Mean? (1954)

Enter Sir Robert (1955)

Never Too Late (1956)

Double Affair, A (1957)

Close Quarters (1958)

Love at All Ages (1959)

# PEACE BREAKS OUT

*A Novel by*

## Angela Thirkell

MOYER BELL
Wakefield, Rhode Island & London

Published by Moyer Bell
This Edition 1997

Copyright © 1947 by Angela Thirkell
Published by arrangement with Hamish Hamilton, Ltd.

All rights reserved. No part of this publication may be reproduced or transmitted in any form or by any means, electronic or
mechanical, including photocopying, recording or any information retrieval system, without permission in writing from
Moyer Bell, Kymbolde Way, Wakefield, Rhode Island 02879
or 112 Sydney Road, Muswell Hill, London N10 2RN.

LIBRARY OF CONGRESS
CATALOGING-IN-PUBLICATION DATA

Thirkell, Angela Mackail, 1890–1961.
    Peace breaks out : a novel / by Angela
Thirkell. — 1st ed.
     p.  cm.
    1. Barsetshire (England : Imaginary
place)—Fiction.  2. World War, 1939–
1945—England—Influence—Fiction.
I. Title.
PR6039.H43P43    1997
823'.912—dc20         96-36738
                     CIP
ISBN 1-55921-188-1 (pbk.)

Cover illustration:
*The Last Day in the Old Home* (detail) by
Robert Braithwaite Martineau
Chapter illustrations:
from *Opulent Textiles* by
Richard Slavin III

Printed in the United States of America
Distributed in North America by Publishers Group West, P.O. Box 8843,
Emeryville CA 94662, 800-788-3123 (in California 510-658-3453).

# CHAPTER I

About half way between Little Misfit and High Rising the pleasant village of Hatch End, close under the steep downland, straggles along one side of the river Rising, separated from it by the road and the water-meadows. The houses are of grey Barsetshire stone fretted with golden lichen, the cottages of anything from decaying stone, through mellow crumbling brick, to a kind of primitive wattle and daub washed in harmonious faded creams and dirty pinks, with mossy, leaking thatched roofs. Over the whole street there reigns a general air of exquisite harmonious crumblingness whose charm is but poorly expressed in the shiny postcards which used before the war to be sold at Mrs. Hubback's, known as The Shop; though poorly as we think of these chromo-lithographic efforts, we have always disliked the pen and ink sketches by the local artist, Mr. Scatcherd, even more. For not only are his works all exactly alike (which is perhaps why they are so well-known) but each carries a few suitable words taken without any particular application from the anthological poems (if we make ourselves clear) of approved bards. His "Rising Rambler" series are particular favourites with the public that used to hike through rural England in motor coaches, with half-an-hour's stop at the Mellings Arms for tea; and among them the picture of the old bridge all on the skew, with Dolly Varden being chucked under the chin by Beau Nash (we give an impression rather than anything so low as a categorical description of the scene) with the caption, "Many a youth and many a maid, Dancing in the chequered shade," was perhaps the most popular. Mr. Scatcherd, who with unusual common sense lives in a well-built hideous little house called "Rokeby," just outside the village, has further shown his sense by bringing his art up to date. The post-card of the Mellings Arms (to give but one example) with a few rude forefathers of the hamlet adumbrated (for the human figure is not one of Mr. Scatcherd's strong points) on a bench outside the Tap with the captain "Troll the bowl," was vastly improved by their metamorphosis as members, or shall we say lay-figures, of the Home Guard, with the simple words, "Britannia needs no Bulwarks." This card was sent by everyone to everyone else for Christmas until paper restriction came into force; and as soon as this ban (invented by a Capittleist and effete government for the enslavement of the people) is removed, Mr. Scatcherd has in mind a yet nobler version in which a one-armed soldier and a one-legged airman, rather vague about the uniform, will be seen clinking mugs upon the bench with those moving words "Home is the sailor, home from the sea." We can confidently predict that this card will bring joy to many a hearth which ought to know better. But few hearths in this half-baked New World have the factual outlook (as their newspapers teach them to say) of Miss Scatcherd, the artist's niece and housekeeper, who turns out and dusts the ground floor back, known as The Studio, once a week, and has often said to her friends what a blessing it is Uncle likes sketching as it keeps him quiet for hours on the stretch as they say.

Hatch End has no Great House, for the shadow of Pomfret Towers lies over this part of the Rising valley. The nearest approach to a squire-house is not even in the village, but lies on the bank of the Rising where the ground slopes gently upwards and has all the afternoon and evening light, whereas Hatch End, nestling closely under the great downs, is in shadow for the greater part of the day and the year; which accounts for the general mossiness of everything and the amount of rheumatics in the cottages, though since the late Lord Pomfret had the water-meadow properly drained and all the sluices and hatches put in order, the cottage floors are distinctly drier. But Hatch House stands well above the river valley, high and dry at all seasons, a square red-brick house with sash windows, a gravel sweep, and a front lawn which is embanked by a brick wall above the old road to Barchester. The road is probably as old as history, always well out of reach of the higher floods, and follows the contours of the hilly land in a series of twisting ups and downs, so that no motor buses use it. This is a source of some quite unreasonable pleasure and pride to its owners, the Hallidays, who have for several generations scoured the country on horse, bicycle and foot, regarding in later years the car of the moment as a useful piece of machinery on occasion and no more, and chiefly used for taking them to the nearest main line station at Nutfield, some six or seven miles away; for the single track line that serves Little Misfit and Pomfret Madrigal ignores people foolish enough to want to go to London, looking upon even Barchester as foreign parts. It is in fact the purest democracy, being a paternal service of the locals, by the locals, for the locals, and no one has ever been allowed to miss a train so long as the guard or the engine driver could see the car, trap, or pedestrian half a mile away. There is of course the inevitable exception to prove the rule, namely the case of Sir Ogilvy Hibberd when he was trying to buy up land before the war; and old gentlemen at the Mellings Arms still discuss, with the long silences broken by a few Wessex words which are their form of Witenagemot, the day when the station-master at Pomfret Madrigal exercised a long dormant right and locked the booking office door in Sir Ogilvy's face at the hour scheduled for the departure of the 9.43, who was still gossiping quietly with the 9.52 down. But of Sir Ogilvy we will say no more. He met more than his match in old Lord Pomfret in the matter of Pooker's Piece and has now gone aloft, in which place his baronial title, which begins with Aber, or Inver, has reduced him to the indistinguishable level of most of his brother peers of later and unimaginative creations, and no one knows who he (or they) were.

So Mr. Halliday rode about a good deal on a hardworking conscientious horse who had no objection to giving the farm-horse a hand with carting dung or wood occasionally; and Mrs. Halliday bicycled or drove an old cob in an old pony trap; and Captain George Halliday of the Barsetshire Yeomanry when on leave rode his father's horse, or the farm-horse or even, in vacant or in pensive mood, the cob, who, he complained made his legs stick out sideways like doing the splits.

"People's legs don't really stick out sideways," said his sister Sylvia, who had been hoping for five-and-a-half years that the war would be over in time for her to go on with her dancing, but did her best for the W.A.A.F.s in the meantime. "They really stick out behind and in front, like running, only much flatter and straighter. And then you turn yourself round like a corkscrew so that it takes everyone in."

To prove which assertion she got up from the breakfast table and gave a fairly good demonstration.

"Cheating an innocent and gullible public, that's what I call it," said Captain Halliday. "English-Speaking Ballet, my girl. Now, look at this."

Rising from the breakfast table he crossed his arms, crossed his feet, sank elegantly and without apparent effort to the floor, rose with the precision of a well-oiled machine, repeated the combined operation three times and sat down again.

"Blast," he said. "That seam in my breeches has gone again."

"I knew it would," said Mrs. Halliday, who minded almost more about damaged clothes than broken arms or legs. "Every time you get leave, George, that seam goes again and I shall have to reinforce it this time. I think," she pursued, contemplating with extensive view all the pieces and scraps of material that were available for patching after so many years of war, "that I might be able to get a bit out of the back seam of your father's old hunting breeches. The tailor left a good wide turn-in at the back when he made them in 1938 because your father was getting so much stouter at that time, and now he has got so nice and thin again that the turn-in is really wasted. And if I unrip the seam of your breeches and machine a good piece of father's onto the back of the seams where the stuff is so worn with being mended so much, and get Hubback to press it well, on the wrong side of course, it would machine up again quite nicely and I could even let it out a bit; the old seam-mark wouldn't show much when it had been pressed with a damp cloth."

By this time her son and daughter, who were used to their mother's household soliloquies, had begun to talk quietly about other matters till the sound of his own name pulled George's attention back.

"So," his mother was continuing, "if you will take those breeches off, George, and let me have them, I am sure I can make a good job of them. But I must have them *now* because of all sorts of things."

"But I'll tell you what you *can't* do," said Sylvia, suddenly emerging from a profound and thoughtful silence. "You can't sit down with your legs beside you."

"I always rather wanted to have a wooden leg when I was small," said George reflectively, "I mean a proper wooden leg like a leg of mutton, so that I could take it off and throw it at people."

"So if you will take off those breeches, George darling," said Mrs. Halliday, getting up, "I'll see about them now."

"Or one could give it to a poor old cottage woman who was too weak to get firewood from the Squire's woods and anyway he'd have had her transported if she had," said Sylvia, warming to the subject, "and be a Ministering Angel."

"I simply can't take off these breeches now, mother," said George. "I don't mean not in the dining-room, for heaven knows nothing is sacred since you and Hubback would try on Sylvia's camiknicks or whatever it was in here because it was the only fire the house last winter, but I'm going down to the village now and I must have my breeches on."

"But the place will get worse," said his mother.

"It won't go any further," said George. "They split about forty times in Normandy and my batman got the little jigger from the adjutant's office that sticks papers together with bits of hairpin and stamped some of them on so that it couldn't come undone any further. I do miss Jones. I hope he'll be there all right when I get back to wherever my lot have gone to."

"I think it is quite dreadful that none of you know how to sew properly," said Mrs. Halliday severely. "It is like that dreadful batman of yours who puts nails through your breeches, right through the material, to hold your braces up when the buttons come off."

"I put the nails in, mother," said George. "They worked awfully well. In fact one of them is still there, because a button you sewed on came off again."

"Then I must have your breeches at once," said Mrs. Halliday. "That settles it. A nail might get shot right into you at any minute."

"So might a button," said George. "All right, mother, I'll give them you tonight."

"You mean 'I'll give you them,'" said Sylvia. "If you say, 'I'll give them you,' it means 'I'll give you to them,' like giving Christians to the lions."

George said it didn't. It meant, he said, "I will give them to you" and if he said "I'll give you them" it would mean "I will give—I will give—" "Oh gosh," he added, "I don't know, but anyway you're wrong. And what's this about sitting down beside your legs anyway?"

Sylvia stood up, and quietly sat down on the floor, the lower part of each leg doubled up neatly on the carpet alongside its upper part.

"Good God," said George.

"Elementary, my dear Watson," said Sylvia, rising as smoothly as she had sunk. "Only I bet you can't do it."

"OW!" said George as he nearly twisted his knees out of their sockets and had to save himself from falling in a heap by clutching at his sister's skirt. "It isn't fair. You've got double joints."

"Double muscles," said Mrs. Halliday, one of whose unexpected gifts was excellent French.

Her offspring stared uncomprehendingly. Mrs. Halliday, who had long ago accepted the fact that her children were by her standards illiterate, and knew that if she said Tartarin they would be no wiser than before, seized the moment of George's discomfiture to tell him that she was quite sure the seam had opened a bit more with all those gymnastics, and he had better let her have his breeches before he went down to the village.

"I say, father," said George to Mr. Halliday, who came in at that moment. "Do save me from your wife. She wants to mend my breeches and I can't spare them."

"Look, my dear," said Mr. Halliday, holding up a pair of riding breeches for his wife's inspection. "It's that button again. Hubback put it on for me last week, but her buttons never last. One might as well use a nail as we used to in the old war. I wish you would sew it on for me, Ellie, if you've time. No—not the back button—that front one."

"I was only looking," said Mrs. Halliday in a fateful voice, which would not have been unworthy of Norna of the Fitful Head in one of her pythonic moments, "to see how much stuff there was on the back seam. All right, Leonard, I'll do it now. And if you will let me have those riding breeches of yours, George," she continued, "I will start the patch at once."

"Oh, all right mother," said George, with a fairly good grace. "I'll put them in your room."

"What's your mother up to?" asked Mr. Halliday. "Is she cutting up your breeches to patch mine?"

"Cutting up yours, father, to patch mine," said George, and went out of the room in better spirits.

"Good God, Ellie! You're not going to touch my breeches," said Mr. Halliday much alarmed.

"It is quite all right, Leonard," said his wife. "George was exaggerating. And don't forget we are having tea at the Deanery today. Will you be in for lunch?"

A little more exchange of plans took place and then Mr. Halliday went away. Sylvia had meanwhile removed the break-fast things and washed them up under the disapproving yet complacent eye of Hubback, daughter of old Mrs. Hubback at The Shop, servant in the Halliday family by right of long village ties as under-housemaid, head-housemaid and now as much a maid of all work as her mistress. Old Mrs. Fothergill was, it is true, nominally cook, but her age and her legs told upon her more and more, and when she was not having a nice cup of tea, or a quiet lay down, or a nice quiet time with the wireless, she was doing something else of a nice and quiet nature. However she was faithful and honest, and as she never went out Mrs. Halliday could always leave the house with a quiet mind.

So George took off his breeches and put on his old grey flannel trousers, very frayed round the turn-ups, and his sister tied her head up in a scarf handkerchief and took her brother George's Burberry, and they prepared to go for a walk by the sunken lane which represents what is left of Gundric's Fossway in those parts, under the steep escarpment of Freshdown, once Frey's Down, and so to the bold eminence of Bolder's Knob where no tree has ever grown since St. Ewold, in an access of slum-clearance, caused the sacred oak grove to be cut down. But all those pleasant plans were swept away, as remorselessly as St. Ewold had swept away the Druids' oaks, by the irruption into the hall of Hubback, holding a large basket in what appeared to the young Hallidays to be an ominous, nay minatory manner."

"As you *are* going down to the village, Miss Sylvia," said Hubback, "you can look in at Mother's and see if there's any biscuits come. And there's some other things ought to have come in by now and if Vidler's boy has been over from Northbridge she'll be able to let you have a bit of fish. Here's the basket and a nice bit of paper to wrap the fish in."

So saying she thrust into Sylvia's unwilling hand a recent number of the *Sunday Express*, with a good deal of dirt and grease on it.

"Oughtn't I to have a cleaner bit for the fish?" said Sylvia.

"Not for Vidler's fish," said Hubback scornfully. "If you was to see the back of Vidler's shop, Miss Sylvia, you'd never touch another piece. You wouldn't credit there was so many flies in the world, and all the year round too. And don't forget the beer, Master George. They can't send now at the Arms, so what you want you'll have to carry. There's plenty of room in the basket."

Without waiting for her, young master and mistress's protests, she went back to the kitchen, giving the door that led to the servants' quarters a hearty slam. But this was taken by the young Hallidays in the spirit in which it was meant; namely, not as a display of temper, but as the only method of making the door shut. Hardly had the noise of the slam stopped resounding through the hall and up the stairs when Hubback opened it again.

"If I've told that Caxton once I've told him a dozen times," she said vengefully, "that what this door needs is a good looking at. If you see him anywhere about you can tell him so."

She withdrew and ostentatiously closed the door quietly. It at once sprang open again.

"Don't say I didn't say so," said Hubback, poking her face through the opening; and slammed the door again till the house reeled.

"Better get out now," said Sylvia, "or she'll send us to find Caxton in the workshop and he'll keep us for hours. Come on."

They shut the front door behind them, for the spring day was grey and cold. Before them lay the velvet-soft lawn with its two great cedars. Beyond the cedars was the low red brick wall with its stone coping and its stone urns at regular intervals, and an eight-foot drop on its far side to the old Barchester Road. In all the springs the young Hallidays could remember, before the German chancellor had changed the face of the whole world with evil intent, the water-meadows in late spring, richly green from the winter flooding, with promise of yellow iris, forget-me-not, and the scent of wild mint crushed as one walked, with dog-roses and meadow-sweet to come, had been part of one's life at Hatch End. Today, when a war against the powers of darkness was well into its sixth year, when the older people were living valiantly with tiredness and even hopelessness as their constant companions, when even the young were wondering if anything really mattered or if one might as well gamble away all one had, a chill spring wind was battering the reeds along the water channels and turning the leaves of the aspens till everything looked as grey as steel, and even the waters were wrinkled with cold, while depressed cows stood with their patient backs to the blast and chewed without enthusiasm.

"Filthy it all looks," said George Halliday.

"Perfectly foul," said Sylvia Halliday. "Come on. If we get Hubback's fish in time, we might go up to Bolder's Knob before lunch."

George knew that a visit to the village made anything else, especially a two-mile walk each way, or two and a half if you kept to Gundric's Fossway and didn't cut up by the chalk quarry, quite out of the question. And he knew that his sister knew this as well as he did and was only playing the game, by now so threadbare and boring, of making the best of things, or looking on the bright side of them; though no side seemed to him brighter or better than any other side, all being pretty dull and depressing. But it was no good talking about these things, so he and Sylvia went down the sloping drive to the road. At the gate they paused, a habit formed in their childhood when to go out onto the road without looking might mean sudden death, not only in the imagination of their nurses, but in the sad fact of the nursery dog who rushed joyfully down the drive and straight under a motor coach of the Southbridge United Viator Passenger Coy., which should never have been allowed to use the narrow Old Road with its sudden ups and downs, its twists and turns. But for a long time no motor coaches had come along the Old Road, no tradesmen's vans came out from Barchester. An occasional convoy that had lost its way in Barsetshire lanes, or coming over the downs, would bump and rattle past in the early hours of the morning, or a car marked Red Cross, W.V.S. or Doctor would pass the gates, but for the most part the road was deserted except for bicycles, and even they avoided it if possible, for there were some hills, notably the hill with the sudden turn in it going down from Hatch House Farm to Nether Hatch, which not even bad little boys could force a bicycle up, let them stand first on one pedal and then on the other as they would. Jimmy Panter, an extremely bad little boy, grandson of Mrs. Hubback at The Shop, had several times ridden down it, but only by keeping both hob-nailed feet firmly on the tyre of the front wheel (whose mudguard he had long ago broken and lost) so ripping the tyre to pieces and getting a good thrashing from his father, Mr. Halliday's carter Panter, who had lost an arm in Ypres salient beside his master, but could handle horses as well as any man in the neighbourhood.

Without further words George and his sister walked a hundred yards or so to where a narrow road, carried high on stone arches, spanned the water-meadows above the reach of any floods. The older wooden bridge, which had been there since time immemorial (or in other words since 1721, the year in which Hatch House was built by one of Mr. Halliday's ancestors, Wm. Halliday, Gent., who had a passion for building, and had married a young lady of property), was carried away in the great flood of 1863, when the waters of the Rising got entirely out of hand and the two sides of the river were completely cut off from one another for seven or eight miles, and a jack-ass was found in a willow tree, unhurt, but extremely difficult to extricate. The New Bridge, as it is still called, was built by the sixth Earl of Pomfret at his own expense; the seventh earl, as we have before mentioned, had the water channels, sluices and hatches put into proper order, and no modern child has ever had the pleasure of seeing a proper flood, though after heavy snowfall or rainfall with the wind blowing upstream the water sometimes laps right over the road at Hatch End and into any cottages that are below road level.

As George and Sylvia walked across the bridge, feeling cross, and also annoyed with themselves for being cross, their attention was agreeably distracted by the sight of Mr. Scatcherd, sitting on a camp-stool like a real artist in the shelter of one of the arches, his feet on a bit of linoleum, industriously sketching. Moved by a common impulse they stopped, leaned their elbows on the parapet, and entered upon the countryman's eternal job of looking at other people working.

Mr. Middleton of Laverings, who being an architect was supposed by such of the county as ever thought about art to be an authority on it, had once said that Mr. Scatcherd was a museum piece and ought to be preserved in a glass case in the Barchester Museum as a type of Late Nineteenth-Century Artist. To his contemporaries this was quite clear. To George and Sylvia it would have meant very little, as indeed it would to most of their contemporaries, had they not been brought up in a home which possessed a complete set of *Punch*. This series showed with most other complete sets the peculiarity of having several volumes missing, but the years between 1870 and 1896 were in perfect condition and from them the young Hallidays had been able to reconstruct a good deal of England's Lost Civilisation.

Mr. Scatcherd was indeed a remarkable relic of the past, or of a conglomeration of pasts. His Norfolk jacket with belt, his knickerbockers buttoning below the knee, his deerstalker hat with several flies stuck in it, would alone have been enough to mark him as different from other men. When to these we add a silken scarf passed through a kind of flat ring, in itself a monu-

ment of antiquity, a drooping walrus moustache, and in bad
weather a heavy tweed Inverness cape, or, hardly expecting to be
believed, mention the green veil with which he swathed his
battered Panama in the summer against midges, it will at once
be realised that Hatch End was highly privileged. And Hatch
End was worthy of its privileges. Real R.A.'s had come over to
Hatch End from one or other of the big houses, and setting up
an easel had roughed in an oil sketch later to be expanded to
thirty square feet of canvas called "The Rising Valley from
Hatch End." Artists of more promise than fame had made oil
sketches apparently through sepia-coloured glasses and shown
them at the Set of Five exhibition held in a room off Tottenham
Court Road, as "The Rising Valley at Hatch End." Other artists
of a good deal more fame than promise had done pen and ink
sketches with a livid wash of black and yellow called "Hatch
End: Rising Valley." Julian Rivers, who had been unwillingly
absorbed by the Army, and been rescued from it as being an
artist of National Importance by people who ought to have
known better, had made a picture of Hatch End and the river
valley from old Tube tickets and some blotting-paper from the
Red Tape and Sealing Wax Office given to him by Geoffrey
Harvey and called it derisively "What we are fighting for." But as
no one except his mother and a girl in trousers who thought she
was in love with him came to the exhibition, the derision was
quite wasted.

Hatch End had watched all those gentlemen at work, and
thought poorly of their efforts, partly because they did the job
that quick it didn't seem it could be any good job, partly because
they did not sit for hours in or outside the Mellings Arms,
slowly drinking what beer there was to be got and saying
nothing, which everyone knows is the way to paint pictures,
drive a cart, shoe a horse, or even mend a car. But Mr. Scatcherd,
ah, there was a man as *studied* what he was doing. Slow and sure,
that was the way Mr. Scatcherd worked, and you could see his
pictures at The Shop any day. And it stood to reason, said Mrs.

Hubback at The Shop, that if a gentleman hadn't got Welling-
tons, nasty things they were, too, and drew the feet, the next best
was to put an old bit of lino under his boots.

"Good-morning, Mr. Scatcherd," said Sylvia from the bridge.

Mr. Scatcherd looked up and courteously removed his deerstalker.

"Good-morning to you, Miss Sylvia," he replied. "You see me
wooing Nature as of old."

"George is on leave," said Sylvia. "Can we come and look?"

Without waiting for permission she climbed down from the
bridge, followed by George, and went through the rushes to Mr.
Scatcherd's arch.

"You will excuse me getting up, or rather not getting up, I am
sure," said Mr. Scatcherd. "Everything falls down if I do. This is
merely an idea, a very rough idea as yet."

"It's *awfully* nice," said Sylvia, looking at his sketchblock,
upon which she distinctly recognised the course of the Rising
among a lot of criss-cross scratchings that were obviously reeds
and bulrushes.

"I am delighted that it gives you satisfaction," said Mr.
Scatcherd. "I always do my best to oblige. You notice of course
the focal point of the trifling sketch."

Neither George nor Sylvia had noticed it, nor could they see
anything which to them looked like more focal than anything
else, unless it were a bulrush which rose rather more proudly
than its fellows. George said would Mr. Scatcherd explain
exactly the idea that lay *behind* it, and Sylvia looked admiringly
at him.

"Now, that is an article that very few people realise the value
of," said Mr. Scatcherd, evidently gratified. "When I make up
my mental accounts—you follow me in this?—" Sylvia and
George said with one untruthful voice that they did—"I put to
the credit side those members of the public who understand
what lies *behind* a sketch. For it is not so much what I put onto
the paper, if you follow me, as the mental conception of what I

am driving at. And here I think I have summed up Everything."

Sylvia said it was quite wonderful. George said it was much better than a lot of exhibitions he'd seen in London, and anyway he didn't understand art much, and he thought they ought to be getting on as they had to fetch the fish and get some beer.

"Vidler hasn't been round yet," said Mr. Scatcherd, shedding the artist and suddenly becoming extremely practical. "I see every single thing that passes on the road. And the Arms ran out of beer last night."

"Good Lord!" said George. "Are you sure?"

"Fact," said Mr. Scatcherd. "But there is another line I might suggest. If you and Miss Sylvia come up to Rokeby I'll show you my latest sketches and my niece will give you some parsnip wine. She made it last year and it's about ready to blow the jar up. You can see Vidler's van from the house."

So depressed were George and Sylvia by the weather and the thought of his twenty-eight days' leave, of which there were only twenty-six left to run, that they accepted with gratitude an offer which in better times they would have declined. Mr. Scatcherd packed his drawing materials into a black-japanned box, put the box, the piece of linoleum and the camp-stool into a suit-case and led the way along the trodden path, with flagstones at regular intervals, through the rushes, up to the road. Here they turned to the left and walked along the village street for about a quarter of a mile to where on a little hillock stood Rokeby, with a commanding view of the road along which they had come.

Rokeby itself had good foundations and a damp course, but otherwise there was little to be said in its favour. It had been built by a Barchester contractor to house his old mother and it was his boast that the bricks were a bargain. Which indeed they doubt-less were, but a very uncompromising one, being of purplish-red colour with flecks of black, like a very nasty German sausage. Its proportions were bad, its slate roof at an abominable pitch, its chocolate-coloured woodwork tastefully relieved with coffee-colour quite revolting, and the meanness of its interior a perfect triumph of what Mr. Middleton called Builder's Joy. Its only redeeming feature, and that a feature which appealed more to romantic youth than to any possible tenant, was a couple of pretence windows on what hardly looked high enough to be the first floor, very small, with black panes and white woodwork, popularly supposed to mask a secret chamber with a corpse in it. In vain had the Barchester Society of Antiquaries, the S.P.A.B., the Georgian Society protested. In vain had the Dean gone to London and spoken to the editor of the *Jupiter*. In vain had Lord Stoke offered several times to buy the site (reputed on no grounds at all to be a British tumulus) and present it to the National Trust. The Barchester contractor, by name Stringer and of a foxy nature, said if all those societies and whatsisnames wanted that bit of ground, it stood to reason there was something up their sleeves and he was as good a man as another and so was his money and if Hatch End didn't like Rokeby they could lump it.

But judgment fell upon Mr. Stringer, for just as the house was finishing, he lost all his money owing to conceited and ill-advised speculation and had to go and live with his old mother, who never stopped letting him know what she thought of him and outlived him by three triumphant weeks. So the house was sold and Mr. Scatcherd at Northbridge, the present proprietor of Scatcherd's Sons, Est: 1824, bought Rokeby cheap as an investment. And as he was a kindly man, he let his ne'er-do-well brother (for so he considered one who had been brought up to the grocery trade and abandoned it to draw a lot of silly stuff), Mr. Scatcherd the artist, live there at a nominal rent, sending his eldest daughter Hettie to keep house for her uncle. If anyone thinks this last was an act of pure kindness, it was not, for Mr. Scatcherd the grocer's eldest unmarried daughter though an excellent housekeeper had a very bad temper. But it all worked very well, for Mr. Scatcherd the artist, who had once spent a week in nervous sin in a cheap hotel at Boulogne, always countered his niece's outburst by telling her how much worse the French Madams were, and so long as he got his meals regular women's whims meant nothing to him. So Hettie got his meals regularly and blew off most of her steam in chapel, where she was reputed to have a powerful gift.

Some of this interesting story was known to the young Hallidays, though like most young they took their elders of every station very much for granted and made no enquiries, shying away from any uncomfortable situations as they arose. But they had never been inside Rokeby before and were rather excited.

"One moment, Miss Halliday," said Mr. Scatcherd, remembering just in time that he was an Artist, and as such entitled to meet the Squire's daughter socially on equal terms, instead of merely saying Miss. "I will deal with the front door. If you and Mr. Halliday would just step back, off the doorstep—"

Obediently the young Hallidays retreated onto a woven wire mat, in which white marbles forming the word POKFRY were embedded, the tail of the R and the bottom of the E and B having been shaken by the furniture men from Northbridge dropping a large wardrobe on them and the loosened marbles having been subsequently extracted by the careful fingers of the Hatch End school children. Mr. Scatcherd, under their fascinated gaze, took a large key from the pocket of his Norfolk jacket, blew into it, saying briefly "India-rubber; it's a wonder how many crumbs it makes," and unlocked the door. It was then that the Hallidays realised the wisdom of Mr. Scatcherd's advice, for the door opened outwards and would have knocked them down had they remained on the wire mat. Almost directly inside the front door a box staircase went up to the top story, with an exiguous doorway on each side of it, just inside the house.

"Parver as you see," said Mr. Scatcherd, "but extremely apter. Mind the bottom step, Miss Halliday, and you'll get into the best sitting-room nicely."

His guests, edging round the bottom step, inserted themselves into a sitting-room as cold and cheerless as every proper best sitting-room should be.

"Hettie doesn't like me to use this room except on Christmas Day," said Mr. Scatcherd. "Come into the Studio."

He led them through a door at the further end of the sitting-room into what was obviously a back kitchen, with a sink under the window and a door into the garden. Upon a large kitchen table were evidences of the tenant's profession, such as a drawing-block, inks of several colours, a pen tray and some pencils.

"And here you see the atterleer," said Mr. Scatcherd, who had not been to Boulogne for nothing. "Where I work out my idea. I'll call Hettie. I expect she's in the kitchen or in her room. She sleeps in the front room, to keep a look out."

Sylvia, much interested in houses, asked Mr. Scatcherd where he slept.

"I have my sanctum upstairs," said Mr. Scatcherd. "There's only the one room upstairs, at the back. The windows at the front are what the French call Tromperloil and I may say, speaking as one who knows a bit about art, remarkably well done. It has a nice dormer window with a view over the chapel burying ground. You'd be surprised how many postcards of that view I've sold. Excuse me."

He opened the door into the garden and shouted "Hettie."

"It's a funny thing," said Mr. Scatcherd, coming in again and shutting the door, "how the man that built this house didn't put more doors in. Still, Hettie and me living here as we do, I daresay it's for the best. For you have no idea at all how people do talk."

As he spoke Miss Scatcherd passed the window and came in by the door. She was a middle-aged woman and if she had not cut her hair short with the kitchen scissors and refused to visit the dentist owing to some religious confusion about graven images, would not have been ill-looking. Both the young Hallidays were rather frightened of her, partly because they had

heard their nurses say something about people that kept themselves *to* themselves in a mysterious voice, partly because
George, when very small, had been taken to chapel by the
under-nurse of the moment and been horribly frightened by a
hymn with a rollicking refrain of,

*We'll all be as one in the Mighty I am,*
*When we've washed off our sin in the Blood of the Lamb,*

which religious canticle had made small George wake screaming
for most of the Christmas Holidays.

"Well REALLY Uncle that's a nice way to bring people to the
house all among your rubbish and things when you knew I'll be
turning the room out tomorrow and everything will be nice and
tidy and there's the best room that I turned out yesterday all
ready but of course you wouldn't think of that and really what
Mr. George and Miss Sylvia will think I can't imagine and just
as I'm getting my things on the line and of course it's beginning
to rain," said Hettie, all in one sentence.

"I say, I'm awfully sorry—" George began.

"It's not your fault Mr. George it's Uncle I'm at," said Hettie.
"And there you go Uncle leaving your things all over the room
when there's a nice hook behind the door can't you ask Mr.
George and Miss Sylvia to sit down it isn't as if we hadn't any
chairs."

With which words she picked up Mr. Scatcherd's Inverness
cape from a chair and hung it violently on a hook. The loop
broke and the cape fell down.

"There," said Hettie, picking it up. "I've been telling Uncle
these three days that loop's on its last legs I told him and what
must he do but go and hang it up by it knowing as well as I do
that I'll mend it as soon as I get a moment to spare and there's
my things out on the line and the rain coming down and Lady
Graham's in the village and happening to meet her in The Shop
she said she was coming here about some sketches or something

good GRACIOUS do you expect me to have fourteen pairs of hands?"

She then rushed out of the door into the garden, where the Hallidays could see her tearing damp flapping objects off the line and cramming them into a basket. The visitors felt uncomfortable and wished they had never come, the more so that their host looked very depressed and had apparently forgotten all about the parsnip wine. Just as they were wondering if they could escape without giving offence, there was a sound of footsteps coming round the side of the house. A small procession of two ladies and three children appeared on the little black verandah and walked into the studio.

"Oh, Lady Graham, it's me and George," said Sylvia. "George is on leave."

"Darling Sylvia," said Lady Graham, giving Sylvia a soft scented embrace. "And dear George. And here is Miss Merriman and Clarissa—darling Clarissa, say how do you do to Sylvia—and Robert and Edith. We have all come to see Mr. Scatcherd's lovely pictures, haven't we, Merry? Clarissa draws beautifully. She gave Mamma a picture of a dove on her birthday, and Robert made a frame and it all fell to bits, didn't it, Robert darling, and Merry glued it together again. You can turn over the pictures, darlings, but don't touch anything."

Her offspring, who appeared to understand these peculiar instructions, at once began to turn over the pen and ink drawings on the table, but with such neat elegant fingers that as Mr. Scatcherd said afterwards you would think it was the pixies.

"Let me give you a seat, Lady Graham," said Mr. Scatcherd, hastily removing drawing materials from the chairs.

"Robert goes back to school tomorrow," said Lady Graham, who took no notice of Mr. Scatcherd's efforts at hospitality. "He is at Eton now and so happy in dear Mr. Manhole's house. James is there too. And John goes back to his school the day after tomorrow, so we shall be quite sad, shan't we, Clarissa darling?"

Her ladyship then picked up Mr. Scatcherd's cloak, examined

it with great interest, sat down upon the one chair which Mr. Scatcherd had not yet cleared, and draped the cloak very becomingly round her, while Miss Merriman, who had known the Hallidays for some years, talked to Sylvia.

"WELL Uncle," said Hettie, putting her basket of damp clothes just outside the door and coming in with a rush. "Letting her ladyship sit on that old chair and hold your cape what her ladyship must think I can't think."

"But it's a lovely cape," said Lady Graham. "I would like to get one like it for darling Mamma. She is not very well, but she had a very happy birthday and we all gave her presents, didn't we, darlings? And now we want to see Mr. Scatcherd's lovely pictures. I am going to have a Bring and Buy Sale at Holdings in the summer and we thought people would love to buy Mr. Scatcherd's pictures and we are going to have a kind of auction. Miss Merriman knows all about it, don't you, Merry? I would always much rather buy a thing, but such a lot of people like to see a thing getting more and more expensive till they feel equal to buying it. Still, it is all for the Barsetshire Regiment Comfort Fund, so if Mr. Scatcherd can spare some of his lovely drawings, it will be quite perfect."

"Mr. Scatcherd was making a new sketch in the water-meadows this morning," said Sylvia. "Do show it, Mr. Scatcherd."

The artist, gratified, began to unpack his suit-case.

"Now Uncle don't you bother her ladyship with your rubbishing sketches and things," said his unappreciative niece. "I'll get up some of my parsnip wine your ladyship and I'm sure your young ladies and young gentleman and Miss Merriman will enjoy it it won't do them the least harm why can't you clear the table a bit Uncle not stand there doing nothing and get some of the glasses out of the best room and why you keep Miss Merriman standing all this time I don't know but as I always say I've only the one pair of hands and can't do everyone's work not if I was paid to which goodness knows I'm not in this house."

Having thus made most of her guests feel acutely uncomfortable and distinctly addled in the intellect, she hustled herself onto the verandah, picked up her washing basket and disappeared into the kitchen. Mr. Scatcherd brought glasses from the front room, Miss Merriman talked to George about the possibility of county cricket that year and Lady Graham gave Sylvia a great deal of information about her eldest daughter Emmy, now eighteen, who suddenly wished to go to an agricultural college and breed bulls.

"I suppose it is a kind of inheritance," said Lady Graham sighing, "because darling Papa used to love breeding bulls. Emmy is spending this summer at Rushwater, which belongs to my nephew Martin since darling Papa died, and of course it would be *most* convenient, because our old agent Mr. Macpherson is devoted to her and would do *any*thing."

Miss Merriman, who had not lived under Lady Graham's roof all through the war without observing her kindly and closely, quite realised the cloud of imbecility in which that delightful creature's talk was apt to engulf her hearers, and came to Sylvia's rescue. Lady Graham relapsed into her usual state of admiring her family and thinking of absolutely nothing at all, and then Hettie came back with a jug of cloudy parsnip wine and some biscuits.

"Biscuits, my darlings," said Lady Graham. "How lovely. We can't get any in Little Misfit this month."

"WELL if I'd known that your ladyship," said Hettie, shocked, "I'd have told Father he would always keep some for your ladyship and I get the broken ones only two points a pound and just as fresh as the whole ones and they do seem to go further and just as well for really with Uncle wanting lunches and things to take out with him I really don't know which way to turn sometimes."

"Merry, we must get some broken biscuits," said Lady Graham.

"We usually do," said Miss Merriman, who since she came to Holdings as friend and secretary to Lady Emily Leslie, Lady

Graham's mother, had gradually taken over most of the house-keeping. "We get a large tin of broken biscuits from the Barchester Stores. It is after twelve, Lady Graham, and perhaps we ought to be getting back."

On hearing this Lady Graham fell into a frenzy of business-likeness, and rapidly chose several dozen reproductions of Mr. Scatcherd's art. So overcome was the artist by his visitor's charm that he wished to present them to the Bring and Buy, but Lady Graham, ably seconded by Hettie, took no notice of him at all and paid the usual price.

"But before I go, Mr. Scatcherd," said Lady Graham, with a radiant smile less brilliant than her mother's but most upsetting to the artist's emotions, "you must show me the picture you were doing this morning."

"It's not really polished yet, Lady Graham," said Mr. Scatcherd. "But if you insist—"

He nervously sorted the drawings in his suit-case, while Miss Merriman, mistress of herself as always, watchful of the family whose protectress she had in a way become during the last six years, thought how like Lady Graham was becoming to her mother. Lady Emily, that wind-blown sparkling fountain, mingling deep love, intense interest, mockery; adorable, impractical and maddening in a breath, could never be repeated. In Agnes the gift of loving (though often wielding to a general mush of amiability), the great interest in other people (though mostly deceptive), were renewed. Mockery she neither had nor recognised, and for all her helpless appearance was extremely practical. But her exquisite unruffled face, as the years passed, had begun to show a little of her mother's hawk glance, a curving of the lips in piercing sweetness; and, as Miss Merriman had just noticed and not for the first time, she had the gift of never losing track of a subject however her conversation might have divagated from it. Miss Merriman sighed; she did not quite know why. But a secretary-friend-companion is not paid to sigh, and Miss Merriman knew where she stood to a hair's breadth and let no one enter her private world, so the sigh was unheard and Mr. Scatcherd, enraptured by Lady Graham's request, had now found the new drawing.

"Come and look, darlings," said Lady Graham.

The three children at once grouped themselves round their mother with such grace that George Halliday suddenly felt that Motherhood was the most beautiful thing in the world.

"It is so delightful to see a real picture before it is finished," said Lady Graham, "and then afterwards when it is really finished one can see what it is. Do tell us *all* about it, Mr. Scatcherd."

"Mother, it's the river," said Clarissa.

"I see the bulrushes," said Robert.

"I see the biggest bulrush," said Edith.

Lady Graham raised her lovely eyes, expressing mutely to the company in general her admiration of her gifted offspring.

"That little lady," said Mr. Scatcherd, who was then assailed by a torturing doubt as to the propriety of such a mode of address, "has hit upon the focal point. Hit it in one, I needn't tell you, Lady Graham, what it is. It may," he continued, screwing up his eyes and looking at the drawing as if it were forty yards away, "give the impression of a bulrush, but that is not to the point. It is the concentration of the observer's interest that is the important thing, and the little critic has hit it in one."

He then wondered if little critic was less suitable than little lady and fell into a kind of swoon, through which he heard Lady Graham's cooing voice uttering idiotic platitudes, till Miss Merriman said firmly that they would all be late for lunch if they didn't go at once.

Roused by a vision of her children starving, Lady Graham got up.

"When that picture is finished, Mr. Scatcherd," she said, "will you let me buy it for the Bring and Buy Sale? And we will make everyone pay a shilling to guess what it is, and the one that guesses it right will get it."

"Suppose no one guesses right," said George Halliday.

"Then we'll make everyone pay to guess again," said Lady Graham. "Now, darlings, we must go. Come and see us before you go back to Germany, George; and Sylvia too."

"It's not Germany, it's Italy," said George.

"Then you must know the Strelsas," said Lady Graham, with what for her was considerable animation. They are cousins of ours, you know, and had a lovely villa outside Florence."

George, feeling a hideous boor, said he hadn't been in Florence at all.

"And, Sylvia, you must come over soon," Lady Graham continued. "My brother David is getting leave from the Air Force on Thursday and will be with us for a few weeks except that with David you never know. He would adore you."

She then wrapped Mr. Scatcherd's Inverness cape round her and prepared to go.

"That is Mr. Scatcherd's cape, Lady Graham," said Miss Merriman.

"How *stupid* of me," said Agnes, letting Miss Merriman remove the cape and give it to Hettie. "Say good-bye, darlings."

In a short chorus of good-byes the Graham family left the house, and a few moments later the trot of a pony's feet could be heard as they drove back to Holdings. To the rest of the company life suddenly felt rather drab. The church clock chimed twelve.

"George! the fish!" said Sylvia. "Oh, Miss Scatcherd, do you know if Vidler's van has been yet?"

Hettie said she couldn't rightly say but Mrs. Panter down the road would know for sure as she had got her washing in early and was ironing in the kitchen and never missed a thing and if Mr. George and Miss Sylvia would come with her they'd soon know.

"It's very kind of you, Miss Scatcherd," said Sylvia.

"Pleasure," said Hettie briefly. "Matter of fact I want some fish myself but it's no good telling Uncle when everything goes right through his head like a bit of butter or I'd have told him to keep a look out when he was doing his sketching and things and nothing to think about this way Miss Sylvia."

The young Hallidays were so confused by Hettie's comparison of butter to a boring agent that they almost forgot to say good-bye to Mr. Scatcherd, who was putting away his sketching materials in a kind of artistic trance, seeing in his mind's eye the heads of the three youngest children in pen and ink on a postcard, reproduced by the thousand and sold all over the country under the title "Angel Faces," which he somehow felt he had seen somewhere.

"You'd better let me have that Uncle," said Hettie, sweeping the notes and silver that Lady Graham had left on the table into her basket. "You'll only be spending it and it might as well go into the bank we're told we ought to save and I'm sure if anyone saves I do though no one thanks me for it."

Mr. Scatcherd looked rather dashed. Sylvia and George felt sorry for him, but there was nothing they could do, so they said good-bye and followed Hettie round the house, out of the front gate and across the road to No. 6, Clarence Cottages, where Mrs. Panter, the wife of Mr. Halliday's carter, was plainly visible at her ironing, just inside the front door.

"Good-morning, Mrs. Panter," said Hettie. "Has that Vidler been up yet?"

"Good-morning, Miss Sylvia and Master George," said Mrs. Panter, putting her iron on its end on the stone floor, wiping her hands on her apron, and taking no notice of Miss Scatcherd at all. "Panter told me you were on leave, Master George, so I said, 'I'll be seeing Master George here before long.'"

Sylvia and George shook hands, both secretly wondering if Miss Scatcherd would mind being ignored. But Hettie, although from foreign parts and the more urban civilisation of Northbridge, quite understood that the gentry must come first and surveyed the scene with an impartial eye.

"Vidler went up to The Shop a quarter of an hour ago," said Mrs. Panter to the young Hallidays. "I saw you go up with

Hettie's Uncle, so I said to Vidler's young man, 'Mind you keep something for Hatch House.' I've got your fish here, Hettie. You can take it, it's on the dresser."

She picked up her iron, licked her finger, touched the iron, listened disapprovingly, put the iron back on the stove, took another from the stove, licked her finger, listened with approval to the hiss, rubbed the fresh iron on an old piece of blanket and went on ironing one of Panter's shirts.

The audience was obviously at an end. George and Sylvia thanked Mrs. Panter, thanked Hettie very much for her parsnip wine, and went to The Shop. Here Mrs. Hubback had a reeking parcel of fish waiting for them and an untidy bundle of washing for her daughter. They then pursued their way, not very hope-fully, to the Mellings Arms where Mr. Geo. Panter—the cart-er's cousin—was licensed to sell beer and spirits to be consumed on or off the premises. The little bar was warm with humanity, a warmth very welcome on so horrid a spring day, and the young Hallidays thought hopefully of beer or even cider.

"Not a drop of anything, Miss Sylvia," said Mr. Geo. Panter regretfully. "Not on the premises nor off. Pilward's have prom-ised me some before the end of the week. Come in on Friday and I'll see what I can do."

There was nothing for it but to say it didn't matter, and the young Hallidays were turning away disconsolately when Mr. Geo. Panter, turning his back upon the other visitors, favoured them with a wink and the information that Lord Pomfret's keeper had left a couple of rabbits with him for Mrs. Halliday and if they could manage them it would save sending the barman up. The barman, who was a young lady in a pullover and a kind of naval trousers highly unbecoming to the female form, looked at George and said it wasn't everyone she'd put herself out for, but if it was to oblige Mr. Halliday, or was it Captain, she didn't mind if she did run up on her bike. George chival-rously said he would hate her to do it and she must have one with him when Pilward's stuff came in, and where were the rabbits.

Mr. George Panter silently led the way to the stables and from a corner produced two rabbits looking very dead. From another corner he produced four quart bottles of beer, wrapped a dirty piece of sacking round them and put beer and rabbits into a large plaited fish basket, remarking that he would chalk it up. George took the basket, handed half a crown to Mr. Geo. Panter with the request that he would have one on him when Pilward sent, collected his sister and went away, while Mr. Geo. Panter returned to the bar.

The return of the young Hallidays was not altogether a success, for according to Hubback, who received her washing with no gratitude at all, cook was in a fine state about her fish and three telephone messages had been received about whose senders Hubback could remember nothing except that one of them was a name something like Bantam.

"Oh Lord!" said George as he and Sylvia wandered out into the garden again to kill time before lunch. "Coming home is all right, but it does get one down."

Sylvia agreed, pointing out at the same time that they had had parsnip wine, got some beer that someone else probably wanted, and had seen Lady Graham, which was always nice. Also that they were going to tea at the Deanery, which might be fun.

George, possessed by melancholy and a nostalgia for Lady Graham, said it mightn't. What he wanted, he said, was lots of drink, a radio-gramophone with a lot of good new dance records, and six dozen ravishing starry-eyed blondes and brunettes all in love with him at once and beautifully dressed in expensive clothes. And a very powerful car painted bright red, he added. Also to make his Colonel clean his, George's leather and brass and webbing and then make him do it all over again.

Sylvia admired his despondency and his nostalgia and would have liked to say what she wanted. But what she wanted, which was either to be an explorer in hot countries, or to have four very nice children and a husband who was rather rich and liked dancing, seemed to her too dull for George. So she only made sympathetic noises. Then George remembered that he wanted two screws, so they went over to the carpenter's shop where Caxton was reading the *Barsetshire Free Press* till it was time to finish his lunch hour. He was a spare elderly man who had worked, as he far too often said, being a man of few words and those far too often repeated, father and son for Hatch House this many a year. As his father had been one of Lord Pomfret's gamekeepers and he was himself childless, this description was generally held to be a figure of speech, and had indeed been invented by the carpenter for the express purpose of luring half-crowns from visitors to Hatch House or tourists at the Mellings Arms. The further to impress his hereditary carpentership upon a credulous world, he affected a kind of square paper hat, like a strawberry punnet upside down, in the almost vanished tradition of the craft. The hat, by a not unnatural confusion of ideas, had led the young Hallidays in their nursery years to call him Mr. Chips, but this name they now kept for their private use, as most of the Brave New World belonged to a generation that had never seen or heard of Happy Families, and in any case only associated the name with a film, if indeed they associated it with anything at all.

Caxton folded the *Barsetshire Free Press*, neatly, put his large plane on it as a kind of paperweight, and shook hands warmly with Master George.

"But you haven't grown, Master George, not a quarter of an inch," he said reproachfully. "There's the mark I made on the door, last time I measured you. No, not a quarter of an inch, nor an eighth."

"Oh, I say, Caxton," said George, standing up manfully for himself, "you can't expect me to grow any more. After all I'm twenty-four."

Caxton said that made no odds. His own cousin Fred, over at Nutfield, grew half an inch at twenty-four when he had the fever so bad; and he had lost all his hair and wouldn't wear a wig. No,

Master George hadn't grown so much as a sixteenth of an inch, as there was the mark on the door to prove.

"I can't have fever on the spot to oblige," said George, "but I'll tell you what I can do. I'll take my shoes off and you can measure me."

As this was exactly what Caxton was itching to do and George well knew it, the offer was after a little proper reluctance accepted. George, leaning against the bench, began to force the shoe off one foot by pushing the heel down with the other foot.

"That's not the way, Master George," said Caxton, his neat and accurate soul disturbed by so unworkmanlike a method. "You'll ruin those shoes; hand-made, too. Unlace them first, Master George, and ease them a bit."

George, realising that in a moment Caxton would be capable of putting his leg in the large vice and taking his shoe off with a chisel and mallet, with a T-square and a gouge in reserve, sat down meekly on a stool, unlaced his shoes, took them off and put them neatly side by side.

"That's better, Master George," said Caxton approvingly. "And now your socks."

"Oh Lord! not my socks," said George, drawing his feet under the stool.

"You can't tell with wool, Master George," said Caxton. "The way the wash felts up the things now, it might make a difference of an eighth easy."

"Out of these socks I will not go," said George. "It was one of the worst shocks in my life when I looked at my own feet when I was about fourteen and realised that they were getting grown up."

"It's a pity," said Caxton. "Spoiling a good job, Master George, that's what it is. Miss Sylvia wouldn't mind."

Sylvia said she was very sorry, but she did mind, frightfully, and simply couldn't bear people's bare feet unless one was bathing and even then they mostly looked perfectly ghastly.

"Well, I'll tell you what I *can* do," said George. "I'll give you one of my socks to-morrow and you can measure how thick it is and subtract it. And now let's see."

He walked over to the shop door where on one of the jambs were recorded the heights of himself and his sister at various ages in indelible pencil. He stood with his back against the jamb, heels well pressed against the wood head erect.

"Time was," said Caxton with melancholy pride, "that I laid the ruler on your head as easy as anything, Master George. It's a job for a ladder now."

He dragged a wooden box to the door, mounted it, and after giving George a number of meticulous instructions as to the way he must hold himself, keeping a ruler flat on his head the while, finally professed himself satisfied, made a pencil mark and got down.

"You can move now, Master George," he said.

"I can't," said George. "I've got stiff all over, catalepsy or something. Oh Lord! I'll never be able to bend my knees again. Help!"

Sylvia kindly assisted her brother to recover from his rigor and he put his shoes on again, while Caxton used his steel measure.

"I've lost my eye," said Caxton. "Six foot and three-eighths it was November three years ago. Now it's fair six foot and half an inch. I wouldn't have thought it of myself."

So downcast was he that George and Sylvia had to do their utmost to restore his self-confidence. George insisted that the socks had done it, while Sylvia pointed out that his thick and rather wavy hair needed cutting badly. But as Caxton took a perverse pleasure in refusing comfort, they gave it up. The sound of the stable clock striking one reached them.

"I say, we must go," said George, "or Hubback will be put out. Oh, by the way, Caxton, she asked me to remind you about easing the service door in the hall."

"You tell her All in good time, Master George," said Caxton, coming out of his despondency. "Miss Hubback knows that there's a time for everything and everything at its time and when the time for that door does come, come it will. If she didn't use her foot to it all the time for which there's no excuse seeing the service slab with hinges I put up for her so she could put her trays down and use her hands, that door wouldn't need easing."

As the feud between the carpenter and Hubback was of long standing, Sylvia tweaked George's sleeve to intimate that he had better leave well alone, so they went back to the house.

"Lord! I never asked Caxton for those screws," said George.

# CHAPTER 2

It was well known in the Close and the County that Mrs.
Crawley's tea-parties at the Deanery were not so much for the
pleasure of herself and her friends, whom she would have
preferred to see in a quieter way, as to express to the world of
Barsetshire her opinion of the Palace, where the fine tradition of
stinginess and inhospitality inaugurated by Bishop Proudie's
wife still held sway, to the fury and scorn of all well-thinking
people. Mrs. Crawley, eighth child of a country vicarage herself
and with a large family of children and grandchildren, had
carried on the subterranean feud between Palace and Deanery
with tact and energy for a number of years. With remarkable
self-restraint she never brandished her family before the Bishop
and his wife with their one depressing son who worked in what
his parents called the Mission Field, though it was an office in
Westminster, and at her yearly dinner for the Palace the best of
the Country and the Close were always invited. Never, except to
such intimate friends as Mrs. Morland the novelist, or Lord and
Lady Pomfret, did the Dean's wife let herself go on the dinner
given once a year by the Palace to the Deanery, but her silence
was extremely eloquent and left no doubt in the minds of the
anti-Palace party about the meager amount of food and the very
poor quality of wine supplied on these occasions. Only once had
she been known to speak a little of her mind when after a
particularly dull and penitential evening at the Palace during the

war she had remarked to old Canon Thorne, who needed shouting at though even then he neither heard nor understood, that the silver and mahogany wine cooler in the palace dining-room was a very fine piece of eighteenth-century work.

"And the Bishop said to me," said Mrs. Crawley with loud and meticulous articulation, "that his predecessor used to have it full of wine for dinner-parties, but he and his wife thought ferns more suitable to a Christian's dining-room."

When it had been sufficiently explained to Canon Thorne that no one was talking about the Bishopric of Ferns, his indignation at this profanation of a wine-cooler, and one with exquisite classical handles and lions feet, knew no bounds, and the whole company assembled had shivered with contempt.

This story had of course a wide circulation, and though it was not a particularly good one was received as a kind of Shibboleth by Close and County and it has become a point of honour with both to re-tell it in and out of season. On this particular afternoon Octavia Needham, youngest and dullest daughter of the Deanery on a visit to her parents with her little boy, was telling the story to an old friend of the family, David Leslie, who as we know was staying with his sister Lady Graham at Hold-ings.

"Even my sister Agnes, who would make excuses for Caligula," said David Leslie, "would be shocked by that story. The Bishop is the sort of person who would cut the General Confession and the Creed out of the service and say it was because there was Er War on. If we aren't careful he will cut them out before long because there's Er Peace on."

Octavia, who was as dull as she was competent, said wouldn't that be rather dreadful. David said it would and lost interest in her, but Octavia, seeing her friend Mrs. Noel Merton across the large drawing-room, had at once lost interest in David, who detached himself and drifted away to say how do you do to his hostess, whom he had not yet been able to reach.

"Octavia has been telling me about the wine-cooler," said David, shaking hands.

"It is a very handsome piece of furniture," said Mrs. Crawley with an air of complete candour, and they both laughed. "But do you know the really shocking thing the Bishop has done?"

David said he didn't owing to having been abroad a good deal, but if it was simony or heresy, he would be happy to become a Common Informer, a person he had always wished to be, and tell the Court of Arches or any other competent body.

"He has arranged," said Mrs. Crowley, sinking her voice and drawing David slightly apart from the crowd, "to broadcast on three successive Fridays."

"Good God, I beg your pardon," said David, "though speaking as one who was long ago and for a very short time a hanger-on of the Wireless Boys in the good old days of Savoy Hill, I should say they had done the arranging not his lordship."

"I daresay they did," said Mrs. Crawley, "for I don't think even the Bishop's wife could approve the subject."

"What is it?" said David. "Or is it one of those subjects that we all talk about without having the faintest idea of its sinister implications."

"It is 'Our Duty'—oh, how do you do, Lady Fielding, and Anne dear. You do know David Leslie, don't you?"

Lady Fielding said a few polite words and passed on with her daughter.

"Ought I to know her?" said David. "I'm a bit rusty about the social world."

"Her husband is our Chancellor," said Mrs. Crawley. "Charming people."

"We all are," said David. "But if I do not at once hear what the proud prelate is broadcasting about, my charm will desert me entirely."

"'Our Duty to a Penitent Foe,'" said Mrs. Crawley, as if she were mentioning leprosy.

"My dear Mrs. Crawley," said David, "while in His Majesty's

Royal Air Force, though alas too old to be a gallant dare-devil of the air, I learnt some new and very offensive words. But not one of them, I assure you, would express my feelings. What would Anselm have said, or Becket? Or, to put the matter on a wider oecumenical basis, what would Pope Hildebrand have said? His idea of treating Penitent Foes was to keep them standing at the back door dressed in a sheet without any boots on in a snow-storm for seventy-two hours, and that was only a beginning."

"Still, you must admit that the Emperor Henry took the wind out of Hildebrand's sails by repenting," said Mrs. Crawley.

"Now, you are what I call a really well-educated woman," said David admiringly. "how true that is. And all our Penitent Foes, blast them, will take the wind out of our sails nicely. When Peace breaks out, you mark my words."

He then lost interest in Mrs. Crawley, who turned to her duties as hostess and welcomed the Halliday family; at least three quarters of it, for Mr. Halliday had basely produced a committee meeting at the Country Club.

"I am so sorry about my husband," said Mrs. Halliday. "I believe it is a real engagement, but he certainly only remembered it because he is frightened of tea-parties. He is coming to fetch me and I intend to stay here till he comes."

Then Mrs. Crawley said how nice to see George and Sylvia and how nice that they had both had leave and wafted them on to the further end of the big drawing room where a small crowd indicated the presence of Mrs. Brandon. But before they could penetrate the massed backs and elbows of their friends, they were detained by Lady Fielding, who wanted to talk to Mrs. Halliday abut the W.V.S.

"This is Anne," said Lady Fielding, who was accompanied by her daughter. "She is doing Domestic Economy at present. Now, Mrs. Halliday, there is this question of the Clothing Exchange. We have a perfect glut of very short pale green sateen frocks and very short pale pink knickers all in quite horrid condition. They come from the evacuee children and none of the other members want them. The cottages say they aren't decent, and they are perfectly right. We shall have to do something about it and about the use of the gas ring at the depot, because Mrs. Betts is being very unpleasant about it and it is her room after all, even if she does charge us a ridiculous rent for it. And Madame Tomkins has had a row with Mrs. Betts and I really can't let Madame Tomkins go, for she is the only good dressmaker in Barchester and makes Anne's things so cleverly. I do hope you are coming to the Committee meeting next week."

The two ladies then fell into matters of high politics.

Meanwhile the young Hallidays were doing their best to make friends with Anne Fielding, and both feeling a little shy of their new acquaintance, which was for them a new experience. It was not that they had taken a dislike to Anne, for they both liked the look of her. It was not that she was stand-offish to them, for her manners, though less slap-dash than those of their friends, were charming without affectation. But they had an impression, though neither of them was equal to defining it, that she was much more grown-up than they were.

"I'm twenty-two," said Sylvia, who believed in direct tactics, "and George is twenty-four."

Anne Fielding said, "Oh"; not at all snubbingly, in fact in a very kind and interested way, but made no further comment.

"How old are you?" said Sylvia desperately.

Anne said she was nearly nineteen.

"Then if we do get peace or anything, I suppose you won't be called up," said Sylvia.

"I'm afraid not," said Anne, flushing slightly. "I did want to be an ambulance driver, but Dr. Ford says it would be out of the question, so I am doing cooking which I love and if only they didn't make us learn economics too, which is all very silly, it would be perfect. I suppose you are a Wren," she added, with an admiring glance at Sylvia's good figure, fair wavy hair and corn-flower blue eyes.

Sylvia realised that Anne was somehow paying her a high

compliment and almost apologised as she said she was in the W.A.A.Fs and George was in the Barsetshire Regiment.

"A great friend of mine called Robin Dale was in the Barsetshire," said Anne. "But his foot came off in Italy, so he is teaching classics at Southbridge."

George had been at Southbridge, so the ice was now broken and they talked very comfortably about nothing in particular till George suggested tea and they went down the noble square staircase to the dining-room, where a passable imitation of tea was set out and the noise was deafening. George was at once pounced upon by quantities of old, or rather, young friends, who would willingly have pounced on Sylvia. But Sylvia suddenly felt a strong protective instinct towards Anne Fielding, who was nearly nineteen and could not be an ambulance driver, so she pushed Anne into a seat in one of the high deep-embrasured windows, ordered her to stay there, reached over several people's heads for tea and such cake as there was, and installed herself by Anne, with cups and plates on the window seat between them. Here again Sylvia was surprised by the grown-up-ness of her new friend. For not only did Anne know who most of the people in the room were, but she seemed to have some private clue to them and spoke with a kind of tolerance of their various characteristics, more than once making Sylvia laugh. Most admirable of all was her repulse of Miss Pettinger. That almost universally disliked headmistress of the Barchester High School, who was by many of the guests present considered to be no better than an agent from the Palace come to spy out the fatness of the land, or in other words to try to poach some of the Deanery guests for the bishop's wife's tea-parties, seeing two young women having tea considered them as her lawful prey, and approaching them with the smile that girls who really had the Honour of the School at heart thought so perfectly sweet, said How nice it was to see Anne, and Celia Halliday wasn't it, and she must hear *all* about what they were doing. At this point Sylvia would have weakly said, "Oh, do come and sit with us,

Miss Pettinger, there's oceans of room and I'll get you some tea," and then repented at leisure. What was her astonishment when Anne, who was nearly nineteen, got up, stepped forward, shook hands with Miss Pettinger and said "How do you do, Miss Pettinger. This is Sylvia Halliday. Did you see Lady Graham? I think she was looking for you," upon which Miss Pettinger had at once made her adieux and gone to throw herself before Lady Graham, who was letting the Precentor tell her about his delightful weekend at the School of Church Music, while gazing at him with the rapt attention which deceived even herself.

"Tiresome woman," said Anne Fielding in a very grown-up way as she sat down again.

"Anne, how *could* you?" said Sylvia, half admiring, half shocked. "Lady Graham didn't really want her, did she?"

"I don't know," said Anne, meeting Sylvia's searching look with a limpid and innocent countenance. "I shouldn't think she did. Nobody could. I thought she was quite horrid when I was at the High School for a few terms."

"She is a foul beast," said Sylvia dispassionately, "and I loathe her. But I couldn't have been brave enough to—" She paused.

"It was a social lie," said Anne, filling up the gap. "I have noticed that mummy is very good at them, and my great friend Robin Dale says they are very important and only people who have no sense would boggle at using them."

Sylvia almost gaped at her new friend's casuistry.

"But don't you feel horrid afterwards?" she said.

"No," said Anne, with a thoughtful, questioning inflexion peculiar to her. "No; I don't. But if I had let Miss Pettinger sit in the window seat I would have felt extremely horrid."

"I know. Contaminated," said Sylvia.

"Like mustard-gas or lepers," said Anne, suddenly a young girl again, and they giggled in a very normal way over such county characters as Sir Edmund Pridham fighting his County Council battles over again to the tired and courteous Lord

Pomfret, or Miss Pemberton from Northbridge with her mush-room hat and large raffia bag keeping a firm eye on her distin-guished lodger Mr. Downing, till Mrs. Halliday came up to collect Sylvia, followed by George.

"Father hasn't turned up," she said to Sylvia, "which is a triumph of experience over hope, and Lady Graham can take us back, which is so much better than the bus. George is staying to supper with the Crawleys. And your mother is looking for you, Anne. She is in the hall."

And in the hall they found Lady Fielding, who was talking to Lady Graham about the Bring and Buy Sale at Little Misfit.

"And that somehow makes me think of Rushwater," said Lady Graham. "I daresay it is because we used to have a Village Concert in the racquet court every year when darling Papa was alive. You know my nephew Martin Leslie owns it now. He was rather wounded in Italy, so he was allowed to come home and look after the place. He is so nice and I am *longing* for him to get married," said her ladyship, gazing piercingly at Sylvia and Anne. "I am taking darling Mamma over on Sunday for the day. Do come with us, Sylvia, and Anne Fielding too. Martin will adore you both. We will have a nice talk about it on the way back. You must both come to lunch first and we will make a plan about how Anne is to get home. Luckily David seems to have a lot of petrol, I cannot think why, so we shall manage beauti-fully."

A stranger would have given the whole affair up and gone mad long before this, but Lady Fielding and Mrs. Halliday knew from experience that under Lady Graham's vague and endearing idiocy there lay a very practical streak; and Mrs. Halliday knew that Miss Merriman would quietly squash all impractical plans and see that everything was neatly arranged. The invitation was gratefully accepted.

"And now," said Lady Graham, "where is David? He brought me here, so he will have to take me back. He is *so* naughty and forgets what time it is."

Her ladyship, having spoken these despairing words in accents of soft, unruffled calm, sat down on a hall chair and looked with gentle appeal at everyone. The elder ladies had every confidence that Lady Graham would not be deserted by Providence, but in George's heart a thousand swords at once sprang from their scabbards to rescue beauty and kindness in distress.

"I'll find him, Lady Graham," he said. "At least I mean if you could tell me what he is like."

"David?" said Lady Graham. "Darling David. He has been in the Air Force all the time though he never flew, at least not driving the aeroplane himself, though of course he had to fly to a great many places, but always with someone else turning the handles. The children adore him."

George felt that Lady Graham's words had a deeply affecting, nay sacred quality, but at the same time gave him no help at all.

"I mean, is he in uniform or anything?" he asked.

"Yes," said Lady Graham thoughtfully. "In Air Force uniform, with half a wing on him."

George sped zealously away. Lady Graham, who had the art of appearing at home and extremely comfortable wherever she was, settled herself upon the uncompromising wooden hall chair and relapsed into her customary abstraction, thinking of nothing at all unless the perfection of one or other of her family crossed her mind. Mrs. Halliday, getting rather impatient, looked at the hall clock, saw that they would have missed the six o'clock bus in any case, and resigned herself. Lady Fielding, a very busy woman, called to Anne that they must be going.

"Can we wait just one moment, mummy," said Anne, casting a quick look towards the stairs. "Sylvia and I are just making a plan to go to the Sale of Work at the Palace because we both have some horrid things we think we could get rid of. Don't you think, Mummy, I could give them that hideous silver buckle that Gradka gave me last year? I have been trying to like it for a long time, but I simply can't. Gradka," she explained, turning to Sylvia, "was a Mixo-Lydian maid we had, who cooked divinely, but we found her a little exhausting, because she was so anxious to get information about literature."

Again Sylvia had the sensation, unformulated, that Anne was of an older generation, of a more civilised age, but Lady Fielding who appeared to look upon her daughter as a child, said it was an excellent plan and she would look through the drawer where she put everything she bought at sales, except things like home-made jam or tomato chutney, and see what she could spare. And now, she said, they must really go.

And even as she spoke George came into the hall, accompanied by David Leslie.

"Oh; Lady Graham," said George, and became dumb.

"Darling David," said Lady Graham, with mild and placid reproach (such reproach as Angels might give, George considered) in her gentle voice. "I have been waiting for you for quite a long time. George was *so* kind and went to find you."

"Oh rot!" said George, going bright red and knocking three hats and an umbrella off an oak chest. "I mean anyone would have found—would have found—him for you," he finished lamely, and then fell into Stygian depths of gloom, realising that by his grossly culpable ignorance of David Leslie's rank, he had forfeited Lady Graham's esteem for ever; which drove him to the nearest equivalent of suicide he could think of at the moment, namely to grovel on the floor collecting the hats and umbrella.

"Flight-Lieutenant they call me," said David, at once grasping the situation and carelessly willing to help an obliging young man. "But it means nothing. They just gave it to me so that I could go for drives in aeroplanes without getting into trouble with the police. Everyone calls me David. Darling Agnes, now that I am here you might as well get up from the chair where you look so nice and come with me to find the car, else darling Mamma and darling Merry and any of your darling children who are allowed to stay up for dinner will think we have been abducted."

Agnes, across whose soft mind an idea had flitted that darling David was making fun of her, smiled tolerantly, rose, adjusted her fox fur in a way that made everyone feel she was wearing at least ten thousand pounds' worth of the richest Imperial black sables, and said good-bye to the Fieldings and Hallidays. David said good-bye to the Hallidays and Lady Fielding.

"And this is Anne," said Lady Fielding. "I don't think you know her."

"But I shall, if you will permit me," said David, looking down in a benevolent way upon a girl whose elegant figure at once met with his approval. Her face he could not well see, for in spite of Double Summer Time the panelled hall was dim.

"May I come and call upon you and Sir Robert while I am here?" he said to Lady Fielding.

"Of course you may," said Lady Fielding. "I merely make the reservation that you know perfectly well you won't."

"Alas! how well you know me," said David. "But beware the Double-Crosser. I shall come though hell itself should garp."

Lady Fielding looked enquiringly at him.

"Though why the Old School of Shakespearean actors say it like that instead of gape, I cannot tell," said David. "Any more than I can tell why Abraham becomes Arbraham at one point in the service. Forgive me, but I see that my sister Agnes is talking to Mrs. Downing, and if she does that Miss Pemberton will walk over from Northbridge to Little Misfit with a raffia hat and a homespun cloak and kill her. Good-bye."

He then dexterously cut out Mr. Downing, hustled—if as he said to his mother after dinner one could really be said to hustle anything so like a soft, warm jelly-fish—his sister Agnes into the car and drove her away.

Perhaps the sun got behind the tall elms in the Close. Or so Anne Fielding felt, so that she was quite glad to leave the party with her mother and go home, which was only to the opposite side of the most beautiful Close in England. The house where

the Fieldings lived had for some years been tenanted by old
Canon Robarts, who had got gently madder and madder till he
died. His last recorded act and remark, namely a feeble blow
upon the bedclothes and the words, which his nurse had to bend
over him to catch, "I've got him now," were by the lower orders
of the Cathedral, the verger, under-verger, bell-ringer, choristers
and so forth, not to speak of Old Tomkins, Madame Tomkin's
father-in-law and jobbing gardener to most of the Close, who
still mowed the level lawns with a scythe, taken as referring to
the devil, whom Canon Robarts was supposed to have finally
squashed in the person of a large blow-fly. But to the higher
orders it was abundantly clear that the Canon was referring to
the Bishop and had died happy under the impression that he
had got the Bishop removed by a special Act of Parliament.

Number Seventeen (for it was a peculiarity of the Close that
every house had a number and no house except the Deanery, and
that only a courtesy title as it were, a name) was one of the most
handsome houses where all were handsome, three stories high,
built of red brick with large sash windows. Over the front door,
which was reached by three wide curved stone steps, was an
elegant shell projection to keep visitors from being rained upon,
and along the top of the house ran a stone balustrade with urns
at regular intervals. At the back of the wide, flagged hall the
most exquisite spiral staircase in the county wound upwards
with harmonious curve of treads, landings and banisters, lighted
from a flattened glass dome like a Chinese umbrella. For more
than six years a black roller blind had been drawn nightly across
this skylight and on two occasions during the war had the blind,
imperfectly fastened, sprung back with a jump, letting the light
stream to heaven and advertise the whereabouts of Number
Seventeen The Close to Whom it might concern. By great good
luck both nights had been wet and windy and the A.R.P. patrol
had been too much occupied in holding their heads down
against the wind and trying to keep their coats done up to notice

what was happening, and on both occasions Lady Fielding, warned by the housewife's sixth sense of something wrong in the house, had discovered the mistake, rushed upstairs and re-drawn the blind. Next day, with a courage which the rest of the Close had admired but would never have dared to emulate with its own servants, if any, she had spoken severely about it to her elderly housemaid, whom, together with the elderly parlour-maid and elderly cook, she had taken on from old Canon Robarts's nieces, who thankfully went to live in a Private Hotel in Bournemouth. The housemaid had said it had come into her mind, like, just while she was having a nice cup of tea with Cook, that there was something like a noise she heard when she come downstairs after doing the blackout and she had had half a mind to pop up and see if that blind was all right, but Pollett had said Care killed the cat and anyway with the night like that old Hitler wouldn't be over, so she hadn't given it a thought till her ladyship mentioned it. This from a servant was the equivalent of a shamefaced apology from an equal, so Lady Fielding remained content with her victory, merely causing a very long cord to be attached to the blind, so that she could herself pull it across the skylight from just outside her bedroom door, and Pollett the parlourmaid need not do violence to her code by going up to the top floor on the housemaid's afternoon off.

Today that worthy creature had in a fit of supererogatory zeal drawn the blind directly after lunch on the specious grounds that what with her time off in the afternoon and people to dinner, how to do everything at once she did not rightly know; and as the Double Summer daylight would linger long after most hardworking people were in bed, the effect in the hall was depressing in the extreme.

"Please pull the blind back, Anne," said Lady Fielding. "It makes one feel like a corpse in the house."

Anne ran upstairs, unfastened the cord and pulled the blind back. Hard uninteresting light flooded the staircase, but anything was better than the gloom of which there would be quite enough next winter without Pollett's ingenious attempts to meet trouble halfway. Anne stood on the landing and gazed at the upward curve of the stairs, which she had often tried to draw, though she had never obtained a result to her own liking. From her nursery days the barley-sugar curve of the staircase had held a secret romance for her. Up and down it had passed in her mind every fairy prince, mythological hero, long-locked Cavalier, dashing and heartless rake, romantic ne'er-do-well, scholar, poet, lover, of her omnivorous appetite for reading, a passion born of a solitary childhood, quickened and fostered by the elderly governess Miss Bunting, who had crowned her life's work by implanting in Anne Fielding some of her own uncompromising rectitude and love of literature. Each figure had kissed her hand, bowed low with a sweep of a plumed hat, held a sword aloft in salute, cast a look of dark adoration from the mantle enshrouding his face; and more than once had a gallant (period unspecified) ridden up the front door steps, down the flagged hall to the foot of the stairs, and reined in his foam-flecked steed at the foot of the staircase. Sometimes he had swung her to his saddle and ridden away with her (the Close having conveniently turned into an immense forest); sometimes, the blood welling from between the fingers pressed to his side, he had fallen dead at her feet in a most attractive way. As she grew older, and during the last year or two she felt she had grown very much older, these visions had faded. But there still remained a secret hope that a figure, embodying in himself every attribute of romance, would one day be at the foot of the stairs. As she reached the bottom step, he would take her hand, raise it respectfully to his lips and look darkly into her eyes. But at this point the imagination of Miss Anne Fielding, nearly nineteen, gave way and beyond a vague feeling that all would be gas and gaiters she left the rest to Providence.

So far the romantic stranger had had no recognisable face. Whether he had a name we cannot exactly say. If he had a name this, like so many other things, was part of the heritage Miss Bunting had left to her last pupil.

The front door banged, which was Sir Robert coming back from work, so Anne ran down to meet him and the vision fled. Sir Robert, an enthusiastic war gardener, had acquired the habit of doing various rather meddlesome and often destructive jobs in his garden before dinner during the summer months and liked his daughter Anne to help him, which she did very pleasantly, though with less zeal and less knowledge. The job for that evening, or rather, as Sir Robert bitterly said, for what was really tea-time if it hadn't been for the Germans, was to cut flowers for the dinner-table.

"And I have told your mother again and again," said Sir Robert, who had the curious perverted habit peculiar to parents of blaming Anne by implication for her other parent's existence, "that the flowers must be cut in the morning and left up to the neck in water, or they won't last."

"Well, daddy," said Anne, nobly sharing the guilt, "mummy had to go to her Red Cross directly after breakfast and anyway nothing had properly come out then, because of Double Summer Time."

Sir Robert said he hoped the late Mr. William Willett would have to spend the rest of eternity in cold, grey Double Summer Time and serve him right.

"Besides," said Anne, "it's much nicer to pick flowers without a gardener looking at one. Tomkins always despises one whatever one does."

Sir Robert agreed, and they cut the flowers and Anne put them in water and then it was time to change for dinner, for though to change was no more than taking off one old summer dress and putting on another, Lady Fielding was very firm about it, and quite right too. To Sir Robert, as head of the family and a very hard-working man, the concession was made that he might slip off his coat and slip on a velvet plum-coloured smoking-jacket, relic of more prosperous days; the word *slip* being ingeniously used to make it all sound easier. But though outwardly a concession it was really a law, and Lady Fielding, so easy-going a wife in most ways, was adamant about the smoking-jacket, saying very truly that if that went Everything would go. For so it has been in every household. Whatever slipshod degradation the Germans have brought us to, each person and each household has a small flag which flies from the very top of the mast even until the vessel is being sucked into the whirlpool; Sir Robert's jacket being one.

Tonight was also a more ceremonial affair, for Mr. Birkett the Headmaster of Southbridge School was coming with his wife and Robin Dale, his junior classical master, whom the Fieldings had come to know well and like during a summer spent at Hallbury, where his father was Rector. Very luckily the School was just within the limit for which a taxi could be hired, and Mr. Brown of the Red Lion had been bespoken for the last ten days to carry the Birketts and Robin Dale to Barchester and back, a deed which had only been made possible by Mr. Brown's Masonic Lodge having a meeting on that same evening. Accordingly at a quarter past seven the dinner party was decanted at the door of Number Seventeen, with strict orders to be ready for the return journey the moment Mr. Brown appeared, as he thought something had gone wrong with his rear light.

"If," said Mr. Birkett, when they had taken their places at the dinner-table, "it is a choice between bicycling to Barchester and back or submitting to Brown's exorbitant charges, I prefer the latter on the whole. But I still hope to tell him what I think of him before I die."

"Another way would be to come by train," said Sir Robert.

"We did think of that," said Mrs. Birkett, "but it would mean getting to Barchester Central at 6:45 and having to catch the 8:03 back if we wanted to sleep in our own beds. And the bus is no good, because it is always full of people from the aeroplane works going in to the cinema by the time it passes us. So Brown it must be."

Sir Robert said the thought of telling people, at some vague future date, exactly what one thought of them, was about the only thing that kept one going through the war. And if, he said, Peace didn't break out soon, he would forestall that threatening event by telling that fool Aberfordbury who sat on a tribunal with him exactly what he thought of him and more.

"Who on earth is Aberfordbury, Robert?" said his wife.

Sir Robert said she knew him well.

"But I don't," said Mrs. Birkett. "I don't think it's a name at all."

"None of the new peers' names are real names," said Sir Robert angrily. "God knows how they find them. If I were offered a peerage, which really might happen to anyone now while he was shaving, I would be Baron Fieldings of the Close. It would at least make it easier for one's friends to know who one was."

"You wouldn't, Robert," said his wife. "I wouldn't allow it. You would be Lord Fielding, but I would only be Lady Fielding, just as I am now. You will have to invent a silly name for yourself."

An agreeable game was then played thinking of all the very unconvincing titles adopted by recent peers and inventing even less convincing ones; though Robin Dale said this was impossible. When the topic petered out, Lady Fielding said she still wanted to know who Lord Aberfordbury was.

"That pestilential fool Sir Ogilvy Hibberd," said her husband. "Lord Aberfordbury of Wopford in the county of Loamshire. Bah!"

Mrs. Birkett, a staunch party woman, said it served him right for being a Liberal and a general discussion took place as to what Liberals were for, Robin Dale obtaining top marks by saying they were invented to split votes. And then the talk, as usual, meandered into food.

"The person I would most like to tell what I think of him," said Lady Fielding, "is the butcher. He has a horrid foxy look and wraps up one's disgusting bit of meat before one can see what it is. Pollett says that the Palace give him ten shillings under the counter and I can quite believe it. So no wonder he despises Number Seventeen."

"Is it grey pork with water oozing out of it this week?" said Mrs. Birkett with animation.

"I almost wish it were," said Lady Fielding. "It is a small cube of magenta beef, very hard, with all the fat cut off."

"Mrs. Carter," said Robin, who lived with Everard Carter the Senior Housemaster, "got what everyone thought was very nasty mutton, till it turned out to be uneatable veal. When I think of heaven I think of a very thick piece of bleeding steak, well grilled on the outside."

"Oh, *Robin!*" said Anne, raising her large dark eyes to his in a kind of reverent ecstasy.

"Kidneys, with a little pool of their own gravy in their cupped hands," said Mr. Birkett, whom no one had thought capable of such a sustained poetic flight.

"The conversation does somehow always get round to food," said Lady Fielding, "and I feel one oughtn't to."

Anne said she wondered if people talked about food in heaven. Sir Robert, returning to his original grievance, said he hoped that in heaven he would have the chance of telling everyone he didn't like exactly what he thought of him; or her, he added.

"Yes, one would have to include the Bishop's wife," said Lady Fielding. "But perhaps she wants the same heaven, and it would be annoying if she got in first. Still, she has so often told me what she thought of me, or at any rate implied it, that it wouldn't make much difference. But it will be lovely to get milk and honey without ration books."

The talk, having reverted to food, got the upper hand of the party till Mr. Birkett began to discuss the chances of the war coming to an end. And as no one could possibly know, and all arguments were based on complete ignorance or fine crusted prejudice, the conversation was highly profitable.

"I have only two demands to make when the peace terms are settled," said Mrs. Birkett. "One is that we shall have Calais because it really belongs to us and the other that we shan't be noble and give all our food to other people, because if we fall down dead, as most of us undoubtedly will as soon as the moral support of the war is withdrawn, we shan't be much use. And we must have more butter, even if everyone else goes without."

"As a public servant in a small way, I must deprecate your remarks," said Sir Robert, "though I agree as a friend. My own suggestion for peace when it attacks us is that children should at once be forced to give up all their ill-gotten and unappreciated extra rations to the grown-ups."

"I saw a whole windowful of oranges going mouldy in Northbridge," said Robin Dale, "because the grown-ups mightn't buy them. And the ones that the children did have they were selling at sixpence each outside the Barchester Odeon."

A determined attempt was then made by the whole party to talk of books, or pictures, or music, but it was a complete failure. Books boiled down to cookery books; pictures appeared to be associated in most people's minds with a vast canvas of a ham, a lobster, a brace of teal, a flask of wine, a cheese with lifelike grubs on it, fresh strawberries with a giant ladybird, and a dead stag thrown carelessly across the lot, while the thought of a small French masterpiece of the two oeufs sur le plat produced a reverent hush. As for music, Anne said boldly that music always made her hungry.

By this time the short meal was over and the company went into the drawing room, flooded with sunshine from the tall sash windows in front, while at its further end the tall sash windows to the east framed the great cedar at the far side of the lawn. Although it was May, it was too chill to go out, and a wood fire was not unwelcome. County news was discussed. Lady Fielding enquired of Mrs. Birkett whether the Mixo-Lydian refugees had gone home yet, and learnt that they were mostly displaying a stubborn resistance to repatriation coupled with a hearty and frequently expressed scorn for the country which had for six weary years fed and sheltered them. Mr. Birkett, who was popularly supposed to talk about the school in his sleep, tried to discuss the Classical Fourth with Robin, but was headed off by Sir Robert, who as a Governor of Southbridge School had a faint claim to Mr. Birkett's attention. So Robin sat by Anne and asked if the Deanery tea-party had been nice.

Anne said it had been quite nice. Lady Graham, she said, had asked her to lunch and was going to take her to Rushwater, and Sylvia and George Halliday were coming too.

"I think it will be a good treat," she said thoughtfully. "Only I do wish Martin Leslie didn't live at Rushwater, because I don't know him."

"Well, all the people you don't know must live somewhere," said Robin, quite sensibly. "I think I heard of Martin in Italy. Blast the Italians. I don't see why they wanted a bit of me."

And Robin looked with bored distaste at the artificial foot whose existence so few people noticed.

"Do you always hate it?" said Anne. Not sentimentally, not with any morbid curiosity, but with a friendly yet bracing interest which Robin found very helpful. And indeed Anne Fielding had been in the last year or so as helpful to him as he had been to her. Time, during the leaden age of the war, had never seemed to move, yet at the same time it seemed to him hundreds of years ago that Robin Dale, crippled out of the army as he bitterly put it to himself, had met the Fieldings and their callow daughter, had liked her, and stood by her at a sad moment in her life and had laughed a good deal with her since, finding when once her young shyness was overcome a most ready response to his own turn of mind. To Anne, only child, for many years a delicate one, Robin's companionship and his deeper if not wider knowledge of books had been an unexpected delight in her rather retired life, and she still turned to Robin for sympathy and interest in most of what she thought, and confided to him various small fears and anxieties that she instinctively kept from her affectionate but very busy mother.

"That," said Anne gravely, "is a great relief. I was rather afraid of Martin."

Robin asked why.

Anne looked at him, giving serious consideration to her motives. Robin thought, as more than one of Lady Fielding's friends had thought of late, how fine a bloom, if one might be botanical, the fragile plant that used to be Anne had produced. The schoolroom child he had first met at Hallbury in her parents' summer residence, all eyes and beak and very few feathers, was becoming a girl that one would look at twice, in the running to be a real beauty. Not the knock-you-down type, but a beauty with the right bones, the right poise, the right manners; a lamp shining through alabaster said Robin to himself, rather pleased with the comparison but doubtful as to whether alabaster was really translucent.

"I expect," said Anne at last, "it was because he is going to breed the bulls at Rushwater. I expect he will have a red face and a moustache and be jovial."

Robin said one must make allowances.

"Lady Graham said her eldest daughter wanted to breed bulls with Martin," said Anne. "Oh, and do you know Lady Graham's brother? He was at the Deanery."

"A very nice fellow but uncommon dull," said Robin. "So is his wife."

Anne looked up and Robin suddenly realized that when novelists compared a girl's surprised glance to a startled fawn they were not writing clichés but expressing a stern fact. Not that he had ever startled a fawn in his life, having very little acquaintance with those elegant-legged people; but Anne's expression reminded him very strongly of the day he had met a deer, or ought he to say hind, in Bushey Park with her child, and how he had offered to the child a piece of a sandwich, and how, just as it had decided to nibble a little, it had discovered that he was a man, turned swiftly upon its little hoofs and nimbled away, followed by its mamma. So had Anne just discovered something that surprised or alarmed her; he could not say which. And as he felt guiltless, he decided not to enquire.

Meanwhile the talk among the elder people had become so animated as to be almost noisy, the cause being Mr. Birkett's rather brilliant description of a farewell party given by Miss Hampton and Miss Bent at Adeline Cottage for Mr. Bissett, headmaster of the Hosiers' Boys' Foundation School, and his wife.

"Dale," said Mr. Birkett across the room. "How many guests did Miss Hampton tell you they had. Was it seventy or eighty?"

Robin got up and joined the group round the fire, followed by Anne. Robin, pulling a chair up for her, wondered what was in her mind now. This was a favorite speculation of his and as a rule he could make a pretty good guess, but this time he was completely baffled. She did not seem to be unhappy, but there was a curious atmosphere about her. Like a sleep-walker said Robin to himself, and then told himself not to be silly as he had never seen anyone sleep-walking and couldn't tell what it looked like. But all this came and went in a flash and he had begun to answer Mr. Birkett before anyone could have noticed the gap.

"There were fifty invitations, sir," he said, sitting down by Mrs. Birkett, "and eighty-five people came, first and last. Brown can tell you how many bottles of gin they had, not counting what some of the Hosiers' people brought."

"The Hosiers' people have learnt a good deal in the last six years," said Mr. Birkett thoughtfully.

"And you from them?" asked Sir Robert, with slight malice.

That, said Mrs. Birkett with good-humoured indignation, was not a fair question.

Sir Robert said Exactly; and that was why he had asked it.

"I should think nobody ever really learns much," said Anne.

The company looked at her with interest, waiting for a

dissertation on this theme. But Anne, having said her say, appeared incapable of further explanation, merely adding, "You know what I mean, Robin."

"In that case, Dale, will you explain this interesting and superficially profound contribution," said Mr. Birkett.

Mrs. Birkett said her husband ought to learn one thing and that was not to talk like a schoolmaster. Sir Robert at the same instant applauded the expression "superficially profound." Lady Fielding, speaking simultaneously with them but in a more authoritative voice, said how very nice it was to hear Mr. Birkett call his junior classical master Dale.

"I quite agree with you," said Robin. "When I visit other schools and hear Christian names being bandied between head-masters and ordinary masters, or which is even more sinister between housemasters and prefects, I feel that the Head is probably saving civilisation."

Lady Fielding said it was just as bad at the Universities. Owing, she said, to her youngest nephew being on Christian-name terms with practically every member of Lazarus College, she had not only taken his tutor for a particularly uncouth undergraduate, but had treated him as such.

At this point Sir Robert, his legal mind shocked by the want of sequence in the foregoing chatter, said he would, if no one had any objection, repeat his question and ask Mr. Birkett if he in particular or Southbridge School in general had learnt anything from the Hosiers' Boys' Foundation School during the last six years.

Mr. Birkett said that Mr. Bissett, the Headmaster of the evacuated Hosiers' Boys, was one of the most upright, unselfish characters he had ever met.

"I daresay," said Sir Robert. "But you haven't answered me. Did you learn anything from him, or, to give the question a wider scope, did he learn anything from you?"

After a short but obviously painful internal struggle, Mr. Birkett said, "No."

"And what a relief it is to say that, I cannot tell you," he continued. "The fact is we spent six years in making allowances for each other and did it very well. Now that it looks as if the war might finish, the Hosiers' School governors are planning to move them back to London. As soon as the mess is cleared up and we have got our own buildings to ourselves again, we shall forget them with joy and thankfulness, and doubtless they will forget us. It can't be done, Fielding; it can't be done. That's all. And the relief it has been to say it I cannot express."

"That's all I wanted," said Sir Robert and there was a short silence while each member of the party reflected according to his or her light that East and West, day and night, salt and sugar were immutably different and so were the accidents or traditions, however one liked to put it, of birth and class; and that however earnestly well-intentioned gumphs might believe in mixing or leveling all ranks, it would never do.

This silence was broken by a nasty grinding, jarring noise outside diagnosed by Mr. Birkett as Brown's taxi, which diagnosis was almost immediately confirmed by Pollett who came in to say it was Mr. Brown and he couldn't wait because of his rear light. So good-byes were quickly said and the Southbridge party got into the taxi and were jarred and clanked back to the School.

"Thanks, Brown," said Mr. Birkett. "I hear Miss Hampton's party went off very well."

A slow Barsetshire smile spread over Mr. Brown's face. He had heard, he said, in the bar, that the party went off with a bang, as you might say. A dozen gin, a dozen sherry, four Scotch and two Cointreau he knew to his certain knowledge, and they did say some of the gentlemen from the School brought their bottles with them.

"And some of those Hoisiers' teachers brought bottles along too," said Mr. Brown. "Miss Hampton she said to me, she said, in the bar it was and no later than last Wednesday evening if I remember rightly, she said to me it seemed quite a pity the Hosiers couldn't stay a bit longer. She said she could have made something of them, she said, if it hadn't been for the war looking as if it might be over. Ah, it's a great pity, sir. Another year here and we'd have made something of those teachers. Thank you, sir. Good-night, sir."

He ground his old gears and jarred and clanked away.

Robin Dale walked over to Everard Carter's house, where it was the friendly custom for any resident master to report himself in the Housemaster's private quarters and kind Mrs. Carter was always delighted to see any member of the school.

"Come in, Dale," said Everard Carter. "Have some whiskey."

"Good Lord!" said Robin, overcome with surprise.

"You may well say so," said Everard. "Miss Hampton gave it to me. A good three-quarters of a bottle left over from her party. And a syphon nearly full. Help yourself."

With a heart overflowing with gratitude Robin half filled a glass and sat down.

Mr. Carter asked if he had had a nice evening. Very nice said Robin.

"And how was that nice Anne Fielding?" said Mrs. Carter. "She is nineteen now, isn't she?"

Robin said just about.

"And you are twenty-seven aren't you?" said Mrs. Carter, looking up from darning her husband's socks.

Robin agreed.

"I was twenty-one when I married," said Mrs. Carter, "and Everard was twenty-nine. I shall always remember my wedding, because Lydia, you know, my sister Lydia Merton, trod on the front of her bridesmaid's dress and a lot of the gathers ripped out and I wished I had a needle and thread as I could have just run it up again in a second."

Full of these beautiful and interesting thoughts, her soft eyes beamed upon her husband with great affection and upon the junior classical master with an air of kind calculation, which might have embarrassed anyone who knew her less well. But Robin was by now so used to her matchmaking propensities that he only said eight years was a very good difference between a husband and wife.

"Lydia is much younger than Noel than that," said Kate, with a charming pride in her younger sister's achievements.

Robin, not to be outdone, said there were thirty years between his father and his mother, who had died when he was very small so that he hardly remembered her.

Kind Mrs. Carter was so unhappy at the thought of a little boy left motherless that Robin had to hasten to assure her that he was quite happy and had not been in the least blighted, and being of a gentle and confiding nature she believed him and became quite cheerful again. The talk roved over school topics, but all the time Robin knew quite well that Mrs. Carter was thinking of the eight years between herself and her husband and the miraculous coincidence of the eight years between himself and Anne Fielding, and upon this slight foundation building matrimonial castles. He did not mind. Ma Carter, as the small boys affectionately called her, would never make mischief or say a word that could hurt. Yet all the same he rather wished the gap between himself and Anne, or alternatively between Mr. and Mrs. Carter, had been slightly larger or smaller.

His feelings for Anne, so far as he had troubled to clarify them, were of a very warm and comfortable nature. He had, during the last year or so, seen an agreeable but gawky fledgling take on elegant plumage, spread its wings and try its notes. The results were eminently satisfactory. Anne had at last come out from under her mother's wing, talked to people, had charming manners, and showed an intelligence which Robin in an elder-brotherly way had encouraged and fostered. If a young school-master thought of marrying he would be very lucky to find such a wife as Anne. On the other hand one still had one's position to make. Of money he had enough for himself with his salary and what his father allowed him, and he knew that several of the assistant masters at Southbridge and their cheerful competent young wives managed on about the same sum. But Anne was different. To apply the words *cheerful* and *competent* to her would be an error in taste. Not that she was sulky and stupid; on the contrary she had a very sweet, even temper and having escaped, owing to poor health in her early teens, the levelling effects of Barchester High School, and having had for a year the great advantage of living at home with a first-rate governess, she was extremely polite and well-read. What kind of life could one offer to such a girl? One of those little cottages in the village where Miss Hampton and Miss bent lived? A husband coming in a little late for meals, busy with examination papers, perhaps talking about end-of-term reports in his sleep? The necessity of consorting with the other masters' wives and talking their talk? Hence, vain deluding joys! Anne should marry a Duke while he, junior classical master at Southbridge School, would remain a one-footed bachelor pedagogue and perhaps give her ducal offspring some coaching in the summer holidays.

From the foregoing attempt to analyse Mr. Robin Dale's feelings towards Miss Anne Fielding, it will we hope to clear that not by any stretch of the too willing imagination could it be said that Robin was in love with Anne. Had that glorious passion filled his heart, he would not for a moment have considered his future wife's happiness or convenience, being fatuously convinced that with HIM her life would at once become a bower of roses. He was very fond of Anne; the fatal word *propinquity* had been responsible for much; and her attention and deference had been very pleasant, though of late he had been amused and also in a way flattered to see her assert her own opinions against his, for had not her reading, since the death of her excellent governess, Miss Bunting, been largely guided by Mr. Robin Dale.

Kate Carter went on with her darning. Everard Carter did the *Times* crossword, which he always pretended to despise, but could not go to bed with a quiet mind unless he had run down the last quotation, unravelled the final snag, and loudly cursed the appearance of a Surrey bowler which was unfair to people who weren't keen on County Cricket. Robin drank his whiskey and let his fancy embroider upon the theme of Anne's children. Yes; he would coach the Marquis and the young lords in Latin and Greek within an inch of their lives for her sake, and in an excess of self-abnegation, determinedly sit below the salt if asked to lunch. And being gay and light-hearted on the whole, he couldn't help laughing aloud at his own thoughts.

Kate, whose attention had been entirely absorbed by a thin place on a navy-blue sock of Everard's, one of those places that you are not quite sure whether you will just darn across now so as to catch it in time or risk for another day's wear, looked up, softly wrinkling her mild brow as she glanced over her spectacles in Robin's direction.

"It's nothing," said Robin, who was devoted to Mrs. Carter and knew it was no good trying to explain what he had been thinking. "I just had a funny thought."

This explanation appeared to satisfy Kate, who used it as a peg on which to hang several anecdotes, illustrative of the brilliant wit of Master Bobbie Carter, Miss Angela Carter and Master Philip Carter.

"Blast the fellow," said Everard, suddenly smashing the *Times* on the floor. "'A remnant painfully toed.' What the devil does he mean?"

"STUB," said Robin.

"Oh," said Everard ungraciously.

He picked up the *Times*, smoothed it, filled in the missing word and said, as he said at least once a week, that it was pure waste of time and he'd never look at the thing again.

"It isn't really cleverness," said Robin. "I looked at Sir Robert's *Times* this evening and he had done it."

"Those lawyers," said Everard. "And to think that I read law till I found I couldn't afford it and became an usher."

"I couldn't have *borne* it, darling, if you had been a lawyer," said his devoted wife. "You would always have been eating dinners, and I can feed you *much* better at home, even with rations and points."

The Senior Housemaster looked at his wife with the kind of married look which makes young bachelors either wish they were married or be fervently thankful that they are not. Robin said he would go to bed.

"One moment, Dale," said Everard Carter. "Young Leslie in the Upper Fourth and his brother have been asked out on Sunday for the day and to bring a friend. I understand that you are to be the friend. I'm driving over that way on Home Guard business and can drop you all at Rushwater."

"Thanks very much, sir," said Robin, who knew that the Housemaster had made this offer with his artificial foot in mind, and had probably invented the Home Guard business, "but there's quite a good train that gets us to Rushwater about three."

"If a boy had asked a master to join him in a Sunday outing in my young days," said Everard, "he would have been put down as a softy, or expelled. How alarming the young are. You can get a train back after tea from Rushwater to Southbridge. It's about the only train on that line that is any help to anyone."

Kate, who could not bear unkindness, said there was a very good 6.53 train before the war from Southbridge for people who wanted to get the 7.33 to London at Barchester Central; but her husband, as a rule ready to agree with all she said, said it was a heathen hour, and then they all went to bed.

# CHAPTER 3

When Lady Graham had made a promise she always kept it. Her vague and charming way of inviting people for dinner the same evening or lunch seven weeks ahead was backed by a good memory, a real wish to be kind, and the collaboration of her mother's secretary, Miss Merriman, whose life had been devoted to sheltering the upper classes.

"Both those nice young people of Mrs. Halliday's are coming with us on Sunday, mamma," she said to Lady Emily at lunch on the Saturday after the Deanery tea-party, "and Lady Fielding's girl. So that is very nice and darling David will drive us all to Rushwater."

"That" said Lady Emily Leslie, "will be five."

"Six, mamma," said Lady Graham.

"The Hallidays, whom you must tell me everything about, make two," said Lady Emily, laying a spoon and a fork side by side. "The Fielding girl is three—"

"Only one, mamma," said Agnes.

"Three," said Lady Emily firmly, adding a saltspoon to her heap, "and you and I make five."

In proof of which she put two fragments of toast by the silver and flashed a smile upon the company.

"And what about me, mamma?" Said David. "After all I'm going to drive, and those lovely days are over when even a chauffeur didn't count as a human being. Six."

To the joy of Lady Graham's younger children who wor-
shipped Uncle David with blind devotion, he took a match-box
from his pocket, struck a match, put it into his mouth, where it
at once expired, and laid the match with the fork, spoons and
toast, to a chorus of "Do it again, Uncle David" from his young
nephew and nieces.

"I can't," said David. "Matches, as your mother is just about to
observe, are worth their weight in gold."

Clarissa remarked in a rather priggish way that people ought
to use lighters.

"True, my love," said David. "But I can't put a lighter into my
mouth so I have to use matches."

"And Merry," said Lady Emily. "Seven. Will your car take us
all, David? I will tell you how we will manage it. You will drive
of course and the Hallidays, who sound rather large, can sit with
you. Then Agnes and Merry can go behind with me and we can
fit the Fielding girl in somewhere, because she is sure to be
small."

"Why, mamma?" Said David.

"She must be small," said Lady Emily. "Anne Fielding is a
small name."

"You may be right, darling," said David, "or she may be a great
wopping girl like Ursule. Do you remember that French girl,
mamma, whose people took the Vicarage the summer John got
engaged to Mary? How that girl did eat. But as I have never seen
Miss Fielding I can't tell."

"But you *did* see her, David," said Agnes. "At Mrs. Crawley's
tea-party just when we were going."

"Bless your heart, one sees so many girls," said David.

Miss Merriman, who knew exactly when she was really
needed and had a gift of withdrawing herself at the right
moment and in any case had had no intention of joining the
party, then said she was not coming.

"You are the only woman I know, Merry," said David admiringly, "who can say No without giving reasons. They all say they have letters to write, or are going to have their hair washed."

"Then," said Lady Emily, dropping as she rose from the table her bag, her scarf and an engagement book with a number of loose papers in it, "that is settled. At least," she added, pausing in the doorway so that no one could get out and the parlourmaid who was rather crossly waiting to clear the table could not get in, "there is still Anne Fielding."

"She looked a charming girl," said Agnes, "though it was so dark in the Deanery hall that I really did not see her. Come into the drawing-room, mamma, and Clarissa will bring your scarf and everything else."

"I will just have my scarf first," said Lady Emily. "Bring it here, Clarissa."

Clarissa, the exquisitely tidy, had collected the scarf and presented it, neatly folded, to her grandmother. Lady Emily, propping herself and her stick in the doorway so that no one could go in or out, took the scarf and began to drape it about her head.

"What we must really settle," she said, "is how Anne is to get here on Sunday."

"She is coming with the Hallidays, mamma," said Agnes, with unruffled placidity.

"That is all very well," said Lady Emily judicially. "But how will she get back to Barchester? David, you must drive her home in your car."

"No, my love," said David. "What's Halliday to me, or, I may add, me to Halliday, that I should cart their female friends all over the county? And you know, mamma, that works of super-erogation are strictly forbidden in the Thirty-Nine Articles."

Undaunted by David's very unfair way of bringing up the Church of England to support his already rock-like determination not to put himself out in any way for anybody, Lady Emily sketched a masterly piece of strategy by which David was to drive her to Barchester for the morning service, take her to

Number Seventeen so that she might satisfy her lively curiosity
as to what Sir Robert and Lady Fielding were like, collect Anne,
drive her to Hatch House, collect George and Sylvia Halliday
and bring all three to Holdings for lunch. From this she was
beginning to adumbrate a plan by which David should, after the
Rushwater expedition, drive herself and Anne to Pomfret Towers that she might there do any meddling that occurred to her
fertile imagination, thence to Barchester, and so home, when
Miss Merriman, considering that her beloved but exasperating
employer had had quite enough rope, suddenly exerted her
secret magic of authority and without apparent effort transferred her ladyship with all her portable property to the
drawing-room, where she handed her over to her old French
maid for her afternoon rest.

"Eef miladi does not rest, il n'y a pas de repos pour moi, ni
pour personne," said Conque, who combined devotion, incom-
petence and rudeness to a degree of which only our Gallic
neighbours are capable, and hustled her ladyship off to lie down.

David, suddenly a prey to one of the waves of affectionate
boredom that his adored mother and his much-loved sister—
and indeed all his friends—were apt to induce in him, thought
of getting his car out. But even as he thought of it he realised
that he had no particular wish to go anywhere or see anybody.
There were lots of people he would have liked vaguely to see if
he could suddenly materialise in their drawing-room and as
quickly dematerialise if not amused. His cousins the Pomfrets,
that attractive Mrs. Brandon at Pomfret Madrigal, the Warings
at Beliers, that handsome Mrs. Merton at Northbridge, the
Marlings, so the list went on. But in each possible port of call his
spoilt fastidious mind found a flaw. Sally and Gillie were so
overweighted by County work and children, Lavinia Brandon's
charming readiness to be made eyes at seemed out of date,
Beliers had such an atmosphere of old age, Mrs. Merton was
great fun but he didn't feel like her, at Marling the old people
were a bit heavy in hand and his cousin Lucy was too robust: and

as for his cousin Lettice, now Mrs. Barclay in a happy second marriage, he couldn't imagine why he had ever imagined he was in love with her. Everywhere he looked it was the same thing. Old people conscientiously doing their duty in a world they didn't understand, a world which did not want them; middle-aged people losing their charm under the endless strain of sons and daughters in danger, public duties, aged and failing parents, and growing discomfort and privation at home, or if they did keep their charm doing so with a plodding determination which ruined everything; young people mostly being so good and doing what they had to do, emerging for leaves in which there was so little fun to be got that they had almost stopped trying to get it. And anyway, not too amusing, thought David, for a girl to get into an evening frock when her hands need at least a month's rest and attention and every restaurant and dancing place is already crammed. Everything in fact was beastly for everybody, except for people like Frances Hervey, who got a frightful kick out of being important and ordering other people about, or old Dame Monica Hopkinson, who had been a queen-policewoman in the last war and still went about in chauffeur's gaiters and lunched with old generals at the Carlton Grill every day.

With such moody thoughts, though we cannot exactly call them exaggerated, David walked down to the village for want of anything better to do. Here he found Mr. Scatcherd seated on his camp-stool, his back to the low churchyard wall, busily sketching. David thought poorly of Mr. Scatcherd's work and did not in the least care what he was drawing, but the demon of idle boredom impelled him to ask Mr. Scatcherd what was the subject of his pencil today. It was pretty obvious that any artist sitting exactly opposite the Mellings Arms was probably drawing it, but David's worse self grasped at the opportunity for a little facile social success, and Mr. Scatcherd was enchanted.

"Since you enquire, sir," began Mr. Scatcherd, which beginning annoyed him very much, for although he knew that his

position as an artist made him the equal of any man, his early
training in his father's old-established grocery business had
implanted in him the habit of addressing everyone as a respected
customer. "Since you *do* enquire, Mr. Leslie," he continued,
though slightly uncomfortable about the whole thing. "I am just
roughing in an idea. Ideas come to we artists and we must catch
them ere they fly."

David said that was a jolly good idea and might he look.

"Only an idea, as I may say," said Mr. Scatcherd, holding his
drawing-book at arm's length and squinting at it with his head
on one side. "But still—an idea."

David without much interest looked at the drawing. As it
bore a paralytic likeness to a three-story building with the words
THE MELLINGS ARMS below the first-floor windows, he felt safe in
guessing that it was a portrait of the village inn, and loudly
admired it.

"Just an idea," said Mr. Scatcherd, with the air of bringing out
a striking and original thought. "And by the way, Mr. Leslie,
could you mention to her ladyship that the views she was good
enough to order are practically completed and I shall have the
pleasure of delivering them well in time for the Sale."

"I didn't know my mamma was an art-patron," said David.

"It is Lady Graham to whom I relude," said Mr. Scatcherd.

"So sorry. I thought you meant mamma," said David. "One
never knows what she will do next. But if she wanted a picture
she'd probably paint it herself with one of the children's paint-
boxes on the dining-room tablecloth."

Mr. Scatcherd did not at once reply, for he was slightly at a
loss. In common with a good many other people he felt that
to say Lady Emily savoured of over-familiarity, though he
knew that to say Lady Leslie would be socially incorrect. He also
knew that an artist was the equal of kings and princes, though
unfortunately there were no emperors to pick up one's paint-
brush, unless it were the Emperor of Abyssinia who was however in the sad position of not being a member of the Church of

England and therefore not a real Emperor; but in spite of this
knowledge his early upbringing had made him speak of Lady
Graham as her ladyship and now there was a muddle.

"Well," said David, already bored, "I must be going. I'll tell
my sister about the pictures. You must get a lot of work done
now the days are so long."

"Ah, well you may say so, Mr. Leslie," said Mr. Scatcherd,
gratified by this tribute to his gift. "But though the days are long,
ars is longer."

With which application of an old tag he resumed his work
and David passed on. For twopence he would have gone back to
Holdings, taken out his car, driven up to London and found
some friends to talk shop with. But duty bade him stay out his
visit to Holdings with his mother and sister, to whom he was
genuinely devoted in his own fashion, and some rather bitter
though perfunctory self-examination told him that he would be
just as bored in London with his R.A.F. Friends. There was no
twopence that anyone could offer him which seemed worth the
taking.

"And a nice state of things for a young man of thirty-seven
who is probably going a bit bald on the top, though thank
heaven very few of the girls are tall enough to see it," he
remarked to himself, and turned aimlessly to the right onto
the long bridge over the water-meadows. When he got as far as
the river he leaned his arms on the stone parapet and contem-
plated suicide. But the Rising was shallow under the bridge,
with a gravelly bottom, and the prospects were not good. Just
then a pleasant trit-trot struck his ear. He turned and saw a
pony-cart coming down the road at a brisk pace, containing
Mrs. Halliday and two young women. Mrs. Halliday pulled the
pony up and called to David.

"I haven't seen you this leave, David," she said. "Keep still,
Brisket. Come back to tea with us."

David, with a charming air of attention, rapidly considered

the rival chances of being bored at Hatch House or Holdings. Why not Hatch House? The girls looked personable.

"Sylvia is on leave," said Mrs. Halliday. "*Will* you keep quiet, Brisket. And we've got Anne for the weekend. Jump in."

"I'll walk up," said David, not relishing the thought of sitting among so many legs and a good many miscellaneous parcels and pieces of luggage.

"Right," said Mrs. Halliday. "Get on, Brisket."

The pony trotted off and David followed. By the time he got to Hatch House Brisket was unharnessed and his passengers were in the drawing-room.

"Good Lord!" Said David. "When you said Sylvia I must have been mad. I didn't see who it was. I was looking at the minnows and rather envying them. How long is it since I saw you, Sylvia?"

"The whole of the war, I think," said Sylvia.

David looked at her and approved. The rather staid uninteresting schoolgirl he remembered had become a very good-looking young woman, tall, with easy movements, good legs, he noticed, shining fair hair and a very attractive face. A relief, if only temporary, from boredom.

"And do you know Anne Fielding?" Said Mrs. Halliday. "She is here for the weekend and you are taking them all over to Rushwater tomorrow, aren't you? George will be in for tea. He is on leave too, so lucky. And I hope my husband will be back soon. He went over to Pomfret Towers about a tractor."

And even as she spoke George came in from helping Caxton with the two-handed saw down at the woodpile, and Mr. Halliday was seen riding past the windows and shortly came in by the back way. And in the middle of a family hubbub and an exchanging of news, Miss Anne Fielding felt a little out of it. So she sat in the window seat and looked at last week but one's *Country Life* passed on from Holdings via the Vicarage by courtesy of the bread every Tuesday. The first time she had seen David Leslie was in the dark; at least it was almost dark in the Deanery hall with all that panelling and the fan-light blacked out. Now she could see him much better. People weren't usually like what you thought they were like. She had not imagined David Leslie like that; but already she had forgotten what her imagining of him had been. When she saw him standing on the bridge she had no idea that it was David Leslie. She had thought he would look older, or perhaps younger, at any rate quite different. It was all rather confusing. But if she went on reading *Country Life* she would be safe and no one would talk to her. Then Hubback brought tea in with the air of a British captive princess walking in a Roman triumph and she had to join the party.

It was all rather noisy and overpowering to Anne until Mr. Halliday, who had very strong ideas about the duties of a landowner abroad and a host at home, saw that the Fielding child looked shy and rather out of it. So he brought his cup of tea to the little sofa where she was sitting and told her about his visit to Pomfret Towers and how he hoped to get a tractor over sometime; and Anne, who was a very good audience, listened in a flattering way and repeated something she had heard Sir Edmund Pridham say about a tractor at Brandon Abbey. Upon this Mr. Halliday at once classified her in his mind as a nice, sensible little thing and his opinion of her rose yet further when he discovered that she held very sound views on the cultivation of sweet peas.

"Daddy is very fond of gardening," said Anne. "And when I wasn't well and stopped going to school and had a governess at Hallbury, daddy used to garden every weekend and I helped him. If anyone tied the sweet peas up the wrong way he was simply furious."

"His sweet peas have beaten mine at every Barchester Flower Show," said Mr. Halliday sadly. "We haven't the soil here — nor the labour."

Then they fell to talking about soils and aspects, and Mrs. Halliday, sitting back behind the tea-tray watching her party, was pleased that the little Fielding girl was making herself agreeable to Leonard, who didn't have many people to talk to now except on his endless committees. An attractive child, but in a quiet way, not to be compared with her tall beautiful Viking Sylvia; or whatever the female of Viking was. And then a louder noise from the other side of the table roused her from her reflections.

The noise was David and Sylvia, who had just made the discovery that they were both non-flying members of the Air Force and had many common acquaintance such as Piggy Hopgood and Tommy Bell and old Chumps Macdougal.

"I ought to have guessed at once," said David, "when I saw you towering over the pony-cart like the Winged Victory only with a better attempt at a head. But I simply thought you were a girl."

"Well, I might have known *you*," said Sylvia, "only I wasn't thinking about you, and you know the way you don't expect to see people unless you do."

David said he fully appreciated the fine nuances implied by her remark, though that, he said, was more due to his own unusual intuitive powers than to her way of putting it. And then George and David discovered that they had both been at the same aerodrome in 1942.

"Our lot were at the sham aerodrome," said George. "The idea was that the Germans would bomb the fake one and kill us, while you chaps went on having hot baths and double rations of everything. Lord! how we hated you!"

"Don't blame me," said David. "I was only a parasite. I haven't the faintest idea how to fly. I got flown about on jobs like a kind of superior typist. Well, thank God it can't go on much longer now."

A rash statement to make, though millions of people were thinking much the same thing. A loud and ignorant discussion followed on the alarming probability of peace breaking out and how ghastly it would be, just as we had got really used to the war.

"The only way of really finding out when peace is coming,"

said Sylvia, "is to have a talk with the baker. He is Hubback's uncle and if he sees peace coming he'll make extra bread the day before and shut up the shop."

"But how will *he* know?" said David.

"He just does," said George. "He's the sort of person that knows when Easter will be. A man who knows that knows anything."

"If only peace meant being demobbed," said Sylvia. "And anyway what's the good of saying peace with all those ghastly Japs about."

"And what will we do with peace when it does break out?" said George. "I mean, as long as the war's on you know where you are. I might get my majority with luck in a few months, but of course peace would come and muck it all up."

"I shall simply turn into a gilded butterfly of uncertain age," said David gloomily. "I sometimes think I'd better go to South America. I've got some land there and some of the Rushwater bulls that went out before the war. I might raise prize cattle and wed a savage woman and she should bear my dusky race, and the fatter she got the more diamond necklaces I'd give her. My nephew Martin is going to get the Rushwater herd going again and Agnes's eldest girl wants to join him. It's all a black lookout."

So quiet did the three young people become as they reflected upon the dangers and horrors of peace that Anne was suddenly startled to hear her own voice talking to Mr. Halliday about politics, though the politics went no deeper then the information that when there was the next General Election Daddy was going to stand for Barchester.

There was no need for her to add that her father was standing as a Conservative, for that was the only thing the people one knew did stand for, unless it was a few queer ones like Lord Bond, who was a Liberal and anyway being a peer merely sat, or that very trying boy of Hermione Rivers's who was an artist and called himself Common Wealth.

"Silly name anyway," said Mr. Halliday. "Why stop to take great breath in the middle? There's one point about those fellows though. They seem to manage to shove their properties off onto the National Trust and go on living there just the same. It's worth considering with Taxes what they are."

"Nonsense, Leonard," said his wife. "You know you'd hate to have people walking past the house all the time or having a Youth Hostel in half of it."

George said that the National Trust would jump at Bolder's Knob and that bit of Gundric's Fossway, but as far as he was concerned he would have man-traps and spring guns if he saw a Youth Hostel anywhere. The younger members, to whom David seemed to belong though considerably older than the others, then made plans for nationalising all the houses of the people they didn't like, and Anne, emboldened by her talk with Mr. Halliday, said she would turn the Palace into an alms-house for old clergymen and their wives and make the Bishop clean the boots and knives in his apron and the Bishop's wife and Miss Pettinger could be scullery maids. This suggestion went down very well and George felt a certain respect for a girl who could think of such sensible things.

"What would be so *awful* for them," said Anne, "would be that they would be eating all the time, because scullery maids are always having cups of nice tea and elevenses all day long. And as they are rather conceited about how little they eat and it doesn't matter if it is nicely cooked or not, it would be a great mortification."

Finding that everyone was listening to her, she suddenly went pink and became shy again.

"If you don't mind," said David, addressing her directly for the first time, "I'll have the Bishop and Bishopess at Pomfret Towers. Sally can never get decent servants and a Bishop wouldn't look bad as a butler. His wife could be under-nurse. Their Nannie would knock the spirit out of any helper in a fortnight."

Then David, restless again, said he must be going, but Sylvia said he must come up to Bolder's Knob first, because Anne hadn't seen it.

David, scenting boredom, said he ought to be getting back to Holdings.

"Don't be silly, David," said Sylvia, her eyes almost on a level with David's as she faced him. "Come on."

Slightly awed by this handsome and probably muscular young Amazon, David said he had so often heard Bolder's Knob discussed at Holdings that he had made a vow never to go there. If however his presence, as he gathered from Sylvia's very illogical remarks, was somehow necessary to enable Miss Fielding to see that historic landmark, far be it from him to be a spoilsport.

"It's not Miss Fielding, it's Anne," said Sylvia. "Come on."

So the four younger people set off up Gundric's Fossway, the chalk track that skirted Mr. Halliday's property and mounted the downs to where the steep green hump, once probably dedicated to Baldur, but for many centuries known as Bolder's Knob, rose abruptly. The lasts ten minutes were fairly stiff going. Sylvia forged ahead. David, just to show that he could do it if he liked, outstripped Sylvia and kindly offered her a hand from above for the final scramble.

"How slow those two are," said Sylvia looking down.

Anne, not so violently robust as Sylvia, was mounting the track at a more sober pace. George, who had a very sacred feeling that by helping any woman (except his mother and sister, and his aunts and grandmother) he was somehow honouring Lady Graham, asked Anne if she felt tired.

"Oh no, thank you," said Anne. "It's only that I can't walk as fast as Sylvia. She has such long legs."

"Showing off," said George briefly. "I say, are you sure you aren't tired?"

But Anne said, quite truthfully, that she was enjoying it, and in a few moments they had joined the others on the summit of the Knob. The cold wind had dropped and there was a promise of milder weather in the air. Round them lay Barsetshire, as lovely a county as any. To the north and east the downs encircled them; Humpback Ridge, the Great Hump, Fish Hill with its stone pines, the Plumstead water tower looking romantic at a distance. To the south and west the downs melted into river valleys, water-meadows, cornland and the low pasture lands. A group of pylons far away looked like minarets.

"What a heavenly evening," said Sylvia.

"Just as you like," said David, "but it's really only four o'clock in the afternoon by real time. Or do I mean eight?" he added anxiously.

There was a tense silence while everyone tried to think.

"Listen!" Said Anne suddenly.

Borne up the Rising valley came four notes from a bell.

"Good Lord!" Said George. "I thought we had tea ages ago."

"It's all right," said Anne. "That was the cathedral. They can't alter the clock because it would burst, or at least Canon Thorne said it would and he knows more about the clock than anybody. The Bishop wanted to have it altered for Double Summer Time, but of course the Dean said he couldn't possibly allow it, so it goes on telling the right time."

"But it isn't the right time," said George indignantly. "It said four, and it's six now. Oh! I see what you mean. It's right by the *right* time. Well anyway when peace comes the Dean will be able to laugh at the Bishop."

This seemed so funny to George and Sylvia and Anne that David felt he must laugh too. Then they all went down the Fossway again and through the garden where Mr. Halliday was hard at work in the potting shed. Anne asked rather timidly if she might help.

"I really must go back now," said David, fearing that he might be asked to pot something, or be set to a kind of stepmother's task of sifting earth. "Lunch one o'clock tomorrow at Holdings. Good-bye, sir. Good-bye."

This last good-bye was addressed to Anne, whose Christian name he had not yet used, a fact which he noted to his own surprise.

"Oh, good-bye, Mr. Leslie," said Anne.

"It's not Mr. Leslie, it's David," said Sylvia. "Come on, David."

Anne hoped she had not been rude and smiled at David. Mr. Halliday, reverently disentangling some thin straggling fibres from a ball of mould, happened to look up and thought Fielding's girl wasn't at all bad-looking when you came to know her. David went off with the young Hallidays, said good-bye to Mrs. Halliday, and walked back by the other path which crossed the Rising where it flowed past the garden at Holdings. As he wrestled with the little iron gate, its bars bent, its hinges loose where many children had climbed and swung on it when nurse's eye was off them, he thought with disapproval of his own behaviour. He had suddenly, for no reason at all, been gauche; a quality for which he had a special contempt. That Fielding girl seemed a shy creature, not really his kind, but she had somehow disturbed his self-possession. This thought pursued him at intervals during dinner, so he exerted himself to be particularly charming, just to show the thought that it was having no effect on him at all.

"How nice it is to have David," said Lady Emily to her daughter after dinner. "He makes everything so amusing."

"Something must be worrying him," said Agnes, placidly re-threading her tapestry needle. "He is in that kind of sweetness, mamma."

Lady Emily, occupied in counting a row of stitches which had unaccountably increased from forty to forty-three while she knitted, did not notice this comment. But Merriman, who was waiting for a favourable moment to take her employer's knitting away and get it straight, thought that Lady Graham had probably, though quite unaware of the fact, said something rather clever. A less perfect woman might have said that Agnes had the occasional moments of inspiration vouchsafed to idiots, but Miss Merriman in her quiet wisdom had taught herself never to criticise even in her secret mind the beings whom it was her appointed task to serve and protect.

On the following morning, being Sunday, Lady Graham, like a very comfortable benevolent hen, took her brood to church. Lady Emily did not accompany them because her rheumatism had been more than usually troublesome and the little church was chilly even in the height of summer, not that there had been a summer to speak of since the war began. One of the many duties which Lady Graham accomplished without any apparent effort was to find an occupation which would keep her beloved but excessively trying mother out of mischief on Sunday mornings so that Miss Merriman could attend divine service. A suggestion by Lady Emily that she should paste an accumulation of family snapshots onto bits of brown paper and make a book of them had been countered by Miss Merriman, who with great presence of mind mislaid the snapshots, knowing well the scene of mess and wreckage that would result if her ladyship were left alone with the pastepot. A second suggestion by her mother of gilding some large magnolia leaves and making a wreath of them as a kind of tribute to Sir Robert Graham, whose birthday fell during the following week, had been put aside by Lady Graham, who knew exactly how much her husband could bear. By her own methods Lady Graham had persuaded Lady Emily that her chief duty to the world was to read Lady Norton's last garden book, *Along My Borders*, and mark any passages that struck her, and after seeing Lady Emily established with an ordinary pencil, a red pencil, a blue pencil and a quantity of loose sheets of paper, she had been able to go to church with a serene mind, Miss Merriman and the children in her train. How Lady Graham managed to get the better of her adored but exhausting and unpredictable mother was the wonder of all her friends, nor can we explain it except by saying that if one could imagine swansdown which combined the strength of concrete and the slipperiness of oil with its own quality of heavenly softness, it would explain a good deal.

David, who had fully intended to be elsewhere when the church party set forth, found himself drawn into his sister's mild but relentless orbit and so into the Holdings pew, which was just behind the Hallidays, for although Holdings was a large house and General Sir Robert Graham, K.C.B., an important person, his family had only been at Holdings since Waterloo, whereas the Hallidays had lived at Hatch House for more than two hundred years and before that in the Tudor stone house which was now the bank, and had owned land thereabouts before Domesday. So Mr. Halliday had the front pew as squire and read the lessons, a position which Sir Robert secretly coveted, though nothing on earth would have persuaded him to say so. And as he had hardly ever been at home since 1939 he would not in any case have been much use.

Lady Graham's children were dispersed suitably among the grown-ups; Clarissa the neat-fingered put coloured slips of paper to mark the hymns for the younger ones; Edith, the youngest, was shaken back into her gloves by Nannie. Uncle David, in the corner nearest the aisle, thought how like one Sunday was to another, one day to another, one year to another and idly thinking of nothing suddenly remembered with great vividness Sundays at Rushwater in past days; his father dominating the little congregation, his mother swathed in scarves, her kind hawk's eyes roving about the church to find an opportunity for distracting her neighbours; his nephew Martin, now the owner of Rushwater, a small schoolboy in an Eton collar, and Mr. Banister, now a Canon of Barchester, always getting his eye-glasses twisted in their cord.

This reverie, which suddenly made David feel that he was very old and had wasted his life, was broken by the arrival of the Hatch House party coming into the front pew. First Mrs. Halliday, looking exactly like the squire's wife, then the little Fielding girl wearing what David's fastidious taste found exactly the right hat for a religious service followed by a lunch party and a pleasure party, then Sylvia more Winged Victory than ever with her burnished hair looking as if a Midas wind had fixed it in golden ripples under her little cap, George a nice boy; Mr. Halliday being the Squire so perfectly that David almost said "Bravo, Sir" as he passed.

The faint smile and slight bow of recognition suitable in sacred edifices passed between Hatch House and Holdings; Caxton, the Hallidays' carpenter, took his seat at the organ, a war-time choir of Miss Scatcherd and two wicked little boys lined the chancel, the Vicar followed hard upon, and the service began.

The Vicar, Mr. Choyce, was an old friend of Mr. Halliday's, who had given him the living (which was in his gift alternately with the Bishop of Barchester) some dozen years previously. Mr. Choyce, who had been languishing in a Liverpool parish, trying to feel that the poor were much nicer than the rich and meeting with little encouragement from his parishioners, who were practically all Dissenters, or total abstainers from any form of religion, was so happy to be in Barsetshire that he made it his life's work to study his patron's every wish, with the firm determination to live at Hatch End till his death, for retirement he did not contemplate, having nowhere to retire to. Finding that Mr. Halliday, though a staunch churchman, was apt to develop pins and needles, the fidgets and the gapes if the service went on too long, the Vicar had gradually evolved a kind of hunting mass which never lasted longer than the chime of the quarter after mid-day. Not that he in any way mutilated the service, but had had by long practice perfected a system of loud, clear and incredibly rapid speech, combined with a reverent celerity in kneeling, rising, and getting to and from the pulpit which was the envy of villages for miles round.

This speed was the more necessary that Mr. Halliday, although an intelligent man on week-days, was apt to read the lessons as if he were a backward child grappling with something beyond its comprehension. There were those who maintained that Mr. Halliday had more than once been heard to add to his reading's such sotto voce glosses as, "Can't understand what the fellow's driving at," but this was stoutly denied by the Vicar, who maintained that the Squire had said quite distinctly, "Here endeth the first lesson."

"Uncle David," said Edith in a whisper as the service proceeded.

David, not wanting to disturb the congregation, made the motion of Hush with his mouth and tried to convey a forbidding expression into his face.

"Uncle David," said Edith, "are they nice hymns?" and she pushed her hymn-book with its coloured markers into his hand.

"You've got it upside down," said David, as ventriloquially as possible.

"But are they nice hymns, Uncle David?" said Edith, always a woman of one idea.

David realising (for he was not really stupid) that his youngest niece had a hymn-book more for the look of the thing than for any practical use it might be to her, turned the book the right way up, looked at the first marker and said, "Jerusalem the Golden." A beatific smile overspread Edith's fat and charming face.

"That's the hymn Nannie's cousin sang, Uncle David, when she was in the hospital," said Edith conversationally.

David was quite fond of Edith, in whom he recognised a capacity for selfish charm almost equal to his own, but Nannie's eye was already boring a hole through his left shoulder and he feared that any moment she might rise, take his hand and lead him out into the churchyard and even seat him on cold tombstones to repent, so he smiled anxiously, made a Hush face again and thrust the hymn-book back into his niece's hand. Edith, a true woman who adored the hand that held her in check, snuggled up to her Uncle David, who against his better judgment and in courageous or some may say foolhardy defiance of

Nannie's basilisk glance, put his arm round her and recomposed himself. At the same moment Mr. Halliday, who had been for the last two minutes fidgeting like a horse before the barriers go down, got up, walked rapidly to the reading desk as if to forestall any attempt on the part of the Vicar to speak out of order, straightened his tie and looked over the congregation in a way that irreligiously reminded David of Rushwater Robert, his father's prize bull, long since a settler in Latin America, looking out of his stall at Sunday morning visitors, long long ago.

Mr. Halliday, having to his own satisfaction quelled a non-existent uprising of free-thinkers, heretics and supporters of the Deposited Prayer-book, announced rather angrily that this was the second lesson, from the second chapter of the Epistle of the Colossians, the sixth verse, and glared again at the congregation. Having satisfied himself that all was well, he read the portion allotted for the day. David, difficult to please, was impressed by the excellent delivery, the fine voice, the complete absence of self-consciousness or affectation in the Squire's reading, and even thought for a moment of becoming a reformed character and leading a new life. But as the reading went on, his worse and better-informed self told him in no uncertain voice that the Squire had, on the whole, not the faintest idea what it was all about. He glanced cautiously about him. The congregation had disposed itself in such attitudes of comfort as wooden pews with very low backs at wide angles can provide, and were quite obviously taking advantage of this respite to reflect in some cases upon next week's ration problems, in some upon whether that hay was coming along nicely and yet again in other cases upon such a jumble of things that it might as well have been nothing at all.

Mr. Halliday, reaching the end sooner than he had expected, shut the book with an injured air and rejoined his family. The moment for the first hymn approached. Mr. Caxton played two lines of the melody. Miss Scatcherd with a quick and masterly scuffle placed herself between the two wicked little boys who had been inciting each other to giggle, and everyone suddenly burst out singing, thought David, and then blamed himself for being too literary.

*Jerusalem the Golden* is emphatically a Good Hymn. There is no need to argue the question. The united voice of church-going England says it is, the united intellect of that body knows that it is. David remembered how he used to cry whenever it was sung at Rushwater because of its exquisite nostalgic beauty, and how he felt free from all sin, and even made resolutions never to tease his sister Agnes again, for at least five minutes after its conclusion. He was touched, more than he would have liked to admit, to find that his niece Edith shared his feelings and was singing with a fervour hardly recognised outside the Salvation Army, her charming fat face irradiated by the light of another world.

It was at this moment that David practically made up his mind to buy some land, marry, and settle down to produce cheap wheat for the millions and a large healthy family who would increase and multiply like Job's, without the initial disadvantage of all having to be killed by the house falling on top of them so that their yet unborn brothers and sisters could take up the burden. In this heavenly frame of mind he remained (so swift is thought, so are a hundred years mirrored in the ink-pool each of us possesses) for at least twenty-five seconds, at the expiration of which eternity two things suddenly recalled him to earth.

The organist, followed and in some cases slightly preceded by his congregation (for Mr. Caxton held strong secret views as to the relative positions of Organist and Vicar during the hymns, and the nullity of the latter official), had pulled out a number of peculiarly saccharine and revolting stops and led his flocks into very high altitudes where only a true soprano, or those who had the good sense suddenly to sing an octave lower, could survive. The voices of praise had died, as they always do at that point, into batlike squeaks or bass rumbles, when to David's amazement a bird's soft effortless notes rose on wings from the pew in front. For a moment he thought the golden Sylvia also had a golden voice. Then he heard her grappling determinedly with the hymn in a muffled way and realised that the lark ascending was the little Fielding girl. It only lasted for a moment. The congregation returning from the unscaleable heights or the silent depths, joyfully crescendoed into "What radiancy of glory" and the bird vanished. David, too susceptible to beauty, though he often looked at it and left it, waited in almost unbearable suspense for the next verse. The small miracle was repeated, and, he felt, for his special benefit, for no one appeared to notice it.

Rapt by this unexpected treat, it was not till the fourth verse of the hymn was well on its way that he realised what anyone less susceptible to exquisite sound would have noticed long before, that his niece Edith, holding her hymn-book upside down and open at the wrong place, was deliberately singing gibberish. He looked nervously round to see if Nannie had heard, but that excellent woman, who was chapel and only went to church in her official capacity, was occupied in disapproving silently of the whole service, item by item. He breathed again. The hymn came to an end, the service proceeded. The collection was made by Mr. Halliday and the other churchwarden, a farmer; the congregation were blessed and dismissed. Nannie pounced upon the children, but Robert escaped and ran back to his side.

"Oh, Uncle David," he said, "how much did you put in the bag? I put in sixpence. Nannie gives us each sixpence to put in the bag. Miss Merriman said there was some Latin that says anyone who gives quickly gives twice, so I always put mine in very quickly. Do you think it turns into a shilling, Uncle David? Oh, Uncle David, how much did you put in?"

"A pound," said David.

"Oh! Uncle David!" said Robert. "Did you put it in quickly so that it would turn into two pounds?"

David said he did, hoping by this means to keep the light of faith burning in his young nephew.

Nannie then approached.

"Come along, Robert," she said, "and don't bother Uncle David."

"He's not bothering me a bit," said David, "We were talking about the collection and he tells me he has sixpence to put in the bag. How nicely Edith sang her hymns!"

But if David hoped to placate Nannie, he had for once quite miscalculated the effect of his charm.

"When I was a little girl, sir, Father gave us a penny for chapel," said Nurse, making David feel that he was rapidly qualifying for the Rake's Progress. "Not that Father couldn't have afforded more, but he always said to let your light shine before men didn't mean showing off."

David, now morally convinced of hell-fire gaping for him and that at no distant date, said weakly that it was a pity there weren't more parents like that.

"Of course," said Nannie severely, "with Lady Graham's children it's quite different. All my young ladies and gentlemen have sixpence. Besides, Father died thirty years ago. Come along, Robert."

"Nannie! Uncle David put a pound in the bag," said Robert. "He said it would turn into two pounds."

"Now come along at once when Nannie tells you," said his guardian ignoring Robert's remark, though David could see quite plainly what she thought of it, and dragged him away to join the nursery party, leaving David convicted of ostentation, deliberate lying and general immorality. Added to which, he felt quite secretly convinced that Nannie knew quite well that Edith was singing nonsense words and looked upon David as a liar who hadn't even the wits to make his lies sound true.

Clarissa, who was allowed to belong to the grown-ups on Sunday, now approached him.

"Oh, Uncle David," she said, "what did you put in the bag? I put in sixpence of mother's and sixpence of my own money."

Her Sunday self-righteousness, coming on the top of so many shattering experiences, was too much for David, who said almost crossly that he had put a pound in the plate because he believed in making large contributions to charity when people could see how generous he was.

"Like our 'Give and Lend, For Hatch End,'" said Clarissa. "I put a halfcrown that I was very fond of into Miss Scatcherd's collecting box, just to show her I didn't like her."

This unexpected light on a niece who he had hitherto looked upon as just one of Agnes's children interested David.

"You mean you wanted to impress Miss Scatcherd, but you wouldn't have wanted to impress someone you liked?" he said.

Clarissa nodded violently.

"When we had the 'Lend all you can, For the Fighting Man' week," said Clarissa, hooking her arm affectionately into David's, "dear old Mrs. Hubbak at The Shop was collecting, so I put a penny in and she said, 'That's right, miss. Do as you would be done by. I'd like to see them boys putting anything in a box for us.' So right, don't you think, Uncle David?"

"How old are you, Clarissa?" said David.

"Fifteen in June, Uncle David," said Clarissa. "On the nineteenth. Will you be here then?"

"I don't know. I shouldn't think so," said David. "But I'll send you a present. Good Lord! I thought you were about twelve."

"Do I look twelve?" asked Clarissa anxiously.

David, seeing that she was slightly wounded, hastened to reassure her. She really, he said, looked like sixteen, but one was apt to think of one's nephews and nieces at the ages they used to be, not the ages they were. Clarissa appeared satisfied. She had taken her gloves off now that Nannie was gone and was fingering some wallflowers that grew in a crevice between two time-worn tombstones.

"Do you know you have charming hands?" said David.

Clarissa spread her hands and looked at them, then at David, enquiringly.

"Elegant and tip-tilted," said David sententiously. He was not sure whether she understood, but she looked pleased and blushed in a becoming way. Then the whole body of Grahams and Hallidays surrounded them. Mr. and Mrs. Halliday, who were going back to Hatch House for lunch, said good-bye.

"I say, David," said Mr. Halliday, drawing David aside. "Did you understand the second lesson?"

"No, sir," said David. He would have liked to add that it was partly because he wasn't listening, but this might have hurt Mr. Halliday.

"Nor did I," said Mr. Halliday. "Still, those fellows wrote in Latin or Greek or something, and it stands to reason they can't always have known what they meant. Deuced hard work for the translators."

"I expect it was often a case of by guess and by God," said David sympathetically, while at the same moment he told himself he was being a hypocrite and making himself a motley to the view, simply from his great desire to be liked, and slipped away from the conversation.

The Hallidays went away towards the bridge while Lady Graham with her family and guests went down the path to the road. Just outside the lychgate Mr. Scatcherd was seated on his camp-stool, his back to the churchyard wall, busily and rather ostentatiously sketching, his head in a very old Panama hat thrown a little back and his block held at arm's length. Dearly would Mr. Scatcherd have liked to pretend that Art had rapt him away into an empyrean where a large chattering party of church-goers seemed a mere delusion, but the younger Graham children hailed him with delight as an old friend, making such flattering comments on his work as obliged him to descend from his heights.

"Mother!" said Robert, "Mr. Scatcherd is making an admiring picture."

Lady Graham, emerging from her normal state of placidly thinking about nothing in particular, smiled with her own peculiar charm at the artist and said, "Good-morning, Mr. Scatcherd. How quick you have been."

It was at once evident to David and Miss Merriman, respectively the quicker-witted and the most intelligent members of the party, that Lady Graham was under the impression that Mr. Scatcherd, having previously attended Divine Service, had with incredible agility sped down the churchyard and out of the gate, put up his camp-stool, opened his drawing-block and made an elaborate pencil drawing of the Mellings Arms, the whole within a period of not more than five minutes. If there had been any real danger both Miss Merriman and David would have gone to Lady Graham's rescue, but in this case, exchanging a glance of sympathetic amusement, they left her ladyship to get out of the muddle as best she could.

"I have been working on this little sketch for some days, Lady Graham," said Mr. Scatcherd. "Only a sketch, of course, but it has what you might call an idea behind it."

"Oh, I thought," said Lady Graham, a shade of disappointment in her voice, "that you had done it all since you came out of church."

This was a very unwise remark, for Mr. Scatcherd was an avowed agnostic and only too ready to be boring about it, though no one took the slightest interest for he was a foreigner from Northbridge and foreigners are well known to be peculiar.

"I was not in church this morning," said Mr. Scatcherd, with the proud fervour of those who know that England is, as far as church-going is concerned, still a free country and that the vicar is only too anxious to be broad-minded.

"The evening service is very nice too," said Lady Graham, "but we all like the morning service, don't we, my darlings?"

At this point Mr. Scatcherd would undoubtedly have burst in his zealous desire to explain to Lady Graham his conviction that organised religion of any sort was a mere mummery, had not his niece come up.

"WELL, uncle!" said Miss Scatcherd, "as if it wasn't trying enough for me your being rude to the Vicar and never setting foot in the church but you must sit in the road like a gypsy and bother her ladyship come along now because I left the dinner in the oven and I'm not going to waste my meat ration getting it burnt and if you're going to be late I'm not good GRACIOUS what will her ladyship think of you sitting there all morning with your pencils and rubbish on a Sunday too I never DID."

At the first sound of his niece's voice Mr. Scatcherd had begun to huddle his sketching materials together, assisted by Robert, while Edith folded the camp-stool and Clarissa picked some long grasses and made an elegant bunch which she gave to Miss Scatcherd.

"THERE uncle," said Miss Scatcherd, finding any subject a good approach for scolding Mr. Scatcherd, "look what Miss Clarissa has given me and all you do is to stand there when the dinner's frizzling up in the oven what her ladyship must be thinking I'd really rather not know it isn't even as if you went to chapel like Nurse but just sitting about outside the church when everyone's coming out good GRACIOUS will you never be ready."

The unfortunate Mr. Scatcherd as well as being hustled by his masterful niece suddenly became conscious of a deadly chill which was Nurse's showing deep though silent disapproval of the mention of her name, and dropped his sketching-block. David, wishing to end a scene which he now found excessively boring, picked up the block and handed it to the artist, who stuffed it into one of his large pockets, raised the Panama and hurried off after his niece. The Holdings party then walked back to lunch without any further delay.

During Lady Graham's absence at church, Lady Emily had made a number of plans for the seating of the lunch party, but as they were chiefly concerned with trying to sit next to the two Hallidays, Anne Fielding and her adored David all at once, Miss Merriman had bided her time and arranged the table just as she, in her wisdom, knew would be best. David, conscious of Sylvia Halliday's golden looks, thought it might be amusing to sit next to her; also to sit next to that Fielding girl who had sung like a bird; but Miss Merriman, who though fond of David in a dispassionate way, saw no reason to spoil him, had him seated between his mother and Clarissa before he could make any protest, so David amiably set himself to please; not a difficult job.

"Mamma," said Lady Graham across the table, "Robert said something you would love this morning. Poor Mr. Scatcherd was sitting outside the church drawing the Mellings Arms and Robert said it was an admiring picture."

"I suppose he meant admirable," said George Halliday, delighted to get into conversation with his hostess.

"Oh no, George," said Lady Graham, turning reproachful dove's eyes upon him. "He meant admiring. It is quite different. Robert has always been so good at words, hasn't he, mamma?"

"I think an admiring picture is *perfect*," said Lady Emily. "Clarissa used to have some nice words. Do you remember the poem she made about the thrush that died, Merry?"

Miss Merriman did not.

"I remember them, mamma," said David.

> "'See our thrush does not arise
> And to heaven he quickly flies.'

I can't think why I remember them," he added thoughtfully.

Lady Emily and Agnes, ignoring their young guests, began to quote several other instances of genius in the young Grahams. David, hoping to find someone to share his boredom, tried to catch Miss Merriman's eye, but that lady was talking to Sylvia Halliday about borrowing a broody hen.

"How *could* you, Uncle David?" said a low, indignant voice at his side.

He turned to his niece Clarissa, whose cheeks were pink, whose eyes were suspiciously bright.

"I don't know how I could in the least," said David, "especially as I don't know what it is I could. What's the matter, Clarissa?"

His niece blinked her eyes violently, and gave them a quick violent dab with her handkerchief.

"My dear! Too tactless," she said, smiling brilliantly. "Let us talk about something else."

Seldom had David Leslie found himself at a loss, especially where the gentler sex was concerned, and never had any shadow come between him and his own family. Clarissa's sudden attack of rage, or embarrassment, or was it both, made him feel acutely uneasy, a feeling unusual to him and rather mortifying. Lady Emily had turned to Anne Fielding and was according to her custom asking a number of piercing questions which from anyone else would have been maddening curiosity but in Lady Emily were only a sign of real interest and good-will. Beyond Clarissa the visit of the broody hen was being arranged by an elaborate system of relays and houses of call, so David felt safe to tackle his niece. To see anyone unhappy or annoyed was a thing he hated; partly from a naturally kind nature, even more because the unhappiness or annoyance might disturb him. In most cases one could slip away from such uncomfortable positions; one could say a few charming words with all temporary sincerity and take one's leave, forgetting very quickly the difficult moments. Possibly, as the war went on, it had become more difficult to skate over social ice that was thin or cracking, but David's confidence in his own immunity had never received so shattering a blow as his niece Clarissa's sudden change from a little girl to a young woman who spoke to him as an equal, and indeed with such grown-up and almost offhand words as made David conscious that he had received a snub and perhaps a well-merited snub.

"Look here, Clarissa," he said, annoyed to find himself treating her as a contemporary and almost appealing for her forgiveness. "I'm awfully sorry about the Thrush poem."

"Rather childish, don't you think, Uncle David?" said the new grown-up voice of this new grown-up niece, who was smiling at him as prettily as ever, only the smile had a diamond-bright quality he did not like. And what was even more disconcerting, he wasn't sure to which of them the word *childish* was meant to apply.

"If you mean the poem was childish, after all you were only a child when you made it," said David.

"Quite," said Clarissa, very politely, the smile a little less sparkling; or so he ventured to hope.

"If you mean I was childish to repeat it," said David in a low voice and almost desperately, "I am quite really and truly and repentingly apologetic. You know, your mother does always repeat all your poems and words; she always has, bless her, though she has less sense of the suitable occasion than any woman I know. Do you suppose Robert minded her telling everyone about the admiring picture?"

"Oh, no," said Clarissa, the hardness almost entirely gone from her voice. "Robert won't ever mind things. Of course I adore mother, but I can't help growing up. If only the war would go on I'd go into the W.A.A.F.s like Sylvia, but it doesn't look as if I'd have much luck. I am going to tell father I must go to boarding-school for a couple of years and perhaps I'll get a scholarship for Cambridge and do engineering draughtman-ship."

In such a calm and conversational manner was this bomb dropped and so good were David's table manners that no one could have guessed how his whole world had turned upside down in a few moments. Clarissa, the fat baby Clarissa, was nearly fifteen, knew what she wanted, would probably get it and was a woman to be reckoned with. And for the first time in his life David suddenly realised that his sister Agnes's divine im-becility might be extremely trying for some of her children. Emmy, as we know, had so far broken away from her family as to become a Land Girl with the ultimate view of breeding bulls with her cousin Martin Leslie. Now Clarissa wanted to try her wings. The boys' feelings did not matter so much. School was setting them free in turn. As for Edith, that stout and enchanting young woman would probably go through life taking it exactly as she found it. Looking across the table at his sister, who was telling George Halliday how well her eldest son James was doing at Eton and how much he loved birds, David wondered with a sudden anxiety if she would ever realise that her children were growing up and the safe family circle, which even the war had not greatly changed, spreading and widening in a new strange world. He would have liked to discuss this matter with his niece Clarissa in the light of the confidence she had just reposed in him, but the lunch table was not the place and at any moment his mother with one of her piercing intuitions might pounce upon their conversation and insist upon discussing the whole matter before the Hallidays and that Fielding girl; so that when she turned to him, at that very instant, he almost jumped.

"I have made a delightful plan with Anne," said Lady Emily, her eyes sparkling with a pleasurable anticipation which David at once diagnosed to be his beloved mother in one of her most meddling moods. "You know that house in the Close where old Canon Robarts used to live, David. I have always wondered what the servants' bedrooms were like, so when you drive Anne back to Barchester after we have had tea at Rushwater I will come too and Anne is going to show me the whole of the top floor, because most luckily Lady Fielding's cook is having her Sunday out. I am going to have my afternoon rest at Rushwater," said her ladyship, letting her table-napkin, her bag, and her spectacles slip from her lap to the floor as she got up, and flashing one of her mischievous defiant smiles at her daughter and her secretary, "so we'll will start as soon as I am ready. Come to my room, Agnes, and look at that piece of embroidery I found. I think it will do for your Bring and Buy Sale. And David, you must amuse Anne."

But David had already determined not to be landed with another very young girl. Clarissa with her unexpected and shattering confidences had been quite enough for one day and the Fielding girl would very likely be dull. So he dutifully picked up his mother's scatterings and managed to detach the Hallidays from the lunch-table so that they could all three talk Army and Air Force shop in the garden. At the same time Clarissa slipped away with the younger children, so that Anne was suddenly deserted. Miss Merriman, who missed very little, came quietly to the rescue.

"Miss Bunting was with you, I think," she said. "She came over here once with the Marlings and I had a great respect for her."

Anne at once felt at home with Miss Merriman, who had liked the old governess and talked in a confiding way that Miss Merriman found slightly touching, until it was time for the Rushwater party to start.

# CHAPTER 4

Sunday dinner at Everard Carter's House had run its course, or to be correct its two courses, which were roast beef, roast potatoes, Yorkshire pudding and cabbage, followed by plum tart and custard. This has a specious sound of being a good Sunday mid-day meal, though in most cases it would have consisted of beef substitute, flannel Yorkshire pudding made with dried eggs, tough potatoes, damp greens, a pie with a leather crust and watery custard powder mess. But under Kate Carter's sway the butcher mysteriously produced Scotch beef earlier in the week so that it would thaw out nicely, the potatoes were soft inside and crisp outside, the cabbage attractive, the plums all home-bottled, the pastry well made and the custard, as well as the Yorkshire pudding, made for a Sunday treat with real eggs. For Mrs. Carter had kept hens ever since 1914 and what with laying hens and laid-down eggs, all the boys in her husband's house were very well fed.

Robin Dale, feeling rather replete and that a chair and a book would be more attractive than an expedition to Rushwater, told himself not to be lazy and rounded up the two Leslie boys, nice boys, but a little dull, as were their parents, John and Mary Leslie. It was already quite obvious to Everard Carter, Robin Dale and Mr. Birkett the Headmaster who knew a great deal more about his boys than they bargained for, that Leslie major and Leslie minor would go through school and later life in a golden mediocrity as good citizens with the right careers, wives and children. It was with more resignation than enthusiasm that Everard Carter put in their yearly reports that they were an excellent influence in the House, and he sometimes wished they would do at least one dashing and disreputable deed a term. Robin had no fault to find with their classics, which would always satisfy the examiners, and noted with some amusement that Leslie major rather ostentatiously took a Greek Testament to church and followed the Second Lesson in it: quite suitable to the outcome of a race of educated landowners.

Robin and his charges arrived at Rushwater Station about three o'clock, where a tall young man with a melancholy face and a slight limp was strolling up and down the platform. The Leslies with restrained joy greeted their Uncle Martin and introduced their classical master to him.

"I've got the car," said Martin Leslie, leading them to a shameful old Ford.

"Oh, Uncle Martin, can I drive?" said Leslie major.

"Certainly not," said Martin. "You both get in behind. You can drive the car inside the park, but not on the road. We've got a new policeman who wants promotion. Do you mind coming in front with me Dale?"

Robin had no objection and they clanked through the little village into the park, where Martin stopped.

"Here, you boys can take her up to the house," he said. "Shall we walk, Dale? It will be better for our nerves, and the park is looking nice."

Robin was quite agreeable; the boys drove off, Leslie major taking first turn at the wheel.

"Extraordinarily competent boys my nephews are," said Martin, "but lord! How uninteresting compared with my Aunt Agnes's children."

"Is that Lady Graham?" Robin asked.

"That's the one," said Martin. "She's coming over this afternoon with some young people, so we may get some decent tennis. Her eldest girl Emmy is staying here to study cattle-breeding. She's a character too. I expect you are pretty good at tennis."

"I hate boasting," said Robin, "but I've got a gammy foot, so I always ask for thirty to start with."

He had said this in his own way, mocking his loss and hoping he wasn't overdoing it; and then as so often happened, he felt ashamed and told himself for the thousandth time that the less he said about his foot the less he would bore people. But to his surprise Martin's melancholy face suddenly lighted up and he produced an extremely agreeable smile.

"Good," he said. "I'll play against you and neither of us need ask for thirty. You may have noticed that I have an obvious kind of limp, which I grossly exaggerate when I want to impress newcomers."

Robin said he had noticed it and he was so sorry and was it a strain.

"Oh, no, those filthy Italians," said Martin. "They were supposed to be being liberated by us, but they jolly well took care to show an independent spirit. But I'm glad to say my men blew that machine-gunner up."

"Where was that?" Robin asked.

"Anzio," said Martin. "Nasty place."

"Good Lord!" said Robin. "Were you there?"

Martin said he was, and did Robin know the beach.

"I should think so," said Robin. "I've got a foot buried somewhere there—what was left of it, anyway."

Upon which they fell into a delightful conversation about the war and discovered a number of common friends and common hatreds, the chief link in this latter category being Sir Ogilvy Hibberd (at that time not yet raised to the peerage), who had come out at no personal inconvenience at all to tell the troops that the Italians were simple children who had been misled by their leaders and that practically all Germans were really domestic peace-loving Christians. Absorbed in their conversation they walked down the drive, crossed the little Rushmere Brook, and so by the side of Rushwater House in all its complacent comfortable ugliness to the terrace outside the drawing-room windows, where they paced up and down, still talking.

"If you didn't think it sinful pride," said Robin presently, "shall we sit down? If we are going to play tennis I like to pamper myself."

Martin said he felt much the same himself, so they sat on a bench against the wall between two of the long windows and continued their army talk. Suddenly round the side of the house appeared a girl in Land Army dress, perhaps a little on the stout side for breeches, but with a pleasant face and a mop of tawny hair.

"I say," said the girl, addressing Martin, "have you got *Stock Breeders' Gazette*? I can't find it in the office."

"Good God, my girl, don't you know Sunday when you see it," said Martin, "and before visitors too? This is my cousin Emmy, that I told you about. Emmy, this is Robin Dale. He brought the boys over from Southbridge."

"Hullo," said Emmy, standing straddled-legged before Robin with her hands in her pockets and looking him up and down in a way that made him feel he was an exhibit at a cattle show and ought to have a rosette pinned onto him somewhere. "How do you do," she added, thrusting a hand at him and evidently satisfied by her scrutiny. "Don't be an ass, Martin. Cows don't take any notice of Sunday and I want to find the date of that show at Nutfield."

"Emmy," said Martin reprovingly, "you are lowering my status before strangers and I haven't the faintest idea where the *Gazette* is. I expect Macpherson has got it. Are you going to play tennis?"

"Are you good?" said Emmy to Robin.

Robin, rightly interpreting this as an enquiry about his tennis form rather than a general Sabbatical enquiry into his moral condition, said he was fair to moderate.

"That's all right," said Emmy, obviously relieved. "I'll play if I don't have to change, Martin, because Rushwater Romany has torn his leg a bit on that barbed wire down the long meadow and I must have a look at it. I told Macpherson we ought to get that wire cleared."

"That's the Home Guard," said Martin. "They would make what they called a strong point there and Lord knows when we'll get it unstrong again. There's Agnes's car."

As he spoke a car stopped at the end of the terrace. Martin and Emmy hurried to meet it, while Robin followed more slowly feeling a little shy of this rising tide of Leslies. David Leslie, the Hallidays and Lady Graham came pouring out of it and then there was a pause while Lady Emily was assisted to alight with such a confusion of rugs, scarves, bags, sticks, other scarves and other bags as gave her ladyship rather the appearance of a conjuror bringing portable property out of the Infinite. Her grandson Martin and her granddaughter Emmy embraced her very affectionately and the whole party began to move along the terrace, when Robin, who was still lingering a little apart, saw yet another passenger get out of the car and look round in a rather frightened way.

"Robin!" said the last passenger in tones of relief and pleased surprise.

"Anne!" said Robin, hurrying forward to extricate her from another of Lady Emily's spare scarves which had got itself wound about her feet. "I didn't know you were coming."

"Nor did I," said Anne. "At least I mean I knew I was coming but I didn't know you'd be here. Oh, I am so glad, Robin, because they are all so large, and the ones that came to meet us are rather large too."

Robin laughed. Anne looked at him with slight anxiety.

"All right," he said. "I quite agree. I suppose being fairly large myself it hadn't occurred to me. Come along."

They followed the others onto the terrace, where Agnes made Anne known to Martin and Emmy. Robin, surveying the scene, thought that Anne looked almost like a creature of another breed, so slight and elegant she was against the handsome stalwart Hallidays, tall David Leslie and his tall nephew Martin, Agnes Graham's maternal opulence of figure, and Emmy's stout form well outlined by jersey and breeches. He was a good height himself too, if it came to that. Even Lady Emily, though rather bowed by age, was rendered so impressive a figure by the number of shawls and cloaks draped about her person and her slightly eccentric hat that beside her Anne looked almost frail. Poor little Anne, thought Robin to himself, and determined to see that she had a happy afternoon and was not trodden under-foot by the Brobdingnagians.

"Now," said Lady Emily, rearranging a scarf round her face and flashing a smile onto the company, "we will make a tour of the house and Martin shall show us everything he has altered. I know, darling Martin, that you have put the nursery rocking-horse into one of the attics."

"I haven't, Gran," said Martin indignantly. "As a matter of fact I had a ride on it only the other day, but both my feet touched the ground, so it wasn't very successful."

"Well, we will all go and look," said Lady Emily.

"Mother darling," said Lady Graham, "you know you ought to rest first. You promised you would lie down before you began exploring."

"But what is so sad," said Lady Emily, deliberately not hearing her daughter's words, "is that the nurseries are empty now. Your grandfather would have hated to see them empty, Martin."

"It's not my fault, Gran," said Martin. "I'm not married and I've never seen anyone I wanted to marry. David can get married and I'll have *his* children here if you like."

David said he saw no reason to have a lot of children just because Martin shirked his obligations as a landowner. What really *was* sad, he added, was that before the war he and Martin would have had a friendly fight after the words that had just passed, and now they both felt too old to scuffle in public.

"But," continued Lady Emily, "I have just thought of a very good plan for altering the furniture in the night nursery, and if you come too, David, we can do it at once."

"I say, Gran," said Emmy, advancing like a corps of Amazons upon her grandmother, "Merry said you were to rest so you'd better come to the morning-room. I've got the sofa ready for you and a hot bottle. Come on."

So surprised was Lady Emily at the suddenness of this attack that she picked up some of her trailing weeds and taking Emily's arm affectionately went with her into the house.

"Good Lord!" said David. "Agnes, that girl of yours is most remarkable. Not in all my thirty-seven or so years have I seen mother pay the faintest attention to what anyone said. Except to Merry of course."

"I think," said Agnes, gratified by any illusion to her off-spring, "that darling Emmy is very like grandpa Pomfret. He always bullied everyone dreadfully at the Towers and used to swear at the footmen. I can just remember him when I was a little girl, with eyes like a pig and rather red hair except for being bald."

"Well, love, you have altered since then," said David, at which Martin burst into a loud guffaw, quite unlike his melancholy face, and Agnes looked faintly perplexed.

As so often happened when members of the Leslie family got together, they quite unconsciously became a compact body, taking little or no notice of outsiders. Martin, who though less quick-witted than his uncle David had a much kinder nature, became aware of an outer circle of guests and hastened to make plans for tennis.

"Six," he said, looking round. "And Emmy makes seven. And the boys nine. Lord! where are those boys? I'd forgotten all about them. They've probably broken the car by now and their own necks as well. Emmy!" he shouted to his cousin, who came out by the drawing-room onto the terrace as he was speaking, "Have you seen the boys?"

"Yes," shouted Emmy. "They wanted to stay with Gran and tell her how they'd driven backwards all up the drive and round the stable-yard, so I told them to go to the tennis court. Come on, everyone."

The whole party straggled through the kitchen garden, in the middle of which was a small pond where a few decayed goldfish still lived.

"Ornamental water," said David to Sylvia Halliday, as they walked past it, "celebrated by having been fallen into by Emmy at a tender age. I wasn't there, but Agnes told me about it so often that I can almost see it happening."

"It was quite dreadful," said Agnes to George Halliday in her sweet unruffled voice. "She might have been drowned if the water had been deep enough."

"I wish I'd been there," said George. "I'd have got her out for you."

"How good of you," said Agnes, her maternal feeling much gratified. "But luckily there was a charming young Frenchman who rescued her. The legs of his tennis trousers got quite wet, so I said, 'Do go in and change your trousers or you will catch cold, monsieur'—what was his name, David?"

"Duval, Durand—something quite ordinary," said David. "Anyway I hate all foreigners. I used to like quite a lot of them, but having all these gallant allies gives one a fair sickener."

"I hate them too; they're always showing off," said George Halliday, with a fervour that surprised his sister Sylvia, who could not know that jealousy of Duval or Durand who had got his trouser legs wet while rescuing Lady Graham's infant daughter, was inspiring these xenophobic sentiments.

"I quite agree with you, George," said Lady Graham, "especially Russians. My husband was on a military mission to Russia before the war and he said he did not like them very much."

"Robert is always so right," said David. "Except the Russian ballet."

His sister smiled at him with a wealth of loving if addle-pated sympathy in her soft eyes, but otherwise his comment passed unnoticed and David reflected rather sadly that of all the company present he and Agnes and possibly Martin were the only remains of a society that had enjoyed the last gleams of a murdered civilization; that all the pleasant, honourable, well-bred young people round them had been brought up on English-Speaking Ballet and—luckily for themselves perhaps—had not immortal longings in them for what was gone beyond recall.

To them opera and ballet would mean the great joy of standing in queues with millions of their fellow-citizens, of huddled high teas before an opera, of audiences in every variety of sloppiness, men in pullovers with wild hair and far too often wild beards, women in trousers or barelegged and in any case with dirty toes and scarlet toe-nails sticking out of sandals, all smoking, all enjoying being in a crowd, having trays of tea on their laps, accepting whatever entertainment was offered to them with equal enthusiasm, applauding to the echo the bad with the good, and always just before the last note of the music had died away.

"I wish I could have seen proper ballet and opera before the war," said a voice at his side.

David turned, and looked down on the Fielding girl.

"And what do you know about them?" he said, speaking kindly as to a child.

"Oh, I don't really know much," said Anne, "but my old governess used to tell me about Covent Garden in the season and the first Russian ballet and I wished dreadfully that I could have been there. People with jewels and tiaras and opera hats and white gloves. And she knew a man who always took two stalls, one for himself and one for his opera cloak. It must have been heavenly." She stopped abruptly, rather alarmed by her own temerity.

"Stout fellow," said David approvingly. "I wish I'd thought of that. If ever we have a decent opera season again, which I think highly improbable having no opinion whatever of the present or future state of the world, I shall always buy three stalls, so that I needn't sit next to anyone. I do hate people who bulge into one sideways."

"Or," said Anne, suddenly feeling braver, "one might get a seat in front and behind as well, because people in front are usually tall, or they have very large heads, and people behind nearly always talk."

David looked down at her with approval. Something in the Fielding girl, perhaps.

"Yes indeed," he said. "There one would sit, in the middle of a quincunx, which I believe is the correct description of the seats you suggest, like God, holding one's own form of creed but tolerating none, if you will excuse the misquotation."

"I *adore* Tennyson," said Anne and then went pink, feeling that she had been too forward.

The party had now come to the tennis court and David was rattling the rather stiff handle of the wire door, and did not reply. To tell the truth he was not sorry for the excuse to break off the conversation, for he was slightly ashamed of himself. He had misquoted Tennyson for his own amusement with, he must admit it, a faint air of superciliousness, assuming that the Fielding girl would not take the allusion. She had taken it at once, and he wondered uneasily whether she had detected the condescension. But there was no time for these fine shades as the whole tennis party surged into the court, where Leslie major and minor were having a knock-up.

"We have managed eleven balls," said Martin rather proudly. "They nearly all bounce. Mother sent me some from America, but they got stolen on the way. She's going to send me some more when she finds somebody flying."

David enquired politely after the health of Martin's mother and her American husband, and began to arrange the games with his nephew.

"Oh, Lady Graham," said Anne, who felt safer with her

hostess than with all the other tall Leslies, "is Martin Leslie American?"

"No," said Lady Graham. "His father, my eldest brother, was killed in the last war and his mother married a very nice American, but Martin was at school in England, because he was to inherit Rushwater when Papa died, so of course he had to live here or the people on the place wouldn't have known him. He has been a great deal in America too, of course, and he only just got back in time when this war began. He is such a darling and adores motors."

Having given this short character sketch of her nephew, Agnes fell silent and sat looking with benign vacancy at the tennis players.

Sylvia and Martin were playing David and Emmy. Sylvia, who had noticed Martin's limp, offered to do most of the running about, an offer which Martin cheerfully accepted. On the other side of the net David, very fond of his niece Emmy but under no illusions as to the quality of her play, ordered her when in doubt to leave the ball to him, which Emmy, conscious of her shortcomings as a tennis player, though supremely confident in her abilities in most other departments especially livestock, was quite glad to do. So the game resolved itself into a kind of duel between David and Sylvia, who were pretty evenly matched. Sylvia was perhaps the better player, having besides pretty style almost alarming strength, but David made up in cunning and experience what he lacked in youth and kept Sylvia on the rush till her colour rose to a most becoming extent and her golden hair fell into great disorder. The set ended after a spectacular rally which made even Agnes pay a little attention and the players left the court, while Leslie major and minor meticulously tested the height of the net and removed a few sticky chestnut sheaths that had fallen from a flowering tree.

"Winged Victory," said David to Sylvia, looking with admiration at her admirable figure in a white tennis frock, her handsome flushed face and her helmet of rippling gold.

"We couldn't have won if you hadn't served those two faults in the last set," said Sylvia. "I expect you were tired."

"Tired!" said David. "Sylvia, whatever I am, I am *not* your grandfather. I was playing badly. Also I was showing off and cheating Emmy of her birthright. It's a lesson to me."

"What of?" said Sylvia.

"I haven't the least idea," said David. "And let this be a lesson to you, my girl, never to ask people what they mean, for they usually don't know themselves. And I shall now tell you that your playing was as superb as your appearance."

"Rot," said the Winged Victory, twiddling her racquet.

"And I'll tell you what, as my cousin Lucy Marling says," said David. "Compliments that I pay in the boudoir, the morning-room, the ballroom, leaning on the railings of Rotten Row or reining up my foam-flecked steed—also in Rotten Row—on its haunches to salute a fair equestrienne, are but idle flattery. But the compliments I pay on the field of mimic battle are from the heart; and very well turned too as a rule," he added sententiously.

The Winged Victory became even redder in the face than before, though very becomingly, gave David a searching look from her speedwell eyes, murmured, "Oh, well," and sat down by her brother.

Meanwhile Martin, a quiet but attentive host, had suggested a men's four of Robin, George and the two Leslie boys. The combination, though well-deserving, was somehow so dull that the audience entirely lost interest and conversed among themselves. Only Anne took no part, overcome by a sudden fit of shyness, while Martin and Emmy returned to the subject of Rushwater Romany's torn leg and Agnes gently bored her adored brother David.

"Are you tired?" said Sylvia to Anne, for whom she felt a certain responsibility as their weekend guest.

"No thank you," said Anne. "I was only wishing I could have been a Land Girl or a W.A.A.F."

"Bad luck," said Sylvia kindly. "And if the war's going to stop you won't have much chance."

"It makes one look so nice," said Anne sadly.

"Nice?" said Sylvia, surprised.

"Well, I mean you and Emmy," said Anne. "I mean you both look so nice and have such lovely hair. I feel *horrid* when I look at you."

"I can't help my hair being tow-coloured," said Sylvia apologetically. "Emmy's is lovely. I wish I'd been a Land Girl. They do really useful work and get a heavenly bleach on their hair and such lovely complexions. Except the spotty ones, but they'd be spotty anywhere."

Emmy, hearing her own name, as one nearly always does, turned from Martin to the girls.

"Don't be a Land Girl," she said earnestly to Anne. "I wish I had dark hair like yours. Mine goes all fair in streaks. And look at my hands."

She spread on her knees a pair of well-shaped hands, roughened and seamed with dirt.

"That's the result of having a good hard wash before you come," she said ruefully. "I don't really mind, but sometimes I *would* like to have clean hands, especially when I see mother's."

"Who *is* happy then?" asked Anne, which made her companions, unused to such philosophical questionings, feel slightly embarrassed.

"Well, I am really," said Emmy stoutly, "because I love bulls and I can live with Martin and help to run the herd even if peace does come. And if he gets married he is going to give me Macpherson's house when he retires. He's our agent and simply won't retire till the war is over, so I hope it will go on for a bit. He'd be miserable if he weren't running Rushwater. Oh, well done!"

Robin, standing up to the net, had just put a ball over neatly where neither George nor Leslie major could reach it and so won the set.

"He doesn't get about very quickly, but he does place the balls," said Emmy.

"Robin only has one foot," said Anne. "The other's artificial."

Emmy said she was most awfully sorry. Then there was a fresh change of players, Robin, the Leslie boys, and their cousin Emmy, and Agnes suggested that the others should come up to the Temple and see the view. Accordingly they went slowly up the hill behind the house by a path winding among beech trees, between lakes of blue-bells, till they emerged into a clearing where stood a high pyramidal monument erected by Martin's great-grandfather. To the north of it the beechwoods and downs sloped up and away for ever. To the south the ground fell away in grass terraces to where Rushwater House lay basking in the spring sun, and beyond it was a vast panorama of gentle English countryside bounded by distant hills.

"It all makes one feel a bit old," said Martin suddenly, a remark which struck everyone dumb, because it seemed so dreadfully true and yet unreasonable.

"Why?" said his aunt Agnes, very kindly, but somehow conveying an atmosphere of wanting to take his temperature.

"Poets and people," said George Halliday quite unexpectedly, "say autumn is sad, but I must say I think spring often gets one down like anything. Something in the air, I suppose."

He stopped suddenly, startled by his own voice and wondering if Lady Graham would despise him for ever.

"I think that is so *true*," said Agnes. "It is just what I meant," at which George fell into a mental swoon owing to the piercing sweetness of her character.

"What you mean, my love," said David, "is that you don't think at all, but wish to be agreeable. Spring can be damnable. But I don't think any of the poets have really got on to it."

"One couldn't say 'In looking on the happy spring fields,'" said Martin thoughtfully. "At least one could, but it wouldn't scan."

"O grief for the promise of May," said Anne, in rather a soft voice as she did not wish to make herself conspicuous.

"By Jove, yes," said David admiringly.

Agnes asked what the promise was.

"It's a bit out of a kind of poem by Tennyson," said Anne colouring as she spoke. "I don't think it's a very good one," she added deprecatingly.

"It's a rotten one," said David, "but I can't think of anyone else who would have had the wits to quote it."

George Halliday gave it as his opinion that Anne would be wizard at crosswords, while his sister Sylvia remarked that she supposed that spring was like puppies and kittens and chickens and would be all right if it didn't grow up.

"What made me feel old," said Martin, "was the Temple. Do you remember the summer those French people were at the vicarage, David, and we were Royalist conspirators against the French Republic? I wonder what happened to them all."

"Collaborating, I expect," said David carelessly. "At least the girl is. What was the name? Ursule, that's it. She would have collaborated like anything with anybody to get sweets or anything nice to eat. I've never met such a whole-hearted eater in my life."

"Mary was a conspirator too," said Martin. "Before she married John."

"So she was," said David. "And the result is those two boys playing tennis. Well, well."

"You were very naughty and unkind to her, David," said his sister Agnes, coming out of a dream of the hot summer when John Leslie had fallen in love with Mary Preston. "You made Mary think she was engaged to you, and she was dreadfully unhappy."

On hearing this interesting echo from past times Martin and Emmy fell upon Lady Graham with a request to have the whole story, but Lady Graham said they must go back as mamma would be getting up.

"And probably painting the front door blue with golden birds on it," said David. "How right you are Agnes."

So the party retraced their steps to the house, where they found Lady Emily sitting on a bench outside the drawing-room talking to her elderly housekeeper, Siddon, who had stayed on all through the war and was now looking after Martin.

"Good-afternoon, my lady," said Siddon severely to Lady Graham. "Her ladyship got up about ten minutes ago and wishes to move the portrait of Mr. Leslie in the hall and put it in the morning-room, so I thought it best to persuade her ladyship to come outside. Tea is ready, my lady."

Lady Graham praised Siddon's action and drew her mother into the house. The others followed and were shortly joined by the tennis players. All the young people made hearty teas and there was a good deal of general talk and laughter.

"Now," said Lady Emily to anyone who happened to be listening, "we must go and see the church before we go home. Mr. Dale, you must come with me and we will have a long talk about John's boys. They tell me you are quite marvellous and do everything with one foot."

Robin expressed his willingness to accompany her ladyship, reserving the question of discussing his pupils.

"And what are you all laughing about?" said Lady Emily, with one of her rapid snipe-fights, addressing the other end of the table where a good deal of suppressed giggling was going on.

"Oh nothing, Gran," said Leslie minor. "I only said Mr. Dale didn't clean his teeth with one foot, and that idiot brother of mine laughed into his tea. So we were all laughing," he finished lamely.

Leslie major said under his breath that he would put his brother's head under the stable-yard pump after tea, a good deal of kicking under the table took place and Martin, watchful always of his guests, got up.

"Then that is settled," said Lady Emily. "Mr. Dale will take me to the church and David and Martin will come too, and Agnes."

"No, mamma darling," said Agnes, with surprising firmness. "I must have a talk with Emmy and visit Macpherson because he has his sciatica rather badly. We ought to start about half past five."

"Oh, poor Macpherson," said Lady Emily. "Agnes, we will start at five-fifteen and stop at Macpherson's house and you and I will have a delightful talk with him."

"No, mamma," said Lady Graham. "I will go to Macpherson, because if you go you won't have time to see if the sweetbriar hedge round father's grave is coming on properly. And don't let mamma tire you, Mr. Dale, because I know how tiring it must be to walk about on one foot."

Lady Emily appearing to be convinced by this very specious reasoning, the company left the tea-room. The Leslie boys invited George and Sylvia to be driven backwards round the park, an invitation which was enthusiastically accepted; Agnes went away with Emmy, and Lady Emily moved with her train towards the front door. Robin, always feeling a little responsible for Anne, paused to see where she was. Overlooked by everyone, even by Martin the good host, she was standing apart, looking a little frightened.

"Coming?" said Robin.

"I didn't know where I was meant to go," said Anne. "I thought perhaps Lady Emily going to the church was rather private."

"I haven't the honour of knowing Lady Emily well," said Robin, "but from what I have heard and seen of her, I think she loves to share everything with friends."

"Would I count as a friend?" said Anne.

Robin said of course she would as she had come with Lady Graham; and as a kind of scullery maid was straining at the leash to clear away the tea things he hurried Anne down the passage and out of the house.

St. Mary's Church stood in a pleasant way within the grounds
of Rushwater House. It had no particular merit. being mid-
Victorian Italian-Gothic with Saxon dog-tooth mouldings in
grey brick over the west door and a kind of campanile at one
side, but it had been built by Mr. Leslie's grandfather at the same
time as the house, and five generations of Leslies had wor-
shipped there. Some rather depressing ecclesiatical evergreens
grew dankly on the north side, making a dismal grove where
small Leslies of each epoch had enjoyed frightening themselves
and their younger brothers and sisters. On the south side the
churchyard was embanked above the Rushmere Brook, and
the sun was gently warming the gravestones. Here Robin and
Anne found Lady Emily leaning on her stick, looking with
affectionate interest at her husband's grave. This monument was
of no interest at all, being the ancestral mid-Victorian burying
plot surrounded by a rather jail-like spiky railing, but since her
husband's death early in the war Lady Emily had with infinite
correspondence, telephoning and summoning the hard-worked
agent Mr. Macpherson to private conferences at times highly
inconvenient to him, so that he had to make on the meagre
petrol ration journeys which were certainly quite unnecessary,
arranged for a sweetbriar hedge to be planted outside the rusty
railings, a hedge which, so old Tacker, the sexton, averred, gave
him more trouble than the whole of the churchyard put together
with her ladyship worriting him in season and out of season. To
whom Mrs. Tacker, who had been a housemaid at Rushwater
House in her youth, said she s'posed he was old Uncle Joe
Staylin and she'd thank him to get her some greens or she'd
never get them washed and on in time for his dinner.

The hedge was by now doing very nicely and it was one of
Lady Emily's pleasures to come over to her old house with her
younger grandchildren and make them pinch a leaf between
their forefinger and thumb and smell the fragrance that remained. As she stood leaning upon her black stick, herself
rubbing a leaf and smelling its fragrance, her keen hawk eyes a

little dimmed, the beautiful thin curved lips in her old lovely face bent in a remembering smile, David thought he had never seen an old age so handsome, so distinguished as his mother's. Looking for someone to appreciate his feelings, he saw the Fielding girl standing a little apart and took a step or two in her direction.

"Just look at my mamma," he said.

Anne looked at Lady Emily and then looked questioningly at David.

"How does she strike you?" said David. "To give you a lead I will tell you at once that I think she's the most beautiful work of art one could see. Like an exquisite piece of alabaster."

"And rather mother-of-pearl," said Anne after a moment's reflection, looking up at David.

"I didn't know," said David, looking down at her with interest, "that anyone could look at one under their long lashes nowadays. And how right you are about mother-of-pearl."

"I think," said Anne, rather alarmed by the allusion to her eyelashes, but pleased by his approval of her words, "that nacrée would be even better for Lady Emily—if it doesn't sound affected," she added.

The Fielding girl was indeed coming out with a vengeance, thought David. It might really be worth cultivating her. He had an impression that she had lived beside the springs of Dove and could do with a little appreciation.

"My mamma," he continued, "has a delightful look of a very maternal falcon. And she can pounce like one."

"I think," said Anne, emboldened by this confidence, "that she reminds one of old happy far-off things."

"Good," said David. "Very good. Are you a Wordsworthian in addition to your other attractions?"

"Only the bits everyone knows," said Anne. "Otherwise I honestly think he is *dreadfully* dull."

"So do I," said David. "At least that's a lie, because I never even tried to read *The Excursion*. Nor do I intend to. Would you like to see the inside of the church? Not that there is anything to see."

To tell the truth, Anne was not quite sure if she wanted to or not. She liked David Leslie. Her old-governess, Miss Bunting, had always spoken of him as her favourite pupil and his name to Anne had a quality of romance. But there was something in his pleasant airy way of treating her—too pleasant, too airy, almost condescending, she secretly thought—that made her draw back. She rather wished Robin would come and rescue her, but Robin and Martin were sitting on the low wall of the churchyard reminding each other of what the lance-corporal had said to the Brigadier on the Anzio beach-head.

"Hi! Martin," David called. "Come and look after mamma. We are going to see the church."

Martin waved a hand amicably at his uncle. David and Anne walked towards the church. Or to be quite truthful, David strolled towards the church with Anne half a pace in the rear, for she felt extremely shy of him and did not wish to presume.

"Porch," said David, pausing at the entrance and rattling at the heavy handle of the church door. "It seems to be locked. I'll have to go round to Tacker's cottage and get the key."

"Oh, please don't," said Anne.

"Would you rather not go inside?" said David. "I admit it's pretty mouldy."

"Oh no, I didn't mean that," said Anne. "Please. I only thought it might be a trouble. I'd really love to see inside. I mean if it's a bother, I don't mind a bit."

Taking no notice of these contradictory flutterings, David gave the iron handle a last rattle. The door opened suddenly and he almost fell into the church down the low step. Anne followed him and looked round. The interior of the church was cream-washed and sufficiently lighted by some rather revolting glass of the Munich school and some greenish leaded windows which gave an aquarium-like atmosphere.

Anne looked at it and didn't know what to say. Mr. Leslie

seemed so clever and so man-of-the-world that she felt whatever she said might be wrong. And then she thought that to say nothing seemed rude, but cudgel her brains as she might, she could think of nothing at all. So she walked into the chancel and began to read the inscriptions on the monuments of departed Leslies. Suddenly she uttered an exclamation which can only be described as a squeak.

"Anything wrong?" said David sympathetically.

Anne could only say, "OH."

"You make me think of Man Friday," said David. "Might one enquire what you are oh-ing about?"

Anne pointed, speechless, to a slab on the north wall of the church on which were the words

TO THE MEMORY OF

MAUD BUNTING

FOR MANY YEARS A FAITHFUL FRIEND AND GUIDE

THIS STONE WAS PLACED BY SOME OF HER

AFFECTIONATE PUPILS.

"Are you looking at Miss Bunting's memorial?" said David. "She used to be our governess. She died a couple of years ago and Gran wanted her buried here, so John and Agnes and I put up the stone. She was a remarkable woman and had no illusions about me at all. It was rather sad that she died among strangers, but it can't be helped. Good old Bunny."

"But she didn't die among strangers," said Anne indignantly.

David looked at her.

"She died with us," said Anne stoutly. "At least she died in the Cottage Hospital, but she was my governess all that year and Mummy would have had her buried at Hallbury, but Lady Graham and Lady Emily wanted it to be at Rushwater."

"I *am* so sorry," said David. "I ought to have known. No, that's not true, because I don't see why I should have known. But I am sure Lady Fielding would have done everything perfectly if

mamma hadn't barged in as she so often does, bless her heart. I
do hope your mother didn't mind."

"Of course not," said Anne. "But *please* don't say strangers,
because we were very fond of Miss Bunting—we truly were.
And she gave me a copy of Keats on my birthday that old Lady
Pomfret had given her," she finished, suddenly finding herself
much nearer tears than she liked.

"I am," said David," a complete and despicable fool. I ought to
have realized about Bunny being with you. I really knew under-
neath, but it all got overlaid somehow. Please don't mind so
much. We will go out into the sun again and see what mischief
mamma is up to. She is probably planting mustard and cress on
Papa's grave because it comes up quickly."

As David was wrestling again with the heavy iron handle to
shut the door Anne said, "Oh Mr. Leslie, please don't tell
anyone."

"No pupil of Bunny's is allowed to call me Mr. Leslie," said
David. "And if I knew what I wasn't to tell anyone, I certainly
wouldn't tell them."

"I mean," said Anne, searching painfully for the right words,
"about my nearly crying about Miss Bunting. I didn't mean to,
only I couldn't bear you to think that she died among strangers,
because we did like her very very much. And she told me you
were her favourite pupil," she added inconsequently.

"Look here, Anne, if you tell me things like that I shall cry
too," said David. "And a strong man in tears is a terrible sight."

"I know," said Anne, sympathetically. "His very being is
racked and beads of perspiration stand out upon his forehead
and his nails are driven deeply into the flesh of his clenched
hands."

"Good God, my girl," said David, suddenly realising that the
Fielding girl was no fool, "you and I are the most perfect
products of dear old Bunny. But if I were really a strong silent
man I would also groan aloud."

And at this they both began to laugh and Anne knew that she

was now grown-up, which fact emboldened her to tell Lady Emily how much she liked the scent of sweetbriar. This led to a conversation on gardening and Lady Emily said Anne must come to Holdings for a weekend and have a really long talk, and Anne, such is the effect of being grown-up, said she would love to come, which was perhaps one of the most dashing things she had yet said, and gave Robin, who overheard her, great pleasure.

Martin, watchful of his visitors' comfort, now began to urge his grandmother towards the house, for Agnes and the car would be waiting, but Lady Emily, more tired than her spirit would admit, leaned heavily on her stick and walked very slowly.

"You take Gran to the seat," said Martin to his uncle David, "and I'll go back to the house and bring the car," for there was a little private driving road to the church, although it was seldom used now except by pedestrians. And he ran, always with his slight limp, in the direction of the house.

Outside the churchyard, against the low wall, there was a wooden seat, put there by Lady Emily's husband for the use of his tenants, and towards this David steered his grandmother. One end of it was already occupied by a deliberately picturesque though rather démodé figure in whom Anne at once recognised Mr. Scatcherd.

"Who is that scarecrow?" said Robin.

"He isn't really a scarecrow," said Anne. "He is an artist who lives in Hatch End. I saw him this morning after church drawing the Mellings Arms, but I don't think he draws very well."

"Let's look," said Robin.

He and Anne went back into the churchyard and leaning on the low wall were able to study from behind the artist at work. Mr. Scatcherd, stimulated by the sight of Lady Emily, whose appearance was of course very familiar to him at Hatch End though he had never been privileged to meet her, at once became so violently an artist that no one could have failed to recognise him. He cocked his head first to one side then the other, screwed up his eyes for a distant view, unscrewed them for the middle distance, put on a pair of spectacles to examine his work, pushed them upon to his forehead and held his drawing block at arm's length the better to judge it, took measurements of the view with a pencil held now vertically, now horizontally, and altogether felt he was making a good effect. His only regret was that he had not brought the battered straw hat and the painter's blouse in which (so he felt) he was Barbizon incarnate; but Hettie had burnt the hat, calling it a nasty mucky old thing only fit for the gypsies, and laid violent hands upon the blouse to make herself a couple of aprons, saying she couldn't be expected to keep herself nice if she didn't and where did uncle think she was going to get the kewpons from for aprons she'd like to know."

"David," said Lady Emily, after seating herself with a vast arranging of scarves and the total though temporary disappearance of her stick among the folds of her cloak, "what is he doing? Is he the district surveyor?"

"Lord no, mamma," said David, lowering his voice in the vain hope that his beloved mother would follow suit. "He's that artist at Hatch End that Agnes gets things from sometimes."

"An artist," said Lady Emily, much interested. "But he doesn't look like one."

"I should say he looked far too like one," said David. "What ought he to look like, mamma?"

"I don't know," said Lady Emily with an air of great candour. "But all the artists I knew were very nice and came to dinner. Papa used to have people like Lord Leighton and Sir John Millais to the Towers when I was a girl and Mr. Sargent dined with your father and me several times when we had the Rutland Gate house. I wonder if he dines out. I will ask Agnes to invite him."

"No, mamma darling," said David. "Merry wouldn't like it."

"Well, I shall go and see," said Lady Emily, hitching herself majestically along the seat.

At the same moment Martin returned with the car.

"Come along, mamma," said David.

"I have only just discovered," said Lady Emily, who had by now sat herself along to Mr. Scatcherd's end of the bench, "that you are an artist. My mother painted quite delightfully in water-colours and did some charming pictures of the Alhambra. You must have seen them at the Towers when you were calling."

David, who realised that his highly maddening mother was under the impression that Mr. Scatcherd frequented the houses of the aristocracy and landed gentry rather as Sir Peter Paul Rubens might have done, looked up at Robin and Anne with an expression of such resigned despair as made them both laugh, though in a very sympathetic way.

"It is very good of your ladyship to say so," said Mr. Scatcherd, much gratified by this speech, "and I called pretty often on my brother's account when his late lordship was alive, but I didn't see the masterpieces to which you refer."

"They were in the yellow morning-room, in gilded frames with buff mounts," said Lady Emily.

"And very nice, your ladyship, for water-colours," said Mr. Scatcherd, "but for black and white, which is my medium, take it from me, you can't beat a big white mount with the drawing rather higher than lower if you take my meaning and a nice plain black binding. You can sell them three times as well if you have an artistic frame. Now take for example this little sketch, only an idea, your ladyship, but what is Art if you don't have ideas: you've no idea the way a nice mount and a black border will improve it. The mounts of course are the difficulty now, but my brother keeps all the best cardboard boxes for me."

"Now cardboard boxes are *exactly* what I need," said Lady Emily. "You must come to lunch and bring me some."

"I don't think my niece Hettie would like me to, your ladyship," said Mr. Scatcherd, "but my brother does send to Holdings on Tuesdays and I'm sure will be only too willing to oblige, especially such an old customer as Lady Graham, though when I say old no offence is meant being only a trade term as you might say."

At this point David hustled his mother into the car as dutifully as possible and collected Robin and Anne, by now in a fine fit of giggles, and Martin drove them back to Rushwater, where the rest of the party were waiting. Robin collected Leslie major and minor and said good-bye to Martin, who asked him to come again. He then said good-bye to Anne and asked if she had had a happy day.

"Yes, thank you," said Anne. "I loved it. Oh, and Robin, Miss Bunting was David's governess. I think he's *very* nice, don't you?"

Robin said he did, gave Anne a fatherly pat on the shoulder and went off to the station with his charges.

By degrees the car was re-packed. Emmy, who had taken a violent fancy to Sylvia because she had shown such sympathy about Rushwater Romany's leg, begged her to come again as soon as she could. Martin asked everyone to come again. David waved his hand and started the car.

"Oh David, stop," said his mother. "I mean really stop not standing still with the engine running, because I want you to hear what I say. What about Mr. Scatcherd?"

David, who was rarely impatient with his mother, much as she deserved it, stopped the car and asked what about him.

"How is he to get back?" asked Lady Emily.

Agnes placidly asked who her mother meant.

"He was making a drawing outside the church," said Lady Emily, "and I told him about mamma's water-colours at the Towers and he said his brother would bring me some of that nice stiff cardboard I always want, and I suddenly wondered if we could take him back and then you could arrange a day for him to come to lunch, Agnes."

"Listen, mamma," said David, almost irritated. "We are already loaded above the Plimsoll line and Mr. Scatcherd's brother is Scatcherd the grocer at Northbridge."

Lady Emily said grocers could be very nice people and one could always manage an extra at lunch.

"I will speak to Robert about it, mamma," said Agnes, "but I don't think he would like Mr. Scatcherd."

"Heaven bless you—and Robert too—for those words, my love," said David, and drove off. As they passed the little turning that led to the church, Mr. Scatcherd emerged from it on his bicycle, his sketching materials strapped on the carrier, his thin stockinged legs working up and down while his cape billowed about him.

"There, mamma, you see heaven helps those who help themselves," said David piously over his shoulder.

The journey back to Holdings did not take long, and Lady Emily, more tired than she cared to admit, did not raise the question of calling at Pomfret Towers, or going to inspect the servants' bedrooms at Lady Fielding's house. David offered to drive the Hallidays and Anne back to Hatch House, but they preferred to walk.

"I shall be here off and on quite a lot," said David to Sylvia. "We must get some more tennis."

"And go for some good long walks," said Sylvia. "If peace did break out I think I'll get released pretty soon and anyway I'll be home for quite a lot of week-ends. Have you ever been right along Gundric's Fossway as far as Low Afton? It's a ripping walk, and we could come back by the Great Hump: there's a place where one crosses the Rising on stepping stones and if the waters are out it's simply splendid. George and I both fell in last time we went there."

David smiled at her with an inward determination not to go for any walk that involved falling into a river at least six miles from home, and turned to Anne.

"Do you think," he said, "that your mamma would take it

kindly if my mamma came and paid a call on her? My mamma will neither slumber nor sleep till she has seen the servants' bedrooms at Number Seventeen. A peculiar passion, but she is like that."

Anne said she thought her mother would like it very much, looked up with a mixture of shyness and confidence at David and said good-bye. She and the Hallidays then said good-bye to Lady Graham and Lady Emily, thanked him for a very happy afternoon and walked away down the village street. Here all was quiet, as most of the cottagers had had a bit of a clean-up and were sitting down to their tea. Outside the Mellings Arms a few hopeful elders were sitting on the bench waiting for the tap to open, in the very unsure and uncertain hope of there being some beer. In the door of The Shop, which was on the sunny side of the street, Mrs. Hubback was sitting in a wicker chair with a white apron on. The young people wished her good-evening as they passed.

"I've got something to say to you, Mr. George," said Mrs. Hubback, managing to give an impression of curtseying while remaining stout and immobile in her chair.

The three young people came over and grouped themselves respectfully in front of her.

"You tell your mother, Mr. George," said Mrs. Hubback, "to get all the bread she wants tomorrow."

"Oh, it's like that, is it?" said George. "Blast. Just as I thought of going up to town on Tuesday. Oh, well. Thank you, Mrs. Hubback."

Mrs. Hubback by remaining stout and immobile in her chair again conveyed the impression that she had bobbed a curtsey, and the three young people passed on.

Anne, less versed in the world than her friends, thought it kind of Mrs. Hubback to remind Mrs. Halliday to get some bread, but did not realise the dire implication behind those simple words, so she wondered why George and Sylvia had suddenly become so depressed, and fell silent in sympathy.

"Well, that's torn it," said Sylvia at last. "A few weeks more and I'd have got promotion and then I could have told that odious Philpott woman all I've wanted to tell her for the last two years. Oh, well."

They continued to walk in gloomy silence, Anne feeling rather small and ignorant beside them. By the time they had crossed the river and were almost at the end of the long bridge over the water-meadows, she could not bear her ignorance any longer.

"Why did that nice woman in the white apron tell you about the bread?" she asked timidly.

George and Sylvia looked at her with interest, as at a small wild animal which had somehow got into the house, and said with one voice, "Peace"; George adding bitterly in what he considered to be an American accent, "And how."

"Do you mean PEACE?" said Anne.

"It was bound to break out some time," said George gloomily, "and it's high time we had some, but of course they had to choose just the most inconvenient moment. Still, I daresay it would be just as bad as any other time. Well, that means good-bye to my majority, I suppose."

Anne was so staggered by this conversation that she did not like to ask any more questions and finished the walk in a state of considerable depression, which was not lessened by a sudden and, as she knew, totally unreasonable apprehension that if peace really happened she would not be able to get back to Barchester. This feeling she knew was extremely silly, but at the moment she would have given anything to be safely in the drawing-room at Number Seventeen with her father and mother. The thought of David Leslie was vaguely comforting, only just across the river at Holdings, but she was sensitive enough to realise that if anything very dreadful happened, his first duty would be to his own relations. What the dreadful happening might be she did not know, nor could she invent any specific catastrophe likely to occur, but a horrid sense of doom hung over her, not even dispelled by the sight of a large cold boiled fowl for supper.

"I suppose you know about the bread, mother," said George when they were seated at the supper table. "Mrs. Hubback told us just now."

His mother said she didn't know, but was not surprised, for the station-master, who had been up with a brown paper package that showed symptoms of going bad if it spent the whole weekend in the parcels office, had said he knew nothing nor did no one else, but if he was going anywhere on Tuesday he wouldn't, a statement which in spite of, or perhaps because of its obscurity, had chilled her to the bone.

Mr. Halliday, by way of cheering everyone, said he had been talking to Roddy Wicklow, Lord Pomfret's agent, on the telephone and Roddy had said he supposed we were for it now.

"Well, peace or no peace," said George, "it's given me the worst guilt complex I've had since I got some ink on the headmaster's Bible by mistake at my prep. school."

At any other time his family would have demanded an instant explanation of this peculiar mistake, but each appeared to be reflecting on his or her blackest sin.

"I suppose peace *had* to come," said Mrs. Halliday, putting the case as she felt very fairly. "But one never thought it would."

Mr. Halliday said people seemed to get on all right if war went on for a long time. There was the Seven Years' War, he said; also the Thirty Years' War.

George said, Come to that there was the Hundred Years' War.

Sylvia said one couldn't compare; George said Why not.

"Well, they were *proper* wars," said Slyvia. "I mean there was a close season and people went into winter quarters."

"Still," said Anne, trying to find what excuses she could for the peace, "it will be nice for people not to have things dropped on their heads."

"And people won't be being killed," said Mrs. Halliday, thinking of George.

George, who was very sensitive to what his mother was thinking, was partly touched, partly annoyed; the annoyance being partly with himself for feeling touched, though this is almost too fine a shade for our pen to express. So to show that he was neither touched nor annoyed he remarked that lots of fellows would be being killed by those foul Japs.

"Quite true," said Mrs. Halliday, cheering up. "We can't really call it a peace till the Japs are done with."

"Then it isn't really peace at all," said Sylvia, also brightening visibly.

Anne said she supposed it would be just as bad as if it were and did Mrs. Halliday think the trains would be running to-morrow, because her mother would worry dreadfully if she didn't come home. Mrs. Halliday was most sympathetic and promised Anne that if there was any difficulty with trains she would drive her back to Barchester herself in the pony cart, after which Anne was able to eat quite a hearty meal of cold chicken, baked potatoes, cold (bottled) gooseberry pie and cream and did not stay awake all night worrying as she had meant to do.

The hideous suspicion of peace bursting upon a war-racked world had already arrived at Holdings via the cowman, who had told the cook with gloomy pleasure that if what they were saying at the Mellings Arms was true, there wouldn't be no trains on Tuesday and he'd think himself lucky if Jimmy, the under cowman, didn't go mafficking off to Barchester on his bike and leave him to do all the milking himself, but if Jimmy did, he'd give him such a larruping that he wouldn't be able to sit on a milking stool for a week. To which the cook replied that there was no need to be coarse and if anyone thought she was going to put herself out about peace she wasn't, not with her two nephews and her cousin's son-in-law out in Burma. After which she had spread the news through the servants' hall at tea-time with embellishments of her own.

"They do say," said cook, with no authority at all for this statement, "that they're going to burn old Hitler like a Guy Fawkes in the Close."

"I should peek my needle in his eye," said Conque, Lady Emily's French maid, whom a six years' totalitarian war had driven to tea with the lower orders, "and speet him to his face."

"Well, Miss Conk," said cook, "it's not English to do that. Poor old Hitler. I dessay he wishes he were somewhere else now. They say he's a secret drinker."

The servants' hall then discussed the private life of the German Chancellor on very insufficient evidence till cook said sitting there talking wouldn't get her supper ready and drove them all away.

Supper at Holdings was also cold chicken and baked potatoes, but the cold pie was bottled plums.

"What a good thing it is that you went to Rushwater to-day, mamma," said Agnes to Lady Emily. "Robert rang me up before supper from London and says he is coming down here to-morrow for a couple of nights. He didn't say why, but I know he couldn't get away unless he could, so I daresay it is peace breaking out. One will really feel quite strange without a war."

The news caused little interest. The Graham children had lived too long in a war to think of any other atmosphere. Not that it had meant much to them, for no bombs had fallen on Barsetshire, beyond one or two strays in open country, and food with a garden and cows had not been too difficult. Uncle David had been flying, it is true, and Martin had been in Italy and come back limping, but one's uncles and cousins might do anything, and in fact, James, now at Eton, had been in as much danger as his uncle or cousin, while Robert and Henry and Edith had forgotten a time when there was not a blackout, and even Clarissa, the half grown-up, did not have any very distinct feelings about peace.

Only two members of the party were a little silent. Lady Emily was thinking of another war, a mere skirmish compared with this war, in which her eldest son, Martin's father, had been killed at Arras. Miss Merriman was thinking of her former employers, the old Earl and Countess of Pomfret, whose only son and only child, Lord Mellings, had been killed on the Northwest Frontier, so long ago, leaving his parents proudly desolate.

"One doesn't know what to think about war," said Miss Merriman, who but rarely enunciated a general opinion, confining herself to being a pleasant, helpful and attentive friend and secretary to Lady Emily.

"There is only one thing to think about them, Merry," said David. "They will always happen. And each war will be worse than the last and each peace more horrible than the one before. Can I have the merrythought if no one wants it, and I'll pull it with Clarissa to see which of us will be married first."

At Rushwater the advance tidings of peace percolated by way of Mr. Macpherson, the agent, who always had Sunday supper with Martin and Emmy. It had come to him through the Secretary of the Barsetshire Stock Breeders' Society, who had heard through the railway that trains might be late during the week and that if any cows wished to travel by rail on that day it must be at their own risk.

"It would happen," said Mr. Macpherson, "just as the Barsetshire W.A.E.C. had got well into its stride. Now we'll have to switch the cows back to peace and they won't like it after five years of war. I'm too old for this sort of thing."

"And what's more," said Emmy, "I'll bet you anything that they'll cut out Double Summer Time and Ordinary Summer Time too, and what'll happen to the milk I don't know."

This horrible thought produced complete silence.

"One thing at a time," said Martin after a pause. "How is Rushwater Romany's leg?"

Emmy reported that it was going to heal nicely and asked Martin if she could have Sylvia Halliday to stay some time because she was keen on bulls. Martin said he would like it very much.

"I like Anne too," said Emmy, her mouth rather full of cold boiled fowl and baked potatoes, "but she wouldn't be much use with cattle; she's too booky."

Martin agreed. He had liked the little Fielding girl, with her large soft eyes and her good manners, but the golden Sylvia had roused a stronger feeling in him. He was too generous to envy his uncle David, but he knew from old experience that if David wished to please Sylvia there would be no chance for anyone else. Still it would be nice to have her at Rushwater and if she got long leave or was demobilised, there might be some sense in peace.

At Southbridge School Mr. Birkett the Headmaster had heard rumours from one or two very highly-placed parents and was wondering what fresh burdens a world at so-called peace would bring, delivering himself to this effect to Everard Carter and Robin Dale, who were supping with him.

"I suppose you'll be sacking some of your temporaries when you get your permanents back, sir," said Robin.

"The permanents have a first claim, of course," said Mr. Birkett, "but you needn't worry. Philip Winter won't come back. He is going to start a prep. school with his wife at Beliers, so you had better stick to your classics here. They are doing quite nicely."

After which they joined Mrs. Birkett and Mrs. Carter, who were discussing the possibility of a peace bonfire with such bits of blackout as were too worn to be used for anything else and the advisability of putting yet more ground under vegetables and fowls in view of the probable horrors of peace. Then the Carters and Robin went back to Mr. Carter's house and Robin went up to his room to work. Thoughts of Anne passed through his mind; pleasant thoughts. She had looked very happy at Rushmore and all the Leslies obviously liked her. Even his two dull pupils had said she was nice. The word nice seemed to ring a bell far away in his mind. Yes. Anne had visited the church with David and had said he was very nice. Well, so he was, and why shouldn't Anne think so? But suddenly he felt that for the fist time since miss Bunting's death there was a gap between Anne and himself, a gap into which Miss Bunting's favourite pupil might step. Not that he was in love with Anne; oh no, not at all. She was too young. But he had become used to being her first friend. Mr. Carton's edition of Fluvius Minucius, which he was studying with much interest, no longer held him.

"BLAST the peace!" said Robin, most unjustly, and applied himself to Mr. Carton's book. But he could not concentrate, gave it up and went to bed, where he lay awake far longer than he liked.

# CHAPTER 5

On the following Tuesday a day of national rejoicing burst by very slow degrees and barely recognised as such upon an exhausted, cross and uninterested world. Not much notice was taken in the country as everyone was busy, few young people were about and there was the usual dearth of beer. In Barchester some of the shops shut early and a number of people, actuated by the peculiar passion nourished by the war for being squashed with numbers of one's fellow-citizens into small spaces, went up to London by the early afternoon train taking a great deal of food and what they called the kiddies. They then took an hour and a half to go by Tube to Piccadilly, eating with some difficulty owing to the crowd as they went, fought their way to Buckingham Palace, where they ate a little more under even more severe difficulties, fought their way back to Piccadilly, sat eating in the Tube for two hours, and having missed the late train to Barchester sat on the platform and finished the food, which the kiddies worn out by national rejoicings were too tired and sick to touch, and finally got the slow 12.35, arriving at Barchester about 7 a.m., having had a lovely time.

But at Hatch End, where most of the cottages had an Alf or a Sid in the Far East, life went on much as usual. Sir Robert Graham came down for two nights, stamped firmly on his mother-in-law's wish to have Mr. Scatcherd to lunch, was pleased to see his wife and family, did some estate business and went back to London. Lady Graham, considering the disturbed state of the world, decided to postpone her Bring and Buy Sale till later, thus leaving the field free for the Sale of Work at the Palace.

The annual Sale of Work (in aid of what no one ever exactly knew) was considered by the anti-Palace faction to be the Bishop's wife's masterpiece. Years ago one of her predecessors, the wife of Bishop Proudie, had after some consideration chosen a conversazione as the cheapest and most showy way of entertaining Barchester Society. The wife of the present Bishop, considering the question of a yearly entertainment, had hit upon the excellent scheme of having a Sale of Work and charging a shilling for admission which included tea. The hope which springs eternal in the human breast of getting more than its money's worth attracted numbers of people who came chiefly to eat, and then finding they could have got more to eat at home without waiting so long for it, worked off their feelings by buying doyleys, raffia goods, crocheted napkin rings and other valuable products of civilization. The Palace in a cathedral town where there is a Bishop is always the Palace, and the aristocracy of Barsetshire made a point of attending the Sale of Work as a civility to the office of Bishop, not to the man and certainly not to his wife, and so it came about that Lady Fielding, who was on no more than bowing terms with the Bishop's wife, was a regular attendant at the Sale of Work and of late years had taken her daughter Anne.

Anne, who had in spite of her fears got back to her parents' house with no difficulty at all, looked all the better for the change, or so her parents thought, and gave them very amusing descriptions of Lady Emily and Mr. Scatcherd, also lively accounts of the church and Miss Bunting's monument adding, with a hardly perceptible hesitation, how nice David Leslie was. Whether either of her parents noticed her hesitation, we cannot say. We rather think not.

Lady Fielding felt very grateful to Mrs. Halliday for having given Anne such a pleasant weekend and was wondering how she could best show her gratitude, for to ask people who lived some miles out of Barchester to dinner was under the present circumstances only a mockery, when Anne asked her mother if she might invite Sylvia Halliday to stay with them for the Palace Sale of Work. The plan seemed excellent to Lady Fielding. Anne wrote to Sylvia. Sylvia by great good luck was having a couple of days off, and all arrangements were made for her to come to Barchester on Tuesday week and stay till the following Thursday. Flown with excitement over her first social outburst, Anne then surprised herself and her parents by asking if they could have a little dinner party on the Wednesday.

Sir Robert, whom his wife always consulted as a matter of form though without the faintest intention of changing her own plans, said Wednesday wasn't a very good day for him as there was a meeting of the Conservative Club at 6 o'clock and he knew the Archdeacon from Plumstead would waste at least half an hour by dragging in Church politics.

"Oh, but daddy," said Anne, "if we have a party on Wednesday, everyone can talk about the Sale of Work and say how ghastly it was."

This point of view had not struck Sir Robert. Gratified at finding in his only child so healthy an attitude towards the Palace and all its works, he admitted that her plea was reasonable.

"And you know, Robert," said his wife, pressing home her advantage, "that you like malicious gossip about the Palace better than anything except gardening."

Sir Robert admitted the impeachment and went away to his office, leaving Lady Fielding and Anne to have a delightful and very grown-up conversation about the party and what guests to invite.

"The first thing," said Lady Fielding, "is to get the men equal to the women. With you and Sylvia we must start with a man for each of you. We might have Robin. And what about George Halliday?"

"Wouldn't it be rather dull for him, mummy?" said Anne. "I mean Sylvia being his sister."

Lady Fielding said he didn't see much of his sister as they were both in the service."

"Besides, he mightn't be able to get leave," said Anne. "He has only just had some."

"Of course we do owe Bishop Joram a meal," said Lady Fielding, thinking of the good-natured Colonial ex-Bishop who now held a canonry in Barchester.

"Isn't he rather old?" said Anne.

"About my age, I should think," said Lady Fielding good-naturedly. "Your turn now, Anne."

Anne, twisting her fingers in a way her old governess would have highly disapproved, began to speak, became very hoarse, choked, and finally said in a voice she did not recognise as her own, a voice which she hoped sounded grown-up and uninterested, "What about David Leslie, mummy?"

At the same time she went very pink in the face, but Lady Fielding, seated at her writing table, her back half turned to her daughter, did not notice these phenomena.

"David Leslie," said Lady Fielding. "He might do if we can't think of anyone better."

At these dreadful words Anne understood why girls leave home and how nice it would be to have a bachelor flat and a small cocktail bar and be dashing. She would have liked to plead for David, but suddenly a wave of shyness overcame her and though she opened her mouth, no words came out of it.

"The trouble is," Lady Fielding continued, quite unconscious of the havoc her last words had made in her daughter's mind, "that one can't rely on any of the younger men. They never know if they can keep an engagement or not, and now with this peace I expect it will be worse than ever. We really ought to ask some of the clergy. We have neglected them dreadfully this year and after all we do live in the Close. And I would like to ask Mrs. Brandon, but I don't suppose she can manage the petrol. Oh dear!"

And Lady Fielding, exhausted by the difficulties of social intercourse, laid down her pen and slewed her chair round towards her daughter, saying, "It's your party, Anne. Do think of someone else."

This request from her all-knowing, efficient mother was most flattering to Anne, but she was still so paralysed by the name of David Leslie that she could only sit and gape.

"There is Sir Edward Pridham," said Lady Fielding, "and old Canon Thorne and Dr. Ford; but we want someone younger for Sylvia."

"If Mrs. Brandon could come, mummy," said Anne, bursting the bonds of her silence with a great effort, "then we could ask Bishop Joram for her and David for Sylvia. Then there'd be me and Robin and you and daddy, to make eight. You know Miss Bunting was David's governess, mummy, and she said he was her favourite pupil."

"There is no one whose opinion I would sooner take than Miss Bunting's," said Lady Fielding. "I don't think I ever knew her make a mistake. And what she would have said if she had heard you say 'me and Robin,' I don't know. Let's try David then."

So full of gratitude was Anne for this change in her mother's mind that she quite forgot to resent her pin-prick about me and Robin, knowing also that her clever mother's slight pedantry was only an outside bit of her and that mummy could always be trusted to help one and was on the whole quite the nicest mother one could have.

All now hung on Mrs. Brandon. If she could come they would be eight; mummy could ask Bishop Joram and she could ask David.

"Shall I ring up Mrs. Brandon for you, mummy?" she asked. Her mother said, "Yes, do." Mrs. Brandon was rung up, the local garage was able to oblige with a car. One step was accomplished.

"Now shall I ring up David?" said Anne, again overcome with self-consciousness as she spoke and hoping that it didn't show.

"I think I had better write," said Lady Fielding. "I really hardly know him."

"But mummy," said Anne, made desperate by a feeling that she could not explain. "I know him quite well now. And Lady Emily is going to come to tea, mummy, isn't she? Oh, mummy, do let me ring up."

Perhaps, thought Lady Fielding, she was not moving enough with the times. Certainly all the young people rang each other up and made plans for their parents to supply rooms, fires, food and such drink as there was, and Anne must do as her generation did. Only Anne had been so long a delicate child and a not very robust girl that she had lived much more under her mother's wing than most girls of her age, and Lady Fielding sometimes blamed herself for fussing too much over her daughter. Anne was nineteen now, or as near nineteen as made no odds. She was getting stronger every year and though Dr. Ford said the Government could not conscript her, she was quite equal to ordinary life and her daily rests were a thing of the past. Possibly she would in any case have outgrown her delicacy, but Lady Fielding had an almost superstitious feeling that the happy turn in Anne's health was largely due to Miss Bunting, and that any kindness shown to a favourite pupil of Miss Bunting's would be a kind of friendly sacrifice to the spirit of that wise and valiant old governess. So she said Yes, and Anne plunged at the telephone, while Lady Fielding went back to her writing table.

Had Lady Fielding not been such a busy woman, shouldering the affairs of half the women's organisations in Barchester with patience and efficiency, she might have been surprised by the change in her daughter's voice as she telephoned to Holdings. But the accounts of the Barchester Branch of the Anti-Non-Interference Society were in a fine muddle owing to the treasurer having borrowed from the purse she kept her mother's housekeeping money in, to repay the purse she kept her own money in, which owed something to the purse she used for the Society's money, and only Lady Fielding could get them straight. She worked very hard for a quarter of an hour or so, hearing sub-consciously a good deal of conversation going on, but paying no attention to it. At last the month's accounts were tidied (though exactly the same would happen again next month as no one had the heart to sack the treasurer, a worthy not-so-young woman in thrall to an exacting mother) and Lady Fielding took off her spectacles, looked at the clock, got up and came nearer to the fire.

"Well?" she said to Anne.

"Oh mummy," said Anne, "Miss Merriman answered the telephone and she said David was away for a few days, so I explained it was your dinner party and very important, so she gave me his number in London and I got on to it and he was there, and says he will love to come. Oh, and I was to thank you very much."

"Splendid," said Lady Fielding. "Now Robin and Bishop Joram and we shall be all right."

"Oh, and mummy," said Anne, "David asked who was coming and I said who, and he said he would bring Sylvia, and I explained she was going to stay here. But it was very nice of him to ask, wasn't it, mummy?"

"Very," said Lady Fielding, absent-mindedly, for it had suddenly come over her that her shy Anne had been pursuing a man who was nearly twice her age from his sister's house to his office or his club in town and taking it all as a matter of course. In any other girl one would have accepted it as a matter of course, but with Anne—. Then Lady Fielding told herself she was a fussy, out-of-date old woman and rang up the Colonial Bishop, who was delighted to come. At lunch time Robin was rung up. The question of transport threatened to keep him away, but after lunch he rang up to say that a master who had just returned from the army had a lot of petrol and would lend him his car for the evening.

"What a lot of fuss you women do make," said Sir Robert, whose lunch had been rather interrupted by his women-folk's telephonings.

Lady Fielding and Anne looked at each other, in a common bond of pity and tolerance for men.

Having made this great exertion, the Fielding household sank back into its usual routine. Lady Fielding went to her various societies or had them to meet in her house. Anne went to her domestic economy classes, and Sir Robert was as busy as ever on his own affairs and those of the diocese of which he was Chancellor and, though this was unusual in him, was late for dinner several times. His wife, who never enquired as she knew that she would be told everything sooner or later, had dishes kept hot for him, quelled with great courage the rising grumbles of the servants and bided her time, which came on the following Sunday when Anne was having supper at the Deanery.

"There is a good deal of talk about a General Election," said Sir Robert when he and Lady Fielding were alone together. "I don't know why there should be, but the Archdeacon thinks Labour is up to something."

"I suppose Barchester is safe," said Lady Fielding.

"It was," said Sir Robert, "as long as Thorne was willing to stand. But he won't this time."

Lady Fielding looked up from her work.

"Heart," said Sir Robert. "The Conservative Association will probably ask me to stand. And the deuce of it is that Adams is standing for Labour. I don't like fighting him. He was a good sort of fellow according to his lights when we were at Hallbury last summer."

"Really, Robert," said his wife. "If you refuse to stand for Parliament simply because the man you are opposing is a good sort of fellow, you don't deserve to get in. Anyway thank goodness Anne has seen no more of his lumping girl. Is this serious, Robert?"

Sir Robert said it was quite serious. Nothing of course would happen, he said, unless Parliament really were dissolved, but he didn't think there was another man who would be mug enough to stand.

"We could afford it," he said. "And I think I'd rather like it. What about you, my dear?"

Lady Fielding said the only answer she could truthfully make was that this was so sudden, also that she would like further notice of the question if her husband expected her to make up his mind for him. Sir Robert said he would tell her everything as it happened, but was not mentioning it to anyone else and the subject was dropped for the time being though both gave serious thought to it, while the inner cauldron of politics bubbled and simmered and threw up a good deal of scum.

Anne, who was not much interested in politics, and vaguely thought that the Premiership was a kind of permanent official's job held for life by Mr. Churchill (in which a good many other people agreed with her) was far more excited about Sylvia's visit and the dinner party than the chances of a new government and thought Tuesday would probably never come. But nothing can thwart Tuesday, nor indeed any other day on its forward path, and in due course it arrived. Sylvia's leave was not cancelled, and she arrived at Number Seventeen for tea in very good spirits. Sir Robert and Lady Fielding were dining out, so the two girls had a kind of high tea and talked about Hatch House and Holdings and Rushwater and all the Leslies, and giggled and altogether enjoyed themselves as befitted their ages.

"I'm looking forward frightfully to your party," said Sylvia. "I haven't been to a proper party for ages. Who's coming?"

Anne named the guests.

"But David is in Paris," said Sylvia.

At these words, the whole world suddenly turned upside-down as far as Anne was concerned, and fireworks chased each other across the ceiling.

"He wrote to me from the Embassy," said Sylvia, in a woman-of-the-world way that Anne hopelessly envied, "but he didn't say about your party. He was going about with Rose Bingham; dancing and things. She's in the Foreign Office."

Poor Anne. A fortnight ago she had been quite grown-up. Now she was like a schoolgirl again, ready to cry at a moment's notice. David, with whom she had talked so dashingly on the telephone, David with whom she shared the secret of Miss Bunting. David who was the nicest person she had ever met except Robin, who was quite different, David in fact; David, David. Also horrible, dreadful, hateful Rose Bingham, whoever she was. But a hostess must not derogate from her hostess-ship, so Anne went on chattering and giggling, but all the time, which gave her a miserable satisfaction, with death in her heart; so what with laughing with Sylvia and secretly despising David, she felt quite light-headed. All of which passed entirely unperceived by Sylvia, we are glad to say.

Next day Mr. Churchill tendered the resignation of the Government. Millions of people felt a sudden sense of desolation, of being children deserted in a dark lonely wood; much as they had felt in it that black winter when their ruler deserted them. Other millions saw the dawn of an even Braver and Newer World, as if the present brave new one were not unpleasant enough. But once the first shock had been taken, conversation in every circle veered round to the unpleasant fact that rations had been cut again. Barchester, nay indeed all England, was at once divided into two camps; the one rejoicing that all our food was going to feed the gallant Mixo-Lydians and other depressing minorities who were busy disliking us for liberating them, the other perfectly furious that our already skimpy rations were to be cut in favour of Foreigners, who lived in Abroad. This difference of opinion cleft every rank of society in Barchester, let alone all England, upwards, downwards, sideways, circularly, zig-zag, in shops, homes, trams, cafés, garages, homes; even in the Cathedral, where the head verger, who had supported Mixo-Lydian refugees all through the war and had no opinion at all of that nation, told the sub-organist, who had no family and was extremely leftist, that he was no better than a Narzy.

But neither politics nor rations affected Sylvia and Anne, who spent the morning working in the garden and chattered and laughed as much as if they had not done it ever since Sylvia came. Anne had gone to bed the night before with a firm determination to be miserable and let no one see, but when her mother came in from her dinner party to kiss her good-night, she could not bear to be unhappy alone any longer, and told Lady Fielding that Sylvia had had a letter from David Leslie from Paris and how sad it would be if he wasn't coming. To which Lady Fielding had answered in a very matter of fact way that letters took a long time from Paris and as David would probably be flying he was very likely to be back at Holdings now. Comforted by the voice of authority Anne had gone to sleep quite happily, and though doubts assailed her at intervals while gardening, she resolutely pushed them down.

At lunch Sir Robert praised the work the two girls had done and suggested a few more jobs.

"Oh, daddy," said Anne reproachfully, "how could you? It's the Palace Sale."

Sir Robert thanked heaven aloud that he did not need to attend that function and told Anne to collect all the gossip she could, especially if in any way to the Bishop's discredit. He then gave each of the girls a pound to buy rubbish with and Lady Fielding, who quite truthfully had an important committee that afternoon, told Anne to be sure to tell the Bishop's wife about it, though she knew she would not believe it, and then gave each girl a pound to spend on her behalf.

"Oh, mummy," said Anne, just as she and Sylvia were leaving the house.

"Well," said Lady Fielding.

"Mummy," said Anne again, standing on one leg in a way that Miss Bunting would have immediately corrected, "do you think David will come?"

"Of course he will," said Lady Fielding; and such was Anne's faith in her mother that she felt considerably relieved and did not worry more than twenty times during the afternoon.

When the girls had gone Sir Robert and Lady Fielding held a short committee meeting together about Sir Robert standing for Parliament and came with a mixture of excitement and regret to the conclusion that it would be his duty if officially asked.

"Well, it's worth a fight," said Sir Robert, "and Adams I know will be a clean fighter, though I wouldn't like to say the same of his supporters. In any case, I shan't lose my deposit. Don't wait dinner for me if I'm late, but I hope to get back in time."

Lady Fielding went to the committee, which was long and troublesome, dealt firmly with uppish members, helped diffident ones, got all her business done and came back tired at 5 o'clock, thankful to have her tea in peace. In more normal times she would have taken a committee and a dinner party in her stride, but after the strain of a long war and the almost greater strain of the recent peace, with all the upheavals and irritations and angers it had brought in its train, she felt her age. And though to be round about forty-five is not at all old, the six years of the war counted as six years of years, and young middle-age has become elderly middle-age, not knowing it till taken off the rack. Lady Fielding would willingly have thrown the remaining good tea-cups onto the marble hearth, hurled the teapot through the window into the Close, screamed at the top of her voice, burst into tears and then, as she sadly admitted to herself, been extremely ashamed and miserable. So she choked down her fatigue and her feeling of hopelessness, drank her tea, and felt a little better.

From her seat by the window she could see the life of the Close going gaily on as usual. The motor mower was making silky tracks with exquisite regularity on the grass, its noise not disagreeable at a distance. Black coats, an occasional black gown (worn more in defiance of the Bishop than from any deep conviction), here and there a pair of gaiters; wives of clergy; children of clergy; several of the Dean's grandchildren being taken to a children's party in perambulators, and on foot; the verger's dog barking at the sub-organist's cat, who was sitting contemptuously on a brick wall washing its face and hands; the gentle click of stonemasons at work on a small exterior repair to the lady-chapel; one of the prebendaries' wives gardening in a disgraceful old hat, a flowered apron and a very unecclesiastical old tweed skirt; a few boys on bicycles; rooks; a steady stream of town people going through the Close on their way to or from the Sale of Work. The sights and sounds were much as they had always been and Lady Fielding thought that if she sat quite still, never moving, hardly breathing, the war and the more dreadful peace would turn out to have been a dream. Full May; laburnum, syringa, flowering thorn, rhododendron, wallflowers against old red brick walls. Peace. Golden peace, not the pinch-beck that was being offered, indeed thrust upon people, in its place. She closed her eyes, a thing she most rarely did except in bed, and half-dreaming felt that if she remained still enough she would be a little girl in a holland smock, playing in one of those gardens in the warm spring sunshine: for she had been born and brought up in the Close and except for the first few years of her married life had always lived there.

A cheerful and very powerful aeroplane, driven by a cheerful and very powerful young man who had already twice been cautioned about low flying over built-up districts, suddenly roared out of nowhere, skimmed the roofs of the Close, circled the Cathedral spire, turned over contemptuously two or three times, deliberately made a noise like the end of the world and disappeared into the blue heights. Lady Fielding controlled herself very well. She picked up an empty tea-cup and threw it as hard as she could at the fattest cushion on the sofa, where it lay placidly for a moment, then deliberately rolled to the ground and shed its handle. This hideous example of the diabolical tendencies of inanimate objects broke the spell. Lady Fielding laughed aloud at herself, collected the cup and its handle and put them on the tea-tray. She then rang the bell.

"Oh, Pollett," she said, when the parlourmaid came in, "the handle came off this cup. Can we get it riveted?"

Pollett said with dark triumph that she'd noticed the handle was cracked last Friday week but hadn't liked to say anything about it and she didn't know no one who could do riveting now that old Mr. Cornstalk in Barley Street was dead.

"Put it away then," said Lady Fielding, "and I'll ask about a riveter. There must be one somewhere."

Pollett took the tray away. Lady Fielding gave herself a mental shake and sat down to her writing table to deal with a pile of the letters that took so much of her time. She heard the front door bell ringing downstairs, then a good deal of conversation in the hall. Pollett could be as a rule relied upon to protect her from unexpected callers, but was evidently getting the worst of this particular encounter. She went to the window and looked out. A car was standing at the door, but cars look much alike from above and in any case Lady Fielding could rarely recognise even her own car, being totally deficient in motor sense. Steps came very slowly up the stairs. Pollett flung open the door, announced "Lady Emily Leslie, my lady, and Mr. Leslie" and disappeared.

"I do hope you will forgive me, Lady Fielding," said Lady Emily, advancing on David's arm with her most enchanting and mischievous smile, "but your daughter said she thought you wouldn't mind if I called. I am hardly ever in Barchester, but we all made a great effort to come to the Palace sale, and Martin and Emmy wanted to come too, so we stopped at your door, and your maid, who is quite delightful, said she thought you were at home, so I said to David 'I'm sure Lady Fielding will let me rest here for a few moments till Martin and Emmy come and pick us up.'"

It was impossible to be annoyed with Lady Emily, even if one knew she was making the most unblushing capital of her age and infirmities and using one's house as a convenient port of call for her grandchildren. Lady Fielding welcomed her and began leading her to the sofa.

"I shall sit here, if I may," said Lady Emily, tugging at a heavy arm chair and much hampered by her crutch-handled stick, "and then I can see Martin and Emmy coming."

"Do let me move that heavy chair, Lady Emily," said Lady Fielding, fearing that her visitor might do herself some serious harm, but Lady Emily had already pushed it towards the window and sat down.

"And now that my mamma has finished moving the furniture," said David, "may I speak? I didn't mean to come to dinner with you at half past five in the afternoon, but my mamma insisted on having my company. As soon as she goes, I shall retire to the Deanery and come back to your kind dinner party looking quite different. Or would you rather I went now?"

Lady Fielding did not really want any visitors at all between her committee and her dinner party, but politeness comes first; and like everyone else she found the peculiar Leslie charm subtly undermining her constitution. So she said nice things and expressed her regret that her husband and daughter were out and offered tea.

"Now, I will tell you why I really came," said Lady Emily, "and no tea thank you, for we had a delightful tea at the Palace."

"A revolting tea," said David pleasantly. "Powdered milk for the common herd is one thing, but when the Bishopess offered mamma a private cup of tea in her own sitting-room, I did think she would ask the cow."

"I believe," said Lady Fielding, dispassionately, "that she calls it her boudoir."

"God bless you, Lady Fielding, and defend the right," said David piously. "Are you sure she doesn't call it her oratory?"

"Quite sure," said Lady Fielding. "It would smack of Popery."

Then they all laughed and felt on safe ground.

"Now," said Lady Emily, who did not believe in wasting time, "I will tell you why I really came. I always have wondered *where* old Canon Robarts put his maids. These houses look big, but then the rooms are large and I know he used the whole of the second floor for his books, as well as the drawing-room and most of the ground floor. Now, how do you manage?"

Lady Fielding, a passionate lover of houses herself, quite understood Lady Emily's interest and asked if she would care to see the servants' bedrooms. "I think it will be safe now," she said. "Will you come too, Mr. Leslie?"

David thanked her, but said he was always frightened of servants' bedrooms in case they were there. So Lady Fielding ushered Lady Emily upstairs, while David sat in the window seat and looked at the Close and wondered idly where the Fielding girl was. He had not exactly suggested to his mother that she could call, but he had played upon her curiosity about the servants' bedrooms quite deliberately; and if he had thought that he would see Anne more comfortably in the afternoon than at a dinner party, well she was not there, and the thought was not worth attention. And then he thought of Paris and the amusing time he had spent with his cousin, Rose Bingham, who knew her world like anything and was hand in glove with all the big noises in Paris, besides having her own very comfortable flat, and then he thought, which he mostly avoided doing, of his future. A flat in town with central heating and valeting and a restaurant and meals in one's own dining-room if one wished was most convenient and he had no intention of giving it up, but sometimes he thought that a small but perfect house in the country was also indicated. There were one or two houses on the Rushwater estate that might suit him, and Martin would always let him rent one, and he would be near Agnes and his mother. With a good cook-housekeeper one could be comfortable. A wife, if she were the right wife, might be agreeable. Someone like the Fielding girl who would sit on an Empire couch—and

he knew exactly where to get the Empire couch he wanted—
and look up at him under her long lashes. A captivating creature
that little Anne; quick, intelligent with depths he had not
plumbed. A line from Byron suddenly rose from old forgotten
readings to his mind about the young ladies who "always smell
of bread and butter." Would Anne be a bread-and-butter wife?
Would she do in London or in Paris? He could not see her
mixing with Rose Bingham's friends. And she was after all only
a schoolgirl. Whether Anne would think of him as a husband he
had not yet begun to consider, but it amused him to sit in the
sunlight making plans, with no real foundation, for his own
pleasure and comfort. So absorbed had he become in his imag-
inings that he did not hear footsteps on the flagged path below,
nor the shutting of the front door and the sound of voices. The
drawing-room door was opened. Anne and Sylvia came in
talking and laughing.

"So you have come at last," said David.

The remark was addressed to Anne, round whom his
thoughts had been roving, but both girls stopped short, surprised to find a stranger in the room, for David's back was to the
light and the afternoon sunlight slanted across the room into
their eyes. In a fraction of a second they realised who it was.

"David," said Anne.

"Hullo, David," said Sylvia, "I thought you were in Paris."

"Bless your heart, no," said David. "Believe it or not I am here.
My mamma is upstairs doing a tour of the bedrooms."

Anne, the slanting afternoon sunlight flecking her view with
golden dust and golden glamour, welcomed David and wondered if she ought to ask him if he would have some sherry, for
it was nearly six o'clock. So bathed was she in the sunlight
that her flush of excitement hardly showed and David merely
thought how very nice the Fielding girl was looking. Really she
would do one credit anywhere. And how handsome the golden
Halliday girl was. How happy in fact could one be with either;
not if 'tother dear charmer were away, but if one could have

both. And, as an afterthought, Rose Bingham too. It was all rather difficult and David preferred to step aside from difficulties.

"Would you like some sherry?" said Anne. "I know daddy would like you to have some and so would mummy."

David said he would like it of all things, so Anne went down to the dining-room and while she was there the front door bell rang again. Through the open dining-room door she saw Martin and Emmy and called to them, for one did not have to feel shy with Martin. He was more like Robin.

"Are we a nuisance?" said Martin. "Gran was coming here and we said we would pick her up. At least she asked us to pick her up. Something about David and a car."

Anne said his grandmother was upstairs with her mother looking at the servants' bedrooms and David was in the drawing-room with Sylvia. On hearing this name Emmy, who had been from her earliest years a young woman of great determination, at once went upstairs, leaving Martin to carry the sherry glasses for Anne, who insisted on bringing the decanter herself, because she said it would be awful if she broke it, but much awfuller for anyone else who did. As they got to the drawing-room door Lady Emily and Lady Fielding came down from the upper regions and they all went into the room together. Lady Emily was glad to sit down, but refused sherry and called David away from talking with Sylvia.

"It is quite easy to understand now," said Lady Emily to David. "There are not so many rooms on the top floor because of one of them being so large. There are shelves in the other room, so I think Canon Robarts must have kept some of his books upstairs and all his servants slept together in the big room. There is one small room with no shelves, so perhaps the cook had it, but one can't really tell. I wish one could, it is so interesting. I wonder if the Canon had a man-servant."

"My mamma was born to bring me to shame," said David to Sylvia, who smiled like a goddess, but as David fully realised, did not quite catch his meaning, which on reflection he thought just as well.

"I can tell you all about that, Lady Emily," said Lady Fielding. "He had a kind of valet-attendant, who slept in a nasty little room in the basement. When my husband and I took the house, we shut up the basement and made the kitchens at the back of the house."

So interested was Lady Emily by these domestic items that she at once asked to inspect the kitchens, but her son David said there was a dinner party that night and she could not possibly go on interfering and in any case ought to be starting for home if she was to have her rest before dinner.

"But you are taking me home, David," said his mother.

Anne heard the news and felt as if she had been given a violent blow. David was going back with Lady Emily. He had avoided the dangers of Paris only to forget the engagement at Number Seventeen. She looked in wild appeal at her mother but Lady Fielding did not notice.

"Now listen, mamma darling," said David. "Well do you know that I am staying to dinner here and that Martin and Emmy are dropping you at Holdings on their way back. But I will take you down to the front door."

Anne's heart soared to heaven in gratitude and also hoped that it would be forgiven for having presumed to doubt his faith.

While the foregoing desultory talk had been taking place Emmy had attached herself to Sylvia with the embarrassing devotion of a young woman of her age and given her a long circumstantial account of the Grade A dairy herd at Rushwater and a pressing invitation to come and stay as soon as possible, holding out as a special inducement the approaching birth of a Jersey calf from whom much was expected. Martin, rather bored by his cousin Emmy's singleness of mind, for though he was a keen and hard-working cattle breeder he found other things to interest him in life, tried once or twice to talk to Sylvia himself, but unable to stand up against Emmy's cow-mindedness contented himself with admiring Sylvia in silence. His grand-mother now summoned him to drive her home, so he said good-bye to Sylvia and added his invitation to Emmy's.

"I'd love to come," said Sylvia. "I'll let you know as soon as I get my next leave. Will David be there?"

"Uncle David doesn't care for cattle a bit," said Emmy scornfully.

"And here he stands unto this day, to witness that you lie, my girl," said David who had overheard her last remark. "Your uncle David went to the Argentine on big-bull business for a whole year while you were an extremely stout little girl, and beat the Argentines at their own game. It was he that raised them to four thousand pounds for Rushwater Rambler, and has practically never been able to look a cocktail in the face since. And let that be a lesson to you against careless talk."

"Did you *really*, Uncle David?" asked Emmy, incredulous.

"Ask Macpherson," said David. "I'll come over to Rushwater while Sylvia is there and show you how much I know."

"If you say when you are coming, I'll manage to get leave," said Sylvia.

David laughed and said if he knew in time he would ring her up, with which she had to be content. Martin, who had been listening seriously to this conversation and wishing he had David's way with girls, then said good-bye, collected Emmy and his grandmother and drove away. It was now nearly half past six and Lady Fielding said she simply must be quiet for a bit, so Anne took David and Sylvia into the garden till it was time to dress for dinner.

Anne had fully intended to be dressed early and ready to meet Robin, who had promised to be very punctual, but the charm of giggling with Sylvia while they dressed made her forget the time, and when she got down to the drawing-room she found David and Robin talking war shop and though pleased to see her, more than ready to go on with their men's talk. So she sat in the window seat sometimes listening, sometimes thinking her own thoughts, till her mother came down, and then Mrs. Brandon came fluffling into the room, thinner than she used to be, but wearing remarkable well.

"We are waiting for Bishop Joram and my husband," said Lady Fielding. "I think you know everyone here, Mrs. Brandon."

Mrs. Brandon was more or less acquainted with everyone in a vague county way, and the party settled very comfortably to desultory talk, till Bishop Joram came.

That susceptible cleric at once fell in love with Sylvia Halliday, whom he had never met before, a proceeding watched by Mrs. Brandon with mischievous amusement.

"The Bishop did fall in love with me once," she said to Robin Dale. "It was at the Deanery, years and years ago when there wasn't any of this trouble about peace."

"I am sure he did," said Robin. "We all do. Did I ever tell you about our Aunt Sally?"

Mrs. Brandon shook her head gently, a gesture which she managed to make extremely attractive.

"A real Aunt Sally, or really an aunt?" she enquired.

"A real Aunt Sally," said Robin gravely. "She had lived in the old stables for hundreds of years and not even the Cottage Hospital Bring and Buy Sale would take her, but Joram said she reminded him of an African idol and nearly cried. So my father gave them his blessings and he took her back to his lodgings."

"I wonder what his landlady thought," said Mrs. Brandon.

"She is a French dressmaker called Madame Tomkins in Barley Street," said Robin. "Anne says she is pretty tough."

"If she made Anne's dress she must be very clever," said Mrs. Brandon admiringly. "She looks so charming. And how is your father?"

Robin said his venerable Pa was pretty well. A little woolly in the intellect sometimes, but the servants were good to him and that kind Sister Chiffinch at the Cottage Hospital kept a friendly eye on him, and he usually went over to visit him from Southbridge once a week.

"A very nice woman," said Mrs. Brandon. "She nursed Delia with her first baby. You know she is going to have another one in August."

Their talk babbled gently on. David amused himself by a private game with Sylvia; not a very kind game as the whole point was for him to say things that he thought she wouldn't quite understand and keep a mental score of his hits or misses. Lady Fielding talked to the Colonial Bishop and Anne sat looking very nice, sometimes wishing she were as beautiful as Mrs. Brandon, sometimes looking at the back of David's head as he teased Sylvia and feeling how very different it was from the back of other people's heads and sometimes exchanging a smile with Robin; which was perhaps the most satisfactory of her occupations. But all the time Lady Fielding was talking to Bishop Joram she had her eye on the clock and her ear on the front door wondering how long she ought to wait dinner for her husband. The hands of the clock moved on and she was just beginning to decide that they must start dinner without him, when in he came with an apology but no explanation.

"You know everyone here, Robert," said his wife.

Sir Robert said Yes indeed and greeted his guests.

"I never heard you come in, Robert," said Lady Fielding.

Sir Robert said that young Needham was having trouble with his car in the Close and the Day of Judgment couldn't have made itself heard while his engine was running.

"Is that the Dean's secretary who married Octavia Crawley?" said Mrs. Brandon. "He came to lunch with me once and lost an arm."

"What an extraordinary effect for lunch to have," said David.

The golden Sylvia looked puzzled, then began to laugh.

"Mrs. Brandon didn't mean he lost the arm at lunch," she explained kindly. "He got it shot off in North Africa. He's the clergyman at Beliers and awfully nice."

David thanked her with old-fashioned courtesy for her explanation and then Lady Fielding herded them downstairs and got them seated. From where she sat at the oval table she was as nearly opposite her husband as is possible with a party of eight and so in a good position to catch his eye. This she ardently wished to do, for it had been impossible to ask him about the result of the Conservative Association's meeting and as the next years of their life might hang on that evening's decision, she wished to know the best or the worst: though which was which she could not at the moment say.

Sir Robert was equally anxious to communicate with his wife, but courtesy compelled him to be as dashing a cavalier as possible for Mrs. Brandon, and compelled his wife to be all attention to the Colonial Bishop. Suddenly such an ear-splitting noise burst out in the Close that everyone turned to look out of the window. In that instant Lady Fielding telegraphed to her husband: "Are you going to stand?" and he, by a masterly piece of pantomime with his eyebrows and his lawyer's rather grim straight mouth, managed to convey to his wife that he was now the officially adopted candidate for the forth-coming election and that he really didn't know if he was pleased or not but there it was and he would do his best.

Lady Fielding didn't know if she was pleased or not either, but thank heaven it was now decided and she could plan the next months or weeks or whatever it was going to be accordingly.

"That was Tommy Needham's car again," said Sylvia, who had the best view of the Close. "He's started it now."

"A very fine fellow, young Needham," said the Colonial Bishop. "He reminds me of a young native chief in Mnganga-land who was a splendid professing Christian."

He paused to help himself to some fish.

"I think it is wonderful of natives to be Christians," said Mrs. Brandon. Robin looked at Anne, who looked gravely at him. If a young woman with large dark eyes could wink without moving a muscle of her face that, Robin thought with some pride in his young friend, was what Anne was doing.

"You are so right, Mrs. Brandon," said Bishop Joram, talking across the table in his zeal. "And this young chief was one of our staunchest churchwardens. He had had both legs bitten off by a lion—that is of course where the parallel between him and young Needham comes in—but his faith never failed and he was carried to church every Sunday and all non-attendants were fined a half bottle of gin."

"And who got the gin?" asked David, losing all sense of dinner-table politeness in his unfeigned interest in the Bishop's narrative and talking across the table.

"The Exchequer," said Bishop Joram. "Mpumpo—that was the chief's name, at least his public name, for of course no one was allowed to know his real name—kept the key of it."

"And what was his real name?" said David, his blood well up.

"Melba," said Bishop Joram. "His father, who was one of my earlier converts, had a record of Melba in *Faust* and liked it so much that he gave the name to his eldest son. In fact all his sons, seventy-five I think it was or eighty-five, were called Melba in private, but of course each had a public name as well. Lady Fielding," he continued, turning to his hostess and lowering his voice, "I have a message for you from my kind hostess, Madame Tomkins. She asked me to let you know that a friend of hers back from Germany had brought her several dress lengths of silk and she thought you might care to look at them."

Lady Fielding thanked the Bishop and said she would call on Madame Tomkins as soon as possible and then they talked about the row between the head verger and the sub-organist and other Close matters.

"And now," said Robin to Anne, "tell me all about the Palace Sale."

"It was Horrid," said Anne loyally.

"I wish the Crawleys could hear you," said Robin. "The Dean looks so tired sometimes with the Deanery always full of grandchildren, and your words would be as good as a tonic. How exactly was it horrid?"

"Well, I don't know how to explain quite," said Anne, "but it was a mean kind of feeling. Rather meagre. Would that explain it?" she added anxiously.

"It would," said Robin. "But I want more details. What was the tea like?"

"Ghastly," said Anne with fervour. "Great horrible buns with pale yellow tops all soggy, and sandwiches with peanut butter in them which is horrid anyway, but even if you did like it there was hardly any there. And a lot of mousy biscuits."

"Mousy?" said Robin. "Do you mean with mice in them, like fly-biscuits?"

Anne said no, tasting of mouse she meant, and Octavia Needham, who was there, told her that the Sunflower Tea Room had made a big batch with some bad flour that had nasty vitamins in it a month ago and nobody would eat them and she was sure the Bishop's wife had bought them all cheap.

"And the Bishop brought a man into the dining-room," Anne continued, "and Octavia thinks it was a man from the B.B.C. because he sounded like that and they had tea with us to be condescending instead of in his wife's sitting-room, but Octavia saw the man putting his biscuit behind the big clock on the mantelpiece and she says the Bishop saw him too but he didn't dare to say anything."

"Why not?" said Robin, amused by the way his young friend was coming out.

"Well, Octavia thinks the Bishop was to do a broadcast in that 'Episcopal Episodes' series," said Anne, "but she thinks the B.B.C. man hated the tea so much that the Bishop won't have a chance. And she heard the B.B.C. man say 'No sherry?' to a waitress that she knows, because she used to be a kitchen-maid at the Deanery, and the waitress told her the B.B.C. man said 'Hell, it's even worse than they told me' and then he went away."

"I am sorry to be ill-mannered," said David Leslie from

Anne's other side, "but Mrs. Brandon is making such eyes at Sir Robert that I have no one to talk to, which is most unfair of her because it puts the whole table out. So may I listen till we get straight again? I adore hearing nasty things about the Palace and I shall repeat them all to my mamma and Agnes."

Anne's heart gave a delightful though disturbing thump. Here she was with Robin, whom she was so fond of, on one side and David on the other, and both talking to her, as if she were a real grown-up fascinating person like Mrs. Brandon. Then, remembering her duties as a deputy hostess in a way Miss Bunting would have strongly approved, she looked across the table and saw Sylvia deserted, Sir Robert on one side of her in Mrs. Brandon's toils and the Colonial Bishop on the other telling Lady Fielding how comfortable Madame Tompkins's lodgings were. Sylvia was behaving very well, looking neither bored nor resentful and smiled across at Anne.

"Oh, Robin," said Anne softly, "Sylvia has got left out. Could you possibly make mummy talk to you, and then Bishop Joram would have to talk to Sylvia. She's all alone."

Robin was sorry to leave Anne, but she was right, and so he turned towards Lady Fielding and managed so to insinuate himself into the conversation that the Colonial Bishop transferred himself to Sylvia and all was peace again. Lady Fielding wanted news of friends at Hallbury, where Robin's father, Dr. Dale, was Rector, and particularly of Jane Gresham, whose husband, Captain Francis Gresham, R.N., had so long been missing in the Far East.

"We have hardly been at Hallbury at all in the last year," said Lady Fielding, "except an occasional weekend. Life gets fuller and fuller here and we went to friends in Devon for Robert's short holiday."

Robin was able to report that Francis Gresham was quite fit again and had a shore job at Plymouth, where his wife had joined him, as little Frank Gresham was now a boarder at Southbridge School. But they intended to make their permanent home at Hallbury, he said, and would live with Jane's father, Admiral Palliser.

"And now," said Lady Fielding kindly, "tell me about your work."

"I like it," said Robin. "I like the boys with a few exceptions whom I think anyone would dislike anywhere. I like the Birketts and I am very fond of the Carters. And we are gradually getting rid of our female teachers, thank God. Two of the old masters have come back, discharged from the army, but perfectly fit for work, and if this peace ever gets going we may have a few more back that are physically fit. I can do tennis, but I can't do football."

Lady Fielding then asked in a very friendly way about his own future. During the year that Anne had spent at Hall's End, the Fieldings' house in Hallbury, with the old governess Miss Bunting, Robin and Anne had become great friends. The Fieldings liked and respected Robin's old father, who had taken a grandfatherly fancy to Anne and given her a ring that had belonged to Robin's mother. They had also come to like Robin very much and had a high opinion of his courage in facing his physical disability and making a success of his little pre-preparatory school. Then Miss Bunting had died and Robin had gone as temporary classics master to Southbridge. Anne's health was greatly improved; they had shut Hall's End and removed to the Close. But they had managed to see a good deal of Robin off and on and he had come to look upon Number Seventeen as a kind of second home and Anne as a kind of friendly confidante who was always ready to listen and sometimes came out with an unexpected piece of helpful common-sense. Lady Fielding, always busier than she meant to be, was glad for Anne to have a friend in Robin, for owing to her delicate health, she had only had a few terms at the Barchester High School and had not found anyone there whom she specially liked.

Whether it ever occurred to Lady Fielding or to her husband that they might be encouraging an attachment between Robin and Anne, we cannot say. Probably not. Anne had remained young in many ways for her age owing to her sheltered life and they had come to look upon Robin as a son, or perhaps a cousin of the house. And in any case Anne and Robin had always remained upon very friendly unemotional terms, felt very safe and comfortable in each other's society; and were not in the least unhappy or anxious if they did not meet for several weeks at a time.

"My future," said Robin, "appears to be settling itself without my interference. Philip Winter, who used to be Senior Classics Master, is not coming back. He is going to start a prep. school at Beliers with his wife, chiefly for boys from naval families."

"Let me see," said Lady Fielding, who liked to get things clear. "His wife's brother will come in for the Priory, won't he?"

Robin said yes, when Sir Harry Waring died, and he understood that he would never be able to afford to live at the Priory and would be delighted to let his sister and her husband take it over.

"And Birkett told me not long ago," said Robin continuing his story, "that as far as he was concerned, I was going to get Winter's job. He said he wouldn't have any trouble with the Governors. And that being so, I shall have quite a decent screw and might get a house later on. So what with my salary and my own bit of money from my mother and what my respected father will leave me some day, and of course watering the boarders' milk and selling their joints to the rag-and-bone man, I shall become a rather well-off crusty bachelor and a well-known Southbridge bore."

"You will have to get married," said Lady Fielding, "won't you? I believe Birkett prefers married house-masters."

"I have considered that too," said Robin gravely, "but I am not quite sure whether one ought to have a house to take a wife to, or provide oneself with a wife in order to get a house. But I shall work that all out in time."

"Well let me know if I can help," said Lady Fielding kindly, and they drifted off into speculations upon the horrors of peace and the prospects of a General Election.

"Robin," said Lady Fielding under the cover of general conversation, "I can't say anything about it, but we might be taking Anne to London in the autumn."

"Oh," said Robin. Then he looked at Lady Fielding, looked quickly at Sir Robert and then questioningly at Lady Fielding. "Yes," said Lady Fielding. "But don't tell Anne. And we may not go."

By this time dinner was nearly over and the company had remained very comfortably paired off. The Colonial Bishop, to whom every fresh love (in an honourable and clerical way) was the best, had gone on falling in love with Sylvia and told her many uninteresting facts about his sub-equatorial diocese. Sylvia listened kindly and if she felt that it was hard lines to be between two old men (by which she meant Sir Robert and Bishop Joram), she did not envy Anne. From time to time she thought a little wistfully of the W.A.A.F., for now that her days in it were about to be numbered, all the companionship and fun, even the hard work, the loneliness on some stations, the bitter winters in huts, the odiousness of the Philpott woman, all began to assume a nostalgic rose-colour.

Lady Fielding took her ladies upstairs to the still sun-lit drawing-room, where they were shortly joined by the men. Anne asked the Colonial Bishop to tell her how Robin's Aunt Sally was getting on and extracted from him a highly unsympathetic account of the only occasion on which he had dined at the Palace.

"I know, my dear Miss Fielding," he said, which made Anne wonder for a moment whom he was addressing, "that it is not easy to get wine or spirits or even beer now, but cold water at dinner and glasses of hot water at half past nine seems to me totally incompatible with the episcopal dignity. The lowest Mpuma—the name of the hereditary slave caste in Mngangaland—would not let a stranger, far less a member of the Church of England, enter his hut without offering to chew some Mgapo for him."

Anne asked what Mgapo was.

The Bishop said it was a kind of preparation of Mkopo, the native millet, fermented with the juice of the Mbola palm in a pit previously filled with the entrails of the Mqaka, a small antelope, and subsequently chewed for three days and nights by the wives of the chief, or as a great courtesy by the chief himself.

Anne said she didn't think the Bishop would have time to do so much chewing and she thought the Bishop's wife had false teeth.

The Colonial Bishop said this was merely a comparison, and that frankly he could think of no comparison between the inhabitants of the Palace and Mngangaland that would not be heavily in favour of his ebony flock. Then Anne told him about the children's dance at the Palace when the Bishop's chaplain had played the piano, which was a very bad piano, because the Bishop's wife had been too stingy to hire a pianist and a decent piano, and could only play one waltz and one polka, and the refreshments were a piece of cake and a glass of tepid lemonade made with lemonade powder for each child, and they laughed a good deal. But all the time Anne, without being in the least envious of Sylvia, was thinking how nice it would be if David would come and sit by her. She was pleased that he should like Sylvia, and thought that Sylvia looked very beautiful, and knew that she could never be beautiful like Sylvia; and she told herself that she had had David all dinner-time and must not be greedy. But her thoughts and sometimes her eyes wandered to where David, sitting by the window with his Winged Victory, was talking in what was evidently a very amusing way; and then ashamed of her selfishness she tired to look as interested as possible by what the Colonial Bishop was saying and hardly heard it at all.

As for David, he was already rather bored. Mrs. Brandon was charming, but not one of his own sort. Lady Fielding he liked, but she was occupied with Robin Dale. Anne with her upward glance was a tantalising object and he desired her further acquaintance, but the Colonial Bishop was well in possession. So he had seized the golden Sylvia, who really looked more splendid than ever in the setting sun, which touched her hair to a deeper gold and enhanced her rose-petal complexion; not to speak of a figure which sunset could neither mend nor mar. And she was of good stock too; better than Anne. The Hallidays had been at Hatch End for longer than the Leslies had been at Rushwater: longer possibly than the Pomfrets had been at the Towers. The Fieldings were delightful people, but they were Barchester as far as one knew anything about their families: not county. There must be a good background to produce them and to produce that outstanding and amazingly attractive child. He had thought of her just a little too much for his own comfort. Now he was deliberately laying siege to Sylvia as a distraction and he was behaving badly and he knew it. He fell into a reverie as the sun sank behind the cedars in the Deanery garden.

Sylvia, with such perfect health and equable temperament that she thought very little about her own looks, faintly envying Anne for being slight and having dark cloudy hair, was not at all embarrassed by the silence, for she rarely had much to say for herself. Accustomed for some years to live among women, having her leaves in a world mostly without young men, she had become rather independent of the other sex, till David, with his open admiration and easy flattery, had come to Holdings to stay with the Grahams. He had looked at her and admired her and Sylvia's heart had also begun to beat faster. She would have liked to say clever things to impress him, but sure instinct told her he had seen too many women to be impressed and that her only chance was to remain, if possible, exactly as she was. And the most difficult thing in the world, as we all know, is to be oneself without being conscious of it, once the self-consciousness has been raised. To break a silence that was beginning to make her uneasy she asked David what he was thinking about.

"Getting married," said David, truthfully but not very considerately.

"Oh, are you engaged then?" said Sylvia, taking her fences one by one.

"Lord, no," said David. "Only sometimes one wonders, that's all."

"What kind of a wife do you want?" said Sylvia.

"Any wife I have will have to be as funny as hell all the time," said David, speaking to his own thoughts, not to Miss Sylvia Halliday.

Sylvia was silenced. Never, she knew, could she be as funny as hell. In fact, she doubted, being a very unconceited girl, whether she could be funny at all, except for laughing with George or with Anne, about silly things, or having silly giggles in the W.A.A.F about nothing at all. In fact she wondered what women who were as funny as hell were really like and began to think if she had ever met one. Lady Fielding certainly wasn't; Mrs. Brandon wasn't; Anne wasn't. Nor was her mother, nor Lady Graham, nor any of the people she knew. The only person she could think of who at all filled the bill was that odious Philpott woman, who to do her justice was always at the top of her form, horrid though she was. If that was the kind of woman David Leslie liked. . . . She left the sentence unfinished in her mind.

As so often happens, all the conversations in the room came to an end about the same time, and there were exclamations about not keeping cars waiting and the lateness of the hour, though the Double Summer Time had not long set. Mrs. Brandon was the first to leave. Then Robin said he must be getting back to Southbridge and bade affectionate good-byes to his host and hostess.

"Will you and Anne come to Southbridge for the School Sports, Lady Fielding?" he said. "The beggarly ushers are allowed to have tea-parties in their rooms. I'll let you know the date as soon as it is fixed. And Sir Robert too of course, if he is free."

Lady Fielding said they would love to come, and hoped the date would be a free one, a hint which Robin understood. Then he said good-bye to Anne and was going away when David said he was coming too. So he waited while David said good-bye with a grace that Robin knew he could never attain and somehow did not wish to attain, and the two young men went down together.

"I say, Dale," said David, "do come out to Holdings sometime. Agnes would love it and I'll mostly be there and my mamma will adore it. Those dull boys of my brother John's come sometimes to Holdings and sometimes to Rushwater. Come with them. How good-looking that Halliday girl is."

Robin cordially agreed.

"And Anne too," said David. "I'd like to see Anne in London. She'd do it well. Sylvia couldn't; she must stay in the country. Well, good luck."

He folded his long legs into his car and went away. Robin got more slowly into the returned master's car and also went away, with a little gnawing thought about Anne being in London if her father got into Parliament, and David being in London and meeting her at parties to which Robin Dale would never be invited.

After considerably outstaying his welcome, the Colonial Bishop went back to his lodgings.

"Well, good-night, Sylvia dear," said Lady Fielding firmly. "You were a great help to the party. Sleep very well. Anne darling, come and say good-night to me in my room before you go to bed."

So when Anne had talked about the party with Sylvia, she padded across in her dressing-gown and slippers to her mother's room.

Lady Fielding was sitting on a sofa and Sir Robert was talking to her through the open dressing-room door.

"Come in, darling," said her mother. "There is a kind of secret daddy and I want to tell you."

Anne's eyes became larger and darker than ever.

"The fact is, Anne," said Sir Robert coming in in his shirt sleeves, "that the Conservative Association has put me up as their official candidate."

"Will you be in Parliament then?" said Anne awe-struck.

Sir Robert said that depended on the electors.

"And your friend Heather's father is standing for Labour, I think," said Sir Robert, "but it isn't officially announced yet."

"I think," said Anne, "that Miss Bunting would have been very glad, Daddy."

"Oh, you do, do you," said Sir Robert, amused. "And why do you think so?"

"Well," said Anne, twisting the sash of her dressing-gown in and out of her fingers, "she would have liked you to help Mr. Churchill."

At this simple creed Anne's parents nearly laughed: but did not quite laugh, because it seemed to them that Anne, speaking for Miss Bunting, might be right.

"That's all, darling," said Lady Fielding. "And a secret just for the present."

Anne kissed her parents good-night very affectionately and went back to her room. Now at last she was really grown-up. She had often thought she was grown-up before, and every time she reached that point, something even grown-upper had happened. Now nothing more grown-up could ever happen to her in her life and she went to sleep prepared to keep the secret even from Robin. As for David he was forgotten in this strange exciting moment in a way that would have caused him considerable if temporary pique if he had known it.

# CHAPTER 6

The whole of England now settled down to grumble, and indeed had everything to grumble about and would have felt very peculiar if they hadn't. May melted into June. Sir Robert's election committee got busy. Mr. Adams's election committee got very much busier, but were a good deal hampered by the irregular attitude of their candidate who refused to go on the lines laid down for him and carried on a kind of guerrilla campaign of his own. Sir Robert and Mr. Adams continued to meet at the County Club and took a good deal of pleasure in each other's society, this scandalising all their partisans.

"It's funny you and me getting so friendly," said Mr. Adams to Sir Robert at lunch one day, "and then having to knock one another about like Punch and Judy as you might say. Still, it's a fair go and a ding-dong go and no malice borne. And if I wake up one morning and find I'm Sam Adams, M.P., I'll be the first to laugh."

"I expect it does feel a bit queer," said Sir Robert thoughtfully. "How is Heather doing?"

"She's doing fine," said Mr. Adams. "She took to Cambridge like a duck to water and there isn't an ology she doesn't know. She wanted to come here and help her old Dad with the election, but the lady that's head of the college said she did ought to go to a reading party. 'Well, Miss Hipcock,' I said— that's her name, Miss Hipcock, though it's not a name I'd choose myself—'well,' I said, 'I don't know that my Heth needs much reading, seeing as I can get her all the books she wants by telling my sekertary to phone up the booksellers, but if that's your idea, I daresay there's something in it.' Well, the long and the short of it seems to be that they want my Heth to do some extra studying and Sam Adams was never one to spoil a ship for a ha'porth of tar, nor a good machine for a ha'porth of oil neither," said Mr. Adams reflectively, "so she won't be here for the election. And I must say I'm just as glad to see her out of it. There's going to be some nasty feeling and I wouldn't like my girlie mixed up in it. Nor yours neither."

"I feel much as you do," said Sir Robert. "I don't think the city will be very pleasant in the next few weeks, and I hope Anne is going to stay with friends in the country for part of the time."

"I liked your girl that summer at Hallbury," said Mr. Adams. "My Heth liked her too. But they aren't going to see much of each other in the future and that's a fack."

Sir Robert looked questioningly at Mr. Adams.

"Men are one thing, women are another," said Mr. Adams.

Sir Robert agreed.

"You and me can meet at the Club, or on the platform, or any other place and speak our minds and no harm done," said Mr. Adams. "But your Anne and my Heth won't be meeting much. They're different. My Heth has the brains and I've got the money to back them, and my Heth is going to go far. But your Anne doesn't need the brains nor the money; and she doesn't need to go far, because she's where she ought to be."

What Mr. Adams had been saying was so true that Sir Robert remained silent.

"Well, that's all," said Mr. Adams. "Sam Adams was always one to speak his mind. And I may say," he added thoughtfully, "that he will likely speak his mind more than his election committee like. If the Labour bosses think they can boss Sam Adams, that's where they trip up on the mat. Well, best of luck, Fielding."

Never before during their acquaintance had Mr. Adams called Sir Robert by his surname. That he should do it now seemed to Sir Robert quite right. One shook hands with an opponent on equal terms.

"And the best of luck to you, Adams," he said, dropping for the first time the Mister, the absence of which he had felt would somehow offend the wealthy self-made ironmaster.

They shook hands warmly, to the horror of one or two members of their committees who were lunching at the Club, and went about their business.

Sylvia Halliday, to her own surprise, was promised an early release from the W.A.A.F. and asked her mother if Anne could come and stay with them as soon as her release came through. The Fieldings were, as we know, quite glad to have Anne out of Barchester during part of the election campaign, and it was settled that she should go to Hatch House after the Southbridge School sports which were to take place at the end of June.

Mr. Birkett, surveying the school which he had served for many years, first as Headmaster of the preparatory school and then as Headmaster of the upper school, felt that things might be worse. They had weathered the storm; faced evacuees, rationing, the absence of some of their best masters, the intrusion of women as teachers, the insanity which overtook every year's Sixth form who feared the war would not last long enough for them to be called up, the difficulties of heating. They had won the battle with the Ministry of General Interference, who had tried to take the school over as a home for the provisional Mixo-Lydian government. They had fought successfully the Air Ministry's plan of putting Nissen huts all over the playing fields in case they could find anyone to put in them. Mr. Birkett, well backed by his Governors, had won a place for Southbridge among the schools whose parents are still base enough to wish to pay for their boys' education. He had won the admiration of the higher ranks of his profession and it was safe to prophesy that he would be the next Chairman of the Headmasters' Conference.

"I hope we shall be lucky in the weather," said Mr. Birkett to his senior housemaster, Everard Carter, who was dining alone with him a few days before the sports, as both their wives were away. "Do you remember the summer Hacker got the Montgomery scholarship? What weather we had for the sports!"

"That was the summer I got engaged," said Everard. "I had a letter from Kate this morning. She says Lydia is very well and Lavinia is just like old Mr. Keith, and the new baby is due in January. I think Kate is arranging for the term to begin a week later than usual so that she can be in at the death—the birth, I mean."

"I like Lydia Merton," said Mr. Birkett. "If it hadn't been for her admirable bridesmaiding I don't think we should ever have got Rose married. What a morning that was, with Rose wanting to go to the Barchester Odeon before her wedding. By the way, Carter, did I tell you that Rose may be back in England at any moment now? Her husband's time as naval attaché in Lisbon is up. They will fly, with the children, so I don't suppose we shall have much warning."

"How shockingly Rose behaved to Philip Winter," said Everard, his wrath rekindled as he thought of the havoc that lovely Rose Birkett had made with his junior housemaster that summer.

"And everyone, including Amy and myself," said Rose's father dispassionately. "John was the only person who could ever manage her. I hope his next job will be at home. It would be very nice to see Rose and our grandchildren."

Then Everard enquired after Geraldine, the Birketts' younger daughter, and was glad to hear that she had a good nannie at last and that her husband was now a full colonel, and so the talk roved over old times and old boys and old friends.

"I wonder," said Mr. Birkett suddenly, "why John Leslie sent those boys of his here. I thought all the Leslies went to Eton."

"I have often wondered too," said Everard. "I think it must be because they are so very uninteresting."

"They are dull boys," said Mr. Birkett.

"I was thinking about Leslie and his wife," said Everard. "They are extraordinarily nice, but so entirely dull. So are the boys. They keep a good average standard in work and games and are eminently respectworthy members of my house, but I sometimes think that if I came in to prayers with my face blacked and rattling a set of bones, they wouldn't notice any difference in me."

"All the better for them," said Mr. Birkett gloomily. "Soon there will be practically no eccentrics left in England, and the mediocre will have it all their own communal way. I hope I'll be dead then. And I'll blow up the school before I die."

" 'Thy hand, Great Anarch,' " said Everard thoughtfully. "You won't be the only one, Birkett. I shall help to lay the train, and I know some old boys who will joyfully abet us. Swan for one, who by the way is back from Africa now, and Morland, and a few more. I wish we had Featherstonhaugh."

And there was a silence for a moment as the Headmastser and the Senior Housemaster thought of the Captain of Rowing, who had gone into the Nigeria police and had been torpedoed on his way home at the outbreak of war. The first name on the school Roll of Honour: the last might be yet to come, for peace didn't seem to have a very good grip of things and the Far East was still at war.

"Morland is in Burma now," said Mr. Birkett. "Laura wrote to Amy the other day. I hope she will come over for the sports. She was a great help to us in the first autumn."

For Laura Morland, the well-known novelist, had come as a kind of unpaid extra secretary to Mr. Birkett in the first term of the war when the whole of the Hosiers' Boys' Foundation School had been evacuated, a loathsome expression but common usage now, to Southbridge.

"It would be just like things if he were killed," said Everard. "The moment peace breaks out anywhere it means trouble. I suppose those filthy Japs will give in soon, but there are bound to

be a lot more casualties. And as soon as the fighting stops, our
boys will kill themselves in jeeps and be spilt out of aeroplanes.
I know their tricks and their manners."

At which Dickensism Mr. Birkett laughed, and then he and
Everard plunged into the time-table for summer examinations.

On the day of the School Sports the weather so far forgot
itself as to give every promise of a perfect mid-summer day. The
sun rose on a soft mist which gradually melted, and there was a
pleasant warmth in its rays. A light breeze tempered the noonday heat; though if one could call it noonday when it was really
only ten o'clock in the morning, said Mr. Birkett, he did not
know; and was then assailed by doubts as to whether he didn't
really mean two o'clock in the afternoon.

By ancient custom the Birketts and the Everard Carters had
large lunch parties for various important people connected with
the school. Sir Robert Fielding, who was one of the Governors,
with his wife and daughter were among the Birketts' guests, as
were the Dean of Barchester and Mrs. Crawley, the Earl and
Countess of Pomfret and Mrs. Morland, who though not officially linked with Southbridge was almost one of the school.

The lunch was all cold, but quite good. Beer had been laid in
by previous arrangement with Mr. Brown of the Red Lion, and
one or two ex-masters and boys on leave from Germany had
brought bottles of wine and liqueurs as a tribute to the headmaster. Anne, who owing to delicate health and war-time
scarcity had hardly ever tasted wine, was slightly nervous of
the hock in her glass, but it tasted so sweetly of flowery
meadows—if these can be said to have a taste—that she felt
much braver.

While the party were still at lunch a very loud noise came
rushing down the drive and pulled itself up with shattering
explosions at the bottom of the flight of steps that led to the
front door, making conversation for a few seconds quite impossible. This noise was followed by footsteps in the hall. The
dining-room door was flung open and in came the most ravish-

ing creature Anne had ever seen. Fair hair perfectly arranged, cornflower blue eyes, a rose-petal complexion, an exquisite figure, legs that would have redeemed the ugliest face, clothes that to the coupon-ridden female guests who were still in most cases wearing pre-war clothes, looked like a glimpse of Paradise: the ravishing creature had everything. Behind her and towering over her was a tall man in naval uniform.

Mrs. Birkett, who was seated sideways near the door, looked round and went quite white.

"Mummy!" shrieked the ravishing creature, dropping a very expensive handbag and hurling herself upon Mrs. Birkett.

A murmur of "Rose," or from the less familiar guests "Rose Fairweather," passed among the company.

"Daddy!" shrieked Rose, extricating herself from her mother and rushing like a rock-bomb at her father.

"Oh, and Dr. Crawley and Mrs. Crawley, how lovely! And everybody! Do you mind if I come by daddy, Lady Pomfret, how do you do."

Blowing kisses at the whole dinner-table she dragged a chair between her father and Lady Pomfret, threw her very becoming hat on the floor and put her elbows on the table.

"Oh, and Simnet!" she cried, as the Birketts' butler laid a place in front of her. "Hullo, Simnet, do be an angel and get my bag. I left it somewhere."

"Yes, Miss Rose," said Simnet. "Excuse me, miss, but have you any luggage?"

"No. We've only come down just for lunch," said Rose. "It's rather meagre, but it can't be helped, daddy. John has a dinner tonight, but I said we must see you and mummy at *once*, so we borrowed the Admiral's car. It's a meagre one, but John got sixty out of it, didn't you, darling?" she called down the table to her husband, who had by now been accommodated with a seat by Mrs. Birkett.

"Don't shout across the table, my girl," said Captain Fairweather, and resumed his conversation with his mother-in-law."

"John is *too* meagre," said Rose, and taking her bag from Simnet began to make up a face which, in the opinion of the whole company, was already perfect. "Is it the Sports day, daddy? How lovely. I knew it was when I saw the tent. Do you remember the year Philip and I were engaged, daddy, and Colin Keith was in Mr. Carter's house? I want to know about *everyone*, daddy."

Enchanted as Mr. Birkett was to see his lovely elder daughter, much as he wanted to hear all the news of his grandchildren, much as he wanted to know his son-in-law's future plans, he sincerely wished that Rose had not chosen the day of the School Sports, or that she could have given him a little warning. It was no use trying to get much information from Rose, but he hoped that he might catch Captain Fairweather alone after lunch. Rose chattered and laughed and looked so lovely that even Lord Pomfret, who was never very well and nearly always felt tired with the weight of his estate, his county responsibilities and his conscientious work in the House of Lords, felt better for the sight; and Lady Pomfret felt she would willingly have the Fairweathers to stay at the Towers, or pull strings at the Admiralty for them, to have such a tonic for her husband.

"I wish we had a quieter day for you and Rose," said Mrs. Birkett to her son-in-law. "I do so want to hear all your news."

"Don't worry, Ma Birky," said Captain Fairweather, using the affectionate nickname by which she had been known when he was in the preparatory school. "I thought I'd give Rose her head today, but we shall come again if you will have us. Rose found someone in Lisbon who wanted to let a flat in Lowndes Square and we shall be there with the children for the present. How do you think she is looking?"

"Lovelier than ever," said Mrs. Birkett. "And just as badly behaved."

Captain Fairweather laughed.

"Elbows off the table, Rose," he called down the room.

"Oh, John, how meagre you are," said Rose, pouting in a most becoming way, taking her elbows off the table and blowing him a kiss.

Then lunch was over and it became everyone's duty to go out to the Sports, the preliminary heats of which were already being run.

Mr. Birkett introduced Rose to Lady Fielding and Anne, who gazed with unselfish admiration on the ravishing creature and, suddenly thinking of David, wondered if Rose was as funny as hell all the time, but came to the conclusion that she wasn't; in which she was perfectly right.

"Mummy," said Anne, "let's find Robin."

So they set out on an exploring expedition to find Robin, while Sir Robert talked about grown-up things with Lord Pomfret and the Dean. The playing field was staked and roped for races; white flannels, most of them rather shrunk and yellow by now, looked cheerful in the sunlight; mothers' and sisters' dresses fluttered, as far as austerity dressmaking would allow, in the light breeze; important parents were in chairs near the tent and lesser parents on benches or sitting on the ground. At the end of the field was a table and here they found Robin.

"How nice to see you," he said, getting up. "It's rather a nuisance that I am stuck here for the time being, but I'll be relieved before tea. How nice Anne looks."

And indeed Anne, in a confection of Madame Tomkins's design made from some of the looted silk, pale yellow with flowers on it, looked very nice indeed.

"You ought to see Mr. Birkett's daughter," said Anne. "Rose she is called."

"Oh, is she back?" said Robin. "I have heard a great deal about her, but I can't look at anything while I am at this table. Will you find your way to my room, Lady Fielding, at the tea interval, or whenever you like. Anyone will show you Carter's house and Matron will be enchanted to look after you."

So Anne and her mother walked about and met friends, or sat in the important chairs and didn't much look at the sports. For except to the immediate relations of Smith minor nothing is duller than watching that young gentleman come in second for the hundred yards under fourteen, unless it is Smith major just not clearing five foot two in the high jump. Various county friends came and talked to them and presently Mrs. Morland joined the party, rather dishevelled by the breeze.

"It is all my own fault, I know, for not cutting my hair off," said Mrs. Morland, as a light wind lifted her hat and let it fall again slightly crooked. "But I should feel quite bald without it. One does get so used to things. When my youngest boy was here he wasn't at all good at games. He always liked the river best. He writes to me quite regularly from Burma and says he likes the fighting. I should if I were a young man."

With such determination did Mrs. Morland say this, and so impossible was it to think of her as a young man, that Anne couldn't help laughing and Mrs. Morland, who had no particular opinion of herself, laughed too. So the afternoon wore on and became gently more boring, and by half-past three Lady Fielding with Anne found her way to Everard Carter's house and walked in through the open door. Matron, who had told the maids they could go to the sports, which most of them liberally interpreted as permission to go to the Barchester Odeon, was lying in wait to greet old parents and was slightly disappointed to see unknown guests for Mr. Dale. But when Lady Fielding mentioned her name, Matron cheered up at once.

"Well, of *course*," she said, leading the way upstairs, "Sir Robert Fielding is one of our Governors and as I said to Mrs. Carter it is always so nice when the Governors and their wives take what I call a personal interest in the school. Mr. Dale is quite one of our nicest masters, Lady Fielding, and you would never know he had only one foot. As I was saying to Jessie, that is the head housemaid who has been here for years, in fact really previous to me, Mr. Dale keeps his socks as neat as if he had all his feet, always so tidy in the drawer. And, I said to Jessie, who is a very good girl though I *cannot* get her to wear her spectacles as the doctor said she should, Jessie, I said to her, don't think you can be less particular about Mr. Dale's socks because one of his feet is artificial. You can never know, I said, which foot he puts which sock on, and a little hole on an artificial foot looks just as bad as a hole on an ordinary foot. It's a very nice room Mr. Dale has, the one Mr. Colin Keith had when he was an under-master here before the war and his sister married Mr. Carter. He *was* a nice gentleman and read his books at night, not always wanting to be off to Barchester like some we had in the war."

And a very nice room it was, with two windows looking into the playground, each deep enough for a small window seat, a bed which though a divan did not look so sinful as those which have no visible legs at all, one armchair, plenty of shelves, a small writing table and a good-sized table spread with peace-time nasty cakes and sandwiches. Anne examined some of the books and looked out of the window while her mother sat in the armchair. After a few moments two boys came in whom Anne at once recognised as the Leslies. They seemed pleased in an uninteresting way to meet her again and asked her if she collected stamps. Anne said she didn't.

"I could have given you some swaps if you did," said Leslie major. "Empire stamps."

"He only collects Empire," said Leslie minor. "I collect European ones. I wish I could get some Mixo-Lydian ones."

"I think I could get you some," said Anne. "We had a Mixo-Lydian maid called Gradka and she writes to me sometimes. I'll ask her if she can send me some."

"Thanks awfully," said Leslie minor. "But please let them be postmarked. I don't collect unused stamps."

He then attached himself firmly to Anne, evidently regarding her as a fountain of benefits, and told her in very boring detail about the new Slavo-Lydian issue which was overprinted on old Mixo-Lydian Customs and Excise stamps, and Anne listened good-naturedly.

"He's got new issues on the brain," said Leslie major scornfully and sat down at the tea-table with a hopeful gleam in his eye.

Just as Anne, for all her good nature, was beginning to wonder how much longer she could bear the conversation, who should come in but Commander Gresham and his wife Jane, introduced by Master Frank Gresham from the preparatory school. Lady Fielding and Anne were pleased to see their Hallbury neighbors and Frank, taking no notice of Leslie minor, began to boast to Anne about his exploits at the prep. school.

"Don't you know the Leslies?" said Anne, prepared to offer an introduction.

"Of course I do," said Frank, "but I can't talk to them. They're Upper School. I say, Anne, the Latin master at the prep. school is a mistress. She's never done Latin verses. We all think she's rotten."

With such artless gabbling did Frank beguile the time, while the Leslies sat with the stoicism of Red Indians before palefaces, refusing to be impressed in any way, till Robin came in with apologies for being late and told Leslie minor to put the kettle on the gas ring.

"Oh, sir," said Frank, "can I use my utility lighter? It saves matches."

He produced his lighter. Leslie minor, ostentatiously ignoring him, took a matchbox from the mantelpiece and struck a match. Frank, apparently not seeing Leslie minor at all, flicked his lighter to a flame and turned on the gas. Leslie minor shouldered Frank in silence and blew out the utility flame. Frank with a quick movement turned the gas out and looked away into the infinite.

"Oh, sorry," said Robin. "Here, Gresham and Leslie minor, it's open season in my room."

On hearing these words Leslie minor turned on the gas, Frank produced his utility lighter and handed it to his late opponent, who applied it to the gas, blew it out and handed it to

Frank. Frank then put the kettle on the gas and both boys squatted by the hearth discussing cricket.

"It's only a House rule," said Robin to the grown-up company. "If boys from another house or the prep. school come in here, they are not supposed to talk to each other till a master says Open Season. If they talk too much he says Close Season."

Commander Gresham asked why.

"I can't tell you," said Robin. "Things like that do happen in schools."

Commander Gresham said they happened in ships too and fell into a talk with Robin while the kettle boiled.

"Sir," said Leslie major, who aloof from a petty strife below his dignity to notice had been looking out of the window.

"Well," said Robin.

"It's Miss Banks from the prep. school, sir," said Leslie major. "I think she's coming to tea."

"Good God, I beg your pardon Lady Fielding," said Robin. "I never invited her."

"She said you did, sir," said Frank. "She said she was going to learn Latin verses with you and you had asked her to tea."

"I'm awfully sorry," said Robin to the company. "I did say something to Miss Banks about giving her some coaching in Latin verses, because she's shaky on her quantities like most women, and I don't want her to corrupt the prep. school before they come up to me. But I didn't mean today."

Lady Fielding and Jane Gresham murmured hollow nothings about how nice it would be to see Miss Banks, who then appeared at the door and was introduced. She was a small slight woman with bad skin and short hair brushed flatly back from her forehead like a man. She was wearing a black jacket and skirt of mannish appearance, a tailored white shirt with a high roll-over collar, and had a bunch of seal-rings hanging at her waist like a fob. Her legs were ungainly and her shoes what can only be called, in the worst interpretation of the word, sensible.

Her coming obviously depressed Robin and so put a damper

on the whole party. Frank and Leslie minor had made the tea and brought the tea-pot to the table, so everyone sat down. Lady Fielding and Jane Gresham worked very hard at making conversation, but Miss Banks was heavy in hand.

"Excuse me, but did I get your name right?" said Miss Banks to Lady Fielding.

That lady, conscious of a slight edge to her voice which she was not quite able to control, said that if Miss Banks had got it as Fielding she was quite correct; and then wished she had not set her daughter such a bad example.

"Then it is your husband who is standing for the Tories," said Miss Banks.

This put Lady Fielding in a quandary. The word *Tories* was obviously intended as a taunt to draw her. She must either accept the want of politeness, or enter into an argument with a young woman whom she had disliked from the first moment she had set eyes on her.

"Luckily," said Lady Fielding, skilfully skirting the question, "Mr. Adams, the Labour candidate, is an unusually capable man and I may say an old friend of ours, so there will be no bitterness as far as he and my husband are concerned."

And that will, I hope, she said to herself, be the end of it.

"We shan't get anywhere by gentlemanly methods," said Miss Banks. "Bitterness is the root of strength and the Tories have got to go. We got rid of Churchill and we shall get rid of his henchmen."

Commander Gresham, a man of few words and not taking very easily to ordinary life after his long wanderings and adventures in the Far East, looked at Miss Banks with distaste and said he thought Mr. Churchill had resigned on his own initiative.

"That," said Miss Banks, shrugging her shoulders in a way which clearly showed her opinion of Commander Gresham, "is of course a matter of opinion. A friend of mine in a very responsible position tells me that Churchill's own party would have voted against him next day had he not resigned."

"Do have a bun," said Robin desperately. "They aren't very nice but they might be nastier."

Leslie major said sotto voce to an unseen audience that some buns weren't very nice and couldn't be nastier, which remark, being obviously directed against the prep. school Latin mistress, made Robin look piercingly at his pupil and wondered if he had more in him than met the eye.

Lady Fielding hastily asked Jane Gresham if she was going away for the summer holidays. Jane said she had written to the Royal Hotel at Oldquay where they had often been, but hadn't had an answer yet.

"You ought to go to the Imperial," said Miss Banks. "A friend of mine was at the Royal lately and says the service is dreadful. You are Frank's mother, aren't you?" Jane nearly said she wasn't, but truth prevailed.

"He is coming on nicely with his Latin," said Miss Banks, "but he has been grounded in quite the wrong methods. We make Latin quite alive and interesting now. Little sentences about cars and aeroplanes and tanks and all the things small boys are keen on, and we have the greatest fun inventing words for them. After all, the Romans had to invent words, so why should not we?"

At this point Anne said to herself, almost aloud, "Ignorance, madam, sheer ignorance," which made Robin look gratefully at her.

"I am sure Mr. Dale will agree with me," said Miss Banks.

Jane Gresham had controlled herself very well up till now, but the fighting blood of a long line of sailors had been boiling up in her.

"Frank did very well in Latin in the school entrance examination," she said in her most county family voice, "thanks to Mr. Dale's coaching."

All the grown-ups plunged into incoherent conversation,

while Miss Banks looked up at Robin in what she considered to be an appealing way and said she must really put herself under him for some coaching and learn his methods. Robin, at the great disadvantage of being a man and a host, said they must talk about it; next term perhaps; and told Leslie minor to put the kettle on again. Anne sat very silent. That horrid Miss Banks, who she was sure knew nothing about Latin, or Governments, or Hotels, was being a nuisance to Robin, and Robin was too kind to be able to defend himself. She longed to fly into Miss Banks's face, or to drag herself along the ground feigning a broken wing; anything to distract her from persecuting Robin.

A noise was heard outside, the door was thrown open and in came Rose Fairweather and her husband.

"Hullo, Lady Fielding," said Rose, greeting her again with fervour, "I'm awfully sorry if it's a party, but I wanted to see Mr. Carter's house because I haven't been at home for ages and we had a splendid party here for the sports ages ago in this room, so Mr. Carter said to go upstairs but I didn't know there was a party. Does it matter?"

A frightful hubbub then arose, consisting of Lady Fielding introducing the senior classics master to Mrs. Fairweather and the discovery, at the same moment, by Captain Fairweather and Commander Gresham that they knew each other. Both naval officers seemed to swell to twice their normal size and half fill the room while they rapidly brought each other up to date about their war careers. Rose at once took possession of Robin, who was astounded by her beauty and her silliness.

"It was Philip Winter that this room belonged to, or else it was Colin Keith," said Rose, sitting down at the table and in her old artless way pulling Robin down by one hand to sit beside her. "Philip was frightfully brainy and we got engaged and it was perfectly meagre because he did nothing but talk about economy and things and wouldn't buy a car so we got unengaged. I was engaged six times before I got engaged to John," continued Rose, looking lovingly at her husband. "Daddy says you are marvellous at Latin and things, Mr. Dale, and I do think it's perfectly meagre your only having one foot. Mr. Carter told me all about it. You ought to get engaged, Mr. Dale, it's marvellous. Who is she?"

This question applied to Miss Banks, who was nearly boiling over at being so ignored by the Headmaster's daughter.

"Miss Banks, who takes Latin in the prep. school," said Robin, introducing that lady.

"How perfectly meagre," said Rose, looking at Miss Banks with an appraising eye and apparently finding nothing in her. "I mean one has to be most awfully brainy to know Latin and things and you must feel a bet meagre teaching prep. boys."

Miss Banks said the First year of Latin was the most formative of all and a friend of hers who had taken a very high degree at Liverpool University was devoting her life to giving Latin lessons to mentally defective children. They responded, she said, in a quite extraordinary manner to her stimulating methods.

Lady Fielding plunged into the silence that followed this paralysing statement and said she was sure it must have been quite extraordinary. She then wished she had not spoken. Robin, who was enjoying his tea-party less and less with this cuckoo in his study, said he was very sorry but he would have to be getting back to the sports soon and asked Lady Fielding if she and Anne would care to see the rest of the house. Miss Banks said how delightful and she would come with them, adding that she wanted to know every *corner* of the school. Lady Fielding, looking significantly at Robin, said she was afraid she and Anne must be going soon and perhaps they might come and see over the house another time.

"Sir," said Leslie major, who had been looking at a pile of gramophone records, "what ripping records you've got."

"Do you like music?" said Anne.

"Rather," said Leslie major. "Mother is awfully musical. Have you got the rest of Holst's *Planets*, sir? I can only find three here."

"A friend of mine, a much older woman than I am," said Miss Banks reverently, "but wonderfully youthful in mind, used to know Holst very well."

There appeared to be no adequate comment on this statement. Anne, knowing that one ought not to allow a long silence at a tea-party, very bravely said that she liked *The Planets* very much.

"My favourite is *Uraynus*," said Miss Banks. "The wonderful far-awayness of the strings!"

We fear that Captain Fairweather , Commander and Mrs. Gresham, Lady Fielding and Anne, though disliking every remark that Miss Banks made, would have accepted this statement at its face value; and as for Mrs. Fairweather she had been for the last five minutes busily employed in re-making-up her beautiful face and on this important task had concentrated her whole intellect. Robin blenched inwardly but could say nothing. Messrs. Leslie (major and minor) and Gresham looked quickly at Miss Banks and then at each other.

"Sir," said Leslie major to Robin in a voice of angelic innocence, "could you let us put *Uranus* on one day? I was thinking of giving it to mother for Christmas and I'd like to hear it."

Miss Banks looked as black as thunder. The naval gentlemen, scenting some kind of disturbance, went back to their naval conversation. Lady Fielding with her trained social sense and Anne, who was an apt pupil, also realised that something was wrong.

"I adore records," said Rose, putting her powder and lipstick away. "I had perfectly marvllous records in Lisbon. The American naval men used to bring them over from New York. Cash Campo and his Symposium Boys have been in New York ever since the war and I had a marvellous one of theirs called *Kiss, kiss, kiss, And You'll Never Do Amiss*. I played it forty times running the night the Admiral dined with us, didn't I, John?"

"If the Admiral hadn't been there you'd only have played it once, my girl," said Captain Fairweather. "Come along now and say good-bye to your people. So long, Gresham, the Admiralty will find me any time."

With loud protest at the meagreness of this command Rose got up, bade farewell to the company and followed her husband, and then the whole party went back to the sports.

"Good-bye, Robin," said Lady Fielding. "Come and see us whenever you are in Barchester. Anne is going to the Hallidays for a bit, and perhaps she and Sylvia will spend a few days at Rushwater."

"In that case I might find my way there with the Leslies," said Robin. "Martin Leslie did ask me to come. Good-bye, Anne, I like your flowery frock."

Anne looked gratefully at him and the Fieldings went away.

It was the headmaster's long-standing habit to have a junior master and a boy or two to Sunday supper as well as the Carters, who always came except when the Birketts went to the Carters. On the evening of the Sports Robin found Leslie major in the Headmaster's drawing-room, quietly reading *Country Life*.

"Thank you, Leslie," said Robin.

Leslie major looked at his classical pedagogue with an inscrutable face which somehow managed to combine innocence with the impression of a very knowing wink.

"This might interest you, sir," he said, showing Robin a photograph of an animal like a huge petrol tin on four sturdy legs with a heavily curled fringe. "It's Uncle Martin's Rushwater Rambler. He got all the prizes at the Barchester Agricultural Show last year and he is going up to the Bath and West of England as soon as they get going again. Do you like bulls, sir?"

"I really don't know them well," said Robin, "and I feel that they would despise me. But I would be pleased to make Rushwater Rambler's further acquaintance."

"Uncle Martin would be awfully pleased if you'd come to

Rushwater, sir," said Leslie major. "I think he gets a bit lonely without anyone to talk to about the war."

Then the Birketts and the Carters came in and Simnet announced supper.

The meal was not so cheerful as usual, for both the Birketts were a little depressed by having seen so little of Rose. Everyone was sorry for them and Kate Carter particularly exerted herself to keep their spirits up by saying how nice the sports had been and how nice it had been to see so many old boys; an unfortunate remark, as both the Headmaster and his Senior Housemaster were reminded of all the old boys that could not come back, and Mrs. Birkett too thought how many Southbridgians there were who would never call her Ma Birky again.

"We ought to have an interesting election in Barchester, sir," said Robin Dale, desperately attempting to help matters. "They seem to expect a heavy poll."

"The Labour people will vote all right," said Mr. Birkett. "Whether our people will is another question. We have had it too much our way and got lazy. I wouldn't give much for Fielding's chances with that man Adams up against him."

Robin said he wasn't a bad sort; which defence of the Labour candidate made Mr. Birkett quite angry, and Mrs. Birkett threw a grateful glance at Robin for having roused her husband.

"How violent Philip would have been about it all," said Everard Carter to the Headmaster. "Do you remember what an out-and-out Red he was the year he and Rose were engaged? He talked Russia in my House till we nearly died of boredom. And now he is a fine old crusted Tory."

The mention of Rose unfortunately sent Mr. Birkett into a fresh fit of depression and Kate looked reproachfully at her husband and said there were going to be some good symphony concerts at the Barchester Town Hall next autumn, some of classical music, some entirely modern.

Robin said not too modern, he hoped, because he felt rather old and conservative at present.

Kate said she thought not what one would call *really* modern. For instance Holst's *Planets*, and when a person was dead you couldn't really call them modern. This reasoning appeared to some of her hearers to have a flaw in it, but no one felt equal to raising the question.

"Mr. Dale has some splendid records of *The Planets*, sir," said Leslie major addressing Everard Carter. "The one of *Uraynus* is particularly good."

Robin could hardly believe his ears and would have liked to kill his pupil and then get under the table. Everard Carter, who rarely showed his deeper feelings, raised his eyebrows and shrugged his shoulders. It seemed to the two masters that Mr. Birkett in his paternal depression had not noticed this horrible barbarism and they secretly thanked their and Leslie major's lucky stars. But the habits of a lifetime are not lightly shed. After a couple of seconds Mr. Birkett's brain registered Leslie major's remark. He raised his eyebrows, looked over his spectacles at Robin's pupil and begged him, far too politely, to repeat what he had just said.

"*Uraynus*, sir," said Leslie major in a clear, cheerful voice. "I wouldn't have said it, sir, but that is how Miss Banks pronounces it, and as she is awfully keen on modern methods I thought perhaps Mr. Dale had taught us all wrong."

There was a moment's terrifying silence. All three masters were, to put it mildly, flabbergasted. Leslie major, the eminently respect-worthy member of Everard Carter's house in Everard's own phrase, the apparently dull son of provedly dull parents, had perpetrated a piece of impertinence worthy, thought Everard, of the days when Swan and Morland devoted their far from despicable intelligence to pulling their superiors' legs, and Swan had quietly driven Philip Winter to desperation by putting on the spectacles that he never put on for his lessons and looking at him through them. It was almost impossible for the Headmaster to make any comment without criticising Miss Banks, and though he did not much care for that lady and was going to have a serious talk with the head of the preparatory school about her, he could not encourage unfavourable criticism of the prep. school staff from boys in the upper school.

Robin looked at Leslie major, but that young gentleman was eating strawberries placidly. Their eyes met for a moment and Robin felt certain that Leslie major was giving him what in war jargon would be called a token wink. Suddenly he couldn't help laughing. The tension of which the men had been conscious relaxed; Mr. Birkett made a real effort and emerged from his depression, and the evening ended as pleasantly as Sunday evening usually did.

The fact that a Polish Government of National Unity had been formed interested nobody except those who wished to believe in it. June came to an end and a few days later Anne Fielding went to Hatch End to visit the Hallidays. Sylvia had shed her uniform but found to her disgust that she was about an inch bigger everywhere and apt to burst out of her summer dresses without warning. This, with a visit to Rushwater in view, was very annoying, and the Winged Victory was on the verge of angry tears when Anne said she thought Madam Tomkins might help her. For the friend of so old a client as Lady Fielding, Madame Tomkins agreed to stretch a point, so Anne and Sylvia went to Barchester by the train from Little Misfit, spent an hour with Madame Tomkins and had lunch at Number Seventeen. The idea of going to lunch as a guest with her own mother seemed so upside-down to Anne that she was almost shy at first, but presently recovering herself chattered away happily. The only blot in the visit was that Sir Robert had to attend a public lunch and could not get away from the office till late.

"Do you think daddy will get in?" said Anne.

"I haven't the faintest idea," said Lady Fielding. "And what is more, I really don't now if I should like London or not."

"I'd loathe it," said Sylvia. "I want to do landwork like Emmy.

I don't mean market gardening. Running a big place with a dairy farm or something of the sort. It's the only way to live now."

"I hope you will find a farm with plenty of sheets and towels and china," said Lady Fielding. "How anyone is to set up house now I cannot imagine, unless their parents can give them furniture. Anne, it is dreadfully sad, but I can't get that cup riveted. I have tried everywhere in the city. We have only three left, not much use if people come to tea."

"I'm sure I could get it mended, Lady Fielding," said Sylvia. "Our carpenter can do absolutely anything and I know he mends china for our cook."

So the cup and its handle were wrapped up and the girls went back to Hatch End, leaving Lady Fielding a little desolate, but on the whole glad that Anne was finding her own feet, even if only in a small way.

When Sylvia and Anne got out of the train they walked across the water-meadows and a plank bridge to Hatch House, where they found David Leslie having tea with Mrs. Halliday and telling her about his visit to Paris.

Sylvia said she had never been abroad.

"Good Lord!" said David. "Come to think of it, thousands of you haven't."

"It's all very well for you, David," said Mrs. Halliday with slight asperity. "You have been going abroad whenever you wanted to all your life and getting abroad during the war. Most of the girls haven't been out of England since 1939."

"You ought to go to Paris," said David, not disputing Mrs. Halliday's statement and addressing himself to Sylvia. "You would adore it, and the French would adore you. They like Englishwomen to be statuesque blondes."

"Well," said Sylvia, "I don't really want to go abroad much. I wouldn't mind exploring, somewhere off the track, but I'd hate a lot of French people gabbling at me. They haven't been much use in this war, anyway."

"I'd love you to meet my cousin Rose Bingham," said David.

"She'd show you Paris. She has a flat there and her faithful maid has kept it all through the war."

For some reason that our readers may be able to explain better than we can, both young ladies immediately took a violent dislike to Rose Bingham, about whom they knew nothing at all, and each decided in her own mind to hate her forever. Then David went away and the girls took Lady Fielding's cup out to the carpenter's shop where Caxton, who thought but poorly of his home compared with a workshop where a man could always lay his hands on what he wanted, was apt to linger as long as there was daylight enough to work by.

Sylvia introduced Anne and the cup to him. Caxton said he could make a nice job of the cup and enquired if the young lady's father was the gentleman that was standing for Barchester.

"I hope you will vote for him," said Anne shyly, but feeling that she ought to do some work for her father.

"I don't vote in Barchester, miss," said Caxton. "East Barsetshire, that's what I vote for. But Mr. Gresham will get in easy enough. There's always been a Gresham in for East Barsetshire."

"Well, there won't be if you and the others don't take the trouble to vote," said Sylvia stoutly. "All the Labour people are working like anything to get their man in."

"What beats me," said Caxton, "is that young fellow calling himself Labour. If he's ever done an honest day's work in his life I'll eat a pound of half-inch nails. I don't hold with those lawyers. I've never been to a lawyer in my life and I hope I never shall. When I made my will I bought a printed paper at the shop and wrote what I wanted and got it witnessed all proper. No lawyer's going to meddle with my affairs."

Anne asked who the Labour candidate was.

"Candidate!" said Sylvia scornfully. "His name's Hibberd. His father got made a lord but I don't remember his name. Not Barsetshire people."

"Well, Miss Sylvia, I'm not saying who I'll vote for, because it's a free country," said Caxton, "but it won't be that young Hibberd, lawyer or no lawyer."

"It doesn't matter whom you don't vote for," said Sylvia firmly, "but whom you do vote for. If you don't vote for Mr. Gresham and don't make all your friends vote, Mr. Hibberd will get in. And then the Government will put a huge tax on tools and say carpenters mustn't work more than six hours a day."

"Well, I do ask you, Miss Sylvia," said Caxton, "what on earth would the use of six hours be? It's all I can do to get through what needs doing without working short shifts. If anyone said to me, 'Caxton, your six hours are up,' when I'd got a nice little job on hand, well there's no saying what I wouldn't do. Chip a bit off his face with my mallet and chisel I would if he came meddling in my affairs."

"Of course you would," said Sylvia. "Now don't forget to vote for Mr. Gresham, Caxton, because if you don't Mr. Hibberd will make it a six-hour day."

Caxton, with a look of great wariness, said again that he wasn't going to tell no one who he was voting for, and anyone who thought he would vote for young Hibberd was mistaken, and if everyone was going voting there'd be a rare crowd at the Mellings Arms and he was never one for crowds and would like to get on with the repairs he was doing for the kitchen and then perhaps that Hubback would stop grizzling at him. And with this he turned on the electric lathe and made such a hideous roaring noise that the girls went away.

"That's our lot all over," said Sylvia. "They *will* not go to the polls. Their hearts are all right but their heads are like mules. I must go and beat people up a bit before the polling day."

Anne, a town child, was deeply interested by this aspect of rural life and began to realise the feeling of responsibility that the landed people still kept for those who lived in their villages and worked on their estates; dimly apprehending a society more deeply rooted than the urban life of the Close or the rather small-town life of Hallbury. With Sylvia she did a kind of political district-visiting, talking to Mrs. Hubback at The Shop, to Mrs. Hubback's cousin the landlord of the Mellings Arms, to cottage women, to elderly labourers, but seldom to the young: for the young were mostly away. Sylvia, she observed, had no particular gift for political argument, but a bulldog tenacity of purpose in bullying people to take the trouble to vote, and a good-natured patience that nothing ruffled.

"It doesn't matter so much which way people vote so long as they do vote," said Sylvia to the Infant School Teacher whom she had caught just outside the church. "People just won't bother."

"Well, really, Miss Halliday, that is rather a peculiar way of looking at it if you don't mind my saying so," said the Infant School Teacher. "In Russiar as they tell us the under-eights are quite politically minded."

"Poor little things," said Sylvia with genuine sympathy.

"Of course this election doesn't affect me," said the Infant School Teacher. "My vote is in Luton. But I do the best I can to make the toddlers politically minded. There is such a nice little song—'We'll all go down the Big Red Road, And meet Joey Staylin there.' The toddlers march to it every day at the physical recreation hour and it is going to be *such* a help to them when they go on to the upper school. The headmistress there has another very nice song, 'My little Red Home in the East.'"

"Well, good-bye," said Sylvia. "And *that* was a waste of time," she added to Anne as they walked on. "I expect it all is."

"Why do you do it then?" said Anne; not critically, but searching for information.

"Oh, I don't know," said Sylvia. "One has to do something and people are such slackers. Come on; we've still got to get a few people before lunch. I wish this election were over."

Everyone in England wished the election were over. Everyone was tired and trying not to show it; cross and trying not to give way to it. Thousands of people, probably tens of thousands of people, who had been removed from their houses by bombing, compulsory evacuation from seaside areas, or from land requisitioned for military purposes; by having to go and look after elderly invalid relations; by being directed (a phrase which deceived nobody) into various employments three or four hundred miles from their homes while other people from other places three or four hundred miles away were directed to the places the first people had come from; by having to move their school, their secretarial college (so-called); by happening to be staying at Ye Olde Bath Chappe at Little-Pigley-in-the-Pound when war began and never having the energy to do anything about it; all these people had, owing to National Registration, become voters in the place of their exile, and now having gone home again were unable to vote for their own candidate and could only express their anger by complaining that there were no proxies for civilians, while Bert and Sid and Alf in Europe, Africa and Asia, were able to exercise their privilege as citizens and vote by proxy in their native town or village for one of several people whom they had mostly never heard of; that is, if the holders of the proxies remembered to use them.

"I suppose you have got Fred's proxy, Mrs. Panter," said Sylvia to that lady, who was as usual ironing just inside her front door.

"I've got it all right, Miss Sylvia," said Mrs. Panter, licking her finger and testing the iron she had just taken off the fire.

"Well, I hope you are going to use it for Mr. Gresham," said Sylvia.

"Of course I am, miss," said Mrs. Panter. "That Fred of ours he was all one for Labour. Never you mind about Labour, Fred, I said to him, you stick to Mr. Gresham. So when he sent me the paper he wrote to me and said I was to put his cross down for that young Hibberd, so when I wrote to him I said if he wanted to vote for Hibberd he'd a ought to have sent the paper to Scatcherd—he's all for Labour Scatcherd is—but I've got your paper, Fred, I said, and I'll vote for who I think proper. Don't you worry, miss."

Having exhausted the heat of her iron, she put it back on the fire and selected another. Sylvia and Anne walked on.

"Isn't that rather unfair?" said Anne.

"Not a bit," said Sylvia. "Mrs. Panter has twice the sense Fred has. It wouldn't be a bad idea to give mothers a vote for each of their children until they get married and have children of their own."

"Then you and George couldn't vote," said Anne.

Sylvia said it would need a bit of working out and they had better go and see Mr. Scatcherd before they went back to lunch.

After knocking several times at the front door of Rokeby and receiving no answer, Sylvia said they had better go round to the back. So they walked along the dank little path overhung by nasty dark evergreens, and round to the little verandah. Looking through the back kitchen or studio window Sylvia saw Mr. Scatcherd working at his large table, so she knocked at the door and went in, followed by Anne, who secretly wondered if one ought to interrupt an artist.

"Hullo, Mr. Scatcherd, are you frightfully busy?" said Sylvia.

Mr. Scatcherd thought of saying something about Youth and Beauty being ever welcome to an Artist's humble abode, but before he could get his higher self onto the job, his lower or grocerial self had said, "Pleased, I'm sure, miss. Pray take a seat," and only by the skin of his teeth did he stop himself saying, "And what can I get for you?"

"I've only come for a moment, Mr. Scatcherd," said Sylvia. "Are you voting for Mr. Gresham?"

"Ah!" said Mr. Scatcherd.

"Well, you ought to," said Sylvia.

"Us artists," said Mr. Scatcherd, "aren't quite like other people. Politics are all very well, but what we say is, Art comes first."

"That's nothing to do with politics," said Sylvia firmly. "If you vote for Mr. Gresham you're voting for Mr. Churchill."

"So Mr. Hibberd says," said Mr. Scatcherd. "Leastways, if you take my meaning, Mr. Hibberd says it's time Mr. Churchill went. And a change does us all good."

"But Mr. Scatcherd," said Anne, braving the sound of her own voice, "Mr. Churchill is an artist too. You ought to vote for an artist."

"An artist in words you mean doubtless, miss," said Mr. Scatcherd. "An ARTIST is a rather different pair of shoes." And he smiled pityingly.

"But he is a *proper* artist," said Anne. "I mean he paints pictures."

Mr. Scatcherd, visibly shaken, said this was quite a new light on things.

"And he has them framed," said Sylvia; though with no grounds for her statement.

Anne said she did think artists ought to stick together.

"That young Hibberd, he may be a lawyer, but he's all for a Ministry of Fine Arts," said Mr. Scatcherd.

"He must be frightfully artistic," said Sylvia, secretly despising herself for using the word. "Did you know he was a Director of the National Rotochrome Polychrome Universal Picture Post Card Company?"

Mr. Scatcherd laid down his pencil and stared.

"Mr. Gresham told me," said Sylvia. "They offered him a seat on the board too, but he wouldn't have anything to do with it."

"The N.R.P.U.P.P.C.C.?" said Mr. Scatcherd, gradually going purple in the face.

"Yes, I suppose it is," said Sylvia, to whom the initials meant nothing except that they make her think vaguely of the Society for the Prevention of Cruelty to Children.

"Do you know what that firm, for body I will not call them, is doing?" said Mr. Scatcherd.

"I don't," said Anne.

"Well, miss," said Mr. Scatcherd, hitching his chair nearer Anne in a very alarming way, "it's out to ruin Art."

Anne, backing her chair a little, asked why.

"Simply to make money," said Mr. Scatcherd. "Doing those coloured photos of all our beauty-spots and selling them cheap, so as real Artists will starve. I'll give you some facks, miss. Before the war I used to make as much as fifty or sixty pounds most years with my black and whites. Easy money you may say, but I can assure you I've often been a week without finding the identical beauty-spot I had in my mind, not to speak of being out sketching in all weathers like the time I got the pewmonia in Northbridge churchyard doing my sketch of the tower from the north-east—one of my most popular bits that was. And now along comes a young whipper-snapper that I wouldn't take as an errand-boy, with his two-hundred-guinea chromo-camera and takes the identically same view as I did, simply stealing it from me, miss, only he missed that little bit where the ventilation pipe comes up, and turns out his photos by the gross. And the public buy these commercial photos, miss, and mine don't sell. And that's your art-loving British public!"

He then laughed so bitterly and sneeringly that Anne moved away a little further.

"WELL uncle what's all this noise about," said his niece Hettie, irrupting suddenly from the verandah, "I only have to turn my back for five minutes an go down to The Shop to see if there's any starch in which of course there isn't and here I come back and find you shouting at the young ladies and Miss Sylvia not even with a chair to sit on good GRACIOUS you ought to be ashamed of yourself and how are you Miss Sylvia?"

Sylvia said she was quite well and she and her friend who was staying with her had only looked in to ask Mr. Scatcherd to vote for Mr. Gresham.

"Don't you worry with uncle miss," said Hettie. "I'll see he votes for Mr. Gresham if I have to lock his trousers up WELL uncle I'm downright ashamed of you arguing with Miss Sylvia and that other young lady I thought you were all for the people and against the lords and there's that young Hibberd's father gone and got himself made a lord and everyone in Barsetshire knows the Greshams have never been lords and wouldn't not if you paid them to don't let me hear a word more about that young Hibberd uncle and if you got your pictures finished for Lady Graham's sale you'd do a sight more good than sitting here idling and gossiping good GRACIOUS it seems I can't go out of the house for a moment but you'll be up to something silly."

Sylvia felt she had done enough canvassing for that day, and having said good-bye to Miss Scatcherd in a less degree, owing to his niece's presence, to Mr. Scatcherd, went back with Anne to Hatch House, both girls very ready for lunch.

"Emmy Graham rang up this morning while you were out," said Mrs. Halliday. "The Ford van is going into Barchester on Friday and Emmy said it would come back this way and take you both to Rushwater. She wants you to stay till Monday week."

Sylvia and Anne expressed great pleasure at this good news, and each wondered if David would be there.

# CHAPTER 7

The weather had been steadily improving and by Friday all Barsetshire was lying sleepily under July sunshine. About four o'clock in the afternoon the Ford van from Rushwater drew up outside Hatch House with Emmy driving and Macpherson the old agent seated beside her. Mrs. Halliday, who was weeding in the front garden, came up in her large kangaroo-pocketed apron and asked them in to tea.

"Love to," said Emmy, stopping the engine with great violence and climbing out of the van. "Come on, Mr. Macpherson."

The agent, who would have retired some years ago had it not been for the war, got out rather reluctantly, for a market-day in Barchester was becoming a burden to him and he longed for his own house and his armchair and his *Times*. Mrs. Halliday, seeing that he looked tired and guessing that a tea-party might bore him, carried him off to her husband's study, otherwise known as the Office, and left the two men together.

Presently Hubback brought tea in to them and Mr. Macpherson accepted a cup.

"I like a decent-sized cup," said Mr. Macpherson, looking with approval at the large flowered cup which held a good half pint.

"So do I," said Mr. Halliday, who rather unfairly had an even larger cup with a view of the Eddystone Lighthouse on one side and "Rule Britannia" on the other. "I've had this cup since I was a child. My old nurse gave it to me. What I can't stand is these drawing-room cups with rims that turn out and over. You know the sort I mean. The tea runs down both sides of your face if you aren't careful."

There was a peaceful silence while they ate jam sandwiches.

"Do you know Fielding?" said Mr. Halliday.

Mr. Macpherson said he did, and Emmy had told him that Anne Fielding was a nice girl.

"So she is," said Mr. Halliday. "A bit shy, but very pretty manners. I believe she had that old governess Miss Bunting, who used to be with Lady Emily."

"Well I remember her," said Mr. Macpherson. "She was the only one that David was afraid of. She reminded me of some of the Edinburgh ladies in my young days; as well-educated as you could find, plenty of character and a tongue like a steel spring. She kept it in check, but when she loosed it, heaven help the one it was loosed upon. There are not many like her now. John's children and Lady Graham's should have had her, but she was getting too old for the very young ones."

"By the way," said Mr. Halliday, "Anne Fielding knows John's boys. She met them at Rushwater and again at South-bridge School the other day. She says they are nice boys."

"So they are, so they are," said Mr. Macpherson. "But you know, Halliday, none of Lady Emily's children or grandchildren come near her, in my opinion, unless it might be David at times. John is a good fellow and I have a great fondness for his wife and their two boys, but there is something wanting. I wouldn't like to admit that a Leslie could be dull, but I sometimes think it is possible. Now Lady Graham's children have more of their grandmother and her family in them. Emmy is very like old Lord Pomfret sometimes. Clarissa and Edith have a good deal of Lady Emily's charm and James, I understand, has already quite a reputation as an eccentric at Eton. It's early to prophesy about Henry and Robert."

"What about Martin?" said Mr. Halliday, amused by the old

agent's frank appraisement of the Leslie family by the standard of Lady Emmy.

"He is a good lad," said Mr. Macpherson, his voice softening. "His father that was killed in the last war was Lady Emily over again. Martin won't be that, but he is a good lad and his heart is in Rushwater. I'm glad Emmy is with him, for it's a lonely life for a young man after the army. If I could see Martin well married I'd be away to Dunbar and lay my bones there with pleasure."

"I wouldn't say that, Macpherson," said Mr. Halliday, for it was well known that although the agent had spoken nostalgically of his native Scotland for the last forty years, it was not known that he had ever revisited it. "You'll find as many excuses for staying on at Rushwater as Andrew Fairservice did for not leaving Osbaldistone Hall."

Mr. Macpherson laughed.

"Ay, there's aye something to saw that I would like to see sawn, or something to maw that I would like to see mawn," he said, and then the talk turned to Barsetshire politics and the town and county elections, till Macpherson heaved himself out of his chair and said it was high time they were away. Emmy was summoned, Anne and Sylvia said good-bye to Mr. and Mrs. Halliday and they all got into the Ford van.

This vehicle combined commercial utility with discomfort in the highest degree. In front there were two seats with broken springs and shiny worn leather seats. The back was used for potatoes, calves, sheep, mangolds, spare parts for the tractor, oil drums, coke, wood, parcels of wool and materials for the W.V.S., harness, milk, the Rushwater Women's Institute competitions in the local Drama League Competition; in fact, as Macpherson bitterly said, everything except a baby elephant. To meet these varied requirements the back seats had been removed and passengers sat on packing cases, dirty tarpaulins, or rolls of chicken wire.

"I'll drive," said Emmy. "You come by me, Mr. Macpherson.

You'll find a couple of cow blankets behind, Sylvia, or there's
Martin's old mackintosh only there's some tar on it."

Sylvia and Anne preferred to sit on some low wooden crates
which were not so obviously dirty as the seats Emmy had
offered. With loud grindings and clankings the Ford got under
way and carried them down the river valley and along by the
little Rushmere Brook, tributary to the Rising, through the
village, into the park where they crossed the brook and drew up
in the stable yard.

The stable yard was flooded with sunshine and warmth. The
mounting-block on which Anne was perched while the van was
being unloaded was for a moment almost uncomfortably hot.
White pigeons were purring sleepily on the coach-house roof,
and taking lazy flights only to settle again in their former places,
while the stable cat stretched along the warm tiles looked
tolerantly at them, gave itself a slight wash and brush-up,
yawned pinkly and went to sleep again. For the first time since
peace had burst upon an apathetic world, Anne felt that peace
was a real thing.

Then Mr. Macpherson got into his own little car and went
home, and Emmy led her guests through the kitchen passages,
dark and beetle-haunted, to the room where they had tea on
their previous visit to Rushwater. Here they found Martin,
having a belated tea after his day's work. Emmy at once began
instructing Sylvia, whom she evidently regarded as a promising
pupil whose education had been neglected, about the farm
routine and the personal tastes and peculiarities of various cows
and bulls, to which Sylvia listened with unfeigned interest.
Seeing that the cow talk threatened to go on for ever, Martin
asked Anne if she would like to see the house and have a walk
round the gardens.

"We don't use the drawing-room now," said Martin, opening
the door into the long room with its six tall windows opening
onto the terrace. "It used to be fun when my grandparents were
living here and lots of people came. They had celebrations for

me when I was seventeen, and a dance with a band and a big house-party and a cricket match. It was great fun. They would have had a twenty-firster for me, but there was too much war in the air and my grandfather wasn't well."

"I am so sorry," said Anne, looking with romantic sympathy at the long deserted room, its shining floor uncarpeted, furniture and lustres in holland coverings, pictures sheeted. "Was David there for the party?"

"Lord, yes," said Martin. "Gran wouldn't have enjoyed it without him. He was here off and on quite a lot; though looking back," he added dispassionately, "it was mostly off, I think. I wonder what the piano is like now."

He pulled the cover off the piano and struck a few notes.

"Not too bad," he announced. "I think Macpherson has it tuned regularly. David used to play it a bit. Have you ever heard him sing?"

"No," said Anne, "I didn't know he did. Miss Bunting never told me."

"I don't suppose Bunny would have called it singing," said Martin, re-covering the piano. "But he sang jazz like a Negro."

On hearing these romantic words Anne nearly fainted.

"I'm not musical like David," said Martin, leading the way through the suite of rooms that opened from the drawing-room. "But I've got a good radio-gramophone if you'd care to hear it, and some fairly good records."

Anne said she would like that very much and that her friend Robin Dale had some very good records.

"I like your friend Robin Dale," said Martin. "I hope he will come here whenever he likes. I'm awfully fond of Rushwater and I mean to make a success of it, but somehow one does miss the army dreadfully."

"Are you lonely here?" said Anne, with such obvious and genuine sympathetic interest that Martin was touched.

"Off and on," he said. "But there's always a job to be done, thank heaven."

"That's what Robin says," said Anne.

Then they visited the library, an octagonal room where books heavily bound in calf reposed behind locked grilles, and there was a door masked from the inside by sham book-backs, including *The Snakes of Iceland* in twenty volumes, which Martin said was a joke of his grandfather's.

"The Leslies are all like that," he said, leading Anne up a wide slippery oak staircase. "They joke with difficulty."

"David doesn't," said Anne.

"David is like Gran," said Martin. "With the Pomfret men it turns to a kind of sardonicness, but Gran is the most amusing person I have ever met and the kindest."

"David is very like her," said Anne.

"David is one of the nicest uncles I know," said Martin. "But not exactly kind. No; one couldn't say kind. This was Gran's bedroom and I adored coming to see her in bed in the morning when I was small and she used to draw pictures for me. And this was Aunt Agnes's room, bless her, the sweet idiot."

This irreverent character sketch of an aunt passed almost unperceived by Anne owing to the dreadful words Martin had just uttered. David was not kind. How could Martin be so unkind, so untruthful, as to say that? She felt almost angry with her host as they finished their tour of the house and went into the garden. But she behaved well and talked agreeably, and presently forgot her resentment in her delight at eating hot strawberries from under the nets.

"And here," said Martin, "is the Estate Office, where I spend a great deal of my life with Macpherson."

They walked in and found Emmy and Sylvia deep in Milk Marketing Board papers.

"I say, Martin," said Emmy. "What did you do with three-eighty-six stroke bee sea stroke eye tea pea stroke ex queue pea tea sea?"

At least that was what it sounded like.

"If you'd looked in the right place you'd have seen it," said

Martin, taking a file from a shelf and opening it on the table. "Here you are."

He handed her the Board's circular 386/BC/ITP/XQPTC.

"That's the one I was telling about," said Emmy to Sylvia, forgetting in her wish to instruct her new helper to thank her cousin Martin.

Sylvia read the form carefully.

"What idiots they are," she said, her finger laid on paragraph five, sub-section eighteen. "That goes bang against the official supplement to BX378 that you showed me."

"By Jove," said Martin, "you're right."

"And what a couple of fools we've been," said Emmy.

"A triplet if you come to that," said Martin. "Macpherson didn't see it either."

And then the three enthusiasts began to talk all at once, though Emmy talked the most loudly.

Anne, suddenly feeling that she was a town dweller, quite uneducated in the eyes of these true country folk, slipped away and wandered about the garden, enjoying the beauty and the peace and the hot afternoon sun (for by the almanac it was only a little after four). In the park the elms and oaks were heavy as thunderclouds in the dark summer foliage against the dark blue, infinitely remote sky. Anne sat down on the terrace, a little tired though delightfully and comfortably so, thinking how heavenly everything was and how happy she would be among such kind people.

Kind; the very word was like a bell. What was the echo it woke in her mind? Who had used it to her? It was Martin. And he had said it about David. He had said that David was not kind. A surge of hot anger rose in her against Martin. She would have liked to be angry with him, but as he was not there she had to get rid of her anger inside herself as well as she could. Of course Martin did not understand David. Nephews, she thought loftily, though Martin was at least eight years her senior, couldn't possibly understand uncles. She had seen David quite a lot this summer and he was Miss Bunting's favourite pupil. Then suddenly, there came into her mind a day when Miss Bunting, discussing the Leslie family in her impersonal way had said, "Mr. Leslie was quite right though, my dear. He always said that David was bone-selfish, though he was very fond of him." At the time she had not paid much attention to the old governess's remark, but now, and most annoyingly, it came back to her mind. And then, having mostly found that the old governess was right in her judgments, she tried to think over the question fairly. And as she thought, or did her best to think, a horrid conviction came over her that perhaps old Mr. Leslie and Miss Bunting and even Martin were right. Had she ever known David do anything except what he wanted to do? If she were unhappy, or had a difficulty in her life, would David help her? She very much doubted if he would. Robin would, of course. Robin would always be there. And she had a strong instinct that Martin, though she hardly knew him as yet, would do all he could to help anyone in distress or perplexity. But David— Well, she said stoutly to herself, it didn't matter if he did not want to help her. She would be gay. And then she could not help laughing at herself, for she knew she could not be gay to order and would always be a little shy of opening her mind to anyone but Robin. Then another echo, quite a horrid one, rushed into her mind. Gay. Why did the word make her feel uncomfortable? And then she remembered how David had said he must have a wife who would be as funny as hell all the time, and all the anger she had felt for Martin suddenly turned against people who could be as funny as hell all the time, and go on being it. Anne knew that she was not funny and she knew that David was not kind, and the warmth went from the sun, the sky was lowering, the trees were menacing, strawberries were tasteless, Rushwater was horrid, and Anne felt desperately homesick and wished she were back at Number Seventeen, safe in her parents' house.

The mellow sound of the stable clock striking seven broke in upon these mortifying reflections. Anne got up and walked back to the house and as she went the warmth, the sunlight were there again, the trees in the park handsome and majestic in their July leafage. By great good luck Siddon the housekeeper was shutting the windows of the great disused drawing-room and, seeing Anne, took her upstairs.

"You are in the Tulip dressing-room, miss," she said, "and there's a door through into the Tulip bedroom, where Miss Halliday is. Bertha will look after you, miss. She was head housemaid here when Mr. Leslie was alive. We had three in those days."

Anne thanked the housekeeper and as soon as she had gone cautiously opened the communicating door. In the Tulip room, to her great relief, she found Sylvia, who was brushing her golden hair violently, almost standing on her head to do so.

"Hullo," said Sylvia, looking at Anne upside-down from among her shining mane. "The Jersey may calve while we're here. I do hope she will."

She then stood up, shook her hair back and combed it swiftly into its natural ripples.

"I wish my hair were like yours," said Anne, perhaps thinking that with hair like Sylvia's it might be easier to be funny.

"Rot," said Sylvia. "If you have fair hair everyone thinks you are a peroxide. Hurry up."

She accompanied Anne back to her room and curled herself up in the window seat while Anne examined the cupboards and drawers and found, to her great relief, that Bertha had put everything where she could find it. Emmy had told them not to change, as there was such a lot to do outside now the evenings were long.

When they had finished supper, which was a good deal interrupted by Emmy reminding Martin that they must give up all the bacon coupons if they wanted to kill the pig, and Martin saying he mustn't forget the meeting of the Barsetshire Road Board on Wednesday, and Mr. Macpherson ringing up to ask if the five acre could be mown on Thursday, and telephone messages from Sir Edmund Pridham and Lord Pomfret and Mr. Marling and Mr. Belton on various county matters, they all went onto the terrace and basked on the warm stone in the evening sunlight. Emmy and Sylvia talked about potato spinners, a subject on which Sylvia came out rather strong as Mr. Halliday had had one of the first in that part of the county. Martin, suspecting that Anne felt a little out of it, asked her about the Sale of Work at the Palace and was amused by her comments.

"I hope you'll enjoy Rushwater," he said. "It's a bit dull now, but I'm very fond of it. When I was away in Africa and Italy I used to think of it on a day like this; all hot and comfortable."

"It has a kind of feeling of going on forever," said Anne sympathetically.

"Like the brook," said Martin, thinking how the level sunlight suited Sylvia's golden beauty.

"More like the land where it was always afternoon," said Anne, half to herself because she was not sure if Martin liked Tennyson or would think she was talking rubbish. But Martin apparently had not heard, so Anne sat quite happily thinking about poetry, because one simply could not help thinking of poetry at Rushwater; and Sylvia and Emmy continued their conversation about potato spinners.

Siddon came out onto the terrace.

"It's Mr. David on the telephone, Mr. Martin," she said.

Martin got up, stretched his long legs and went into the house. Emmy and Sylvia drifted from the potato spinner to the prospect of a few partridges later on and the trouble the foxes gave without a proper hunt, and Anne went on feeling that she belonged to a lower civilisation. But she felt this quite comfortably and without shame, for after all life was very pleasant in Barchester and in the Close, and it would not always be afternoon or summer at Rushwater.

"What did Uncle David want?" said Emmy when Martin came back.

"Only to say Rose is back," said Martin. "The F.O. have

transferred her to London and they will be dispensing with her services soon. But she is keeping her flat in Paris. David is bringing her over on Sunday."

"Good old Rose," said Emmy, "I haven't seen her for ages. I expect she's had a marvellous time abroad. She may be in time to see the Jersey calve."

"Do have a little sense of fitness, Emmy," said Martin. "Rose doesn't know a bull from a cow. But it's always amusing when she comes. John's boys are coming this Sunday, aren't they?"

Emmy said they were.

"Then I'll ask Robin Dale to come with them," said Martin, looking kindly at Anne. "I'll ring up the school now."

He got up again and went, with his slight limp, into the house.

"It's a shame Martin has to limp like that," said Sylvia to Emmy. "Can't they do anything?"

"They haven't yet," said Emmy. "But Rose said she knew a wonderful man in Lisbon who had cured lots of people that got stiff legs and things in the war. I must ask her about him again. I could run Rushwater quite well for a month or six weeks in the autumn with Macpherson. And you could come over and help me."

Sylvia said she would love to.

Anne again felt out of it. Also slightly confused, because she wondered who Rose was. It could hardly be Rose Fairweather; yet Rose had been in Lisbon and this man who cured people with stiff legs and things was in Lisbon.

"I expect Rose has brought some marvellous clothes from Paris," said Emmy, continuing her artless prattle. "Not that I'd be seen dead in them," she continued, looking with some complacence at her own serviceable legs in corduroy breeches, green woolen stockings and stout shoes.

"That's all right," said Martin, coming back and sitting down by Anne. "Your friend Robin will come. You'll like Rose. She was here for my seventeenth birthday party. She is great fun."

"I am so sorry," said Anne desperately, "but please, who is Rose?"

"How stupid of me," said Martin. "My cousin Rose Bingham. She has been abroad most of the war, Paris and Cairo and Lisbon and Washington and everywhere."

Anne now knew the worst. The horrible Rose Bingham who was as funny as hell all the time was coming. David was bringing her. He would probably marry her out of hand at Rushmere church, bringing a special licence with him, and whisk her away in a very expensive private aeroplane to Paris, or Lisbon, or one of those places that other people went to. A doubt then assailed her as to whether Sunday was a day on which one could be legally married; but she put it angrily away, desiring to savour the bitterness of despair to the utmost. There was no one to whom she could unbosom herself. Martin was the horrible Rose's cousin. Sylvia might have sympathised, but Sylvia was deep in winter feeding with Emmy.

She suddenly felt that everything was useless, and so far forgot Miss Bunting's training as to give up any effort at conversation. Martin, thinking that Anne was probably tired, hitched his chair nearer to Sylvia's and was soon deep in oil-cake and straw. Anne, miserably realising that she was a social failure, got up and walked slowly away. No one noticed her absence. In solitary misery she walked down the garden to where a terrace was built above the Rushmere Brook, a gazebo at each end. Here, had she but known it, David Leslie had given a perfunctory and most unromantic kiss to Mary Preston, now the mother of Leslie major and minor, on the night of Martin's seventeenth birthday dance. And had she but known it, David had been kissing people up and down town, off and on, for more years than her whole age; though even had she known it her feelings for David would have been unaffected, for David was just David. She then cried a little from sheer self-pity, which gave her rather a grown-up and romantic feeling, and then, a slight breeze having sprung up, she returned to the more sheltered terrace where no one had noticed that she had been away.

Emmy, who had not much use for the finer shades of politeness, yawned got up and shook herself, and said she was going to bed. The rest of the party followed her and Anne very much enjoyed talking to Sylvia through the communicating door, like young ladies in novels, and quite forgot that she meant to be unhappy.

The weather, by some unaccountable oversight, remained hot and still. Day after day the elms and oaks looked darker and heavier against the dark cloudless blue sky. The roses were buds at daybreak, shameless flaunting blooms by mid-day, scented carpets upon the earth by nightfall. Nature so far forgot herself as to provide warmth, unending strawberries and peas and young beans. All was golden sunshine, life, a piercing sweetness. The only tarnish on Anne's happiness was the thought that at the end of the week Sunday would come, and with it the horrible Rose Bingham. But she did her best to forget that separator of companions and terminator of delights.

It was not Martin's fault that Anne was a good deal alone. Nor was it Sylvia's or Emmy's fault, for though they were both extremely well disposed towards her, the affairs of farm and dairy kept them busy throughout the long day, and by the evening they were all pleasantly fatigued; and also pleasantly disposed to discuss at great length what they had been doing during the day and what they meant to do on the morrow. Luckily for Anne, Mr. Macpherson took a fancy to her and she accompanied him on a good many of his estate activities, listening to his talk, or sitting quite happily in the car while he went into farms or cottages. And sometimes they climbed the hills behind the house together, where Mr. Macpherson noted what trees would have to be felled and where the new planting was to be done. From him Anne learnt a good deal about the Leslie family: what a pity it was that Martin's father had been killed, how well Martin was taking over the responsibility for the place,

how proud old Mr. Leslie had been of his prize bulls and his
first-class milkers and how Martin was nearly as good a judge of
cattle as his grandfather had been: how fond he was of Mrs. John
Leslie, the mother of Robin's pupils, how he hoped to finish his
life in the place to which most of it had been devoted.

"But I thought you wanted to lay your bones in Scotland, Mr.
Macpherson," said Anne, parodying, we fear, the old agent's
favourite theme.

"To tell you the truth, Miss Anne," said Mr. Macpherson,
who stuck to his pleasant old-fashioned way of addressing
young ladies, "I have no very particular feeling about my bones
one way or the other. But I would like to die here, and I should
preferrr," said the old agent, whose voice became more Scotch
when his feelings were stirred, "to die when the hay is in, and the
corn cut and thrashed and stacked, and the winter feed earthed
up, and Mrs. Siddon has bottled all the fruit and vegetables and
made all the jam. I could fold my hands and go then," said Mr.
Macpherson, who was quite obviously thinking of what would
have to be done next.

"But you can't die this year," said Anne seriously. "There's the
planting to be done on Hangman's Hill and the new roof for the
potting-shed, and you know you said the Rushmere Brook
needed cleaning out, down by the keeper's cottage."

"You are maybe right, Miss Anne," said Mr. Macpherson.
"But there's one thing I fear I shan't see, though I'd much like to
see it, and that is David settled. He's a grand lad and I am as fond
of him as if he were my own son, but he has had all the rope he
needs; forbye his hair is beginning to get a bit thin on top," said
Mr. Macpherson meditatively.

To Anne this comment was so dreadful, so soul-racking, that
she nearly got out of the car and went home. But as they were
now slowly climbing Hangman's Hill by a track never meant for
cars, the machinery was making such a noise, not to speak of the
view getting more beautiful every moment, that she found it
better to say nothing and stay where she was.

The little car, expressing at every step its unwillingness to go any further, at last stopped, panting, on the top of Hangman's Hill, the most considerable eminence in those parts. Before 1914 there would have been no view, so thickly was it wooded, but during the last war most of the timber had been felled and replaced by quick-growing conifers which were as quickly removed when they reached the point at which they were worth selling. Anyone who had known Hangman's Hill forty years earlier would have experienced a severe shock on finding the beeches and the thorns replaced by larch and fir, the tall ones in regimental lines, the small ones rather squashed together in nurseries waiting to be planted out. And such an observer would have lamented the romantic gloom which even at mid-day overspread the hill, and might have gone so far as to quote from Cowper's threnody on poplars and make an allusion to the Woods of Westermain: which would have given him the utmost pleasure and done no harm to anybody. But that same observer, if the intelligent and well-educated man we take him to be, could not, even in the middle of his grief, have failed to notice the exquisite prospect now opened to his view in more than one direction, nor the skilful way in which Mr. Macpherson had disposed long open rides among his conifers, each with a different enchantment to the view. To the north the downs rolled away, one green humped bulk behind another where sheep-bells rang. To the east and southeast were glimpses of the arable land, now turning golden. To the west and south-west lay the green water-meadows bordering the River Rising, then the roofs and towers of Barchester, crowned by its soaring steeple; then low downs intersected by valleys of streams of rivers and on the farthest horizon in a glimmer of golden mist, the real hills, well beyond the county but a part of its landscape.

"Oh, Mr. Macpherson," was all Anne could say; but this comment, inadequate though it may appear, entirely satisfied the old agent.

"And well you may say so, Miss Anne," he said. "I cannot

truthfully say that I am responsible for the landscape, but I sometimes feel that we have understood each other, and that a part of my work here will go on when I am dead."

This struck Anne as so fitting to the time, the place, the season, that she felt a delightful sense of romantic melancholy, of looking on happy autumn fields and thinking of days that were no more, and she could have cried with the greatest pleasure, but Mr. Macpherson said it was high time they were getting back for tea. So they remounted the little car, which, chattering with rage, pursued its homeward path down the track heavily scored by timber waggons, and did not stop complaining till they got onto the farm road again.

The plan for the afternoon was that Anne should go back with Mr. Macpherson for tea and that Emmy, Martin and Sylvia should join them there. Mr. Macpherson's house was exactly what we should all like, with none of the drawbacks. It was a small Regency house partaking slightly of the cottage orné in that it had very improbable stucco battlements and a small church porch. It was painted cream and its small but elegant verandah on the south side was green. To the north it was sheltered by rising ground and a belt of well-groomed trees. Before the verandah a lawn sloped down to the Rushmere Brook. There was a mild rose-garden, a very good little walled fruit and vegetable garden, and no kind of provision whatsoever for playing any kind of game.

"Oh!" said Anne as they drew up before the elegant little iron gate in the fence. "Oh! Mr. Macpherson!"

Pleased by her admiration the agent offered to show her his house. It consisted of a wide hall, a drawing-room which looked out onto the verandah and had a tiny conservatory communicating with it at the further end, a dining-room, and a room where Mr. Macpherson kept his pipes, such papers as he did not keep in the Estate Office and complete files of the *Scotsman* and the *Stock Breeders' Gazette*. Upstairs there were three bedrooms and a surprisingly modern bathroom.

"That," said Mr. Macpherson, when he had displayed its glories to Anne and taken her out to sit on the verandah, "was a present to me from Mr. Leslie on my sixtieth birthday. He said, in worrds I am prroud to rrrepeat," said Mr. Macpherson, letting his feelings and his Scotch tongue get the upper hand of him for a moment, "that I had given good service to his father and to himself, and if I felt like marrying when I retired I ought to have a nice bathroom for the future Mrs. Macpherson. That, you will understand," he said, looking firmly at Anne, "was just by way of a joke, for I never yet saw the woman I'd have married."

Anne said that was a great pity.

"I couldn't exactly say," said Mr. Macpherson cautiously. "There are points about marriage, but had I married I might have left a widow, and I may tell you, Miss Anne, that an agent's widow can be a sore trial and expense to an estate. No; when I die this house will be free and Martin can give it to anyone he thinks suitable. Only one thing I have said to him about it. The new agent—and I doubt if he will be able to afford one for some time—must live in one of those new houses in the village. This house is too good for the agent. Now, if Martin marries, Emmy might like to live here for a time, for she will never be happy away from Rushwater. I would like to see Martin married. The lad is too much alone and though Emmy is a fine girl, she is a harum-scarum creature. He needs a wife who will look after him with that leg of his. Ah well."

At this moment, to the intense joy and excitement of Anne the town-child, Emmy in a pony-cart and Martin and Sylvia on horses came up to the side gate where an elderly kind of groom-factotum took their horses and led them away.

An elderly woman then brought tea onto the verandah and Mr. Macpherson asked Emmy to preside, which she did with something less than her mother's grace, but with great hospitality and goodwill.

"I say, Mr. Macpherson," said Emmy, "I think the Jersey is

going to calve by tomorrow night. I'm going to sit up to-morrow anyway. So's Sylvia."

"Sylvia certainly mustn't," said Martin. "I am responsible for the cow. Emmy can help if she wants to. And old Herdman will be there. He hasn't missed a calf since he came here as a boy in the year of Queen Victoria's first Jubilee."

Mr. Macpherson said Herdman was bad with his lumbago again, so Mrs. Herdman had told him that morning.

"He'll turn up all right if he's wanted," said Martin. "He has a theory that if a man—by which he means himself—spent all his life in the cowshed and didn't have to go home and find the misses had been washing the kitchen floor, making a man get the perishing colic in his innards, he'd never have nothing wrong with him. He may be right, I haven't tried it."

"Mrs. Herdman is *dreadfully* clean," said Emmy. "Her kitchen is always swimming in soapsuds when I go there. You know that cottage is a disgrace, Martin."

"I know it is," said Martin ruefully. "I wish to goodness I could build a few better ones, but I can't get permission to do anything, let alone the labour."

"Never mind," said Emmy. "Perhaps we'll have better luck with the new Government. The Conservatives are bound to come in again, even if it isn't such a big majority, and then they'll have to pay some attention to housing and things."

"Do you think a Conservative Government will come in?" asked Anne.

"Of course," said Emmy and Sylvia in one breath.

Martin looked sad and said nothing.

"If you ask my opinion," said Mr. Macpherson, "Gresham will get in for East Barsetshire; but I wouldn't bet on it and I wouldn't bet on any constituency except Mr. Churchill's and perhaps South Kensington. It's going to be a landslide as it was in 1906. None of you remember that. Stalybridge was the first sign of how the current was flowing against us, and then all the dykes went down. We'll see it again. What does Sir Robert think, Miss Anne?"

Anne, feeling a little frightened at being suddenly appealed to about politics, said that Daddy had said it would be a hard fight, but that Mr. Adams would be a clean fighter, whatever his supporters might be.

"Sir Robert is right," said Martin. "I've had to meet Adams on some county matters and I have rather a respect for him. He has the courage of his opinions too. He addressed a large meeting at the Barchester Mechanics' Institute and told them that if Barchester returned him he wouldn't vote for a single measure that gave the working classes something for nothing. He then said he had always been a working man himself and had paid his way wherever he went, and he didn't want to be taxed to help a lot of unmentionables to get everything free. Then he said he wasn't going to vote for sending our food abroad, or for lending money to Mixo-Lydia, or broadly speaking for anything."

"What happened?" said Anne.

"I thought there was going to be a free fight," said Martin, "and having been trained to fight under Army Regulations I didn't much like the look of it. But a lot of his men from the ironworks were there and they sang *Annie Laurie* in parts at the top of their voices and then *God Save the King*, so we all got home without having our heads broken. Adams told me he was very proud of the Works Choral Society."

"I expect he will win," said Anne. "Daddy thinks a lot of the same things that Mr. Adams does, but he can't say them so well. I mean daddy can't help talking like himself. I mean I can't quite explain," she finished lamely.

"I know," said Emmy, who had been listening with an interest she rarely showed for anything outside the cow world, her capable hands outspread on her corduroyed knees, "Sir Robert and Mr. Adams say the same things, but Sir Robert says them in a gentleman's voice and Mr. Adams doesn't, so Mr. Adams will get in."

"And that's the humour of it," said Martin, and Anne cast an appreciative glance at him, which he received with pleasure.

"Well, anyway, we'll know soon," said Emmy getting up. "Come on, Anne, I'll drive you home. I brought the pony-cart on purpose because I thought you'd be tired."

The equipages were brought round. Sylvia and Martin mounted their horses and rode away. Anne thanked Mr. Macpherson for her happy afternoon and got into the pony-trap. Mr. Macpherson stood at his gate to see the cavalcade depart. Much as he liked Anne, it was the riders whom he followed with his eyes, and as he went back into the house he thought that perhaps one of his dearest wishes might be fulfilled and he could hand over his life's work with a conviction that it would be continued by a generation he might not live to see.

"Would you like to drive?" said Emmy to Anne.

Anne said she would love it if the pony didn't mind.

Emmy said old Bramble never minded anything, the reins were put into Anne's hands and old Bramble, who knew his own mind and never paid the faintest attention to anyone who rode or drove him, went off at the brisk cheerful trot that he reserved for going home.

"I hope she won't calve tomorrow morning," said Emmy after a short silence.

Anne, rather thoughtlessly, asked why.

"Church," said Emmy briefly. "Of course it *would* be a Sunday the day she chose to calve. I know what I'll do. If she's all right tonight I'll go to early service and then I'll be ready if anything happens. I don't want to have to go out in the middle of morning service, because Mr. Bostock hasn't been here long and he comes from a potato country where there isn't much dairy-farming, so he wouldn't understand. Mr. Banister that used to be here understood cows properly and so did Bishop Joram. I'll have to get the new vicar a bit cow-minded."

Anne had not realised that her parents' friends, Canon Banister and Bishop Joram, used to be vicars of Rushwater and this made an interesting subject for conversation between herself and Emmy, who had a plan for taking the vicar round the cowsheds every Sunday after morning church, even if it meant keeping him to lunch, so that cow-mindedness might gradually sink into his being.

"And if she doesn't calve tomorrow morning, I hope to goodness she'll leave it alone till the evening," Emmy continued, "because David and Rose are coming, oh and your friend Robin and the boys, and I don't want to miss Rose. She's quite uneducated about cows, but she's awfully amusing. Do you know her?"

Anne, whose inner mind was suddenly like a green plum-pudding with spikes of yellow and purple coming out of it, said she didn't.

"Could you explain who she is?" she added. "Everyone says Rose, but I don't know if she is Mrs. or Miss or what."

"She's our cousin of course," said Emmy. "At least mother's cousin though I think it's a kind of second cousin. Her mother is a kind of cousin of Gran's."

"Who is her mother?" asked Anne desperately.

"Aunt Dorothy," said Emmy, at the same time giving a tug to the right-hand rein. "Don't be an idiot, Bramble. Stable-yard, not front door."

Bramble tossed his head as one who scorned his employers but was willing to humour them, trotted into the stable-yard and stood still with such violence that he nearly knocked their front teeth out against the bar the reins go over.

In the dark kitchen-passage Anne met Siddon, the house-keeper.

"Dinner's not till eight, miss," she said, "because Mr. Martin has to go to a Parish meeting and Miss Halliday is going with him. He had forgotten to mention it, miss, so he rang up. I expect you'll be glad to have a rest before dinner, miss."

"I'm really not tired, thank you," said Anne. "But if you aren't too busy, Mrs. Siddon, may I see your room? I've never seen a proper housekeeper's room."

These artless words gave a grim pleasure to Siddon, who then took Anne along another dark passage, expatiating as they went upon the number of beetles and cockroaches that used to live there in the good old days.

"Mr. David and Mr. Martin used to have beetlehunts at night, miss," said Siddon pausing, "when the servants had all gone to bed, and I can tell you, miss, I was one to be particular about that, and so was Mr. Gudgeon, that was our butler then but he lives with his sister now at Bovey Tracey, the young gentleman used to come down in their shooting boots and turn on the lights all of a sudden, and the passages were like—well, like the sea at Margate only black, miss, if you take my meaning. And the young gentlemen used to trample on them, really quite unpleasant I should have thought, and they'd lift this matting, this very coconut matting we're standing on now, miss, and sweep all the beetles out with housemaids' brooms, and walk on them too. And then they'd go and have a glass of beer with Gudgeon in his pantry."

"But what happened to the dead beetles?" said Anne.

"I couldn't say, miss. They was all swept up before I came down in the morning, that's all I can say, because someone would have heard about it if they hadn't been. Excuse me, miss."

She passed in front of Anne, opened a door and stood aside for Anne to pass.

The housekeeper's room was long, with a window at one end looking upon the stable-yard and a large bow window at the side commanding an uninteresting shrubbery. A large table spoke silently of stately lunches and suppers when Rushmere House was full of visitors with valets and maids. Photographs of Lesllies of all generations hung on the walls, from old Mr. Leslie as a young man in a Norfolk jacket and breeches and gaiters to Edith attendng a meet of the Rising Otterhounds in her perambulator. Anne admired them heartily.

"I'd like to show you my special album, miss, if you have the time," said Siddon, who had taken a fancy to that quiet little Miss Fielding with such nice manners. "It's the one I keep for the Family Groups."

From the top of a cupboard she took a gigantic album bound in purple plush with open-work brass hinges, and laid it on the table. "Will you sit down, miss?" she said. "You'll see it better. And I'll sit down too, if you will excuse me, miss, for I'm not as young as I was. Now, here we begin with the photo of the staff soon after I first came, on the occasion of young Mr. Leslie's marriage, that is, Mr. Martin's father that was, who was killed in the last war. You wouldn't know that for me, I daresay."

Anne had to admit that she would not have recognised in the round-faced, stiff-collared, long-skirted, heavily be-aproned young woman with coils of dark hair, the thin, imposing housekeeper who was beside her.

"I'd defy anyone to know it was me, miss," said Siddon rather proudly. "I've lost a lot of flesh since those days. My family were terrible ones for losing flesh. Mother was a fine, stout young woman, but at the end she was no more than a bag of bones. Now, here's the Family on the terrace the day the Prince of Wales, that is King Edward the Seventh that was, came to shoot."

And she continued to turn over the pages while Anne, not knowing most of the guests or celebrities, amused herself by picking out David at every stage, from a kind of picture frock and Gainsborough hat onwards, noticing that he always looked different from everyone else: as, thank heaven, most of us do, or life would be even more difficult than it is.

"Here's one you'll like, miss," said Siddon. "Mr. Martin's seventeenth birthday party. That was the year Mr. John became engaged to Miss Preston, a very nice young lady. You know their two young gentlemen at Southbridge School, miss, don't you?"

Anne said she did, and thought how very nice David looked.

"And there's her ladyship," said Mrs. Siddon. "She always photographed beautifully. And Mr. Leslie, and Mr. David with Miss Rose and Miss Hermione. We did think, miss, there might be something between Mr. David and Miss Rose, but you never can tell with these things."

Anne, a sudden sick pain for which she could not at once account gripping her stomach, asked who Miss Rose was exactly.

"Lady Dorothy's twin daughter, miss," said Siddon. "Miss Hermione married Lord Tadpole just before this war and they have what I am given to understand is a very nice place, Tadpole Hall, near Tadcaster. But Miss Rose hasn't married as yet, though they do say she had several very good offers. Such a nice young lady and always a cheerful word for everyone. And dresses so nicely. Her maid used to say it was a pleasure to look after a young lady that did her so much credit as Miss Rose.

Anne listened politely. Her outer self heard what Siddon was saying; it also looked at the photographs and could not but admit that Rose Bingham, even in the fashions of those days, was an extremely good-looking girl and worthy to be photographed next to David. As for her inner self, it was behaving so badly that she pretended it was not there.

"I'm so sorry, Mrs. Siddon," she said, as the housekeeper turned to the next page, "but would you explain who the Binghams are. You see, I don't really know the Leslies very well, at least I hardly knew them at all till I came here that Sunday, but Miss Bunting used to talk about them."

If Anne had hoped to improve her position by mentioning Miss Bunting she was mistaken, for the housekeeper had the natural contempt of the staff for any governess that happened to be about, looking upon them as necessary drawbacks of life. But she understood and approved Miss Fielding's interest in family ramifications and hastened to make them clear.

"You'll remember the Duke of Towers, miss," she said. "Lady Dorothy was his second daughter. There were no sons, which was a great mistake, and the title went to a nephew. The duchess was a Miss Foster, a cousin of Lord Pomfret, who was Lady Emily's father, so Lady Dorothy and her ladyship were cousins, and Miss Rose and Miss Hermione, who were as like as two peas except that Miss Rose is dark and Miss Hermione is fair, were quite part of the family. I hear that Miss Rose has done wonders in the war, being in the Foreign Office. You'll like her, miss."

Anne knew that she would hate her. And with this agreeable thought in mind found it extremely difficult to look at the photographs with the interest that politeness demands. Mrs. Siddon noticed that she was flagging and attributed it to fatigue.

"There, I've been keeping you too long, miss," she said. "You're tired out and no wonder. Mr. Macpherson and Miss Emmy don't know what it is to be tired and they don't expect anyone else to feel different. Now you go and have a nice bath, miss, and lie down before dinner and you'll feel quite yourself again."

So Anne went upstairs, had a bath, and curled up on the chaise-longue at the foot of her bed with the first volume of *A Step Too Far*, the novel written by Lady Emily's mother which had shocked Mr. Gladstone, and looked at the sunlight upon the cedars and the great tulip tree beyond the terrace, and her thoughts became more confused and less bitter till she slid into a gentle sleep, from which she was roused by Sylvia coming in at ten minutes to eight looking so handsome, so tanned, so golden, so glowing, that Anne felt here at least the horrible Rose Bingham would meet her match.

"I've got to change," said Sylvia. "I'm so hot in these breeches," saying which she flung everything onto the floor of her room, splashed rapidly in and out of the bath, combed her hair vehemently, shook herself into a chintz house-frock and said she was ready.

Martin and Emmy had also got into a kind of semi-evening attire, and Martin had routed a bottle of white wine out of the cellar. The talk at dinner was still mostly about cows, though Martin firmly suppressed his cousin Emmy's desire to discuss the less interesting technicalities of contagious abortion; and though Anne could not feel really at home in it, the fragrant wine made her very tolerant. After dinner they sat as usual on the terrace. Moonlight mixing with twilight; warmth, scent, drowsiness. All Anne's anxieties were lulled, as the ceaseless tides of cow talk lapped idly

above her head, varied occasionally by an allusion to the meeting
Martin and Sylvia had been to, and some very pertinent suggestions from Sylvia, to which Martin listened with interest.

So, thought Anne, life should always be. Warm, peaceful, cow-
minded. Only it would be nice, said her inner self, to have someone
to talk to about books and poetry; also someone who really understood what one was saying without one's having to explain it.
Someone like Robin. In fact, if Robin were here it would be
perfect. And tomorrow he would be coming. And if that horrible
Rose Bingham were coming too, she would want to see Martin and
Emmy, and one would perhaps have a walk with David. Various
passages from her favourite poet, Lord Tennyson, floated through
her mind, all enlarging upon the beauty of an English summer; the
hay, the corn, the trees, the warm air, the flowers, the exquisite
peacefulness of high summer, its transiency. In fact an idyllic life,
whatever idyllic might mean. The talk went on in the long twilight
lit by the moon, no breath stirred, it was the magic hour; and in it
Anne knew that no other life was possible—if only David were
there, and of course always Robin.

"I'm sorry, Mr. Martin," said a voice behind him, "but that
Daisy's broken through the fence again and got into the vegetable
garden. That great danged fool, sorry ladies I'm sure, Ted Poulter
didn't shut the kitchen-garden gate properly and he's gone off to
Barchester on his bike, so I thought I'd better tell you, sir."

"Oh, all right," said Martin, getting up. "You get a couple of
sticks, Brown, and I'll come along. And may heaven blast Ted,"
he added in a gentle voice. "I'll be back soon."

"Ted will have to marry," said Emmy, "then he wouldn't be
out at all hours like this. I'll speak to his mother about it. He's
been walking out with Lily Brown quite long enough."

"What about a cottage?" said Sylvia, who seemed to know all
about the Poulter and Brown families.

"Oh, that's all right," said Emmy. "Old Brown died last
November and Mrs. Brown always said she'd go to her sister at

Rushwater Parva if Lily married. Of course she won't want to when it really happens, but I'll see that she does."

Of this dragooning method Sylvia highly approved, adducing the sad example of Mrs. Hubback at The Shop, who still had a bed-ridden and distinctly half-witted mother in the best double-bed upstairs, although she was a grandmother herself. Cows, said Emmy, embarking upon an entirely new subject, had more sense. No one ever heard of a grandmother cow living with its old mother, at any rate not in the same stall. Which led, not unnaturally, to an exposition of the gravid Jersey's pedigree, about which Sylvia seemed to be almost as well informed as Emmy.

"How *do* you know all that?" said Anne admiringly.

Sylvia said you could always know things if they were interesting enough. She knew radio-location all right because it was interesting, and she remembered the cow's pedigree because it was even more interesting than radio-location. And crops were awfully interesting, too, and fertilisers and tractors and things like bottling vegetables and laying down eggs and winter feed for the stock. In fact her list of things to be interested in might have gone on for ever, if a very frightened little girl in a faded pink cotton frock had not approached the terrace with a kind of desperate courage.

"Please, Miss Emmy," said the little girl, and then stopped, obviously about to burst into tears.

"Hullo, Aggie," said Emmy. "Come along and tell me what's the matter and stop crying. She's called Agnes after mother," she added to her guests. "Nearly all the cottages have one of our names and it gets a bit confusing. They always ask Martin first if they may. There's a Martina at the post-office, she's five, and a Davida and a Davidette at Hacker's Corner, they're twins. Well, Aggie, what is it?"

"Please, Miss Emmy," said Aggie, rubbing her face on her sleeve, "mum said to come up and tell you, miss, because there's been an awful accident."

Anne could see the light of First-Aid Lust burn in her friends' eyes and felt very incompetent and hoped earnestly that she would not have to hear the details.

"It's DREADFUL, miss," said Aggie, beginning to cheer up as she unfolded her tidings of dismay. "All the blood and all, and mum said please would you come quick, miss, because she can't abear to see blood. Nor can I, miss," said Aggie proudly.

"Well, where is the accident?" said Emmy, with a coolness that Anne much admired.

"Please miss, down our garden," said Aggie. "It was a big stone dad put on the top of the coop to keep it down in the wind and when mum was moving the coop it fell right down on her, miss, and she was shrieking dreadful and mum can't abear to touch anything, that's in pain, miss, so she said to come up and tell you."

Emmy stood up.

"Now who did the stone fall on?" she said. "And hurry up. There are three younger than Aggie, though I can't think how her mother managed it even if one is an illegitimate child of a sergeant at Brandon Abbas," said Emmy in a rapid parenthesis to her two friends.

"The broody, miss," said Aggie, beginning to cry again. "Mum only let her out just to have a little run like and the stone fell on her and her inside looks all nasty. I couldn't touch it, miss, not if you was to ask me, nor couldn't mum."

"Sacré tas d'imbéciles," said Emmy, whose French, owing to long conversations with her grandmother's maid Conque was very fluent if not academic. "All right, Aggie. I'll be down in a moment. Run and tell mother. Lord!" she continued, as the tear-stained Aggie sped homewards, "those women are fools. First they put a large stone on the broody-coop because they are too lazy to nail a few boards on. Then they try to move the coop with the stone on the roof, and then they haven't the sense to wring the hen's neck when it falls on her, or even cut off her head with the chopper. They're the ones that are going to put in a Labour Government. I shan't be long."

Emmy went away and was seen a moment later bicycling to the village with a face that boded no good to Aggie's mother.

"She's a stupid woman," said Sylvia. "Oh, bother; the midges are biting my legs. She's as near half-witted as possible and her husband is, too. He's labourer and one of the best hedge-layers in the country."

Anne, much impressed by Sylvia's knowledge of these details, asked her how she knew.

"Oh, I don't know," said Sylvia. "One just does know. After all, father has farmed all his life and it's much the same here, only bigger. But Martin's a much better farmer than father. I don't mean only being more up-to-date and being better off, but—well, I can't explain it, but he simply *is* a farmer and all the things that go with it."

Anne could not quite understand this explanation, nor perhaps could Sylvia, but it sufficed. The long daylight was at last fading, the midges became more persistent. The two girls sat silent, their thoughts running over their happy visit to Rushwater and the amusements of the morrow and the visitors that were coming.

"It's awfully nice that David is coming tomorrow," said Sylvia. "He said he'd show me the inside of the Temple, where he and Lady Graham used to play when they were small."

If so wicked a passion as jealousy could have lodged in Anne's very kind heart, now was the moment. But being a humble creature, who realised her friend's beauty and her forthcoming-ness, she only said how nice that would be and tried hard to feel it. Lines from her favourite poet, Lord Tennyson, floated into her mind. "We were two sisters of one race, She was the fairer in the face," she said aloud to herself, if we make ourselves clear. Not that she and Sylvia were sisters or in any way connected, but it somehow seemed fitting. And if David did fall in love with Sylvia and Sylvia died, it would be rather nice to marry David and then stab him three times through and through, though she did not propose to go so far as to wrap him in his winding-sheet and lay him at Lady Emily's feet. But some kind of revenge on one who was base enough to be nice to Sylvia and herself while toying with the horrible Rose Bingham, was clearly indicated. If only Robin were there, he would understand.

Through the dusk Mrs. Siddon approached.

"I am very sorry to inconvenience you, Miss Halliday," she said, "but that stupid girl Diana dropped a pot of tea just freshly made on her foot, and she's screaming the kitchen down. I've done what I could, miss, and rung up the doctor, but he's out. Could you kindly come and have a look? I've got Miss Emily's first-aid cupboard in my room."

Sylvia rose with joyful alacrity and went hurriedly into the house with Mrs. Siddon. Anne was left alone on the terrace in the gathering dusk, her legs severely assailed by midges, her mind assailed with almost equal gravity by sad reflections on her complete uselessness. A cow broke a fence and got into the kitchen garden; Martin was fetched. A hen was mangled by a large stone falling on it; Emmy was sent for. A servant dropped a tea-pot on her foot; Sylvia was summoned. Looking at things dispassionately, Anne could not imagine a single thing in which she would be of any use. If Robin were there she could put this distressing moral problem before him and he would understand, sympathise and comfort. But Robin was not there. She was also alone with several millions of midges. So far they had only attacked her legs, but she feared that if she lingered outside they might attack her face and make her all blotchy next day, so she went disconsolately into the morning-room and sat down in a large chair, not daring to turn on a light and read, for the curtains were not drawn and midges would come rushing in to the light, and she was afraid of offending Bertha if she drew the curtains herself.

Eternity passed. When it had been going on for about ten minutes, Martin came into the room, turned on the lights, and seeing Anne, naturally asked why she was sitting in the dark. Anne said she was afraid the midges would come in. Martin laughed, quite kindly, drew the heavy curtains and sat down.

"Did you catch the cow?" said Anne.

"Oh, we got her almost at once," said Martin, "and before she'd done too much damage. But I had to go over to Hacker's Corner. There's an old man there who is dying, at least he has been dying to my certain knowledge for fifteen months, but he doesn't seem to get on with the job. And whenever he feels a bit dull he sends for me to receive his last breath. He was head cowman here in my grandfather's time and one has to do something about it, but he is a plaguery nuisance. And what's more, he doesn't even know who I am. He always calls me Master Henry because that's what the men used to call my grandfather while his father was still alive. Well, well. Where's everybody and why are you alone?"

Anne explained that Emmy had been sent for to kill a maimed hen and how Siddon had fetched Sylvia to attend to the kitchen-maid's foot.

"Kitchen-maids aren't usually called Diana, are they?" said Anne. "Is it one of your family's name?"

"Oh, that girl. It isn't Diana, it's Deanna—after the film star. Well, Sylvia, how is your patient?"

Sylvia, who had come in while he was speaking, said the burn wasn't bad and the girl ought to be quite fit for work in a day or two and could get about on Sunday if she rested her foot as much as possible. She then sat down and began to look at *Country Life*. Martin at the same moment took up the *Times*, which he had not yet had time to look at, and a thought flashed into Anne's mind of how like a married couple they were; like mummy and daddy at home, reading or writing quietly, in the enjoyment of one another's company. But this domestic scene did not last long. Emmy came clumping in to announce that she had wrung the hen's neck, plucked her and hung her up by the legs, and there was no reason why her owners shouldn't eat her, though she would take a lot of boiling.

"Isn't it very difficult to pluck a hen?" Anne asked.

Emmy, picking up a library book, said not if you did it while they were warm. If you left it till they were cold the best way was to plunge them into boiling water and the feathers came off like onion skins. She then enquired briefly about the cow, said Deanna was a fool and wouldn't wear her glasses and she would speak to her, and relapsed into desultory reading. But she yawned so much and so uncontrollably that her cousin Martin sent her to bed, which seemed to Sylvia and Anne a good moment to go to bed themselves."

"I'll lock up. Good-night," said Martin to the three girls.

"Aren't you coming up?" said Emmy between her yawns.

Martin said not yet. The cow and old Herdman had taken too much of his time and he must do some work in the Estate Office, as Sunday would be a busy day.

"Wake me if the Jersey calves," said Emmy, from the depths of a final, jaw-rending yawn.

"She won't," said Martin. "Get along to bed."

Sylvia was soon asleep. Anne, next door, lay awake for some time, considering the peace and quiet of country life. To her town-bred mind it was almost terrifying. Beauty, trees, water, hills, sun, scents, all conspired to make a haunt of ancient peace. Then parish meetings, cows, hens, kitchen-maids, old men at Hacker's Corner, all came tumbling in with ceaseless demands on the judgment, skill, patience, time of the landowners, upon whom every person and every animal and every piece of work on the place seemed to depend. How far more peaceful was life in the Close, even if one's parents were very busy people. How much more peaceful was life at Southbridge School, where everything had its appointed hour. It was all very interesting, very difficult to understand, and she thought gratefully that tomorrow she would be able to talk to Robin about it. And tomorrow David would come. And on David's name she slid into oblivion.

# CHAPTER 8

The Jersey did not calve that night. So all the people who had said they knew she was going to calve said they had really known all along that she wouldn't; which all came to much the same thing. Deanna's foot was doing nicely and she sat at the back door with her bandaged leg on a stool and shelled peas and beans and washed the new potatoes and did a great many other odd jobs for cook, who was her aunt and stood no nonsense. Word came up from the village via the cowman's lad that a new broody had been found to replace yesterday's victim. Word came over from Hacker's Corner to say that old Cruncher had drunk a quart of cider at eleven o'clock last night and said he'd cheat the sexton yet. No one was permanently disfigured by midges. Emmy went to early service and ate a very large breakfast afterwards to prepare herself for all emergencies. Martin, Sylvia and Anne went in a more trustful spirit to the eleven o'clock service, visited Mr. Leslie's grave and Miss Bunting's memorial tablet, and took the vicar to see Rushwater Romany, who was looking over the half-door of his house and wondering how a ring had got into his nose, and deciding that it was on the whole a mark of glory, given to him as tribute by his subjects, Martin and the cowman, and denied to the cows, who were only women.

The vicar, who though unused to cattle was almost too eager to learn, put out his hand to pat Rushwater Romany's forehead, but the bull tossed his head and then puffed violently through his nostrils, which made the vicar withdraw his intended caress. Martin and Sylvia, who were tolerant of human frailty, thought the vicar had had enough for the present, but Emmy, who had no use for shirkers, insisted on taking him round the cowsheds, so the others went onto the terrace to wait for the party from Holdings.

At about ten minutes to one a car was seen coming through the park. It drew up near the house and Lady Graham got out, followed by Clarissa. Then came David. He did not at once come to greet his relations, for he was helping a female figure to alight from the car; a figure who, Anne knew, must be the horrible Rose Bingham; a figure from whom she would have liked to avert her eyes in scorn, but whom curiosity compelled her to consider with breathless interest and anxiety. Another young man, whom Anne could not quite see, followed them.

"Darling Martin, how lovely this is," said Lady Graham. "And Sylvia and Anne, how lovely to see you both. Mother didn't come, Martin. She was a little tired, so I left her with Merry and brought Clarissa instead. And now I am longing to hear *all* about what you have been doing. And where is Emmy?"

Emmy then came round the corner of the house leading the vicar rather as if he were a bull who had only got a second prize, and seeing her mother, flung herself violently upon her.

"Darling Emmy," said Lady Graham, melting in the most loving way from her stalwart daughter's embrace. "And the vicar, too. I was so dreadfully sorry not to be able to come to *your* service, Mr. Bostock, but I simply *have* to go to the service at Hatch End or our vicar would be quite annoyed. Martin must tell me all about it. Was it a lovely sermon, Martin? I am sure it was."

The vicar, who had not been long at Rushwater and was not yet used to Lady Graham's incursions into religious matters and life in general, stammered dreadfully in his efforts to explain that one could but do one's best, but was too often but too sadly conscious that one was not giving of one's best; and then became so depressed about the way the words "too" and "but" and "best" seemed to have got the better of him that he became quite unintelligible and knew that Lady Graham would despise him forever.

Meanwhile the three other occupants of the car were slowly approaching and Sylvia with a yelp of pleasure recognised in the unknown young man her brother George.

"Hullo, George, I didn't know you were coming," she said.

"I wasn't," said George, "but I had to go to church with the parents and Lady Graham was there and she said would I like to come over with her and see you, so I said of course I would. It's just like her to think of a thing like that. Who's that she's talking to?"

This remark, accompanied by a baleful glance at the vicar, showed Sylvia that her brother was still romantically devoted to Lady Graham, so to make things easier she said it was no one; only the vicar, she added.

"What's his name?" said George, adding in a grudging way, "I suppose I'll have to call him something."

"George," said Lady Graham, "this is our vicar who gives us such wonderful services at Rushwater. And this is George," she added, turning to Mr. Bostock, "who was so kind and came with us because darling mother was so tired and we had a spare seat in the car because Clarissa doesn't take up much room. You must know George's people at Hatch House."

Having performed which highly inadequate introduction, she left them to dislike each other as much as one can dislike a man whose name one doesn't know and who is obviously on more friendly terms with a goddess than oneself. And now David was at Anne's side, saying, "Anne, you must know Rose. She is dying to meet you."

Flight was useless. Anne was not without courage. She held out her hand to the horrible Rose Bingham and said how do you do. She could not look her in the eyes, for Rose was tall, just the right height for David, Anne thought bitterly. She was elegant, her dark sleek hair was perfectly arranged, her eyebrows had a perfect arch, her dark eyes were luminous, her nose what one could only call, even if it sounded like a bad novel, aristocratic, her mouth an exquisite shape, her camellia complexion ravishing. Her figure was perfect, her stockings silk, her shoes just right. And just right were the linen coat and skirt she wore, the thin woollen lace jumper, the single string of pearls, the diamond clip. Anne suddenly felt like a cottage child and despair descended upon her soul, making her colour very prettily.

Rose extended a hand of exquisite softness with polished nails of a discreet pink suitable for a day in the country and said in a slightly husky voice which Anne, against her own will, could not but find very attractive, "How do you do. You are Anne Fielding, aren't you? David is mad about you. We must have a long talk about him."

"Oh—thank you," said Anne.

The whole universe was whirling about her. She had liked the feeling of Rose's hand; it felt strong and safe. She liked her voice, she admired her face, her figure, her clothes, everything about her. She felt that she was friendly, that this was a prelude to a new kind of grown-up-ness; that a talk from which David was to be excluded would be the most grown-up thing that had ever happened to her.

"How old are you?" said Rose.

Anne said nineteen.

"I wish I had looked as nice as you do when I was nineteen," said the horrible Rose Bingham. "David, do you remember how awful I looked at Martin's seventeener? Mother would make Hermione and me have our frocks from that awful Madame Tessé and we looked like plum-puddings. Martin dear, how nice to see you and Emmy again."

Martin introduced Sylvia.

"I want to have a talk with you about Eve Philpott," said Rose. "She was in the W.A.A.F.s with you, wasn't she? I hate that woman like hell. And talking of hell, what is the vicar's name? He's new here and I never can remember it."

Sylvia said it was Bostock.

"It couldn't be anything else," said Rose, lighting a cigarette with the most elegant and expensive lighter Anne had ever seen. "And George is your brother, isn't he? He is frightfully in love with Agnes. They all are. We must have a terrific talk about Philpott after lunch."

The gong, once the favourite instrument of the old butler Gudgeon, but now only used on ceremonial occasions, sounded from the hall and the whole party went in to lunch. Emmy had wanted to arrange the seating, but when Martin had pointed out that her mother, who was in many ways increasingly like Lady Emily, would insist on re-arranging it to suit her own taste, Emmy had recognised the justice of his criticism and given up her plan. The result was a huddle of guests near the door who showed considerable reluctance to choose seats for themselves; all but Lady Graham, who having seated herself said she must have darling Emmy on one side of her because she never saw her now and the vicar on the other, at which Mr. Bostock, giving George what that young officer thought to be a look of malicious triumph though it was really only short-sightedness, said that miracles did happen even nowadays. George said it depended on what you called miracles, but as he didn't really know what he was saying himself, it was just as well that the discussion could not continue, and he sat down in a determined way next to Emmy, where he was only removed one place from the adored being and could show contempt for Mr. Bostock across the table. Rose and Clarissa, lovingly arm-in-arm, came next to George; Martin sat between Clarissa and Sylvia, then came David, while Anne with mingled feelings found herself between David and the vicar.

"And now, Mr. Bostock," said Lady Graham, "we must have a delightful talk about the vicarage. My mother will be so interested to hear about it."

The vicar, who had found the vicarage useful to live in but had not otherwise much considered it, said it was very nice.

"That is so like you," said Lady Graham, turning her lovely eyes full on the vicar without really meaning anything at all, for as she hardly knew him she could hardly be expected to know what was like him. "I expect you always think of other people."

The vicar would have liked to say, "I always think of you," but as he had only met her twice, he thought it might sound untruthful.

"But what my mother really wants to know," said Lady Graham, "is whether that little room on the top floor with a skylight is still used for a servant's bedroom. She wanted Mr. Banister, who was our dear vicar until he became a canon and that delightful Bishop Joram came, to keep apples there, but he only had two small apple trees in the garden, not enough to devote a whole room to them, so nothing happened."

"I'm awfully sorry, Lady Graham," said Mr. Bostock, "but I haven't any servants. Mrs. Poulter sometimes comes in the morning and clean things and cooks my lunch and I do the rest myself. And the days she doesn't come I can get a really excellent meal at the Bull's Head."

"Oh dear," said Lady Graham, much affected by these domestic arrangements. "Emmy," she said, turning to her eldest daughter, "Mr. Bostock needs someone to look after him."

George Halliday, who was also of this opinion though on different grounds, smiled sardonically, or at any rate made a face which was intended to that effect.

"I say, you're going to choke," said Emmy, pouring water into his glass with such goodwill that it splashed all over his plate. "That's all right, mummy. Ted Poulter's got to marry Lily Brown as soon as possible—"

"Oh dear," said Mr. Bostock, distressed that the shame of one of his flock should be so suddenly sprung upon him and in a public place.

"—because it'll stop him always going off to Barchester after his work and wasting his money. He and Lily had better live with you, Mr. Bostock. I can't think why I didn't think of that before. Lily can do the house and Ted can give a hand in the garden. Only mind, you mustn't give them man and wife wages. Ted is earning good money and they'll have a house for nothing and all their food. I'll speak to Lily's mother about it."

Whether the vicar really wanted a newly-married young couple to come and live with him and eat his food we shall never know, for he already knew Emmy well enough to realise that like her respected and autocratic great uncle, the late Earl of Pomfret, she always did what she meant to do, or made other people do it for her.

"And Mrs. Brown can have her sister from Rushmere Parva to live with her," said Emmy, "so that's settled. Mummy, did Gran like the picture I drew for her of Rushwater Romany in the paddock?"

Mother and daughter fell into a murmured conversation about the family, so the vicar, being forced to absent himself from felicity awhile, turned to Anne and said he thought she knew Canon Banister, his predecessor, or it might be more correct to say his ante-predecessor, at Rushmere. Anne said Oh yes, she did know Canon Banister and he was very nice and went about everywhere on a bicycle. And, said the vicar, if he were not mistaken she was the daughter of the Diocesan Chancellor. Anne, after a mental gasp, remembered her father's office and said she was. They had a little mild gossip about the Close and so by easy degrees came round to the Palace, about whose female ruler the vicar knew a highly discreditable story which Anne treasured to take back to her parents.

"Oh, Mr. Bostock, did she really do that with you and the Archdeacon?" she asked.

"She did," said the vicar. "He was there on Monday night and I was there on Tuesday night, and the housemaid said she was so sorry there was an inkspot on the sheet, but it was the Archdeacon who did it so perhaps I wouldn't mind."

"Oh, how *lovely*," said Anne. "I must tell mummy and daddy."

"And I can tell you something else," the vicar began, but at the same moment David said to Anne, "You haven't said one word to me since we began lunch."

"Oh, I am *dreadfully* sorry," said Anne, going crimson. A young woman with any self-respect, with any knowledge of the ways of society would, she knew, have said, "Well, you haven't said much to me either," or even more dashing, though perhaps a trifle pert, "Why should I?" But poor Anne could only say what her silly, slightly dazzled heart put into her mouth.

"And what do you think of Rushwater?" said David.

"Oh, I love it," said Anne. "I simply adore it. Only such a lot of things happen all the time that one gets rather muddled. I mean cows and hens and cottages and kitchenmaids and horses and midges and everything. But I have been frightfully happy."

"How well you put it," said David. "I adore Rushwater too. But three days of life at twenty cow-power tension drive me back to the comparative calm of London or Paris."

"Do you think everyone feels like that?" asked Anne.

"Not the right ones," said David. "People like Martin and Emmy and the Hallidays and my Marling cousins don't notice that anything is happening. They just do their job and get on to the next job. Heredity a good deal. Then you get someone that runs off the track, like myself or Rose. Rose is the toughest woman I know, but a week of Rushwater and she'd even stop making up her face from sheer exhaustion. Wouldn't you, Rose?" he said across the table.

"Wouldn't I what?" said Rose.

"Die if you lived in the country," said David.

"Of course I would," said Rose. "Life is too terrific in the country. Give me Paris, or London, or even Lisbon or Rome, and I'll put my feet up and relax."

"I know someone that was in Lisbon," said Anne, plunging into society.

"Do you?" said Rose, in a much softer voice than she had used to David; a kinder voice, Anne thought. "Who is he?"

"It's only a girl," said Anne apologetically. "At least she is married. Her name is Rose Fairweather."

"Is she a great friend of yours?" said Rose.

"No, not really," said Anne, wishing she had let Society alone. "But her father is the Headmaster of Southbridge School and a great friend of mine is a master there and we went to the sports and Rose came in the middle of lunch and I thought she was so lovely."

Having made this uninteresting, gauche and school-girlish speech, she wished she were dead.

"I know the girl you mean," said Rose. "Her husband dances terrifically well. She doesn't. She has plenty of glamour and she's as beautiful as she's dumb. The Portuguese called us Rose of the Night and Rose of the Day. I saw a good deal of her at official parties, but that was all."

She then resumed her conversation with her cousin Clarissa. Anne felt tears of shame stinging her. It served her right for talking across the table, an action always strongly deprecated by Miss Bunting. Her eyes were suddenly opened to the fact that the lovely Rose Fairweather was not only a nitwit, but second-rate. Not that Rose Bingham had meant to be unkind, but it was abundantly clear that to the Rose Binghams of this world the Rose Fairweathers hardly existed, spinning like fretful midges, as one of her favourite poets, D. G. Rossetti, had written. But no one seemed to have noticed her shame and there was by now a good deal of general talk across the table in every direction. David had turned his attention to Sylvia, the vicar was telling Lady Graham that he was using the little room with the skylight to keep his cricket things and his squash rackets in, but could easily put them somewhere else if she or Lady Emily thought it advisable. George was boring Rose a good deal by telling her about some shooting he had had while in billets in Norfolk, to which Rose listened with an air of interest that did not deceive her cousin David. And then the party gradually drifted back to the terrace to drink coffee and wait for the Southbridge contingent.

"Did I hear you mention squash?" said David to Mr. Bostock. "We might have a game. Not directly after all this lunch, but before tea. Miss Halliday plays a good game and so does her brother, and we could get my elder nephew when he comes. Sylvia," he continued, staying a little apart from the others while he spoke, "don't forget we are to look at the Temple. When we have had our coffee, do you think? Anne," he said, moving to where she sat, "we must make our pilgrimage to Miss Bunting's memorial or my mamma will never forgive me. Would you come?"

Anne said she would love to.

"Emmy, my precious," said David, "if you can stop confiding in your mother for one moment, your Uncle David would like to see Rushwater Romany. And this is Real," he added, "because I do know a bit about bulls."

"Rather!" said Emmy. "Oh, and Uncle David, the Jersey may calve at any moment."

"Then we shall not visit the Jersey," said David. "What's sport to her is death to me. Rose, what are you doing?"

"Nothing," said Rose simply. "I shall go and see Siddy some time and tell her about Hermione's children and she will say what a pity it is I don't find a nice husband, and I shall have that delightful impression that I have lived it all before in one of my past lives."

"And darling Agnes," said David affectionately, "will catch old Bertha and go over all the bedrooms and nurseries and cry when she sees the rocking-horse. Lord! when I think that I used to be invited to see Clarissa in her bath, it makes me feel how old I am."

His niece Clarissa looked at him in rather a bored way and said something to her cousin Rose that made her laugh.

"I have made a very unpleasant discovery lately," said David to his nephew Martin.

Martin asked what it was.

"Sit down and I'll tell you," said David, who had noticed that Martin's limp was having one of its bad days. "I have discovered that I am a back number. Clarissa, whom I knew very well in her bath some baker's dozen of years ago, has become someone to reckon with. She has no respect for me at all and will break several hearts before she gets married and probably afterwards."

"Good lord!" said Martin.

"It's no use good-lording," said David, almost pettishly. "Clarissa has very neatly put me in my place more than once and this very moment is saying something to my disadvantage which is making Rose laugh."

"You might get married," said Martin, at once making a kind of plan for David. "Then your wife could scratch Clarissa's eyes out."

David said it was a good idea, but he didn't feel like it. He must have a wife, he said, who would do him great credit and never bore him. And come to that, he said, it was high time his dear nephew got married. He expected an indignant disclaimer of any such idea, but to his surprise Martin said, rather wistfully, that he would like it very much; so long, he added, as it was someone who would get on with Emmy, as she had obviously made up her mind to live at Rushwater forever like the Ladies of Llangollen.

"I see what you mean," said David, "though nobody else would. Well, we'll see what we can do and have a double wedding at Rushwater and Agnes can cry while Merry does all the work and mamma interferes."

Then he got up and walked towards Sylvia, wondering what his nephew Martin had in his mind, or rather whom. Was he by any chance in love with the little Fielding girl? If he were, David would certainly not spoil his chances, but as he was not supposed to know anything he would pass some of the afternoon in making the Fielding girl come out of her shell; always an amusing occupation.

Then Robin and the boys arrived, having borrowed a car from the same obliging junior master back from the wars who had lent it for the Fieldings' dinner-party. Leslie major and minor greeted all their relations affectionately, the Hallidays as equals, the vicar as one of the permanent duties of life, and asked if they could go on the roof.

"Only in tennis shoes," said Martin, "and you are not to walk round the parapet on the outside because it makes me feel sick. And we'll be wanting you for some squash before tea."

The boys asked if anyone would like to come with them and George Halliday at once volunteered.

"Have you got a good head, sir?" said Leslie major. "Emmy got stuck once on the bit we call Great Gable and began to cry and we had to rope her to get her down."

"Well, I don't want to come, anyway," said Emmy, overhearing this aspersion on her character. "And I didn't cry. And anyway I've got to be about because of the Jersey."

"Emmy prefers child welfare to adventure," said Leslie minor in a pitying way. "Come on, sir."

"I say, don't call me sir," said George. "My name's Halliday, or George."

"Excuse me, George," said Leslie major with a sudden and surprising deference, "but are you any relation of the Halliday who was at St. Jude's?"

"Well, I was at St. Jude's for a year before the army caught me," said George.

"Then you *are* The One," said Leslie minor suddenly.

"My brother isn't very bright," said Leslie major apologetically, which made his junior hit him and be hit back, with incredible rapidity and no ill-feeling. "What he means is there is a master who got invalided out of the army who was at St. Jude's and he used to do a lot of climbing and he said there was a fresher called Halliday who climbed right round the quad on the first floor."

George looked sheepish but pleased.

"It was rather a good rag," he said, accepting the Leslie boys as fellow-craftsmen and ignoring the rest of the company completely. "I hired some black tights and a cloak and got all the way round. The windows are pretty close together and there's a good ledge about five inches wide and a fair amount of drain-pipes. The worst part was getting past the Master's study, because he was sitting up late that night working and his curtains weren't drawn because of that awful Double Summer Time. I think he saw something, but by the time he had taken his reading spectacles off and put his long-distance ones on I was outside the Bursar's rooms and he always draws his curtains at six o'clock all the year round."

"Why did you have tights and a cloak, sir?" said Leslie minor.

"Shut up! Didn't you hear him tell us not to say 'sir'?" said Leslie major in a loud aside. "But why did you, sir?" he added.

"So that if anyone saw me they'd think I was Dracula," said George Halliday, which eminently reasonable explanation satisfied the Leslie boys, who joyfully dragged him away to show him the glories of Great Gable.

"David, darling," said Lady Graham, "you will be quite happy, won't you? I must go and have a little talk with Siddon and then I am going over the house with Bertha, so I shan't see you till tea-time. I will tell Siddon you are coming to visit her, Rose darling."

And Lady Graham went into the house.

"How I do adore that woman," said her brother David to Sylvia. "If I ever meet anyone as divinely silly, I'll marry her. Sylvia, we had a plan to visit the Temple, hadn't we?"

Robin was talking to the vicar, who knew his father. Rose and Clarissa were pursuing their endless conversation. Martin seeing that Anne looked deserted pulled a chair over to her. Anne was grateful, for the sight of Sylvia and David walking together in the chequered shade made her gently sad, though she would not for a moment have deprived Sylvia of the treat. So she asked Martin, with whom she always felt safe, to explain the Leslies to her from the very beginning, which he did with such success that she said, "Then I suppose if you don't get married, Leslie major will have Rushwater."

Far from being offended by this anticipation, Martin felt rather proud of his pupil and said he would very much like to get married himself and cut his cousin out, only he didn't know if anyone would care to marry him, limping about like a beggar all the time.

"Oh, don't say that," said Anne, much distressed. "I promise you it hardly shows a bit and anyway if a person was in love with a person they wouldn't care *what* they looked like."

Martin smiled, rather touched by her earnestness, and said she had cheered him up a good deal, and if anyone did care to marry him he would tell her at once.

"First?" said Anne, incredulous of the honour offered to her.

"Absolutely first," said Martin, giving her hand a comfortable squeeze, and then they talked about books. And of course, just as would happen in a novel, Robin heard through his talk with the vicar disjointed fragments of this conversation and wondered if Anne had begun to discover that she had a heart. He would have a deep affection for her heart, whithersoever it led her, and if it did lead her to Martin, she might do far worse, and Martin was a thoroughly good fellow, and a better match for Sir Robert Fielding's daughter than a schoolmaster. And then he gave himself a good deal of unnecessary pain, talking pleasantly the while, by reflecting how unsuited Anne with her city upbringing and her delicate health, though thank goodness that was really a thing of the past, would be to the grinding life of what was really a farmer's wife with all the responsibilities of the wife of a landowner.

So the two conversations went on and then the four talked together till Martin, the conscientious host, said they must collect some people for squash, or there wouldn't be time before tea.

"You are playing, Bostock," he said, "and the Hallidays and one of my young cousins. They are on the roof. Someone will have to fetch them.

"I will," said Anne. "I'll go up to the old nursery and shout. They'll be sure to hear me. I think David took Sylvia to the Temple."

"I'll go and find them," said Martin. "I'll leave you with Dale, vicar. You might as well go to the squash court and then I'll know where to find you. On any other occasion," he added vengefully, "my young cousins would be hanging head downwards from a crocket, but of course just when I want them they are invisible. Don't go on the roof, Anne. Only shout."

Anne said she would be far too frightened to go on the roof, a confidence which Robin heard, and which most unreasonably added to his depression. But he put a good face on it and went off towards the squash court, discussing the advantages and disadvantages of having a young married couple living in the vicarage.

David and Sylvia walked slowly up the winding track in the beechen shade towards the Temple, talking of radio-location. Sylvia supplied most of the information while David asked intelligent questions and thought that a life on the farm and among cows had made her if possible more golden in her beauty than before. Her face, her arms, seemed to be powdered with golden dust over a darker shade of gold; her hair rippled in golden waves. Her legs, on which David was pleased to see silk stockings, were as finely shaped as the rest of her. Altogether, he decided with the eye of a connoisseur, she was a perfect beauty, and if her face expressed a healthy satisfaction with life in general more than intellectual longings, well, that was all right for a hot July day with nothing particular to be intellectual about.

Presently they emerged from the trees and onto the sun-baked hollow where the Temple stood. David tried to open the door, but it resisted firmly.

"I'll do it," said Sylvia, and taking an Amazon's grip on the tarnished door-handle, turned it with such force that it came off in her hand.

"Well, you *have* done it," said David. "Now we'll have to tell Martin. Thank God there is still an estate carpenter. We'll have a go at the windows."

The ground floor of the Temple was lighted by four enormous sash windows of such weight that no one had ever been able to open them, and if opened by the carpenter it was impossible for human power to shut them. But on examination David found that some panes had been broken, together with their woodwork, and loosely boarded over. A couple of kicks and a wrench removed the boards and he was able to creep in, followed by Sylvia.

"It's extraordinarily dull, isn't it?" said David, dusting himself. "And extraordinarily hot."

"I expect it's because of the sun shining so hard on all that glass and the windows not being open," said Sylvia.

David said he thought it very probable and was assailed, as he so often was, by a wish to be somewhere else and with somebody else. But politeness forbade him, though even politeness did not always have this effect, to leave his guest, so he offered to show her the upper storey, which could only be reached by a ladder leading to a trap-door.

"I'll go first," he said, "because the trap-door has probably stuck. And look out, Sylvia. The third step is missing, like *Kidnapped.*"

"Oh, that's *Treasure Island*, isn't it?" said Sylvia. "I saw a film of it."

If David had not been above Sylvia on the ladder-stair, he would have made some charming excuse and taken her out of the Temple and killed her. But he was already battling with the trap-door, stiff from long disuse, while dust and flakes of plaster from the ceiling rained down on them both. The trap-door suddenly burst open, one half falling back against the wall of the upper room, the other getting unmoored from its rusty hinges and falling on the floor with a bang that made the plaster fly more than ever and roused an enormous, panic-stricken gang of spiders and daddy-longlegses to mass hysteria.

"It's pretty awful, isn't it?" said Sylvia, emerging from the opening.

Indeed, it was not a place to choose for a fine afternoon, but to David it still meant romance. The writings and the very bad pictures on the walls were the work of himself and his brothers and Agnes. A line from a French sonnet still visible in pencil reminded him of the summer those French people had taken the vicarage, the year Martin was seventeen. Lord! how long ago. Agnes's children had played there before the war, but since that time the Temple had been deserted, its plaster flaking, its stone crumbling, its woodwork rotting. There were some ominous cracks in the walls and David determined to ask Martin to have them looked at. The Temple must not fall into disrepair before the next generation could play in it; though where the next generation was coming from, no one could say.

"I don't mean awful, exactly," said Sylvia. "I mean it's a bit lonely. I mean it feels lonely. At least I mean it would feel lonely if it was a person."

David looked at Sylvia with a respect which had hitherto been lacking in his relation with her, though always the gentleman. The girl was coming out. Not only was she an admirable creature to the eye, but she appeared to have some finer shades of thought of which he had not guessed her to be capable.

"There ought to be five or six children here at least," said Sylvia in a very determined voice, as of one who was going to do something about it at once.

"Quite right, love," said David. "Let's off to town and purchase some."

The allusion evidently meant nothing to Sylvia, but all the

same David was interested. They went down the ladder backwards, cautiously, and crawled out of the window. David then gave the boards a few bangs so that they were more or less firmly fixed over the gap.

Sylvia was standing outside the Temple on the hot stone pavement, shading her eyes with one hand as she looked over the land. David came and stood beside her, silent, under the spell of a nostalgia for lost childhood, a nostalgia that Sylvia's words had roused. His height was almost matched by the tall Sylvia. She turned her head and their eyes were almost on a level. Their hands touched, lingered together.

"Sylvia," said David.

He had not in the least meant to say it, and certainly not in that particular voice, and was excessively annoyed with his nostalgic self for its behaviour.

"David," said Sylvia.

And as she had nothing else to say and was too comfortably warm and lazy to bother to think of anything, they remained rather ridiculously hand in hand upon the idle hill of summer, speechless.

"Yes, five or six children certainly," said Sylvia after a pause. "Or perhaps ten."

"Ten is a large number," said David, "but you shall have as many as you like."

As Sylvia made no comment, he assumed that her ambitions were satisfied. He then rather wished that his golden beauty would let go of his hand, for his fatal boredom was rapidly gaining upon him. But the golden beauty appeared to have no such idea and chivalry forebade him to withdraw his hand if she wished to hold it. It was all rather embarrassing and a distinct nuisance.

Meanwhile Martin had been walking, not too fast, for the day was hot and his leg reminded him of its existence more than he liked, up the hill under the beechwood cover. As he came blinking from the green gloom into the hot July sun, he saw his

Uncle David holding Sylvia's hand and heard them discussing how many children they were going to have. It was no business of his and he was furious with himself for his involuntary eavesdropping. There was nothing for it but to kick some loose pieces of stone as noisily as possible and speak to them; of course in a very natural way.

"David," he called across the clearing. "Are you going to play squash? They are waiting for you and Sylvia."

The hands so lately clasped came undone without any effort on their respective owners' part and apparently with no consciousness of anything unusual having occurred.

"I say, Martin," said David. "Just one moment. There are some nasty cracks in the upper room. I think you ought to have the Temple looked at. On the east side."

Martin moved round to the east.

"There's a crack outside too," he said. "Some of the lead clamps have fallen out. It's the place where the boughs of the big beech hit it in that storm when the barn was struck when I was a boy. I'll get a man onto it to-morrow."

"It's all rather in a mess," said David. "I took Sylvia inside and the ladder is rickety and the trap-door is broken. All rather sad."

"There are a lot of sad things at Rushwater," said Martin, thinking of the many improvements and repairs that an estate needed and the difficulties in getting men and material, not to speak of the money. But among the sad things he did not include the sight of two people hand-in-hand before the Temple, for it was a thing he should not honourably have seen and must forget.

"And one is that blasted leg of yours," said David. "Why on earth did you come sweltering up the hill, Martin? Why didn't you send one of the boys? Come on, Sylvia. We'll keep the others waiting."

But he would not let Martin hurry his pace down the hill and Martin was vaguely grateful, though his gratitude felt to him as if it came from a great distance and was tired. If he did not talk much to Sylvia it was not because he felt unfriendly to her; he only felt lost and wished the day were well over.

By the time they got to the racquet court Anne had, by dint of screaming from various attic windows, collected George Halliday and Leslie major. Leslie minor had elected to stay on the roof and see if he could climb the hideous little pointed turret with a weathercock on it. As the turret stood on a flat leaded roof with a parapet, he could do himself no harm unless he fell off and broke his legs, said Anne, which cold comfort seemed to satisfy his host.

The vicar and Sylvia were already hard at it, with George and Leslie major waiting their turn and Martin acting as audience-umpire, rather glad to rest his leg.

"We were going to see the church, weren't we?" said David to Anne, as they walked back to the terrace.

Anne wasn't quite sure if she wanted to go and see the church. It would be very peaceful to sit and talk to Robin. But as they got nearer the terrace she saw that Robin was talking to Rose Bingham, just as if he had known her all his life and apparently amusing her.

"I'm taking Anne to the church," said David, as they passed the talkers.

"I'll come too, Uncle David," said Clarissa, who was resenting with all the unreasonableness of an advanced young lady in her teens the fact that her cousin Rose was finding entertainment in a grown-up man's talk; a schoolmaster too, with a wooden leg, said Clarissa scornfully to herself. And she got up and followed the church-going party.

Anne, who had almost decided to stay with Rose Bingham and Robin, suddenly felt aggrieved that Clarissa was disturbing her and David's private visit to the church, a visit which a moment ago she had thought of escaping. Clarissa slipped her hand affectionately yet mockingly into her uncle's coat pocket and so walked beside him, chattering about Paris and Rose's flat where she was to go on a visit when things were better. Names of people unknown to Anne floated into the conversation and for the thousandth time the grown-up Anne Fielding suddenly found herself a shy schoolgirl again, and all because of a girl fully four years younger than herself. Still, Clarissa was David's niece, and the world Clarissa and David belonged to was not Anne's world; a fact to be recognised and accepted by Miss Bunting's ex-pupil.

Presently Clarissa withdrew her hand from David's pocket and they turned their steps to old Mr. Leslie's grave, where the sweetbriar was showering its perfume on the warm air. Anne crushed a leaf between her fingers and breathed the sweet scent. Clarissa did the same. David plucked and gave a little sprig to each of his companions.

"How sweet of you, Uncle David," said Clarissa in her charming society voice. "It is *too* delicious. I shall put it in your buttonhole."

Reaching upwards a little, she put her sweetbriar in her uncle's buttonhole, arranging it with elegant fingers. David accepted the attention gracefully, but had to admit that his niece Clarissa had beaten him at his own game. Was she giving him the sprig as a token of affection from a dutiful niece, or was it her way of showing him that his gift was worthless; or, even more mortifying, to show him that she knew that he knew that both gifts were a mere piece of idle showing-off?

"Your hands are as charming as ever, Clarissa," he said, as she finished her arranging and stood back to look at it.

Anne was not comfortable. She felt a mocking antagonism between uncle and niece but could not explain it. She turned aside and without thinking of what she was doing began tracing the letters on an old flat-topped family grave, a kind of stone chest on four bulbous stone legs, sagging towards one corner where the ground had given way.

"I am a fool; also a blindworm," said David's voice conversationally at Anne's elbow. "Do you know, I had never properly noticed your hands."

Anne looked up, startled.

"They are quite exquisite," said David, taking one of them and holding it lightly while he looked at it. "I adore fingers that are so elegant and turn up at the ends and have almond nails. I cannot at the moment think what flowers they are like, but certainly a flower. Perhaps one of those slim tulips that turn outwards. You and Clarissa shall have first and second prize for hands."

Without the least suspicion of pressing or wishing to retain her hand he laid it on the tombstone again.

"And now we will go and see Bunny's memorial," he said, "and then, I think, tea."

Anne had never felt so uncomfortable in her life. To have her hand taken by David and admired ought to have filled her with indescribable rapture, instead of which she felt as if the David who was Miss Bunting's favourite pupil had suddenly vanished, or had never existed. David was still David, but Anne was woman enough to know, though she could not have put it into words and would have been ashamed to utter them if she could, that David was using her as a pawn in the game of pin-pricks that he was playing, and very unkindly playing, with his niece Clarissa. Clarissa, whom she was more than willing to like, would now dislike and despise her; and though Clarissa was four years younger than she was, she was also a much older creature; older, Anne thought in a quick confused way, because the Leslies had so long a tradition behind them and had an understanding of life as part of their birthright. David understood life, so did Lady Graham in a different sort of way; so did all Leslies, down to Leslie minor, who, having decided that to climb a hideous little pointed turret was the most important thing in the world, was quietly devoting a hot Sunday afternoon to this uninteresting employment. Anne Fielding did not understand life and never would, but she did understand good manners and the duties of a guest, so she accompanied David and a scornful Clarissa into the church, where lived the little tablet which kept

Miss Bunting's name alive. David, suddenly bored with young girls, went and played the organ to himself, while Clarissa, seeing flowers in a state of languor on the altar, went to the vestry, collected a long-spouted watering-can, filled it at the vestry tap and replenished the vases.

Seldom had Anne been more perplexed. The happy Sunday to which she had looked forward with such excitement had turned to dust and ashes. David—though evermore David— could be unkind, more than unkind. He had hurt Clarissa, he had made Clarissa dislike Anne. How could one ever be happy again after such a searing experience? She wondered in a respectful way if one could pray about it as one happened to be in a church, but came sadly to the conclusion that she didn't know what she wanted to pray for, except to go back to a quarter of an hour ago and none of the things to happen that had happened. And if the vicar did chance to come in and find anyone praying in his church, he might think it presumptuous. Sad, bewildered, a little afraid, all Anne could find to say was, "Oh, Miss Bunting," and wait to see what happened. Nothing happened. David's music flowed on. Anne tiptoed down the aisle and out into the sunshine where Clarissa was making daisy-chains with her neat elegant hands.

"Uncle David will go on like that for ages," said Clarissa. "Let's go back."

Her voice was again a society voice, but Anne felt that she was less like an elegant savage animal showing teeth and claws, and was relieved.

"I went to look at Miss Bunting's monument," said Anne, making conversation according to the old governess's precept.

"I wish old Bunny were alive," said Clarissa in a tone of savage intensity, which however did not seem to be directed against Anne.

"So do I," said Anne.

"Why do you want her alive?" asked Clarissa lightly.

Anne wondered idly why Clarissa asked and thought that

whatever she said would probably be wrong, but that the truth was perhaps the safest, so she said, "Because she always knew what to do. She was my governess for a year before she died."

"How stupid I am," said Clarissa, still in her society voice but with much more kindness. "Mummy did say something about Bunny being with you, but as I didn't know you then I didn't think about it. Good old Bunny. We all adored her."

Encouraged by this Anne ventured to say, "Please, why do you want her to be alive too?"

"Because she was the only person that didn't spoil Uncle David," said Clarissa. "Of course we all adore him, but he is too frightfully selfish. Gran and mummy don't see it of course, poor darlings, but I do and so does Rose. I wish Bunny had been here just now and she'd have scolded him till he was ashamed. At least I don't believe anyone could make Uncle David ashamed, but anyway she'd have made him behave. Stupid showing-off at his age."

At this blasphemy Anne expected the heavens to fall, but having other things to do, they didn't. And after a moment's silence, which felt to her like years, she came to the conclusion that Clarissa was right. David was David: but Miss Bunting would not have approved his conduct that day, and Miss Bunting could not err.

"I like your friend Robin Dale," said Clarissa, evidently considering that the subject of David was disposed of and that she and Anne were leagued in confidence. "And the boys say he is a very good sort," which pleased Anne very much. "I wish I were a boy."

Anne asked why.

"Not really," said Clarissa, "because they take so long to grow up. But then I could do what I wanted."

Anne asked what that was.

"Engineering draughtsmanship," said Clarissa. "I mean to make daddy send me to a proper boarding-school for two years and I'll get a scholarship to Cambridge. And in the holidays I want to go into a real works and learn things. Gran and mummy will think it's too ghastly but Merry thinks I had better try to have my own way because everyone will have to do a job probably. I wish I knew anyone in a works."

"I do know someone who has a works," said Anne, "but I don't think you'd exactly like him perhaps."

"Do you really?" said Clarissa, as much impressed by Anne's acquaintance with the engineering trade as Anne was by Clarissa's precocious bright ease of manner.

"He is called Mr. Adams," said Anne. "I know his daughter too, at least I haven't seen her for some time, but she is awfully clever at mathematics and got a scholarship."

"You know Mr. Adams?" said Clarissa, stopping dead. "At Hogglestock?"

"They were near us at Hallbury one summer," said Anne, "and he is standing against daddy for Barchester."

"Oh, bother politics," said Clarissa. "Look here, Anne, can you get me introduced to him?"

Anne, now feeling quite grown-up again and fully conscious of her four years' seniority, said she must ask mummy and anyway Clarissa couldn't go into a works yet, but she would promise faithfully to do all she could for her when the time came.

"Thanks terrifically," said Clarissa. "I say, don't take any notice if I fight Uncle David a bit. I'm really awfully fond of him, but he needs taking down. I've been talking to Rose about it and she quite agrees it's time he came to heel. She's going to do something about it. She's terrifically clever and nice."

# CHAPTER 9

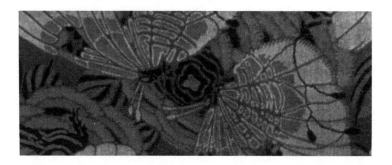

Robin and Rose had remained peacefully on the terrace, finding each other rather amusing, till Martin came across the lawn and asked Robin if he would mind umpiring for George Halliday and Leslie major.

"The vicar just beat Sylvia, but only just," he said. "So he is going to show her his plans for the new central heating in the church as a consolation prize."

Robin went off to the squash court and Martin sat down by Rose and said nothing.

"What's wrong?" said Rose, lighting another cigarette.

"Why?" said Martin.

"You look rotten," said Rose. "Is your leg bad?"

"Oh, damn my leg," said Martin.

"Thanks," said Rose. "And now you can tell me what it is."

The vicar and Sylvia walked slowly across the lawn in the direction of the church, waved their hands, and disappeared behind some shrubs. Martin, having answered their signal, slumped down into his chair looking so old and haggard for one so young that his cousin Rose, who was very fond of him in her own way, felt almost disturbed.

"I expect I'm only stupid," said Martin.

"You are. Terrifically stupid," said Rose, without raising her husky low voice or showing any signs of emotion. "Now, what is it? Come on and take your fences. Is it money?"

Martin laughed and said: "No more than usual."

"And it's not your leg," said Rose. "I suppose it's Sylvia."

Martin looked at her with reproach and appeal mingled.

"Well, I'll have to drag it out of you," said Rose. "Won't she marry you?"

"I haven't asked her," said Martin.

"Ask her then," said Rose.

"I can't now," said Martin.

"Good God, my dear boy," said Rose, who was at least two years older than Martin, "one can always ask. Have a little sense."

"I went up to the Temple to fetch Sylvia for squash," said Martin, "and David was holding her hand."

"My dear boy, even Othello wouldn't have worried about that," said Rose. "Did you ever know David when he wasn't holding someone's hand, or kissing it? He will do it once too often. But don't worry, it won't be with Sylvia."

"I behaved like a cad," said Martin with gloomy relish. "I heard them talking and I didn't try not to listen."

"We all do that," said Rose. "Don't be so silly."

"It was what they were saying," said Martin.

"Well, what *were* they saying?" asked Rose, never raising her voice or quickening her lazy speech, though she was longing to smack Martin.

"They were talking about children," said Martin, his voice hard, his eyes averted from his cousin.

"A stinking subject," said Rose. "Little beasts, getting all the oranges and cod-liver oil and free this and that and Saturday morning cinemas, God blast them, and thinking they are important. I wish our old Nannie had the handling of them. 'Eat what's on your plate or you'll go to bed till you do' was her method. And we all adored her."

"Not like that," said Martin. "It was about how many children they were going to have."

"Look here, Martin," said Rose. "If you are going crackers, do it quickly and get it over. Why on earth shouldn't Sylvia and David discuss the size of their families? I'll tell you here and now that when I marry I'll have three children as fast as possible and that's the end. My dear boy, one must look ahead a bit now."

"It wasn't the size of their families; it was their family," said Martin, examining with great interest a lady-bird who was walking up his coat sleeve.

It would have given Rose a good deal of pleasure to pick up a chair and hit Martin over the head with it, but it would not be sporting to attack a cousin with a limp who thought his heart was broken, for it was now abundantly plain to her that David had been at his tricks again. That he was in love with Sylvia, or she with him, Rose did not for a moment believe. She knew her David too well, and her considerable worldly experience told her that Sylvia might have been dazzled by David, but had not for a moment thought of loving him. In fact she doubted whether Sylvia had yet thought of loving anybody.

"I agree," said Martin, in a careless way, "that children are an infernal nuisance. But," he added, steering the lady-bird in the direction it didn't want to go, "I've been thinking lately that a few little chaps of one's own about the place wouldn't be a bad thing."

"You've been going to the Barchester Odeon too much," said Rose coldly. "If you want to get married and cut John's boy out of the place that's reasonable, and it's high time you did, or Emmy will bring her cows into the house. If you want to marry Sylvia, *ask* her, you soft gobbin. The girl can't jump down your throat."

"I shouldn't have any chance against David," said Martin, though not quite so despairingly.

"Good God, have I got to spell everything for you in words of one letter?" said Rose. "David can't help exerting charm and you know that as well as I do. But girls are such fools. Poor Mary nearly didn't marry John at all, just because David kissed her at your seventeenth birthday dance."

"David kissed Mary?" said Martin, to whom the idea of Uncle David having kissed his aunt by marriage before she was even engaged seemed at the moment like a confirmation of all his fears.

"Ask Agnes," said Rose. "And don't be an ass. Don't worry about David; I'll do that. Just concentrate on Sylvia and don't be a sentimental fool; and stop being sorry for yourself. It's teatime."

She got up, gave Martin a not unkindly pat on the shoulder and walked away. Martin told the lady-bird that its house was on fire and its children at home, but the lady-bird said that it was living at the Butlin Insect Holiday Camp and its children were all at the cinema, and anyway Martin appeared to be taking it for its wife who was away with her mother over the week-end and he would thank Martin not to move his arm so much. Martin gently removed it onto a leaf, which annoyed the lady-bird so much that it voted labour at once.

The whole party now began to gather for tea. Lady Graham had passed her afternoon very comfortably discussing various repairs and changes with the old housemaid Bertha and visiting the nurseries where she and Martin's father and John and David had played, quarrelled, ridden on the rocking-horse, turned on the Poly-phone or monster musical box, and kept dormice and canaries; where her children, visiting their grandparents, had done much the same; and had agreed with Bertha that it was high time Master Martin married. There was nothing, said Bertha, she would like more than to be carrying trays up to the nursery again. Lady Graham, remembering the house-splitting disputes between her children's nurse and the kitchen about trays, and how Bertha would have died sooner than demean herself to do work which belonged to Bessie the third housemaid or to Ivy the nurseymaid, said how delicious that would be and did Bertha remember where those old red damask curtains were that used to be in Lady Emily's bedroom. She also had a nice gossiping talk with her daughter Emmy, who had held aloof from the guests, keeping a kind of daylight vigil over the Jersey, but had kindly come in for tea.

Anne and Clarissa were the last to arrive, as they had found a common bond in poetry, and had both learnt Omar Khayyam by heart, which seemed a very good foundation for eternal friendship. While they quoted at each other Clarissa had made several more daisy-chains, and these she distributed among her friends and relations at the tea-table, who resigned themselves amiably to sitting garlanded like sacred cows in India, as Leslie major said. The vicar wondered if one ought to call cows sacred on the Sabbath-day, but by that time Clarissa had lightly thrown a daisy-chain over his head and he had to thank her.

"And the longest one for Uncle David," said Clarissa, putting the chain carelessly round her uncle's neck and slightly disarranging his hair.

David stroked his hair back rather pettishly.

"Never mind, darling, there isn't really much there," said Clarissa, who was still standing behind him looking down on the top of his head.

Luckily no one overheard this remark but Rose, who laughed a very small, low-toned laugh. David, unwilling to recognise the fact that his niece Clarissa had put a public affront upon him, swallowed his mortification and talked to Leslie major about cricket.

"Oh, Martin," said Sylvia. "I think Mr. Bostock's idea about the new central heating in the church is splendid. There's plenty of room for a furnace in that little room under the chancel steps where the gardening things and hand barrow whatever its name is I mean the thing you wheel coffins on live, and then there could be a pipe running right along the Rushwater pew."

"Splendid," said Martin, smiling pleasantly, but not with the enthusiasm Sylvia had expected.

"One of my earliest recollections is how cold that pew was in winter," said David. "Nurse always put my gaiters on for church

and on Christmas Day I took the nursery nail-scissors with me
and cut all the buttons off."

There was some laughter, but David had an uneasy feeling
that no one really cared and that he was not being appreciated.
Before he could do anything about it Lady Graham, looking
benignly yet searchingly round the table, asked Leslie major
where his brother was.

"I don't know, Aunt Agnes," said Leslie major. "When I came
down to play squash he was on the roof."

"Oh, Lady Graham," said Anne, "he was going to climb that
little tower thing with the weathercock on it."

The whole company at once realised that Leslie minor, who
had never been known to miss any meal, had fallen off the turret
and was lying spread-eagled on the leads with all his limbs
broken and his head split in two.

"I'd better go and look," said Robin, pushing his chair back
with a horrible feeling of guilt, for the Leslie boys, though in
their cousin's home, were nominally under his charge in term
time.

"You can't climb with that foot of yours," said Martin, also
feeling a horrid sense of responsibility. "I'll go." And he got up.

"You can't climb either with that leg of yours," said George
Halliday, actuated less by philanthropic motives than by a wish
to shine in Lady Graham's eyes. "Let me go, Lady Graham. I'll
search every inch of the roof. I swear."

The vicar, also much concerned for the fate of a nephew of
Lady Graham's, suggested ringing the church bell. It might, he
said, attract the lad's notice.

"More likely to bring the Home Guard out," said David.
"They haven't got used to being out of work yet."

"Yes, do go, George," said Lady Graham. "Only do be careful
when you go up the little staircase that goes up to the leads,
because I know there is a hole in the carpet and you might catch
your foot in it. I saw it to-day and spoke to Siddon about it."

"I swear I'll be most awfully careful, Lady Graham," said

George, and like a marquis of the ancient régime on his way to the guillotine walked with head proudly erect to the door, which was opened at the same moment in a disconcerting and baffling way, and Siddon came in, rather squashing George behind the door.

"I thought you'd want some more hot water, my lady," she said. "And the other young gentleman wants to know if he can have the honeycomb if you've done with it. It's the last I have, my lady."

"That great idiot my young brother," said Leslie major (who had shown no anxiety about his minor's fate), hastily scraping the rest of the honeycomb onto his plate. "Tell him it's all gone, Siddy."

"Do you know where he is then?" asked Martin.

"In my room, Mr. Martin," said Siddon. "I was sitting at my tea and there was a pair of legs outside the window and he'd climbed down from the roof by the drain-pipe, my lady, as black as a sweep he was. So I said he must have a good wash in the scullery and then I'd give him some tea. He's just Mr. David over again, always up to some sort of mischief."

Rose laughed in a detached way.

"David was a dreadful boy, wasn't he, Siddy," she said.

But although Rose was a near relation of the family Siddon was not going to discuss her Mr. David before the younger generation, so she merely smiled at Rose in an I could an if I would way and went back to the house-keeper's room. George sat down again.

"That was very naughty of him," said Lady Graham mildly. "And poor Mr. Dale must have felt quite worried," at which George Halliday and the vicar, who had both made useful suggestions, felt murder in their hearts. "I think, David, we ought to start by six, or a little earlier. And now, Mr. Bostock, will you be very kind and go over to the church with me, if it isn't too often for you in one day. I do so want to see your plans for the central heating, because darling mamma will want to know everything."

The vicar wanted to say that no one could go too often to church who had the pleasure of escorting Lady Graham, but it didn't sound quite convincing in that form, so he contented himself with describing his central heating plan at great length and saying what a charming person Miss Halliday was and how intelligent.

"And she really seemed to know as much about cows as your eldest daughter, Lady Graham," he added.

"Darling Emmy. She was christened and confirmed here," said Lady Graham. "It was so lucky, because the Bishop was away at an Economic conference at the time and we had a perfectly charming Bishop whose name I have quite forgotten."

The vicar wondered for a moment if Lady Graham meant Oecumenical, but came to the conclusion that so exquisite a being could not err, and that it was more than probable that a man like the present Bishop of Barchester should have gone shoving himself into Economic conferences. In which he was perfectly right, for the Bishop in addition to his many other gross defects thought that he understood finance, and had made several very ill-advised statements in the House of Lords, much to the annoyance of his party.

"Darling Papa's grave looks so peaceful," said Lady Graham, looking with tender eyes at the sweetbriar hedge.

The vicar said that all graves had that wonderful look of peace. Of peace, he repeated.

"Except the ones that are covered with horrid little spiky chips of marble all over," said Lady Graham, roused by the thought to what was for her considerable vehemence. "They must be most uncomfortable. I shall pick a few pieces of sweetbriar for mamma. Will you have one, Mr. Bostock?"

The vicar reverently received the sweetbriar from her hand.

"I shall treasure it," he said, too overcome to say more.

"It doesn't last long in water," said Lady Graham, "but if you press it till it is dry it lasts quite a long time. I had a piece pressed in my prayer book till it fell out and got lost. But you don't have a prayer book, I expect. I mean you wouldn't need one, knowing it all so well by heart, except of course the parts that one doesn't often meet. And now you shall explain the *whole* of the central heating to me before we go."

Robin, relieved about the fate of Leslie minor, now took possession of Anne, with whom he had not had much talk. They had news to exchange. Robin of the school, Anne of pastoral life. Then they wondered what the voting next week would bring forth and whether Sir Robert would get in. Anne said she almost hoped he wouldn't, because he wouldn't really mind so dreadfully, but Mr. Adams would be so dreadfully disappointed if he didn't. Then Robin told Anne as a great secret that Miss Banks had been sacked and was going to leave at the end of the term, having alienated everybody, even Miss Hampton and Miss Bent at Adeline Cottage, who had loudly denounced her as not being able to take her liquor like a man.

Anne said she thought that anyone Miss Hampton and Miss Bent didn't like must be exceedingly nasty. And as the ladies of Adeline Cottage were noted for the catholicity of their friend-ships, Robin thought that Anne was coming on nicely in knowl-edge of the world.

"And one more quite terrifically secret secret, as Miss Bing-ham would say," said Robin.

"Clarissa says terrifically too," said Anne. "I expect she picked it up from Miss Bingham. I think Miss Bingham is *very* nice, don't you, Robin? Not really frightening a bit."

"If she doesn't frighten you, that's all right," said Robin. "I must admit that she frightens me a little, though she is very amusing. I feel she is about a hundred years older than I am."

"I wonder if David is frightened of her," said Anne.

"I expect he is used to her," said Robin. "She is extraordinarily vital, though she squeals so quietly. I shouldn't think she ever feels tired."

Anne had the same feeling, that Rose Bingham would always be at the top of her cool, self-confident, poised form.

"She would be as funny as hell all the time," she said absently.

"Good Lord! my girl, what language you have been picking up!" said Robin. "This comes of living among cows."

"Oh, no!" said Anne, distressed that Robin should so misjudge her kind hosts. "Martin and Emmy aren't a bit like that. It was something David said to Sylvia."

"If I don't catch those boys, they'll be digging a tunnel to Australia, or stealing an aeroplane and flying to the North Pole," said Robin. "I must look for them. Come on."

Rose Bingham, accompanied by Clarissa, paid her visit to Mrs Siddon, showed the photographs of her sister Hermione Tadpole's babies, and was told it was high time she found a nice husband like Lord Tadpole.

"Wait a little longer, Siddy," said Rose, "and I may have a surprise for you," with which oracular words she shook hands warmly with the housekeeper and went back to the morning room, Clarissa at her heels.

"Look here, Clarissa," said Rose, blowing some cigarette smoke away, "you mustn't be so cattish to David in public. It won't do."

"If you mean saying his hair is thin on the top, it is," said Clarissa. "One doesn't usually see the tops of people's heads, and when I looked at his I couldn't help saying it, because really, Rose, he is quite horrible."

"Go on," said Rose.

"I can't quite explain," said Clarissa, coming and plumping herself down on a pouffe at Rose's feet, "but he seems rather old to be showing-off so much."

"Go on," said Rose.

"Well, you know what I mean," said Clarissa. "He is funny about people when they can't answer back. And he was *beastly* to Anne this afternoon. That's why I said about his hair."

"How was he beastly?" said Rose.

"It doesn't sound like anything when you say it," said Clarissa, wrinkling her pretty brow in her efforts to explain, "but I'd been standing up to him—"

"You had been very impertinent to him," said Rose, merely stating a fact.

"Only because he had been impertinent to me first," said Clarissa. "And he didn't like it, so he tried to make me nasty to Anne and the dreadful part is that I nearly was. And he tried to make us jealous of each other just for fun, which I think was horrid and mean and terrifically despiseworthy," said Clarissa vehemently.

Rose said nothing. Then she lighted another cigarette.

"David is becoming intolerable," she said again merely as a statement of fact. "He has always been bone-selfish—Uncle Henry used to say so, though David was his own son—and he's bone-spoilt. And if he isn't careful he will be a bone-nuisance in a few years and bone-unpopular. Clarissa, you must not be impertinent to David. I am going to give him a lesson that he will never forget to the end of his life, because I shall take exceedingly good care that he doesn't."

Clarissa looked up at her cousin Rose.

"Never mind how," said Rose. "You shall know quite soon. I will not have him teasing that nice little Anne Fielding, or anybody else."

"I like Anne," said Clarissa. "I really did like her the whole time, only David was so beastly. And she knows Mr. Adams at Hogglestock, the one that has the engineering works."

"The man who is standing against her father?" said Rose. "What queer people other people do know. It's high time you went to school, Clarissa."

"I'm gong to," said Clarissa. "Merry agrees with me. She says I've had enough governessing. I can get round daddy. It's mummy and Gran."

"I shall be on your side," said Rose. "Don't worry. Now we will go and say good-bye to the boys."

So they went onto the terrace, where several of the party were sitting.

"I hope the boys haven't gone," said Rose.

"They went to say good-bye to Rushwater Romany," said Anne, "so Robin had to go and hurry them up."

"Let's walk and meet them," said Rose, an offer which Anne found very flattering. "Clarissa likes you very much."

Anne blushed with pleasure.

"I like her too, terrifically," she said. "I nearly didn't like her, because David—"

She stopped, afraid of offending her companion.

"Because David was making mischief, I suppose," said Rose negligently. "He is the most charming man I know and the most careless about hurting people. Don't worry about him, Anne."

"I don't really," said Anne. "Only he does say things I can't understand. He said he could only marry someone who was as funny as hell all the time and I didn't like it. And he was really horrid to Clarissa," she added, with what for her was considerable violence. "He tried to make us not like each other on purpose. At least I thought he did."

"I shan't let him do it again," said Rose. "When things are a bit easier you and Clarissa must come to Paris and stay with me in my flat."

To this Anne could only say Oh! in a very schoolgirlish way, and then Robin appeared with his pupils and they all went to the front of the house.

"Come again soon," said Martin to Robin. "There'll be some shooting later if you feel like it."

Robin thanked his host, who looked, he thought, thoroughly worn out by his Sunday entertainment, told Leslie major he certainly was not going to drive and got into the car.

"I say, sir," said Leslie minor to George Halliday, "could you come to Southbridge ever? It's fairly mouldy, but no one has managed to climb the chapel roof yet."

George, although he thought it improbable that a complete

stranger, in broad daylight, would have much chance of Alpine work, said he would love to come when he got leave again, or he might be demobilised fairly soon.

"He said not to call him 'sir,' you idiot," said Leslie major. "Thanks awfully for coming on the roof, sir."

"Oh, Mr. Dale," said Lady Graham, suddenly wafting herself out of the hall down onto the steps. "I told Siddon to put some eggs and fruit in the car. I know you must need them with your foot. And do come to Holdings one Sunday. Robert would love to meet you."

No one had ever yet discovered whether General Sir Robert Graham, K.C.M.G., was pleased to see any guest, but if his wife said so, so it must be. Robin thanked her, the Leslie boys waved and shouted and the car disappeared down the drive.

"Now," said Lady Graham, "we must be going too. Mr. Bostock, I do so want you to come to Holdings. Mamma would love to see you. I know Sunday is a quite dreadful day for you, but it is the only day my husband is ever at home."

Overhearing these words George Halliday felt much sympathy with King Henry II, except that Mr. Bostock was not an Archbishop; but reflecting that he would drive back with Lady Graham while Mr. Bostock was taking Evening Service, he relented slightly.

Mr. Bostock, in a very dashing way, said it would be quite possible for him to drive over to Holdings one Sunday and how much he would like it, upon which George Halliday's brow became dark.

Then the Holdings car went away, leaving the world to Double Summer Time and Mr. Bostock, who soon went over to the church for Evening Service in a highly addled frame of mind.

Everything felt rather flat. Anne and Sylvia's happy visit would be over next day; the lovely idyll of a hot July would come to an end. Anne would be very glad to see her father and mother and to help them bear the success or defeat that would be announced in a few days, but she liked Martin and Emmy and the farm life and Mrs. Siddon and even Rushwater Romany. But having been taught by Miss Bunting that one should always be considerate of others, she had noticed how low-spirited Martin had become during the afternoon, though always kind, and thought perhaps two visitors on the top of all his work had been bad for his leg.

Sylvia also would as a matter of course be glad to see her people but she did not at all wish to leave Rushwater. The Jersey had not yet calved, there was a good deal to be done in the kitchen garden, where they were shorthanded, the question of the central heating for the church to be seriously gone into with the vicar, the Milk Marketing Board to be dealt with, and a thousand things about the place that needed her helping hand; although, had she paused to reflect, she would have had to confess that things had gone on in their own way at Rushwater before she came, and would probably go on after she had gone.

Supper was very quiet except for Emmy, who splendidly immune to social atmosphere talked about the farm in general and the Jersey in particular till even Sylvia was rather bored. As the sun set a breeze had sprung up and watery mists were veiling the sky.

"Too cold to sit out," said Martin. "It will rain tonight. Old Herdman has got lumbago again, and that always means bad weather coming."

"He simply *can't* have lumbago if the Jersey—" Emmy began, when her kind, good-tempered cousin suddenly damned the Jersey quite ferociously, said he didn't care if she calved or not and he was going to light a fire in the morning-room. This he did and sat not reading the *Stock Breeders' Gazette*, while the girls chattered.

"I'm going to sit up all night," said Emmy. "I told Herdman to come and shout under my window if he needed help. I'm going to bed now to get some sleep. What shall we call the calf, Martin? I thought of Ruritania. Rushwater Ruritania would do for a bull or a heifer."

"All right, anything you like," said her cousin Martin.

"Mind you wake me, Emmy," said Sylvia. "if there's any fun. It's my last chance."

"No," said Martin. "I will *not* have Sylvia in the cow-shed at two in the morning. I'll hear Herdman if he comes."

"What on earth's the matter?" Sylvia said, who had never seen Martin out of temper or even out of patience before.

Martin said nothing was the matter, and he wished people wouldn't ask him silly questions.

"I'll sit up with Emmy," said Sylvia firmly. "Oh, and Martin, don't forget about the Temple. David said those cracks were really serious."

Martin got up, folded the *Stock Breeders' Gazette* neatly, put it in the paper-rack, said Good-night inclusively without looking at anyone, adding, "Damn the Temple," and limped out of the room.

There was a horrified silence as his step was heard going down the long kitchen passage.

"He's gone to the Estate Office," said Emmy. "He often does in the evenings. If the Jersey calves—"

On this Sylvia suddenly burst into tears, said she hated Jerseys and calves and wished she had never been born and rushed upstairs.

"She needn't get so excited," said Emmy to Anne. "It's awfully interesting really. Would you like to come?"

Anne hastened to protest that she wouldn't like to come at all and hoped she wouldn't wake in the night because she would feel so frightened. Emmy, with friendly scorn, said Anne had better go to bed and she was going herself now, but would not undress. Anne went up to her room and tapped at Sylvia's door. A muffled voice said Come in, and she found Sylvia in a dressing-gown with red eyes and impeded utterance. Anne begged to know what the matter was, to which her friend replied that it was Martin and he was a beast. Anne said perhaps his leg was hurting him.

"That's no reason for being beastly," said Sylvia. And then bursting into tears again said she was a beast too, and if Martin's leg was hurting it was all her fault because he had come all the way up to the Temple to find her for squash.

"Please, Sylvia, do stop," said Anne. "Emmy's next door, and if she hears you she'll come in and tell us awful things about cows. Please, please, Sylvia."

Sylvia, thus appeared to, checked her sobs and said she would be all right now and Anne must go to bed. So Anne went back to her own room and undressed. When she was in bed she sleepily thought over the long happy day; happy till the very end when poor Martin's leg had made him so cross. Robin, she reflected, was never cross, though an artificial foot must sometimes be worse than a limping leg. Then suddenly she remembered that Robin had been going to tell her a very special secret. Somehow the talk had changed and the special secret had not been told. She wondered what it could be and wondering fell asleep.

The Holdings party were soon back. Lady Graham asked George to stay to supper, but he suddenly felt unworthy and mumbled something about his people expecting him.

"Then you must come another Sunday," said Lady Graham, who appeared to George to have a halo and very soft white wings. "Perhaps that would be better, because this is just the one Sunday that Robert couldn't get down and he would like so much to see you. Come to lunch on Sunday, when that nice Mr. Bostock comes."

No longer had Lady Graham a halo or wings; but though a fallen angel, George's heart was torn with pity for one who could so far forget herself as to make a gross social gaffe. So he went home and was rather short with his parents.

Lady Graham at once became absorbed by her family, so Rose and David strolled down the garden to where a lawn skirted the Rising and there was a seat. The breeze had not yet become unpleasant, dragonflies were darting about over the water, everything was green and quiet.

"Well?" said Rose.

"What do you mean exactly?" said David.

"You know quite well," said Rose in her slow husky voice. "You have behaved abominably today."

"I haven't," said David, like cross child.

"You have," said Rose. "You have been showing off all day and we are all ashamed of you. Even Clarissa."

"Clarissa is a little devil," said her uncle.

"Possibly," said Rose, looking at her beautiful, well-groomed hands. "But why raise her devil? And why make Martin unhappy? A gammy leg and Rushwater and no money are quite enough."

"I didn't do anything to Martin," said David. "I swear I didn't. I only took Sylvia's hand up at the Temple. Lord! one always takes pretty girls' hands."

"You have been taking pretty girls' hands up and down town on and off for about twenty years," said Rose coldly. "It doesn't look so funny now you are getting a bit bald on the top."

"Not twenty years," said David appealingly.

"You were certainly doing it at seventeen," said Rose. "I was a beastly little girl in the schoolroom then with very sharp eyes. And you made that nice little Anne Fielding extremely uncomfortable."

"Good God! Rose, what right have you got to lecture me?" said David. "You have made lots of people uncomfortable."

"Not schoolboys," said Rose. "Only grown-up men who were asking for it. But that is neither here nor there. You have got to stop it, David."

"But I can't," said David.

"You'll have to when we are married," said Rose.

David stared at her.

"I think you have asked me about seven times," said Rose, without raising her voice or hastening her speech. "The last time you asked me was after Lettice turned you down, just before she married Captain Barclay. This time I am going to say yes."

"But I haven't asked you," said David, alarmed.

"That again is neither here nor there," said Rose. "We are gong to be married. It is all most suitable and we will do all sorts of amusing things when this foul peace is over. I believe you told

Anne Fielding that you wanted a wife who would be as funny as hell all the time."

"Do you mean it seriously?" said David, getting up in his agitation.

"I do," said Rose. "Wait a moment till I put my bag down."

She laid her bag on the seat and stood up. Miss Merriman, who had been to Evening Service and was walking back by the river path, observed with interest an embrace which left Glamora Tudor and Hash Gobbet in *Burning Flesh* nowhere at all.

"May I be the first to congratulate you?" said Miss Merriman, who had never been known to lose her composure. "Nothing could be nicer. Lady Emily will be delighted and so, I am sure, will Lady Dorothy.

"I'd forgotten about mother," said Rose. "But she's not much trouble. And I shan't let her come and stay with me for my babies. She's practically been turned out of Tadpole Hall. Tadpole wouldn't stand for it."

"Nor will I," said David with prompt gallantry, determined not to show surprise at anything.

The next person they met was Clarissa, taking her dog for a walk.

"Would you like to be a bridesmaid, Clarissa?" said Rose.

Clarissa asked whose.

"Mine," said Rose. "Rose Leslie sounds prettier than Rose Bingham so I'm going to marry David."

"Was that what you meant?" said Clarissa. "Oh, lovely, lovely," and she hugged her cousin Rose violently. "I say, David," she added, "I'm awfully sorry I was beastly this afternoon."

"So am I," said David. "Rose told me off so odiously that I had to say I'd marry her."

Clarissa put her arm affectionately through her uncle's and they all walked on to the house, agreeing to keep the engagement till after dinner, because if Lady Emily and Agnes knew, the servants would never be able to get at the table to clear away.

After dinner Lady Emily was installed as usual in her large

chair, with a table on each side of her covered with books, painting materials, flowers, letters, knitting, in which last art she made no progress at all since she had taken it up in the second year of the war and had nearly exhausted Miss Merriman's inexhaustible patience. Lady Graham reclined elegantly on a sofa with her embroidery, and Clarissa sat at her feet, mending some house-linen with exquisite stitches.

"Darling mamma," said David, sitting down as near his mother as the table, footstools and shawls would allow, "would you like to hear some good news about me?"

Lady Emily looked up at her son, her kind falcon's eyes shining with anticipation, her beautiful thin lips ready to smile.

"I am going to be married," said David.

"Wait a minute," said Lady Emily, shutting her eyes to assist her memory. "Not that woman whose name I can't remember, darling," she said anxiously.

"Good God, mamma, not Frances Harvey," said David, at once guessing his mother's meaning. "And anyway she is in Athens now, being an infernal nuisance, I gather, at the Embassy. Mamma, darling, I hate to disappoint you, but it's someone much nicer."

Lady Graham had stopped embroidering. Clarissa went on darning her linen with bent head, while Miss Merriman, knitting, looked on at another scene in the history of the family she had tended so well.

"Do help me, Rose," said David.

Then Lady Emily knew at once and Rose, getting as near her future mother-in-law as she could, kissed the fragile, handsome face very lovingly.

"Dear Rose," said Lady Emily. "Welcome. How pleased your uncle would have been. Darling David, this is perfect. Thank you both. Bless you both."

The bright falcon eyes were a little dimmed, but it was with sheer joy. Lady Graham, who by now had realised what was happening, came and kissed Rose and David in her own soft way and beamed approval.

"There is only one thing that isn't perfect," she said, "and that is Robert not being here. But I shall ring him up and he will be delighted. He had better give you way, Rose," for Rose's father had died meekly and uncomplainingly a good many years ago, not much missed by his masterful fox-hunting wife.

"That would be lovely," said Rose. "I did think of flying over and being married at the Embassy in Paris, but perhaps it would be better at home. I must ring mother up to-night."

"Give dear Dodo my love," said Lady Graham, "and say how pleased we all are. We had better have the wedding here, mamma, don't you think?"

"Wouldn't Rushwater be better?" said Lady Emily. "Martin wouldn't mind and there are more bedrooms empty."

Lady Emily and her daughter then discussed the wedding as if David and Rose were not there and Lady Dorothy Bingham did not exist, till Rose said she thought St. George's, Hanover Square, would be the best, because everyone was coming back to London. And then, said Lady Graham, they could have the reception at the Grantchester, who always managed to get food and some drinks somehow."

Lady Emily looked sad.

"Listen, mamma darling," said Lady Graham. "I will ask Robert. He always knows what to do. And he knows a lot of people on the board of the Grantchester and he shall get a couple of suites and you and Conque can drive up and be quite comfortable and you will see a lot of friends."

"Whose wedding is it, Rose?" said David to his affianced. "Yours, or mine, or your mother's, or my mother's, or Agnes's?"

"I don't mind in the least so long as it is your wedding and mine," said Rose. "David."

"I never thought anyone could make my name sound so attractive," said David. "Yes, Clarissa, I shall have to give you a present if you are a bridesmaid. What would you like? Two turtle doves, or a partridge in a pear tree?"

"Oh, Uncle David, could I have paste clip-on earrings?" said Clarissa.

"You shall," said David, "and they shall be specially chosen to suit you, and if they don't suit the other brides-maids they will have to lump it."

Then the question of bridesmaids had to be considered and Miss Merriman made lists and was helpful, and there was a delightful, comfortable, simmering kind of excitement till Conque came in to help her mistress to her bedroom and Miss Merriman went away with them.

"Oh dear, I had forgotten Emmy," said Lady Graham. "She goes to bed early so I will ring her up tomorrow morning. Good-night, darling David; good-night, darling Rose. Come along, Clarissa darling."

Having offered her incredibly soft face to be kissed, she went off with Clarissa.

"And bed for us too—in the more refined sense of the phrase," said David, yawning. "Lord! how sleepy being engaged makes one. Are we really engaged, Rose?"

"Really and always," said Rose, "till marriage us do part."

They went upstairs. On the landing Nurse was lurking, apparently, as David afterwards said to Rose, with the laudable intention that they should not be alone till St. George's, Hanover Square, should, on a date not yet settled, make them one, but really to offer congratulations.

"Miss Conk brought up the good news, Mr. David," said Nurse, "and I am sure I wish you and Miss Rose every happiness, and Edith will be quite excited when I tell her tomorrow morning, and we must write to James and Robert and Henry about their new auntie."

"Thanks awfully, Nurse," said David. "I'm a very lucky man."

"I'm sure you are, sir," said Nurse kindly. As David passed on to his bedroom she said to Rose, "You remember Ivy, Miss Rose, that was undernurse here so long? She took a place as single-handed nurse when the boys had all gone to school and there was only Edith except in the holidays, but she is thinking of giving notice because the lady she is with hasn't heard from her husband in the Far East for four years and Ivy won't stay if there isn't another baby. So if you should be thinking about a nurse, miss, I think you would find Ivy a nice willing girl and can take them from the month."

Rose thanked Nurse warmly, and then scandalised that worthy creature by going to David's room and telling him her suggestion, which made them both laugh immoderately. Much to Nurse's relief, who had been hanging about in case summoned by the shriek of a woman in distress, David came to his door fully clothed except for his jacket and bade a final goodnight to his betrothed.

Miss Merriman, having settled her employer, left her to Conque's administrations and went to her own room. Her thoughts went back to the day, three, four, five years ago—one lost count of time during a war—when Mrs. Marling and her daughter Lettice Watson had come over to see their cousin Emily, bringing with them the Leslies' old governess, Miss Bunting; and how she and Miss Bunting had discussed, without mentioning a single name, the possibilities of marriage for Lettice and David. Lettice had re-married, happily. David was going to marry, a little late, but very well, very suitably, and she felt that Miss Bunting would have approved.

As if their minds had moved together, David tapped at her door and came in.

"As a gentleman I must apologise for being in my dressing-gown," said David, "but I wanted to tell somebody how happy I am."

"That was very nice of you," said Miss Merriman.

"I have been thinking of old Bunny," said David. "She told me I couldn't fool all the people all the time. How right she was."

"She saw more than most people," said Miss Merriman.

"So do you, Merry," said David. "Well, having said my say, I shall now go away again. I suppose I shall find I really am engaged to-morrow morning?" he added anxiously.

Miss Merriman said he would, bade him good-night and kindly pushed him out of the room.

Through the open window of her bedroom she could hear soft steady rain. The summer was over.

The rain continued all night, the temperature fell. Nature had got things in hand again and was doing her best to help the cross, exhausted people of England to enjoy the first summer of so-called peace. Emmy, coming down to breakfast as usual at eight o'clock, found Martin and Sylvia already at the table. They looked wet, dirty and very tired, and were having their breakfast in a very uncomfortable way, holding hands across the table and feeding themselves with their spare hands. As Emmy came in they unclasped and pretended to look like ordinary people.

"Hullo," said Emmy, whose pre-occupation with herself and cows made her not notice other people much unless they were doing something useful in a cowshed, garden or field. "What a nasty morning. It's a good thing the Jersey didn't calve last night."

"She did," said Martin. "And I've got something to tell you, Emmy."

"The calf has two heads!" said Emmy, whose mind ran entirely on practical lines.

"No, that's all right," said Martin. "It's about Sylvia and me. We—"

"But what do you mean she calved then?" said Emmy. "I told Herdman to wake me."

"He couldn't," said Martin, adding under his breath the word Darling which was not meant for Emmy.

"What do you mean he couldn't?" said Emmy, her mouth rather full of fish-cake. "I told him to shout under my window if he needed me."

"He did shout," said Sylvia, "and I hadn't gone to bed yet, because I was thinking about things—"

"Angel!" said Martin, seizing a moment when his cousin Emmy was drinking her coffee in gulps.

"—and I went into your room," Sylvia continued, "but I couldn't wake you, so I dressed again and came down and then Herdman saw a light in the Estate Office, so we found Martin."

"What time was it?" said Emmy suspiciously.

"About one," said Martin. "I hadn't gone to bed yet, because I was worried about some things—"

"Poor lamb," said Sylvia softly.

"—and poor old Herdman's lumbago was pretty bad, so I sent him home and we did the job."

"It was *lovely*," said Sylvia, her eyes gleaming at the thought of her interesting vigil. "And when the Jersey—"

"That's enough at breakfast," said Martin. "You are as bad as Emmy."

Emmy said she would never forgive Herdman for not waking her.

"You must, Emmy," said Martin, "because Sylvia and I made such friends while we were sitting up with the Jersey that we got engaged."

Emmy stared, first incredulous, then half-convinced, and on the whole slightly contemptuous of people who could waste time on getting engaged while a cow and a calf were at stake. A sudden thought struck her.

"A bull or a heifer?" she asked anxiously.

"The finest little bull-calf I've ever seen," said Martin. "Rushwater Romany would be a proud man if he had the faintest idea it was his child."

It was then that Emmy rose supremely to the occasion.

"I say, Martin," she said. "I think we ought to give the R a miss this time and call him Churchill. It might bring him luck," she added, thinking not of the bull-calf but of a great Prime Minister whose party, so the omens foretold, would probably be swept from power by the millions of tired, impatient and mostly irresponsible people whom he had served.

Martin thought. The tradition of the R had never been broken since his great-grandfather had bred the first great prize winner, Rushwater Ramper. But there are moments when loyalty and gratitude must come first.

"Good girl, Emmy," he said. "Rushwater Churchill it shall be, and I wish those election results were out."

"I say, what did you mean you're engaged?" said Emmy, who had not forgotten Martin's news, though more important things had for the moment obscured it. "Do you mean that you and Sylvia are going to get married?"

Martin said that was what he intended to convey.

Emmy, finding words inadequate, got up, gave each of them a violent kiss and then began to cry loudly.

"It's all right," she mumbled, between her shrieks, her sniffs and her gulps. "I'm only so *awfully* pleased, and that beast Herdman not waking me and everything that I can't help it. Can I be a bridesmaid?"

"I'd love you to be a bridesmaid," said Sylvia, "if you'll promise me something."

"All right, I promise," said Emmy, "unless it's anything awful like my having my hair permed for the wedding."

"Will you go on living at Rushwater with us?" said Sylvia; and Martin felt deeply content with his bride.

At this Emmy cried more loudly than ever till quite suddenly she stopped, gave her face a kind of polish with an oily duster from her overalls pocket, and said she must ring mummy up. As Lady Graham was at the same moment trying to ring her daughter up there was some confusion and delay, but luckily the girl at the exchange, who had heard about Flight-Lieutenant Leslie's engagement from a friend at the Hatch End post-office who had got it from the Grahams' cowman, realised the importance of what was happening and got both lines clear.

When Emmy came back Martin and Sylvia were still holding hands across the table, but this time they did not unclasp.

"I say," said Emmy, "what do you think, David is going to

marry Rose and they want me to be a bridesmaid but it's to be in London and I don't know if I ought to go, because of the cows if Herdman is going to be bad with lumbago again. And Rose wants Anne to be one too."

Martin suddenly went quite pale and haggard. He knew this happiness could not last. Sylvia, in the reaction from their night of stress with the Jersey, had said she would marry him. She meant to be kind, God bless her, and beauty dwells with kindness as we all know, but of course when she heard that David, who only yesterday was trying his arts—oh yes, Martin knew the charm his Uncle David had for women—on her was really intending to marry Rose all the time, her heart would be broken; and either she would annul their engagement, or else marry him, pine, and die within the year, leaving perhaps one puny babe, sole relic of his love.

"Oh, Emmy! how *splendid*," said Sylvia. "I do think Rose is so nice and so beautifully dressed and just the right age for David. Oh! everything is *heavenly*. Martin darling, what is the matter? Is it your leg?"

Martin, suddenly transported from the dungeon of Giant Despair to the Delectable Mountains, said his leg was hurting a bit, but it was nothing, and of course Emmy must be a bridesmaid even if all the cows died.

Anne, who had overslept herself after the long, happy day and the agitation of the evening, now came in, was informed by three people at once of the events of the night, and though still only half awake was delighted that so many of her friends were going to marry each other and was engaged as bridesmaid for both marriages. Then they all went to look at Rushwater Churchill and presently Martin had to go to Barchester in the Ford van and dropped Sylvia and Anne at their homes, and the happy Rushwater visit was over.

# CHAPTER 10

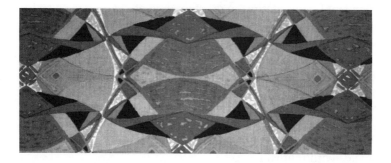

Emmy had done her best for Mr. Churchill, but as the election results came tumbling in it became clear that six years of increasing danger and discomfort, for part of which time they had stood alone against a world of deadly enemies, cautious friends and swithering neutrals, had left the peculiar English so desirous for a change of any kind, so blindly making themselves believe in promises of everything for nothing (except even higher taxes and discomfort), and Mr. Churchill's friends were swept away by huge majorities and the Brave and Revolting New World came into its own. Emmy, whose faith was of the bulldog kind, was however convinced that Rushwater Churchill had saved the ex-Prime Minister's seat for him, though as Martin pointed out, it must have been pre-natal influence. A minister (without portfolio) who should have known better spoke of "my Government" instead of His Majesty's Government without one protest being made, and England lurched on her way.

In East Barsetshire Mr. Gresham got in with a good majority and Mr. Hibberd went back to the City and continued to ruin Mr. Scatcherd's profession. In Barchester Sir Robert Fielding was beaten, partly because no power on earth could stop Mr. Adams getting in, but also because of a young man who had made over his estate to the National Trust on condition that he should live in it, he and his heirs, with no responsibilities for evermore, and suddenly burst into politics as a National Independent Crank, stating on no grounds at all that a vote given for him would be a vote given to Mr. Churchill, which quite took in a number of people who did not reflect that a vote given in Barchester would not have any effect in Woodford. This unpleasant young man forfeited his deposit, we are glad to say, but he had previously managed to unsettle a good many citizens who had thought of voting for Sir Robert. So Mr. Adams got in with a good thumping majority and he and Sir Robert shook hands with mutual respect.

"Now that it's over, I must say I am rather relieved," said Sir Robert. "To be Member for Barchester is a fine thing and I am sure you will look after us, Adams."

"I may say there's no one I'd sooner have been beaten by than you, Fielding," said Mr. Adams, "but as I'm in I'll do my best. And no one can say that my committee told more lies or made more promises than yours."

Sir Robert laughed.

"We all promised free everything, except perhaps free love," he said, "and we all knew we couldn't give anything. It's going to be hell for your lot, Adams, and I don't envy you. But I think you'll stay for five years. Everyone will be too tired and too busy scraping along somehow to want another General Election. How is Heather?"

"Between you and I and the gate-post," said Mr. Adams, "though it isn't public yet, my little Heth's gone and got herself engaged."

Sir Robert asked who the lucky man was, despising himself the while for deliberately speaking Mr. Adams's language.

"It's young Ted Pilward," said Mr. Adams. "He's a good lad and my Heth and he have been good friends for some time. He'll be out of the army by next year and going into his dad's business. Old Pilward is a good customer of mine. Many's the thousand pounds' worth of castings and parts we've turned out for the brewery. Mother would have been pleased," said Mr. Adams, who did not often speak of the wife who had died when Heather was a little girl. "Your Anne will be the next, I expect."

Sir Robert said he hoped not, as she was only nineteen, and went away. Mr. Adams then addressed his committee, thanked them for their support and said Sam Adams was a plain man and believed in plain speaking and knew a thing or two, and if they thought he was going into the lobby the way he was told they would have some surprises, and if everyone treated his employees fair, the way he did, there wouldn't be any need for all this labour unrest, and he only wished Mr. Churchill would take the leadership of the Labour Party and then England would get on all right. These very un-party words were eagerly taken down by the young man from the *Barchester Chronicle* who had got himself registered as doing work of national importance, and less eagerly by the elderly man who represented the *Barchester Free Press* and had no convictions or illusions about anything, and doubtless there would have been a fine commotion in Barchester next day, had not Councillor Budge of the Gas Works, a man of prompt action, taken them both to the Mitre, kept them there till closing time and seen them both not only home but into their beds.

"Adams is a rum bird," said Sir Robert to his wife. "I wouldn't be in the least surprised if he turned up on the Opposition Benches one day. There's nothing so conservative as a good Labour man. And now, that's that. What do you and Anne think about it?"

"Mixed, Robert," said Lady Fielding. "It might have been fun. But I think this Parliament is going to be very tiring whichever side one is on, and you have quite enough work here, and London will be dreadful, all fuller than ever of foreigners. And something quite dreadful might have happened like your getting a peerage and having a title like Lord Aberinverglenboldover that nobody can remember and they don't know who you are. No, Robert; I am very sorry, dearest, but really I'm very glad."

"And what about Anne," said Sir Robert.

"I'm most dreadfully sorry, daddy, about you being disappointed," said Anne, kissing the side of her father's head in affectionate if perfunctory way, "but I think Barchester is really nicer than London. I did love being at Rushwater so terrifically, and if we go to Hallbury Robin will be there for the school holidays and he is going to teach me Latin."

Sir Robert and his wife smiled at this natural if parochial view of politics and the talk passed to the two weddings, which were to be in September, and what the bridesmaids' frocks would be like.

The next really exciting thing that was to happen in Anne Fielding's life was Lady Graham's Bring and Buy Sale at Holdings, which was finally arranged for the third Wednesday in August. Anne was invited to stay at Holdings on the previous night so that she and Clarissa could have a comfortable talk about the dresses and what sort of stuff could be got without coupons and whether Madame Tomkins could be persuaded to give them priority. She was also to help Miss Merriman to arrange the many articles, pleasant and unpleasant, that had been contributed.

A very horrid rumour of still more peace was floating about in Barchester and indeed about all England for a few days before Anne's visit, filling everyone with deep misgivings about trains and more especially about the grocer and the bread. Public opinion was divided, some saying They would certainly have peace on a Tuesday so that one could get the rations done on Monday, others saying that they knew for certain that the King had asked for peace to happen on Friday, so that everyone could have a nice long weekend. Yet others, and these a very large class including all the housewives of England who had been working for sixteen or seventeen hours a day ever since the war began, looking after children and aged relatives, standing in queues, walking a mile to the bus and taking an hour to get to the nearest town only to find that the whelk oil or chuckerberry juice or whatever it was that they were told their children must have wasn't in and it was two hours before the bus went back and anyway they had been given the wrong certificate, slaving at W.V.S. in their meagre spare time, suffering evacuees, taking in lodgers because their husband was only getting army pay now, cooking for everyone, fire-watching, being wardens, being mostly too tired to eat, seeing Italian and German prisoners of war riding happily about the country in motor lorries while they pounded along on bicycles against wind and rain or lugged heavy baskets on foot, seeing mountains of coal and coke at the prisoner of war camps while they were down to two hot baths a week and very little soap for the washing and the laundry only coming irregularly every three weeks, seeing Mixo-Lydian and other refugees throwing whole loaves into the pig-bin and getting the best cuts at the butcher's, keeping their children nicely dressed while they got shabbier themselves every day, too driven to consider their looks, unable to have their houses properly cleaned and repaired, having to be servile to tradesmen and in many cases to tip them in money or kind, seeing one egg in eight weeks with luck, in a state of permanent tiredness varied by waves of complete exhaustion, yet never letting down anyone dependent on them; this great, valiant, unrecognised class, the stay of domestic England, all knew that THEY would burst peace on them whenever it was most inconvenient and went about their shopping listlessly, waiting for the tiger to spring.

"I have a quite dreadful feeling that peace will be tomorrow," said Lady Graham as they all sat in the garden after tea on Tuesday.

"It's our own fault if it does," said Miss Merriman, who was hardly ever known to complain or criticise, "for arranging the sale. We might have known that any day we fixed would bring bad luck."

Nurse, who had come out to fetch Edith for her bath, said no one seemed to consider anyone's feelings nowadays and she wouldn't be surprised if Hitler hadn't been at the bottom of all this peace after all.

"Cook said, No bread," said Edith, who was given to poetic outbursts.

"What do you mean, Edith darling?" Said her mother.

"Really Edith, the way you do repeat thing," said Nurse. "We had tea in the kitchen, my lady, for a treat, and cook was passing the remark that they were saying at The Shop we'd better get our bread in today as there'll likely be a run on it tomorrow. Really, some people don't seem to have any consideration. Say good-night, Edith."

"Good-night Merry and eat a cherry,

"Good-night Clarissa and don't cut yourself on a scissor,

"Good-night Anne, come again as soon as you can," said Edith, accompanying her verses by a king of hipping dance.

"Good-night, darling Edith," said Lady Graham, kissing her youngest daughter with great affection.

"Come along now, Edith," said Nurse, secretly very proud of Edith's lyrical gifts, but determined not to let her know it.

"Oh, mummy! I'd forgotten you," said Edith running back. "Good-night mummy, I love you with my *whole* tummy."

"Come along, Edith," said Nurse, justly outraged; and withdrew her young charge.

Next morning the very worst had occurred. News of the outbreak of Peace had been announced in a grave yet refined manner to England at midnight through the courtesy of the British Broadcasting Corporation, who being used to keeping peculiar hours themselves did not realise nor care that the great mass of people were in bed and asleep at that time, nor that, in spite of all the Beveridge and Social Security fuss, there were a number of people who couldn't afford a wireless at all. The next editions of this news were heard by the people who had to be up early and get breakfast for their husbands, or go to work early themselves and they were in too much of a hurry to bother; some shouting to Tom for the love of mike to turn off that filthy noise as they couldn't hear themselves speak, others reflecting gloomily that it was the hell of a lot of good their knowing it was Vee Jee Day, they meant Vay Jay Dee, oh, blast it whatever it was then, as the shops wouldn't be open when they went to work and would be empty and probably shut into the bargain at the lunch hour. By the time the later announcements were made, exasperated housewives said Oh God! another Peace and we've only half a loaf and Sheila and Dick coming to supper; so that by the time the newspapers arrived with the announcement that there would be a kind of public holiday, a number of people in suburbs and dormitory towns had already started by train to earn their daily bread in London, Liverpool, Birmingham and other places. Some of these discovered through the conversation of other passengers and a general feeling of apprehension that their office or works would probably be shut and angrily got out at the junction, there to await the very slow 10.40 down train and go home. Others, not having been warned, got to their destination and if employers swore loudly and attended to the correspondence themselves, if employed swore even more loudly because the pubs weren't open yet (chiefly male) and the tea-shops were all sold out of cakes and mostly closed for the day (female).

They then all walked aimlessly about London, swelling the already gigantic crowd of Esquimaux, Tibetans, Americans, Free French, Tierra del Fuegans, Poles (who owing to each supporting a different kind of Government seemed even more numerous than they were), Mixo-Lydians, Canadians, Slavo-Lydians, Australians, Indians (which to the English mind roughly included any Persians, Arabs or South Sea Islanders who happened to be about), Argentines who had loyally come into the war the day before, Chileans who were all called Eduardo O'Coughlin or Ignacio Macalister, a clergyman who had once lived on Tristan da Cunha, Irish labourers out of whose large wages paid by the Saxon Oppressor Dark Rosaleen was doing very nicely while her sons pursued a divil-may-care policy of sitting on doorsteps all day smoking and contemplating the repairing jobs they had been imported to do, Lapps, Swedes, Broccoli, Calabresi, Chinese who being used to three million people dying of famine or being drowned in floods were unimpressed by crowds, some Russians one supposes, practically the whole of the Balkan states, the head chief of Mngangaland, who was in England with a large retinue to put his eightieth and favourite son to Balliol, and the President of the Republic of Sangrado, so-called from the great Liberator Shaun O'Grady (murdered 1843). And all these people walked up and down London all day, with very little to drink and little or nothing to eat, and squashed each other loyally in front of Buckingham Palace, irritably in the Strand, angrily in Trafalgar Square, furiously in the Tubes as long as they were open, and drove the long-suffering Metropolitan Police nearly demented by being funny at night in Piccadilly Circus.

Meanwhile in the residential suburbs of London bakers' shops were practically looted and mothers of young families went home with angry tears to make such scones as they could when they had meant to get the fat ration this morning, my dear, and how on earth was I to know it would be peace when Tom and I are sleeping like the dead at twelve o'clock at night and goodness knows I haven't a moment to listen to the wireless when I'm getting him and the children off and he always takes the newspaper with him and of course the milkman has only left us a pint to-day and what the good is of having three children under ten if you can't get their milk don't ask me, my dear. Whereas in transpondine Squattlesea and other less residential parts of London the bakers were working full time because their fellow-citizens, being as Communist as they were, would have wrecked their shops if they hadn't, and the public houses mysteriously had beer for quite a long time after closing hours if you knew how to get it.

In Barchester the day passed off in comparative peace,

though with an amount of irritation that six years of war hod not yet produced. The Close was convulsed by the news that the Bishop had asked the Dean to allow the organist to play the Red Flag after evensong as a sign of gratitude to our Wonderful Red Comrades, which piece of meddling the Dean had very neatly countered by asking the precentor to include in the service the hymn beginning "Lord God Omnipotent" which is sung to the tune of the Russian Imperial National Anthem, and announcing that instead of a voluntary after the service there would be a two minutes' silence in memory of the Barsetshire dead, after which the congregation were asked to leave silently and reverently. Luckily the Deanery's annual dinner party for the Palace had taken place a week earlier and the Palace's annual dinner party for the Deanery—if you could call it a dinner party with soup made from a packet and tap-water to drink, said Mrs. Crawley—was not due till February, which gave things time to simmer down.

But we are anticipating and must return to Holdings where Lady Graham and Miss Merriman held counsel as to the advisability of cancelling the sale. Lady Graham thought that everything would be so upset that nobody would come. Miss Merriman considered that everyone who possibly could come would come so that they could tell other people how annoying it all was. Miss Merriman was usually right, the sale had been made widely known and one didn't want to disappoint people, so it was decided to go ahead.

The sale was to be held in the large room with long windows onto the garden. It had been known since the late eighteenth century as the Saloon and was now used as a kind of store for unwanted furniture and pictures till such time as it was possible to live in the whole house again, while a smaller room was used as the family drawing-room. Three or four large trestle tables had been put up, and here Miss Merriman, Clarissa and Anne spent the morning in arranging all the nasty things to look as nice as they could, which wasn't saying much, for few people had anything pretty left to give and all sales relied largely on the jam, cakes, fruit and vegetables brought in by the Bringers, who then themselves became Buyers of other people's vegetables, fruit, cakes and jam.

"That horror has been all round Barsetshire to my certain knowledge since Lady Pomfret gave it to the Pomfret Madrigal Women's Institute sale in 1941," said Miss Merriman, holding up an olive green earthenware vase at least two feet high with a spray of bulrushes painted on it. "It will go all round Barsetshire again I expect."

Clarissa asked if she might improve it.

"You couldn't," said Miss Merriman, looking with fascinated loathing at the vase, "but do try."

So Clarissa fetched some gold and silver paint and with her neat, elegant fingers touched up the bulrushes in silver and painted the word PEACE in gold, slantingly.

"I think that is just about right for a sale," said Clarissa, putting her paints neatly away; and Miss Merriman thought that Clarissa was growing up very fast and must certainly go to school that autumn and become a child again for a year or two, while improving her mathematics and science if she really wanted to do engineering draughtsmanship.

As they worked they chattered about the weddings and how sad it was that David and Rose couldn't come to the Sale. Still, Martin and Emmy were coming with farm produce and Martin was going to bring Sylvia's engagement ring with him.

"How pretty your ring is, Anne," said Miss Merriman.

"Mummy said only to wear it for evening or occasions," said Anne, holding out her right hand to let Miss Merriman inspect the ring more closely.

"It must be an old one," said Miss Merriman. "It is one of those Regard rings. A lovely little thing."

Clarissa asked what a Regard ring was.

"Ruby, Emerald, Garnet, Amethyst, Ruby, Diamond," said Anne. "Robin's father gave it to me—old Mr. Dale. It belonged to Robin's mother, who died when he was quite little. And I thought Lady Graham's Bring and Buy Sale was rather an occasion, so I put it on."

Miss Merriman again expressed admiration and Mr. Scatcherd came into the room carrying a parcel.]

"My humble contribution to Lady Graham's sale," said Mr. Scatcherd to Miss Merriman. "I should be much obliged to you, miss, if a reserved price could be put upon my sketches. One must keep up the standard and I should not like to see them go for less than her ladyship purchased them from me for."

Miss Merriman, who quite understood what he meant, said she would see that a reserve was put on the drawings.

"Especially," said Mr. Scatcherd, undoing the parcel and laying the contents on the table, "this one. It is the one I was doing the morning her ladyship happened to look in and see me about the sale. If I LIVE," said Mr. Scatcherd, "I mean in the artistic sense of the word, for of course one might have a heart attack or be run over any day and mors is quite common in an omnibus as the saying is though I dessay it was horse buses they were thinking of, not motor buses in the Olden Times," said Mr. Scatcherd with a scholarly air, "if I LIVE, this is what I shall live by."

"I remember it," said Clarissa, coming to look. "It's the Rising and some bulrushes. Are there really any bulrushes as tall as that, Mr. Scatcherd?" She added, pointing to the centre background of the picture.

"Ah, it takes a Lifetime to understand sketches," said Mr. Scatcherd. "Look again, miss."

Clarissa looked again.

"Ah!" Mr. Scatcherd repeated in a superior way, with a kind of sneering smile which exhibited his rather cheap uppers to their fullest extent.

"I know," said Anne. "It's the spire of the cathedral, isn't it, Mr. Scatcherd? Only one doesn't really see it from here, does one?"

"Now, here is a young critic who understands Art," said Mr. Scatcherd, by-passing in a cowardly way the question of the spire. "Are you one of the family, miss?"

Miss Merriman, who wanted to get on with the arranging, said this was Miss Fielding, who was on a visit from Barchester, and it was so good of Mr. Scatcherd to bring his drawings and she hoped he would come in the afternoon and buy something.

"Not Number Seventeen, The Close?" said Mr. Scatcherd, getting so near Anne that she slid to the other side of Miss Merriman. "I know Number Seventeen inside and out, every corner. The postcards I've done of Number Seventeen, Miss Fielding, would surprise you. When I say 'inside,' I've never had the pleasure of being in the house, Miss Fielding, but the Eye of the Artist sees a lot through the windows in summer and what the Eye doesn't see the Imagination can imagine. My sketches of the interior of the drawing-room with a nice Jacobean buffet and a spinet is quite one of my best sellers."

Anne was just going to protest that there was nothing Jacobean in the drawing-room and certainly no spinet, but luckily for her (for Mr. Scatcherd would have pitied her ignorance and despised her), Hettie who had been up to Holdings about a hen to sit on some ducks' eggs and was passing the open French window, heard her uncle's voice and came in, calling heaven to witness without a single comma that if uncle could give trouble he always did and hadn't he the sense to see Miss Merriman and the young ladies were busy instead of standing there talking about his painting and rubbish good GRACIOUS did he think no one had anything to do but to listen to him and to come along at once if he wanted his dinner.

Mr. Scatcherd, unable to make his voice heard, tried to make the kind of face Socrates might have made while Xantippe was, in Miss Lucy Marling's favourite phrase, telling him what; flung his cloak round him to theatrically that not being buttoned at the top it all fell onto the floor, picked it up and followed his masterful niece.

The ladies then disposed his sketches to the best advantage, provided raffle tickets for his view of the cathedral, washed their hands and went in to lunch.

It had been arranged earlier in the week that Robin Dale, who was spending the school holidays with his father at Hallbury and had lately bought a cheap little car from a young man on leave who had spent his all on wine and women and wanted some cash, should come to Lady Graham's sale and drive Anne back to Hallbury where her parents were also spending a few weeks, thus saving her the tiring roundabout journey by train to Barchester with nearly an hour's wait. The sale was to be from two to five with tea sixpence at one end of the Saloon and when Robin arrived at half-past two he found Anne selling raffle tickets for the green earthenware vase. Robin said he would buy all the tickets if he might be allowed to break the vase, but Anne, who was taking her duties seriously, said that would not be fair and five tickets was the ration. So Robin bought five tickets and went to pay his respects to Lady Graham, who was in the small drawing-room mildly trying to control her mother, who was profiting by Miss Merriman's absence at the sale to make hay of the books, drawing and painting materials, letters, scarves, so carefully arranged by her secretary; also to knit an Air Force blue scarf into a state of inextricable and triangular confusion.

"Mother darling, here is Mr. Dale," said Lady Graham. "You know he is the Latin master at Southbridge and he came to Rushwater with John's boys."

Lady Emily, always enchanted to meet new people, begged Robin to sit down and talk to her. To sit, owing to the barricades of portable property with which Lady Emily had surrounded herself, was not easy, but with her daughter's help a breach in the fortifications was made, into which Robin was able to introduce a small chair.

"I am so glad those dear boys of John's are learning Latin with you," said Lady Emily. "I feel it is extraordinarily important, though I do not really know why. My father learnt Latin at

Eton. I cannot remember who taught him, but I remember he was a very distinguished scholar because he became a Bishop afterwards and had a very good cellar. Papa bought some of his port after he died and I believe there is still some of it at Pomfret Towers. Papa translated a poem by Ronsard once and had it privately printed. Of course not Latin exactly, but I expect you know French too, Mr. Dale."

Robin, feeling as giddy as anyone usually did who met Lady Emily for the first time, said he did know French a bit, but not enough to teach it.

"Of *course* not," said Lady Emily, with an earnestness that meant nothing at all. "My maid Conque, who has been with me for forty years, still can't speak English. It shows what an extraordinary language French is."

Robin said it did, hoping to win favour thereby.

"And are you by any chance connected with the Allington Dales?" said Lady Emily.

Robin said his father, who was Rector of Hallbury, had a great aunt called Lily Dale, but he didn't know much about her.

"But then your father is Dr. Dale!" said Lady Emily, enchanted to have an excuse for going into relationships. "I remember meeting him at the Deanery a long time ago with your mother, a lovely young creature. How is she?"

Robin said he was dreadfully sorry but she was dead, at which Lady Emily's face became all compassion; but a long time ago, when he was quite a little boy, he added.

"Poor boy, poor boy," said Lady Emily, laying her frail hand with its heavy jewelled rings on his knee. "And poor Dr. Dale. My second son—the one whose boys are at Southbridge—lost his first wife soon after they were married. She was the most enchanting person and we all adored her, but they had no children. John was in the most bitter distress, and if he had not met Mary Preston—her mother is the sister of Agnes's husband and Mary is a darling and we all love her—I think he would have become a kind of hollow mask, though he was always most

loving to me," said Lady Emily, a veil coming over her bright
falcon's eyes as she thought of her child's misery, though long
since stilled and probably forgotten with his very nice wife and
his children.

Robin did not know what to answer. He could not truthfully
say "poor boy" of himself, for he hardly remembered his mother,
his boyhood and school days had been happy, and he and his
father were excellent if not intimate friends. But all this was
rather difficult to explain in one breath and he did not like to
intrude his own deficiency in sorrow upon Lady Emily, to
whom the old griefs were still young in her remembering of
them. Luckily the pause was not too long before her ladyship,
always wanting to know about people, asked Robin if his father
had married again.

Robin said No; not but what, he added, he thought his father
certainly would have if he had wanted to.

"You must bring him to see me one day," said Lady Emily.
"We could talk about old times and your lovely mother."

"I'm afraid Papa wouldn't be up to it," said Robin. "He is over
eighty—he married very late in life, but I think he and my
mother were very happy—and very frail. But I will give him
your kind message."

Lady Emily then fell into a welter of plans for going over to
Hallbury, and Robin had to explain that though his father was
not in the least mad, he was very apt to forget or jumble names
and dates and places, and was in fact distinctly woolly in the wits
except for church matters, on which his mind remained perfectly clear, though his physical powers were failing.

Lady Emily's sympathy was so prompt, so understanding,
that Robin confided to her that everyone was wondering if his
father would have to retire soon; how Robin hoped this would
not come to pass, because he thought his father would die of a
broken heart, quite apart from old age, if he were separated from
his beloved St. Hall Friar's Church; and that a horrid rumour

had reached him through the Deanery that the Bishop was going to be difficult.

"The Bishop!" said lady Emily. And then her ladyship expressed her opinion of that prelate with some vigour. "My dear Mr. Dale, it must not be. I shall tell Gillie to enquire into it at once, and he shall tell the Duke of Omnium to speak to the Archbishop"; for Lady Emily's distant cousin young Giles Foster, who had succeeded to the Pomfret earldom after her brother's death, had become a power in Barsetshire, not so much through his possessions as by his hard work in the county and his utter reliability in any matter into which he entered.

"Bishop Joram, I think you know him, who was vicar of Rushwater for a time during the war," said Robin, "is extremely kind about coming over from Barchester to help, and Papa likes him. So I hope everything will be all right. But thank you very much, Lady Emily, for your kindness. I don't know how to thank you properly."

"And you lost a foot at Anzio, so little Anne Fielding told me," said Lady Emily. "And there is Martin with that leg of his though he never complains, and I sometimes think of my eldest son. He was killed at Arras. He was Martin's father, you know. The Flowers of the Forest."

There was a silence while Lady Emily looked far back into the pasts and Robin thought of the Leslie boys and all his other pupils, and wondered at what age another war would catch them with its blind, senseless fury. He saw no particular hope in the prospect.

"Before you go," said Lady Emily, coming back to the present with a very practical air, "I should like to give you a copy of Papa's translation of the poem by Ronsard. We will go to my room and find one. Will you give me your arm?"

Without waiting for an assistance which Robin hardly knew how to give, so encompassed was her ladyship by the barricades round her chair, Lady Emily began to get up. As Robin told Anne afterwards it was rather like a game of spillikins, except that Lady Emily cheated and always played again after she had disturbed the pile. Three books slid gently to the floor, a glass of water with two paint brushes and a rose in it tilted with maddening slowness, though just so fast that Robin could not catch it in time, and fell into a basket of knitting. A reading lamp crashed to the ground and Robin, trying to get nearer his hostess, caught his foot in the flex and nearly fell into the fireplace.

"Oh dear, do be careful, Mr. Dale," said Lady Emily, who had by now managed to stand up and was dropping shawls and scarves like icicles when the thaw begins. "You will hurt your foot."

Without pausing to ask whether she meant his real foot or the pretence one, Robin picked up some of the impedimenta and followed her respectfully across the hall to her own sitting-room, which looked rather as if a dealer in old furniture and clothes had been trying to find the philosopher's stone over a period of years.

"Merry tidies it every day," said Lady Emily, "I cannot *think* how it gets so untidy. Now, I know Papa's Ronsards are on the top shelf in the corner, because I put them there only last week. Will you look, Mr. Dale?"

Robin looked and said he was very sorry he couldn't see them.

"You are perfectly right," said Lady Emily. "They can't be there for I distinctly remember having moved them to make room for something else. I know."

She advanced triumphantly, leaning on her stick, to the large table, lifted a piece of old wine-coloured velvet and exposed a little pile of thin books. She took one, and saying to Robin that she would write his name in it, sat down at another part of the table where pens, pencils, paste, chalks, drawing-pins and co-loured inks lay pell-mell.

"Green for Ronsard, I think," said Lady Emily, taking up a pen and dipping it into an ink bottle. "Though why green," she added with an air of great candour, "I really do not know."

"Perhaps because of its verte nouveauté," said Robin, a phrase suddenly rising to his memory.

Lady Emily flashed one of her most brilliant bewitching smiles upon him and her flowing handwriting embellished with arabesques, wrote some words.

"We will let it dry," she said. "It always looks nicer than if you blot it."

Robin looked over his shoulder and read, "To Robin Dale this book written by his dear Father. Emily Leslie."

"I think," said Robin, though tentatively, for he was beginning to feel as most of Lady Emily's friend did that with her all things were possible, "there is a kind of mistake, Lady Emily. It was Lord Pomfret who translated the poem, not my father. At least, I don't think he did,"

"How foolish of me," said Lady Emily. "I must have been thinking of your dear father, or of something quite different. I often do. I will alter it."

Below the inscription she added the words, "Fool that I am. It was Papa that translated the poem."

"There," she said, handing it triumphantly to Robin. "Give your father my love and tell him that I have never forgotten your mother; that lovely creature. And now if you will ring the bell for Conque I shall go to my room."

Robin rang. Conque came in her usual grudging way and took possession of her mistress's loose property. Lady Emily said good-bye and Robin went to see how the sale was getting on.

The sale was going pretty well. The neighbourhood had rallied loyally and a few friends had come from Barchester by train, really to see Lady Graham, though they bought nobly as well. But the friends further away mostly hadn't any petrol to spare, or if they had, felt too tired to make the effort after dealing with the food problems roused by Peace. Lord Stoke, who never missed an opportunity of going anywhere, had driven over from

Rising Castle in a dog-cart, bringing Mrs. Morland with him and an elderly groom on the back seat, which turn-out aroused a great deal of comment, most of it we regret to say of a disparaging nature, from the general public who thought a horse was funny.

"I wouldn't have come over," said Lord Stoke to Lady Graham, "if I hadn't known you could put the horse up. When I was a young man you could drive all over England and put your trap or your horse up properly. Now, except for the Omnium Arms at Hallbury, I don't know an hotel within miles that has even one loose-box. My rule is: go and see your friends that farm. They'll be able to look after a horse. I told my man to take the dog-cart over to the farm. Well, well, you've a sale, haven't you? Anything I can buy?"

"Lady Graham, having waited patiently for her distinguished old friend to finish talking, for owing to his deafness it was useless to say anything till he had talked himself out, said at the top of her voice that she was so glad he had sent the dog-cart over to the farm and the bailiff would take great care of it and the horse and look after the groom. She then welcomed Mrs. Morland and begged them both to come and have tea in the drawing-room before they went.

Lord Stoke, whose knowledge of the county was extensive and peculiar, made himself quite happy in his own way by giving the best-looking of the village helpers five pounds and telling her to buy some rubbish for him and take tickets in all the raffles, and then melted away towards the farm, where he caught the bailiff and had a long and delightfully depressing talk about the future of agriculture in England. Mrs. Morland, seeing Anne Fielding, for whom she had taken a great liking, went and talked to her.

"Will you introduce me to Mrs. Morland, Anne?" said Miss Merriman.

"But don't you know each other?" said Anne, surprised that two ladies, both inhabitants of Barsetshire, each so distinguished in her own way, should not be acquainted. "Oh Mrs. Morland, this is Miss Merriman."

"Would you mind if I told you how very much I like your books?" said Miss Merriman, shaking hands with Mrs. Morland.

"Not really," said Mrs. Morland, with her air of desperate candour. "I mean I am frightfully pleased, but it always seems to me so peculiar that the sort of people one knows should like one's books, because they are really intelligent."

"Do you mean the people or the books?" said Miss Merriman.

And then both the ladies laughed and got on very well, each respecting in the other something she could not possibly do herself.

"I have brought you, if you don't mind," said Mrs. Morland, scrabbling about in a large bag and extracting an untidy parcel, "three of my books for the sale. I wish I could have brought more, but my publisher Adrian Coates can't get any more paper and I can't get copies of my own old books. These are some I happened to have by me. I wish they were eggs or something useful."

Miss Merriman thanked Mrs. Morland warmly and said if she would autograph them it would greatly enhance their value. Mrs. Morland, flattered and surprised, undid the parcel, put the books on a table where second-hand novels were being sold and pulling out a fountain pen signed them all.

"Thank you very much," said Miss Merriman. "But they are too good for this stall. We will raffle them."

Clarissa, who had been looking on, hoping to be allowed to shake hands with the creator of Madame Koska, in whose dressmaking establishment so many delightful crimes and conspiracies took place yearly, threw herself into the business of raffle tickets and with the help of Anne and the Infant School Teacher, who was very littery—at least that was how she described herself—had within a quarter of an hour sold two pounds fourteen shillings and sixpence worth of tickets, which gratified the well-known authoress very much.

"Because that," she explained, "comes to more than they cost at a bookseller's, so my publisher can't say I am underselling him."

"Even Miss Merriman, who had kept the whole of the domestic accounts for Pomfret Towers and metaphorically cast her shoe over most financial problems, was staggered by Mrs. Morland's statement, but decided to treat it as a proof of genius.

"It was Clarissa," said Anne, presenting her friend.

Mrs. Morland shook Clarissa's hand warmly and said she would send a copy of her next book, which kind action confirmed Clarissa in her wish to go to boarding-school, as she would there be able to boast about it.

As most of the goods on the tables were now sold, Miss Merriman decided to announce the names of raffle winners before tea, at which news Mr. Scatcherd's anxiety rose to fever point, for the fate of his masterpiece was in the balance.

Clarissa drew the tickets out of a horse's nosebag, itself one of the articles being raffled, and read, "Mr. Scatcherd's picture. Number Twenty-two."

All those who had not lost their tickets looked anxiously through them.

"Well to GOODNESS," said the exasperated voice of Hettie Scatcherd, "if it isn't my number anyone might have told me not to be fool enough to take a ticket for anything of Uncle's I'd be sure to get it oh good GRACIOUS now we've got to have it back on our hands as if there wasn't enough of your rubbishy stuff about the house any way Uncle and what her ladyship will say after being so kind as to buy those things of yours for her sale I don't know oh my GOODNESS!"

Lady Graham, who had been talking with the Hallidays and Martin about Sylvia's wedding, which was to be at Hatch End, of course, came over to see what all the noise was about. Miss Merriman explained the unfortunate coincidence and Lady

Graham said if Miss Scatcherd didn't mind she would re-buy
the picture for whatever it had fetched in the raffle and present
it to the Infant School. On enquiry it was found that Hettie's
was the last ticket sold and that twenty-two sixpences were
eleven shillings. This sum Lady Graham accordingly paid to
Miss Merriman as Honorary Treasurer, the Infant School
teacher said it would brighten up that dark place where the
children left their coats nicely, and Mr. Scatcherd, pleased to
think that his masterpiece would assist in forming the minds, if
any, of future generations, though he would have preferred to
see it hung in the National Gallery, was dragged back to Rokeby
by his niece, who didn't believe in spending money on tea when
she could have it quietly at home.

The gentry then went into the drawing-room, leaving the
commons to have tea in the now almost denuded Saloon.

"Where is Lord Stoke?" said Lady Graham.

"With Emmy," said Martin. "As soon as she heard he was
here she went off to the farm to talk cows with him."

Leslie major, who had bicycled from his home on the other
side of Barchester with his brother, said he would go and find
them and before long returned with the wanderers, who had
been enjoying themselves vastly.

"Nice girl of yours," said Lord Stoke to Lady Graham. "She's
got a head on her shoulders. We were talking a bit of business. I
hear you are looking out for a good heifer in calf, Martin. Send
Emmy over to see one or two I've got. And how are yours,
eh? Emmy says you've called the new bull-calf Rushwater
Churchill. Quite right too. If Churchill had been in, we'd never
have had this peace."

At this revolutionary remark most of the company stopped
talking and stared.

"I know *exactly* what Lord Stoke means," said Mrs. Morland,
ramming her hat onto her head in a way which anyone who
knew her would have recognised as a preparation for some of her
most irresponsible and Sibylline utterances. "When this Gov-

ernment came into power—I will not say we put them into power," said Mrs. Morland, "for I voted Conservative and so did everyone I know except a few people like that dreadful Major Hooper who thinks that what he thinks *matters*—I decided that as the People of England, though I really do not know what I mean by that nor does anyone else, wanted a Government like that and as it was His Majesty's Government we ought to support it. So I did support it, except of course when I voted Conservative in the bye-election, but that was quite different because it was voting for one man, not for a whole Government; and I would be supporting it still, not that it has ever supported me," said Mrs. Morland bitterly as she swept a bit of loose hair behind her ear, "until this *dreadful* Vay Jay Dee—I mean Vee Jee Day—well, you know what I mean. And when," Mrs. Morland continued, putting her hat a little crooked and giving the impression of rising to her feet and being nine feet high, although she was sitting at the tea-table, "I saw the way They managed it; when Anne Knox started for London and got as far as Barchester and had to come back because the papers hadn't come and they very rightly don't listen to the wireless, though I daresay we shall all be compelled by law to listen to it soon, in which case I shall go and live with Lord Stoke because he is deaf; then I Lost Faith. Not that I ever had any," said Mrs. Morland simply, "but I do want to be loyal and after all the Government is the governing power however you look at it. And people finding all the bread gone just because the Government thought it would show off instead of letting us know the day before, and then we could have stayed in bed an hour longer or something. So I stopped being loyal. I mean to the Government, not to the King, who makes me cry whenever I think of him," at which loyal effusion most of her hearers felt they could easily cry too. "So," said Mrs. Moreland, reserving this thunderbolt for the last, "I joined the Women's Section of the High Rising Branch of the Barsetshire Conservative Association, for I felt it was the very worst I could do. And now the Government can do what it likes."

So strongly did this patriotic and defiant speech affect her audience that but for the powerful voices of Lord Stoke and Emmy they would all probably have joined the nearest Conservative Association at once, and Anne and Clarissa might have become members of a Youth Group. But the cow-keeping interest overbore all such secondary considerations, and Lord Stoke, Emmy, Martin and Sylvia bargained about the heifer at the tops of their voices, owing to his lordship's deafness; which made Martin, who was not very good at shouting, think how lucky he was to have won a wife like Sylvia who was not only an angel and very kind and very beautiful, but could bellow down Lord Stoke on his own ground. And as he looked at Sylvia with adoration and gratitude, she suddenly looked at him with protection and adoration in her eyes, and Mrs. Halliday said to Lady Graham how very lovely Sylvia's engagement ring was and how clever of Martin to find it, and they fell again into wedding talk while Mr. Halliday discussed *The Three Musketeers* with Leslie minor.

Then Robin said to Anne that they ought to be getting back, as his father liked his dinner rather early, so good-byes were said.

"It is really good-bye to everything nice forever," said Mrs. Morland in her deepest tragedy voice, "from today onwards."

"Don't be a fool, Laura," said Lord Stoke, who had happened to hear her. "World's got to go on somehow."

"But it is all going to be horrid forever," said Mrs. Morland. "We shall have a horrid winter and probably the Government will send all our coal and all our food to the Russians or the Mixo-Lydians, and there will be millions of conferences with millions of foreigners eating what's left and commandeering all the hotels. And no clothes, and everyone being rude. And we shall be so tired," said Mrs. Morland sadly, "that we shan't even try to protest. And Tony will probably be killed in India because of Fakeers and Yogis and Gandhis and things rioting and the army being sent for and not allowed to fire on them till they have all been murdered."

"Yes, it is all *dreadful*," said Lady Graham sympathetically. "But you will write another book, Mrs. Morland, won't you, and we shall all read it aloud, shan't we, Clarissa darling, with Gran and Merry."

"Come along, Laura," said Lord Stoke, who had been looking out of the window. "The cob doesn't like standing."

"Oh, Lord Stoke," said Clarissa, bringing forward the green vase with the bulrushes, "this is yours."

"It's not mine," said Lord Stoke indignantly. "Never set eyes on it in my life."

"But you bought a ticket for it, at least you gave Betty Hubback some money to buy tickets," said Clarissa. "It's the only raffle you won, but Betty bought some jam and things for you and they are in the dog-cart."

"Excuse me, sir," said Leslie major, noting Lord Stoke's marked dislike for the vase, "but if you don't need it, could I have it? The Matron in our house has a birthday next term and it is just in her line."

"Who are you, eh?" said Lord Stoke. "Leslie's boy? Here you are and don't let me see it again."

"Beast," said Leslie minor, though without heat. "I wanted it for Matron myself," and he attacked his brother in a friendly way on the doorstep. The vase fell and was shattered beyond mending.

Lord Stoke climbed up into the dog-cart where Mrs. Morland was already seated, the elderly groom got up behind and they went away. Then Anne embraced everyone with fervour and promised to telephone to Sylvia and Emmy and Clarissa about wedding preparations nearly every day; and then she and Robin got into his cheap little car and drove towards Hallbury.

\*       \*       \*

The weather, which had at first been grey and cold, had gradually cleared. The breeze had dropped, everything was warm and comfortable again. Not that one could trust it, but one could enjoy the present moment. Robin and Anne had a great deal to talk about as they drove and not till they had by-passed Barchester did Anne remember something she had forgotten.

"Oh, Robin," she said. "I have remembered something perfectly dreadful."

Robin, who was not seriously alarmed, asked what it was.

"You remember at Rushwater we were talking about secrets," said Anne, "and you said you had a special secret secret to tell me and somehow you never did. Is it still very secret?"

Robin said not very secret now, because it was all settled. The Housmaster of the Junior House was resigning next year because an uncle wanted him to go into a very good family business and Mr. Birkett had formally offered him the post with the approval of the Governors.

"And will you take it?" said Anne. "Oh, Robin!"

Robin said he had accepted it. The house itself was a nice one, not too large; the matron was well disposed and as the Leslies were there he hoped they would give him a good character.

"And what with my salary and my own money that my mother left me and what I can squeeze out of the boarders by watering the milk," he said, "I shall be quite well off. I shall go there in September next year, or possibly in the summer term. It all depends on how long Kitson's uncle will wait. But no violent hurry."

Anne expressed the greatest delight at this news and they imagined some very good ways of stinting the boys' food and fuel and washing, so that Robin could get very rich.

"And you'll need a wife, won't you?" she asked.

She had said this once before when the possibility of a housemastership was raised, but lightheartedly. Now, suddenly, she felt uneasy; as if she had made a social blunder. Perhaps one ought not to ask people, not even Robin, about getting married. Robin spoke of something else. The afternoon did not seem quite so warm, so bright, to either of them.

"It's very exciting to be two bridesmaids," said Anne, feeling that she had better talk. "I mean Sylvia's and Rose's. David is going to give Clarissa and me and the other bridesmaids real paste ear-rings. I do think David and Rose getting married is one of the most exciting things that ever happened. I almost knew in a kind of way that it was going to happen, because of something Rose said to me, and I jumped with joy inside, because David had been rather horrid to me and Clarissa—not really horrid of course, but a little schoolboyish," said Anne from her lofty nineteen years. "But the minute he was engaged to Rose everything was perfect and I am terrifically glad. Martin and Sylvia isn't quite so exciting, but it's the nicest thing that could possibly happen and Sylvia is going to ask me to stay at Rushwater when she is married."

Part of Robin answered Anne suitably. Part of him noted with amusement the word *terrifically*, Rose's catchword of the moment. Another part wondered why it suddenly felt so cheerful and was informed by yet another party that it had made a complete fool of itself by ever thinking that Anne had any kind of feeling for Martin or for David. Then the four different parts of Robin became one and he urged his cheap little car joyfully over the level crossing and up the steep Hallbury High Street.

"Let's go to the Rectory first," said Anne, "and see Dr. Dale. I expect he would love to hear about the weddings."

So they left Anne's suitcase at her parents' house and drove up Little Gidding, that narrow crooked lane whose name was of immemorial antiquity, to the Rectory stable yard, where Robin put the car away.

The warmth of a four o'clock August sun, though by Pretence Time it was six, was so delightful that they sat down on the stone mounting-block to bask before going up to the Rectory, talking

of the sale and this and that, and Anne told Robin how much
her Regard ring had been admired.

"Do you remember," said Robin, "when my father gave you
that ring on your birthday and you had it on your engagement
finger?"

"He said I could be engaged to him till I was really engaged,"
said Anne, looking pensively into the past.

"And you said you didn't think you were old enough to be
really engaged then," said Robin, "so you put it on the other
hand."

"And mummy said only wear it for evenings or occasions,"
said Anne, "and I thought Lady Graham's sale was an occasion,
because I'd never stayed at Holdings before, so I put it on. I love
it."

She held out her right hand, upon which Ruby, Emerald,
Garnet, Amethyst, Ruby, Diamond sparkled in the sun.

"May I look at it," said Robin and without waiting for an
answer took it gently off her finger.

"Do you think I am old enough for being engaged now?" said
Anne.

"I think so," said Robin. "But it all depends on whom to, and
it depends on you a good deal."

Anne looked at him with interest.

"You see," said Robin, "I think I know a good job for you, only
it would mean being engaged."

Anne's gaze was fixed on him and questioning.

"If I take on the Junior House next year," said Robin, as warily
as if he were approaching a small bright-eyed bird with crumbs
or a worm, "a wife would be extraordinarily useful."

"She could help you with the House," said Anne, looking
away at the gooseberry bushes.

"I suppose she could," said Robin. "But I was really thinking
how very nice it would be to have someone to talk to after
school, and when the boys have gone to bed. I have thought
about that a good deal."

"You mean you might be lonely," said Anne, her gaze still averted, but not unkindly.

"I might," said Robin. "My papa is never lonely as far as I can make out. I suppose he is so used to being lonely since my mother died that he really doesn't notice it. One might get quite used to it in time."

Anne turned her head towards Robin and looked down upon her ringless hands, lightly clasped upon her lap.

"Do you mean that I could be the one?" she asked, looking up at him under her lashes in the way David had admired and which made Robin nearly die with love.

"I do," said Robin. "If you could consider yourself engaged to me, I would feel perfectly safe about loneliness."

"So would I," said Anne after a pause.

And then she rubbed her face gently against Robin's coat sleeve and said nothing.

"I love you, I love you, I love you, I love you," said Robin, with all his heart, but quietly, so that the bird should not take wing and disappear.

"Then I had better have my ring upon the proper hand, please," said Anne, holding out her left hand.

"You have the loveliest hands," said Robin, slipping the Regard ring onto her third finger.

"David said they were even nicer than Clarissa's," said Anne, talking to gain time.

"An hour ago I'd have said Blast David," said Robin, "but now I simply don't care. Anne, my darling."

As Anne did not appear to resent this remark, he kissed her hair with great devotion.

> "*'O love, O fire! once he drew*
> *With one long kiss my whole soul through*
> *My lips, as sunlight drinketh dew,'*"

said Miss Anne Fielding, ever mindful of her favourite poet, Lord Tennyson.

"Well, he didn't," said Robin indignantly. "He simply kissed the top of your head. Listen, my own precious, divine angel. The church clock has struck half-past six and we must be moving. Come and see my papa and tell him you are engaged to me, and then we will go and tell your people."

"I hope your father won't mind," said Anne.

"If it comes to that, I hope yours won't either," said Robin, "nor your mother. But I think everything will be all right, and they can't un-engage us."

"If they do, I'll wait till I'm twenty-one and then I'll run away with you," said Anne.

Robin said he was delighted to find that he had chosen such a practical wife, and they walked up the garden to the Rectory.

Just outside the french window of his study the Rector was sitting in an armchair, a book on his knees, the sun shining beneficently upon him. Kind Sister Chiffinch from the Cottage Hospital came forward to greet them.

"I've been paying one of my little friendly visits to the Rector," she said to Robin, "and he had a fancy to sit in the sun. He was asleep till just now. And if it isn't Miss Fielding, as I suppose I must call her now she is a grown-up young lady."

Robin, falling into her manner of speech, replied that she might have to call Anne Mrs. Robin Dale some day, upon which Sister Chiffinch, cautiously going yet a little further from Dr. Dale lest she should disturb him, expressed her extreme delight and said she had always foreseen the engagement.

"Well, I didn't," said Robin with great candour. "Did you, Anne? It suddenly came upon me like a flash."

"It was partly a flash, and partly not being surprised in the least," said Anne, considering the matter carefully.

"Excuse me, Sister," said Robin, "but I simply must kiss Miss Fielding at once," which he did, though in so gentle a way that Anne found it very agreeable.

"And how is my papa, Sister?" he asked.

Sister Chiffinch said he seemed quite cheerful, but very much weaker than when she had last visited him. Robin's face grew troubled.

"If papa has to resign, it will kill him," he said.

"Mr. Dale," said Sister Chiffinch earnestly, drawing him a little apart. "I don't think Dr. Dale will need to resign."

Robin looked at her and wondered if he understood.

"The machinery is running down very quickly," said Sister Chiffinch. "He is with your mother most of the time, Mr. Dale, back in their early married days. But he will be pleased to see you and to hear about his new daughter-in-law-to-be. My friend Sister Heath, who is on holiday here, is coming to spend the night at the Rectory and she will ring up Dr. Ford if it is necessary. But I don't think it will be."

Robin still could not quite understand whether her words were of good or ill omen. Everything seemed suddenly to be strange; except Anne.

"Come and talk to papa," he said, taking her hand. "Papa, here is Anne Fielding."

Dr. Dale, who was looking at something very far away, roused himself to courteous attention.

"Anne Fielding," he repeated. "Yes, I think I know her. How are you, my dear?"

Anne said quite well thank you, and looked to Robin for help.

"Papa dear, Anne and I are engaged," said Robin.

"'From this day will I bless you,'" said the Rector, using the words of his favourite prophet, Haggai, whose words were lying open upon his knees.

"Oh, *thank* you," said Anne. "And I am engaged with your ring, Dr. Dale."

She held out her left hand with the Regard ring upon its third finger.

"Yes, I know your ring," said the Rector, speaking as if to himself.

"He is very tired," said kind Sister Chiffinch in a low voice.

"Take Miss Fielding home, Mr. Dale, and then come back. I shan't go till Sister Heath comes."

"Good-bye. I will come and see you again soon," said Anne.

The Rector looked at her and through her at something very far away.

"The lovely creature," he said, in a voice that was hardly more than a breath.

"It is your mother he means," said Sister Chiffinch to Robin, always speaking low. "He has thought she was near him all day."

Anne kissed the Rector's forehead and went away with Robin. Sister Chiffinch returned to Dr. Dale, who had very quietly left a world in which he was too tired to remain. She looked after Robin and Anne with compassion. But they were young and would not be unhappy for long.

# COLOPHON

This book is being reissued as part of Moyer Bell's Angela Thirkell Series. Readers may join the Thirkell Circle for free to receive notices of new titles in the series and to receive a newsletter, bookmarks, posters and more. Simply send in the enclosed card or write to the address below.

The text of this book was set in Caslon, a typeface designed by William Caslon I (1692-1766). This face designed in 1725 has gone through many incarnations. It was the mainstay of British printers for over one hundred years and remains very popular today. The version used here is Adobe Caslon. The display faces are Adobe Caslon Outline, Calligraphic 421, and Adobe Caslon.

Composed by Alabama Book Composition, Deatsville, Alabama.

*Peace Breaks Out* was printed by Edwards Brothers, Ann Arbor, Michigan on acid free paper.

Moyer Bell
Kymbolde Way
Wakefield, RI 02879